Barbara Morgan
June 2013

THE CRYING SISTERS

BY MABEL SEELEY

MYSTERIES

The Listening House (1938)

The Crying Sisters (1939)

The Whispering Cup (1940)

The Chuckling Fingers (1941)

Eleven Came Back (1943)

The Beckoning Door (1950)

The Whistling Shadow (1954)

NOVELS

Woman of Property (1947)

The Stranger Beside Me (1951)

THE CRYING SISTERS

A MYSTERY

MABEL SEELEY

Afton Historical Society Press
Afton, Minnesota

Designed by Barbara J. Arney
Pre-press by Mary Susan Oleson

This first Afton Historical Society Press
reprint edition is limited to
two thousand copies.

Library of Congress Cataloging-in-Publication Data

Seeley, Mabel, 1903–1991
 The crying sisters : a mystery / Mabel Seeley.
  p. cm.
 ISBN 1-890434-26-4
 1. Minnesota--Fiction. I. Title
PS3537.E2826C49 2000   00-029274
813'.54--dc21   CIP

Printed in Canada

The Afton Historical Society Press is a non-profit organization
that takes pride and pleasure in publishing
exceptional books on regional subjects.

W. Duncan MacMillan   Patricia Condon Johnston
      president   publisher

Afton Historical Society Press
P.O. Box 100 Afton, MN 55001
800-436-8443
e-mail: aftonpress@aftonpress.com
www.aftonpress.com

THE CRYING SISTERS was an immediate success when it was published in New York in 1939. It was Minnesota mystery writer Mabel Seeley's second novel in as many years, and she was on a streak. The year before, her first book, *The Listening House,* had catapulted Mabel Seeley to the front ranks of American mystery writers. In 1940 she would sell her third novel, *The Whispering Cup,* to Hollywood.

The critics loved her. Howard Haycraft in *Murder for Pleasure: The Life and Times of the Detective Story* (1941) predicted that Mabel Seeley would "pilot the American-feminine detective story out of the doldrums of its own formula-bound monotony."

"It is not the least of her achievements [he wrote] that she has dared to use, and with striking effectiveness, the most commonplace of settings: a drab Minnesota lake resort [the locale for *The Crying Sisters*], a grain elevator [*The Whispering Cup*], a cheap rooming-house [*The Listening House*]. Akin to this restraint is her ability to create breath-taking moods of suspense and fear . . . by a technique of brooding understatement not unlike the cinematic methods of Alfred Hitchcock, whom, indeed, she resembles in many ways."

There was every reason to expect many more fine novels from Mabel Seeley, said Haycraft, and indeed there would be four additional mysteries,* until, when she was in her early fifties, Mabel put away her typewriter. She was in

*The Chuckling Fingers (1941), Eleven Came Back (1943), The Beckoning Door (1950), and The Whistling Shadow (1954)

the East, promoting her final book, *The Whistling Shadow*, when she met lawyer Henry Ross. Mabel had earlier been married to Kenneth Seeley by whom she had a son, Gregory, but that marriage had ended in divorce. In 1956 she married Ross.

So why did she quit writing? "Writing is hard work, and she felt she was burned out," Ross recalled following Mabel's death at age eighty-eight in 1991. "Her books were well-received critically, and they were commercially successful, but she liked being married better."

Ironically, the heroines in Mabel's mystery stories had usually been clever women who solved crimes while falling in love with men who considerately encouraged them in their work. In *The Crying Sisters*, Janet Ruell is a small-town librarian on vacation who goes looking for adventure and finds it. Jilted eight years earlier and still single, she is running away from a proposal from an unambitious forty-year-old bank cashier named George Train:

"Get away. Never go back." That was the tune the wheels ran to on tires that seemed to stick and melt against the paving. "Get away. Never go back. Any chance for adventure you get this month, take it. Any man that smiles at you, smile back. If you never get anything else gather up one adventure for your life."

Janet, of course, finds adventure in spades in this well-crafted mystery with a double plot. Does she also find romance? I'll only say that Mabel Seeley's stories do not disappoint.

The Afton Historical Society Press is delighted to be able to bring Mabel Seeley's classic stories back to print. Mabel's brother, Franklin Hodnefield, generously lent us first edition copies of her books and also provided the photograph of his sister that appears on our dust jackets. We are also grateful to Mabel's son, Gregory Seeley, for helping us obtain the rights to reprint his mother's books from Bantam Doubleday Dell.

Patricia Condon Johnston

DRAMATIS PERSONAE

JANET RUELL, *librarian on vacation, who asks for adventure and gets it.*

STEVE CORBETT, *highway engineer, who goes to a resort on business.*

COTTIE CORBETT, *his son, whose age is two and a half.*

JOHN LOXTON, *owner of the Crying Sisters Resort*

EDNA RUDEEN, *the unfriendly resident of cottage one*

FRED WILLARD, *pale and withdrawn occupant of cottage two*

MARJORIE WILLARD, *ex-nurse, now entirely a wife*

EARL JORDAN, *blond bond salesman in cottage three*

MRS. CLAPSHAW, *elderly resident of cottage four*

BITS and JOANIE CLAPSHAW, *her grandchildren*

AL SPRUNG, *son of the former owner of the resort, cottage five*

HARRY LEWIS, *portly resident of cottage six*

CAROL LEWIS, *who was also once a nurse*

ELMER, *John Loxton's boy-about-camp*

SHERIFF CARL BOXRUUD, *who in that locality is law*

CHET LEEGARD, *the sheriff's deputy*

MR. NIDDIE, *who keeps a tavern, the Flaming Door*

HOXIE MUELLER, *who was sorry he did what he did*

DAVE SPENDLER, *who never said what he thought*

DR. EVALD HANSEN, *physician and coroner*

JOE E. VIND, *county attorney of Poleckema County, Minnesota*

I STILL PINCH MYSELF and say it isn't true. I still wake at night to reach for the tangible proof within touch of my hand. If anyone should say to me, "Those things didn't really happen to you last summer; they're just part of some story you've read," I'd probably have dazed moments of wondering if I couldn't distinguish between reality and fiction any more.

Because what happened to me last August went so far outside anything I'd known all the rest of my life that even while it was going on I often thought I must be imagining.

On one day—Saturday, the thirtieth of July, to be exact—I was Janet Ruell, a respectable small-town librarian, driving north in my new car from Eldreth, Minnesota, for the first vacation I'd ever taken without my mother. My life had been openly humdrum and secretly desperate—the way life in a small town is for a girl who's still unmarried at twenty-nine.

And then the next day I was agreeing to go to an unknown resort under conditions which—well, Eldreth would have looked at them slant eyed.

Agreeing to go. There's no getting away from the fact that I went to that resort of my own free choice. Even when I chose I knew something was hidden under the surface of what was offered me. I went of my own volition into those days when I heard death crying in the night, when I saw it indicated by a plantain leaf and discovered in a plaything, when I saw it rising in a muddy bundle from the lake. The time was to come when I

1

felt myself living in the very house of death and eating at its table. And in the end . . .

I wonder if I'd have had the courage to take what Steve Corbett offered me if I'd had premonitions.

If it hadn't been so hot on that thirtieth of July I'd never have stopped at the Coldspring Tourist Cabins and so never have met the boy and the man at all. I had an entirely different destination in mind when I left Eldreth at seven that morning; two Eldreth teachers had recommended Graymoose Lodge on Lake Superior.

The sun threw white-hot ingots at me out of the east as I drove down Eldreth's main street, thanking heaven I wouldn't see it or the library again for a month. When I stopped on the curve around Rochester for gas the attendant told me it was ninety-seven. He was stripped to the waist. I sat looking at his freckled shoulders as he wiped my windshield; there was a drop of perspiration on every freckle.

After that I just abandoned myself to being hot. Cows drooped in pastures, leaves hung as if they'd lost their skeletons, fields faded visibly as the sun scorched out the green. I drove through Minneapolis to Lyndale without even looking at the tall buildings. In the afternoon I was a cooking waffle between two irons, the steely paving and the chromium sky; heat from below pressed up and heat from above pressed down until the juice oozed out of my bones and each eye was a separate furnace.

And while my physical being sizzled my mental state reached a boiling point and went up in steam, too. I'd been working up that pressure for a long time. I think it was George Train's proposal to me the night before that made me reach the steaming stage. George Train. Forty. Eldreth bank cashier and no ambition to be anything else. A neck that looked as if his hair had been clipped

2

under a bowl. He'd hinted that we'd reached a sensible age; of course I'd want to keep my job and not bother with children.

I had hated Eldreth for eight years, ever since Ted Williams jilted me and I heard the first whisper, "You can't tell me there isn't a reason." That whisper had changed with the years; it had become, "She still holds her head pretty high for a jilted girl, don't she?" Small towns never forget, not when they can take malicious triumph in remembering. I'd stuck it out, partly because I never can bear to give up in a fight, partly because I had a job there and my mother wanted me to stay until she'd lived out her ailing life. Well, I had.

Now she was gone I was offered George Train, Eldreth's only unmarried male older than I was, as an apology for the life I'd had so lightly taken from me.

"Get away, never go back." That was the tune the wheels ran to on tires that seemed to stick and melt against the paving. "Get away. Never go back. Any chance for adventure you get this month, take it. Any man that smiles at you, smile back. If you never get anything else gather up one adventure for your life."

Then I thought dully that nothing exciting could ever happen to me.

The small sign announcing the Coldspring Tourist Cabins loomed up on my left just before five o'clock. At the same time I seemed to feel a breath of breathable air. I was close enough to Duluth so the land was a desert of gravel with thin beige weeds, but back of the sign I saw what looked like an oasis: a darkly green hollow with big oaks around it, small white cabins under the oaks and a larger porched white house in front.

Three more hours of driving would bring me to Graymoose, but three more hours seemed intolerable. I made one of those sudden decisions.

A stout woman with reddish hair and wattles came out of the

3

white house when I stopped before it. She told me I was lucky, this was the coolest spot in the state. I drove down into the hollow and, miracle of miracles, it was cool there. Red water from some underground river churned up through red sand; the air at the spring's brink had the scent of ice. I lay on my stomach so I could put my face in the water; I forgot Eldreth and George Train.

By the time I went to supper I was almost human. The table was on the house porch—a long white table set farm style with about twenty places. Vaguely I noticed family groups down the table sides, and across from the place I took, a very small blond boy in a dark blue wash suit, propped on books. I cut once into the Swedish sausage on my plate and had the piece halfway to my mouth when a frog jumped out of the little boy's clothes somewhere and landed where the sausage had been.

My fork dropped on the table, and the next instant I was holding a gravy-smeared frog, feeling its heart's wild beat against my fingers. Instinct got me that far then let me down; I sat at a total loss. The by-sitters went into orchestrated hysterics, with a loud shout of laughter from the man beside the little boy furnishing the bass.

"Not *raw* frogs, *please*," I said with italics.

The boy was standing on his chair, obviously about to follow the frog across the table into my plate. The man jerked him back.

"It's my srog!" the boy said in a clear imperative. "He's all my srog. I want my——"

The frog had been gathering himself for a convulsive effort. It got him out of my hand and to the middle of the table; his next leap took him over the boy's head. After that, with the small boy leaping first, everyone jumped toward or away from the frog. The wattled woman won; she held the door open.

By the time I'd scrubbed my hands and returned to a new assortment of food—no gravy by request—the boy was back on his

4

books. He wasn't eating; his hands were tucked under his blue wash-suited legs. He was one of those thin pale youngsters with a head too big for his neck and shoulders; he wasn't crying, but he kept focused on me the most accusingly reproachful big blue eyes I'd ever wilted under. He couldn't have been three; he still had his baby hair, thin and colorless and fine, parted manfully at the side and brushed over.

Youngsters sidle around Eldreth library all day; I knew their minds as well as their spilling pockets. I knew I'd been completely inadequate.

I smiled across. "After supper should we go down by the frog's house to see if he's back?"

He lit up immediately. "I got my srog by the srog's house. Let's go now."

From someone he had learned to speak. Except for a few baffling sounds, the consonants came clearly, and each syllable was given its full value.

I promised. "We'll go the minute you finish supper."

He lit into a plate that had been untouched before. It struck me then that something was missing—his mother. He seemed alone with the khaki-clad man next to him. The man was putting away blueberry pie in a quick, definite, aloof way, apparently withdrawn to some dark inside recess of thought that left his face empty but still belligerently hard. He was perhaps thirty; the eyes were dark under thickly browed overhanging banks of socket; the brown hair stood up a little like tufted grass before it brushed over. When he turned sidewise the light struck the plane of his left cheek, and I saw he had a hole in his face, an odd depression in his left cheekbone, shaped like the bowl of a teaspoon, but deeper.

He raised his eyes then and caught me looking at him; at once he started staring me down as if I were thoroughly contemptible.

5

I know how I look. My hair is yellow, just plain yellow, long and straight. I wear it twisted in ropes around my head; that's as plain as I can make it. Since a childhood illness I've had two patches of red over my cheekbones and when I'm tired or hot, shadows as dark as mascara darken under my eyes until they nearly reach the red. I know it's theatrical. That's one thing Eldreth held against me.

I stared haughtily back.

He settled into his chair and almost absently kept that scorn on his face.

From beside him a small voice asked slowly, "See srogs now?"

I'd forgotten the boy. The child had quit eating; he was holding his back stiffly erect, but his head drooped until he caught it back with a jerk.

"Of course we'll go now." I stood up, but instead of sliding from his books he answered with a sigh.

"I guess I lazy." His head went sidewise to the table; I think he was asleep before it touched.

The man scooped up the child without a word, turned and strode off. He walked with a sort of effortless competence, quickly, scarcely lifting his feet from the ground. He wore the khaki shirt and breeches and high boots as if he'd been born in them, married in them, and if he should die would be buried in them. He was perhaps five feet eleven and he was very wide; the khaki shirt covered shoulders that looked knobbed like the padded shoulders of football players.

"Some travelers ain't friendly that way," the wattled woman consoled beside me. I awoke to the fact that I'd again been made to look graceless.

She added, "Poor kid, an orphan with a daddy like that."

"Perhaps his mother doesn't feel like eating."

"No, there ain't no woman with 'em."

Man alone with a little boy. The mother dead perhaps, the child tended by that dark, resentful, unfriendly man, learning that exquisite speech.

Something there that didn't fit.

The camp's washroom was at the rear of the main house; I walked toward it late that night for a last-minute shower bath. The moon was too small a melon rind to give much light; most of the cottages, too, were dark. But as I passed one that was still lit I saw a curtain lift inward on a breeze, and inside a man's bent back. It was unmistakably the man who had the boy; he was polishing something with a cloth. He raised what he was working on and I saw it.

A revolver.

It halted me where I stood. Guns to me meant holdups and gangsters. My first impulse was to rush to the wattled woman and tell her what I'd seen, but with my hand on her door I remembered that men could have permits to carry guns. Somewhat warily, and feeling nervous at slight sounds, I returned to my cabin, abandoning the idea of a bath. My imagination worked overtime a bit, but the last thing I would ever have thought was that that revolver would come into my possession.

After breakfast the next morning I made just one trip into the heat that wavered and streamed over Minnesota, and decided that whatever other people did I wouldn't leave the spring that day.

The car was gone from the cabin where I had seen the man; I never expected to see him again. I sat on a red rock by the water and exhausted the Sunday papers, from Soglow's *Little King* to an account of the suits being brought by the victims of a month-old airplane crash in St. Paul, and a Sunday magazine story of missing heirs, which led off with the tale of one James Maartens, once a well-known man about town in St. Paul, who had disappeared the day after his father's death and never returned to claim an inheritance of a quarter million. I thought if that were my quarter of a million it wouldn't be unclaimed very long.

It was when I wandered toward the big house in sheer boredom that I saw that although the car was gone the little boy wasn't. He was out in the sideyard alone in a red seersucker sun suit, sitting flat on the grass with his thin legs before him, resting back on his hands and looking sullen. As I came across the yard he got on his hands and knees and scrabbled over to a patch of shade. The wattled cabin keeper's voice came from the porch.

"Little boy, get back in the sun!"

He yelled obstinately and loudly, flinging his head back, "No!"

"Want me to take you back?"

"No!" he yelled again, and moved so the sun just hit his legs.

He was limp from sweating, and his shoulders were more than pink. I hesitated, but after all I had decided it might be all right about the gun, and I couldn't see any child get seriously sunburned. I slammed the porch door behind me and said so. The woman shook her wattles and went on peeling potatoes.

"I can't help it. His father said keep him in the sun."

"He doesn't look used to hot sunshine."

She shrugged. "I got to do what I'm told. His dad paid me two bucks for watchen him whiles he went off."

"I'll take the responsibility."

I started off to get the boy, but she made me tell her who I was and what experience I'd had with children before she gave a grudging consent; she seemed afraid I'd claim the two dollars.

The boy came willingly to my cabin, where I gave him a sponge bath and let him nap. When he woke he was an enchanting chatterbox. He told me his name was Cottie, that his daddy gave him a train and could make the car go "hurryer" and "hurryer," but not a word that suggested who or what his father really was or why he carried a gun. The afternoon we spent by the pool, both of us soon sopping because Cottie wanted me to hold in my lap all the frogs he caught. He was astoundingly quick, but the frog supply never got large; a frog would leap, he would make an almost identical leap, I would leap to keep him from drowning, and all the prisoners would leap for freedom. Whereupon Cottie would shriek with mixed regret and glee and we'd start over.

It was just as I'd made a particularly wild grab for his muddy bottom that I came up to see his father standing on the south shore of the pool, his eyelids as straight as his mouth, and the hollow in his cheek almost flat.

"I told Mrs. Golloy to keep that kid in the sun."

Cottie ran to throw himself like a climbing monkey halfway up the man's leg, with howls of greeting. The man lifted him, still shedding fury my way.

It might not be a good idea to have the possessor of a gun too furious at me. I defended myself.

"If I hadn't kept the boy in the shade he'd be in a hospital tonight with a sunburn that would make a fireburn look sick. Don't you know people can die from too much sun?"

"I know kids need all the sun they can get."

"Not between ten and two o'clock when it's one hundred and six."

Cottie put in a placating "She held my srogs, Daddy."

His father turned and walked off. In his anger the roll was intensified; I thought his feet had at some time learned to cling to a deck. The small face looked seriously back at me over the man's shoulder.

The two weren't at supper, and the car was again gone from

9

their cabin. Minneapolis was within an evening's drive; again I thought I'd never see them again. Time had never been as interminable as it was that evening; I wandered out to the pool in the faintly moonlit dark; not a soul was there, but I stayed a while. Coming back along the cabin row, I saw that the car was back at Cottie's cabin, and quickened my step; that gun would then be back in camp, too.

A man sat on my doorstep. He stood up as I came near, his dark shoulders stretching widely to both sides.

He said, "Miss Ruell, I'd like to see you about my kid."

I surprised myself by feeling alert but unafraid. "How do you know my name?"

"Mrs. Golloy told me."

My reasoning self balanced his manner, the gun he no doubt had on him, and the fact that he was Cottie's father. Then the part of me that had been uppermost yesterday sent a flash of liquid quicksilver across my chest. I didn't have much to be robbed of, and my life wasn't so pleasant I couldn't bear to have it changed.

I could at least find out what was offered.

"Come in." I passed him to unlock my door and switch on the uncovered bulb in the ceiling. He followed, but he didn't sit down when I pushed a chair at him or when I sat down; he just went off into a silence that seemed to last five minutes, with his eyes not on me but over my head.

When he did talk he said, "You're too fond of drugstores."

It wasn't what I'd expected, but I've learned to take that remark. "I don't get my face in a drugstore."

The first thing I knew he had a handkerchief in his hand and was rubbing it, hard, over my right cheek. I swiped with my hand at his fist and got to my feet.

"What possible——"

10

He said, "I don't mind a little paint, but yours would have been too much," and stowed the handkerchief calmly in his pocket as if I weren't giving him a wildcat glare. "I'm taking the kid to a lake for a month. He could use a girl—use a woman to look after him. I'd pay thirty a week."

I had one of those caught-unaware sensations—the mind with a large space filled with gray mist. Was this a guise adventure could take?

I asked incredulously, "You want to hire me as a nurse-maid?"

"You'd have to be more responsible than a nursemaid."

"I'm a librarian. On my vacation. Why should I——"

He said without any change in his face or voice, "I saw you liked the kid."

For the first time I realized why the evening I had just spent had been so long.

I asked slowly, trying to piece together my emotions, "You'd be willing to leave the boy with me?"

"No. I'd be there, too."

Suspicion reared its head. "I don't own anything to be robbed of and I——"

He smiled in the middle of that, humorlessly, just the wide mouth stretching back to show the line of white meeting teeth.

"I'm not interested in anything you own or you either."

He didn't seem to be. Except when his eyes flicked over me to read my thoughts, he kept his gaze away from me as if I were an abomination he could scarcely bear to look at. Absurd anger worked up in my chest; I wanted to fight back at him, not with my innocuous virginal respectability that he would only scorn, but with some daring that would force even his respect. I tried not to yield.

"It's impossible. I don't even know your name."

11

"If that helps you any—Steve Corbett."

"You work somewhere, I suppose?"

"Highway engineer. I handle my own jobs."

I wasn't supposed to know he had a gun; I couldn't very well come out with that.

"If I could write for references——"

He said steadily, "No."

"Could I choose the resort? I know one where——"

"I've already rented the cottage."

"Where is it?"

"At Crying Sisters Lake."

That was the first time I heard that name, the Crying Sisters. Even then it hit my ears with an eerie, suggestive sound.

The whole thing was ridiculous. "Do you realize you're asking me to go alone with a strange man to a strange resort? It just isn't done."

"Isn't done." He looked at me then, shrugging. "That's your answer all the time, isn't it?"

He turned to go.

All the desperation I'd been seething under the day before hit me. In the split second it took him to make the one step to the door I looked again at the Eldreth life ahead of me. Breakfast with George Train. Butter on George's mouth from the toast; he always got butter on his mouth. Hurrying to the library at nine, standing aside at the door to let some of yesterday's stale air out before I dived in. Watching Mrs. Binns to see she dusted the back stacks. Checking *Love Is a Rose* from sloppy Mrs. Lindblom's card, suggesting she'd like *Stardust in Her Hand*. Hunting up *Dilly the Silly* for Budge Lindblom, Mrs. Lindblom's dahlia-cheeked stolid four-year-old, not mine. Never any child of mine. Getting down *Nancy of Wyngate* for Jean Schwartz; she'd want *Party Girl* instead.

Having Wentworth Olson bring in a new *Tecos Tom* with the binding ripped, watching his already wise eyes see me keep my tongue hushed. No one fines the son of the town's one factory owner; no one smacks him down, just once, to make a decent boy of a good youngster who's rapidly becoming ungood.

No man ever came into Eldreth Library. Except George Train.

My hand went out of its own accord toward Steve Corbett's retreating back, and my tongue said, "Wait, I'll go."

CHAPTER TWO

HE TURNED BACK slowly, but as if all his bones were oiled and moved in greased sockets. "Okay, I'll give you this." A hand went into his breeches pocket and came out with a length of dark blue metal in the palm.

The gun. He was offering *me* the gun. My eyes leaped from the weapon to his unreadable face. I'd taken an uncertain step forward, but I backed now until the edge of the bed hit the insides of my knees, feeling I'd like to back farther.

"That's silly. I wouldn't know how to use it."

He flipped the weapon to hold it toward me handle first.

"You don't have to know how to use it. If it seems a good idea just point it and pull the trigger. It does the rest."

"But I don't want to get into anything where I'd have to use a gun!"

"You won't. It's just to keep you from thinking I might start making passes."

The gun had a hypnotizing effect on me; too much so for me to be bothered by his words.

"Is it loaded now?"

"Try it and see."

Somehow it was in my hand, and I was lifting it to look down the little black hole.

He said steadily, "I'll trust you to see the kid doesn't get on the receiving end. What you do to yourself is your business."

The metal was warm; warmth from it seemed to flow into my

hand. I got that spurious feeling of power firearms give, as if I could afford to be reckless, as if with the gun in my hand I could dare to go anywhere. I'd have the gun, not he.

He'd turned again to the door, throwing back over his shoulder, "Leave here at nine in the morning. Take 169 north."

I tried to struggle toward common sense. "I must at least know I'm not getting into any crimes."

"You won't. All you'll get into is taking care of the kid. Get that in your head and keep it there."

He didn't add good night.

I stood with the gun in my hand, trying to get the picture.

What had I let myself in for?

Was it just a month of being a high-class nursemaid? Of cooking Cottie's meals, putting him to bed at night, seeing he didn't drown in the lake?

The gun stood against that.

I tried to put a frame of reason around the man's actions. There he was, a man alone with a little boy. Probably a widower, although he hadn't said so. He realized he couldn't care for the boy at a lake alone.

That was reasonable, but the gun wasn't. Minnesota lake resorts are famous for being as safe as churches. I'd heard of a few that were wild, but never one where it was advisable to carry a gun.

There had to be something else in the wind than a simple month at a lake resort. He'd never give me a gun to protect me against himself; if he was that safe I wouldn't need a gun. No, something about that month was going to be dangerous.

I knew it then as well as I knew it later. But just the same, as I tossed that night on the baseball-stuffed mattress, my moments of thinking I had better back out were fewer than my moments of

15

liking the excitement. The last eight years had given me confidence in my self-reliance. I thought I could look out for myself.

I'm not nearly that confident now.

Looking back, I can see in the happenings of the next day those that had a bearing on what was to come and why they were as they were.

The Corbetts had gone before I went to breakfast; no mistaking what I felt as I looked at the space where their car had been—it was the thud of disappointment, and on the heels of that an upswing of relief.

Of course we couldn't be seen joining forces here; it would look illegal to the wattled woman.

I left the camp at nine exactly, still set and ready for adventure, the gun in the handbag on my lap.

But as I drove on I felt my courage weakening. For one thing, the heat was unstiffening. It hit like a blanket wrung from boiling water the moment I struck the highway. The sun hung red and swollen, and toward the west the sky was matted with what looked like wadded mountains of dirty wool. Not only uncertainty but storm lay ahead.

Moving along that thin gray, greasy worm of highway, with what might be my last chance to back out drawing close, common sense rushed back at me with a vengeance. Go off with that strange man, even if he did have an appealing child? It was precarious and fantastic. I'd have to give it up.

Almost undoubtedly I'd have stuck to that if it hadn't been for the name Cottie called me.

The car appeared, drawn up at the side of the road, after I'd driven an hour. A scrap of bright blue moved beyond it, exploring a bush. My car had barely stopped before the blue scrap was hanging to its right window sill and the boy's face looked in at me with its half-shy, considering smile of acquaintance.

"Mamma, can I sit in a front seat by you?"

What happened in my interior was exactly as if a gigantic spoon had stirred once around. I pushed damp hair—heat and dampness at least were real—back from my forehead, and tried to orient myself.

"What did you say?"

He nodded rapidly. "I can't sit in a back seat, Mamma."

The first work my mind did was to tell me he hadn't thought that up himself.

I pushed the door open, sending him with it, and got to solid ground as he swung back.

"I'm not your mamma, you can't——"

The moment he was able to he started scurrying inside on all fours until he was in the middle of the front seat.

"See? Isn't too tight, Mamma."

I began again, "You mustn't call me——"

Behind me his father said evenly, "I told him he could. He does what I say. He calls any woman mamma. It's just a name to him."

As soon as he spoke I saw a meaning in the name, and turned to face the man. His look this morning was exactly as I had first seen it—unapproachably remote. He carried a huge Gladstone in one fist and had a load of clothes—coats, sweaters and blankets—over the other arm. I got in one glance that he intended to move his entire outfit into my car, and have us go as a family.

"Perhaps," I said grimly. "But it doesn't escape me that if Cottie calls me mamma, then anyone who hears him will think I'm your wife."

"I won't."

It was cold enough to douse me the rest of the way back to sanity. "I'm sorry, I've changed my mind. I'm not going."

His answer came with the tired reasonableness of a construction boss rebuking a steel riveter who complains he is afraid of high places.

"Aw, quit being a sissy pants."

Sissy pants! Before I could recover he had elbowed me aside, ordered, "Cottie, move over," and was inside my car, hooking hangers over the back window ledges.

What I finally got out, with an obscure idea of warning him, was, "I've still got the gun."

"So what're you kicking about?" A glimpse of his mouth, between coats, showed it grinning wryly.

I held myself together to say carefully, "Is there any reason why you should be so hard boiled, or why you're so anxious to have me appear as Cottie's mother?"

His voice came muffled and still tired. "What the hell difference does it make? Saves talk. What other reason is there?"

I can see, now, how expertly he handled me, how exactly he conveyed the right amount of disinterest in me, how he goaded me into staying. Then I knew only that I continued to stand by, feeling torn by indecision, while he piled groceries and suitcases into my trunk; found myself trailing his car to the next small town with Cottie bounding joyously on the seat beside me, on a lookout for cow barns; found myself waiting while his car was stored.

The man returned to stride purposefully toward my door and jerk it open.

"I'll drive."

I sat tight. I had let myself be goaded into staying, but I still had sense enough to know I had more power over what happened to me if I kept the wheel.

"This is my car."

"That's why we're using yours, so you can see you've still got it. But any car I'm in I drive."

18

"No."

He said again, "I'll drive," and slid into the seat forcing me over.

Before I could say what I thought of this new arrogant usurpation he had the car going, and fast. I did open my mouth, but my face was full of Cottie; he hadn't moved over; instead he'd started climbing over me.

"I has to be in the middle," he explained impatiently. "Mamma, too tight. Mamma, I'm too tight."

I moved to the right-hand side.

"Nice now," Cottie said, and stood up. "I see a cow barn," he announced. "And two cows and two cows and two cows."

Anger always ties my tongue. I felt myself swelling outward with resentment like a hot balloon about to burst.

The trouble was there wasn't anything to *burst at*. The man drove like a demon; the speedometer swung to seventy, eighty; the car was as steady in its flight as if it flew in a groove, unswerving, its only second movement a slight rise and fall. I felt I could have screamed at the man, could have beaten at his face, and that expressionless brown cast would have stayed as it was. Only my hands would have bruised against the hard, unyielding substance of his flesh.

My right hand did hurt; in my impotence I had been pounding it on the handle of the door. I caught the hand away to my lap and forced myself to quiet.

As I quieted I discovered that unexplainably I was swinging back to the attitude I'd had the night before. I wanted to go ahead with this now. Dimly at first, then clearly, I saw that what had just happened wasn't reasonless conflict.

It was a link in a chain.

That I should be asked to go with the man and the boy at

all—that was the first link. That I should be given the gun—that was the second. That I should be maneuvered into appearing as Cottie's mother—that was the third. The man wouldn't go to all that trouble unless he had a reason.

Again a desire to know that reason, know where all this would lead, swept me. I told myself, all right, I'll stick. But it will be for my own purposes. I'm going to enjoy this.

I turned to Cottie. The boy's head was moving like a sniffing pup's in his efforts to see what went past. I looked out, too, to learn anything I could from the countryside. The meager farmsteads were far between here, in their stead miles of unbroken woodland, the trees a more olive green than the trees of southern Minnesota. We passed one tragic stretch of blackened stumps, and then miles of gray upthrusting rock covered thinly with bush. It was wild country enough, with the red heat haze over it, and the dark oppressive clouds now reaching almost to the sun.

Once Cottie drew away to balance against his father's shoulder; when I turned he was staring at me from under low lashes, almost furtively.

"Mamma. Isn't Mommy."

So mamma wasn't just a name to him! Something I might learn. I asked quickly, thinking the man might stop me, "You have a mommy?"

The small blond head moved up and down. "Mommy's all gone."

Mommy was gone, and he called me mamma. I had an entirely illogical, intuitive wisp of apprehension. Was I to be all gone, too? Was that the end link in the chain? Then I looked again at the boy, tended, protected, taught to be good—he was no lure. "Mommy's all gone." Those were exactly the words said to children whose mothers were dead or divorced.

Cottie's thoughts had brightened, too. "Doobie isn't all gone."

"Who's Doobie?"

The blue eyes became incredulous. "Don't you know Doobie?"

"I'm afraid I don't."

"I do. Daddy knows Doobie, too. Don't you know Doobie?" He stared anew, aghast at my lack.

"Doobie looks after you at home, doesn't she?" I guessed.

The head nodded again. "She slaps my hands, too, when I'm naughty but she doesn't slap my ears."

The man growled once, a sound that must have come through his neck because he didn't open his mouth.

For a long time that was all I knew of Cottie's background: that his mother had gone away and he had been tended by a woman named Doobie. Of all the links I finally held that was one of the most important.

It was after eleven when we sped through a village named Maple Valley, and almost immediately after that swung from the highway into a sandy side road, with a signboard at the fork.

CRYING SISTERS LODGE
LEFT 2 MILES
CLEAN HOUSEKEEPING COTTAGES
Good Boats—Good Fishing

My expectation heightened; we were close now to the unknown destination to which the man was taking me.

As if our leaving the highroad was a signal, the sun went out, the dirty gray wool covered all the sky, the maple and birch trees pressing in closely to the sides of the car darkened, and a wind

21

whipped up behind us, bending the trees forward. Within a mile the storm broke. The gray wool spouted water, the sound on the car roof was the thunder under a cataract.

The car slowed instantly as the winding curves ahead were swallowed up in water, and I reached to wind the windows up. Beside me Cottie made a small sound. He had sat down in the center of the seat, squeezing himself small.

I said cheerfully, "Here's a nice big rain. Now it'll be cool."

He said, "I like little rains better."

His father spoke, too, for the first time since he had taken the wheel. "You're a big kid. You're not afraid of rain."

The boy stiffened valiantly; I put out a hand to him, but he said, "Don't hold me, Mamma. I'm big."

The car crawled now over a road winding in S curves; I hadn't seen a sign of a house, not even a clearing, since we left the highway; just the dense trees. The two wipers swept incessantly at the windshield, but even then the glass was too water runneled for vision.

That was the way we came to the Crying Sisters: sheeted in swift blank falls of water, deafened by the beat of water on the roof, sightless except within our narrow compass.

CHAPTER THREE

MY FIRST IMPRESSION of the resort which was to be the backdrop for so many of the horrible incidents in the chain was that all the forces of nature had staged a protest at our coming. Rain slashed, trees lashed frantically, the crash of harried lake water mingled with the thundering drum of rain; earth itself seemed to be withdrawing from us, so hidden was it by water.

Hidden. That was the word that characterized the Crying Sisters, up to the very end. Even when the sun shone, even when I thought I saw all there was to see clearly, still the reality was hidden.

It appeared first as a clearing, into which the car swung from the hemming trees. At one spot an open gate was just visible, very close to the car.

CRYING SISTERS LODGE

The top board carried the name in black. The car went down a small incline and stopped where the only things within sight were a set of what appeared to be showcases set out before a long log cabin, emerging dimly from the water-saturated air beyond.

Cottie was on my lap looking out. "What's 'at?"

"Indian relics in that case," his father told him. "You can see them when the rain stops."

He seemed entirely unaffected by the violence surrounding him; he sat talking about Indians as easily as if he had nothing on his mind but being a parental encyclopedia. For the attention he gave me I might not have been there. I continued to look out, telling myself that it was the storm alone that disturbed me. The house emerged more clearly now: a two-story house of gray logs, its porch buttoned to the roof in curtains.

The rain slackened after half an hour. As soon as it did so Steve Corbett left the car, sprinting between the showcases to the screened porch door. He went in without knocking.

If I could have seen anyone in the log house I thought I would have felt more easy, but no movement showed beyond the dark screen of the door. When Steve Corbett came back he was stuffing a horn-tagged key in his pocket.

Rain quieted rather abruptly as he started the car again. Ahead appeared a rutted track with a grassy center, leading up a rise. On the left was a reach of lawn ending in a rim of trees. Through the trees I saw the lake, restlessly gray, rising and falling from sharp white heights. On the right were more of the log cabins, smaller than the first. I had a lift of relief; several of the cabins had cars alongside, and cars meant people. What I had begun to be afraid of was no people.

At the top of the rise we passed two cottages that seemed empty, then swung to stop beside the last cottage of the string.

"The last one?" I had to make that protest.

"Quiet up here. Cottie, wait until I get the door unlocked before you scoot through this rain."

For once Cottie clung to me. I reached for a blanket in the back seat, and when his father had the porch screen unlocked wound us both in it and ran. Inside the blanket Cottie laughed and bounced, and on the porch he was out of my hands at once, as slippery as one of his frogs, for an immediate exploration of the cabin.

I looked, too, trying to see in the cottage some clue to why Steve Corbett had come here.

24

There wasn't much of it to tell anything: In front, a porch the length of the cabin, with a cot at one end, a rough kitchen table and chairs next to it, three bright canvas beach chairs, a three-burner oil stove, a sink beside the door. Canvas curtains inside the screening kept out the rain. In the house wall was a door leading inward, and in the corner near the sink an icebox and a cupboard.

The single inside room showed unfinished log walls, two windows, a peaked roof overhead, two iron beds with a limp orchid curtain on a wire between them, one old rocker, one varnishy chest of drawers. The beds had only orchid mattresses and pillows; the closed room smelled of hot moist wood, moist feathers, moist cotton.

I've been in just enough lake resorts to know that it was the very model of all cheap lake cottages.

It reassured me somewhat; I felt my tautness loosening, thought that perhaps the place was all right, and the gun just a bit of quixoticism on Steve Corbett's part. I heard him, on the porch, making the most fatherly of remarks:

"Cottie, leave that oilstove alone."

Then he addressed me. "You and Cottie will use the beds inside; I'll sleep on the cot out here. You can hook the screen door between if it makes you feel better, or even close the wood door."

I looked at the screen door; it had a stout hook on the inside. With the revolver I thought I should be reasonably safe.

I'll pass quickly over that afternoon; it wasn't until deep night that that next significant and mystifying link attached itself to the chain.

Not a soul came near us. Cottie's father carried in the luggage in a lull of the rain. While I unpacked and made beds he prepared lunch: cocoa from canned milk and an omelet; it was done with as few waste motions as if he'd learned how in a Detroit factory. We ate on the porch, Cottie talking to me as his father grew more and more abstracted and remote.

When I took the boy in for his nap the man retreated to the cot and stayed there, smoking a crusted pipe, staring moodily out at what trees and water were visible through a rain that thickened again. I finished unpacking; the only thing difficult to place was the gun. I climbed on my bed, finally, and slipped it behind a board that met the wall in a V just below the open rafters of the ceiling. Cottie couldn't get it there, but I could get it quickly from my bed.

On the porch I abstracted a wicked-looking knife from the cutlery drawer; it had an eight-inch blade ending in a point. As I reached to put it on top of the cupboard I noticed it had a nick in the blade; someone had used it roughly.

When Cottie woke we cut a city full of houses, fire engines, policemen and cows from newspaper—play I'd used a hundred times, but different now with this eager child I could hardly keep out of the scissors, and the dark man not even watching from the cot.

Steve Corbett shook off his abstraction to talk pleasantly to Cottie as he ate supper—a meal I made—but to me he addressed only the words necessary to two people eating at the same table. That was all right with me; if he ignored me I could ignore him.

After I'd put Cottie to bed for the night I didn't leave the inside room. I'd openly hooked the door as I went in. Steve Corbett's only utterance that evening was to call good night to his son.

I undressed in the dark as soon as Cottie's breath was even and quiet. In bed I settled to thinking about the situation now. As far as the afternoon went I had been right in calming myself; I was simply a nursemaid.

But if Steve Corbett had come to this lake to enjoy himself he was making an odd beginning. If ever I had seen a man sunk in deep, involved pondering I had seen that man that afternoon.

And whatever he pondered wasn't pleasant; he'd sat hunched, brooding, distant.

What could his purpose here be?

Cottie. So far the cabin had been an excellent hiding spot. Suppose he had been kidnapped. Suppose——

I pushed my thoughts in that direction, but they went lamely. I hadn't heard of any kidnappings lately. Cottie hadn't been hidden at the tourist camp. The boy and the man were too familiar. And Cottie in his way was as imperious as the man—if that wasn't heredity it at least showed long association.

I resolved lukewarmedly to look out for news of a kidnapping.

What other purpose could there be? I was obviously a source of disinterest. My car was small bait for robbery, the little money I had was in traveler's checks, and traveler's checks were what Steve Corbett would expect of what he called a sissy pants.

I still thought of that name with tightened lips.

Hide-out after robbery. Hide-out for an intended robbery. We weren't far from Duluth. I'd always thought thieves skulked. There was nothing skulking about Steve Corbett.

I thought with a shock that it would be easier to suspect him of murder than of robbery.

As I lay in my bed the man was not ten feet distant on the porch outside. I found my mind uncontrollable; through it marched a scene of death, incoherent, formless. A woman, lying, sitting, standing. Dark. A dark man striking quickly, now reaching with strangling hands for her throat, now pushing home a knife, now pointing a gun. Perhaps I dozed a little and all the vague, unfastened fears I'd had that day and the night before took in my mind those dark pictorial forms. It must have been that. But as I write this, knowing what I know now, I am almost convinced that thought can be transferred, that one mind can sense the emotions and forces that drive through another physical organism. I know now that in Steve Corbett's mind that night——

But I didn't know that then. Then I roused to shake off the nightmare, to shake loose from any thought of Steve Corbett or his purposes. I forced myself to listen instead to the taffeta rustle of the trees and the lake. The rain seemed to have stopped for good. The night was refreshingly cool after the heat. Just before I dozed I heard a car's motor, going or coming.

When I woke it was to an entirely different sound.

I woke, not lying but sitting in my bed. My first motion, even before my mind had waked enough to tell what had roused me, was to leap the three feet that separated Cottie's bed from mine. He was there, rolled like a cocoon in his flannel blanket. It was so dark in the room I couldn't distinguish the edge of the bed from the floor, but I moved my palms along the warm soft roll; he felt relaxed and safe; his breath came quietly and steadily.

That couldn't have taken an instant.

From outside the house, distant, came a woman's muffled scream.

That was what had wakened me; the sound of an earlier scream was still in my ears as the second one came.

All my suspicions of the resort, all my previous tension, jumped back.

I stood straight, shaking. Not Cottie. But someone screaming somewhere. An extended scream that sounded like terror and that ended so abruptly it might have been choked off.

The pitch blackness outside didn't tell me anything. At the bedroom door I listened, first for another scream, and then when that didn't come, for the heavy breathing on the porch that would be Steve Corbett asleep.

I couldn't hear that, either.

28

I heard the lake, the trees. I listened so intently Cottie's breath sounded loud; the watch on my wrist sounded loud. Nothing else.

I called in a whisper, "Mr. Corbett!"

No answer. I whispered louder, "Mr. Corbett!"

Still no answer.

What should I do? Help might be needed by that woman who had screamed. Steve Corbett was the one to go. I would have to wake him from his soundless sleep.

I went back and got my gun, and with that held nervously before my chest, unhooked the door and guided myself along the porch wall to the cot.

"Mr. Corbett," I whispered again. I put my left hand down to where his shoulder should be, but it found nothing. My hand went on down until it touched the cot. Quickly then I knew: the cot was empty, the covers tumbled back. The occupant had been gone so long there wasn't even any warmth in the bed.

I stood up, my mind filling with a chaos of terrors. Steve Corbett was gone, somewhere into the moist, unbroken dark that surrounded me, leaving Cottie and me in the cabin alone. And out where he was a woman screamed.

For seconds I stood at the porch door, trying to work up my courage to run to the next inhabited cottage. Should I leave Cottie there alone? I stood torn and distraught. Finally I pushed at the door; I must do what I could no matter what I ran into in the dark before me.

The door didn't give. My fumbling fingers found the hook; it hung unfastened.

Steve Corbett hadn't taken any chances. He had padlocked the cottage on the outside, leaving me a captive with Cottie in a locked prison.

I thought that I, too, like that unknown woman, should

29

scream. But who would come? I was immediately certain, with that necessity for thinking the worst that goes with all night sounds, that that woman had screamed in terror for her life. Was it in terror of Steve Corbett she had screamed? Was it for that he had come here?

If that was so, what would happen when he was through? Would he come springing back for Cottie? Me, what would he do to me? He wouldn't want me any more. Or would he? Was that my purpose, to be window dressing for an escape? Father, mother, small boy—did he think that domesticity would disarm suspicion?

It would have to be my car in which he'd escape. It still loomed black just before the door. Whether he left me here or took me along I'd be considered an accessory. What defense could I make? That I had come here with him——

I must have been at the door an hour before a sharper noise sounded above the slapping of the lake.

I fled, not on reason, on instinct—fled to the inner room, hooked the door, stood with the revolver ready to protect myself as best I could.

I heard the rusty turn of the key in the padlock, the small whine of hinges, the slide of the screen being hooked on the inside. Then the turn of the key in the padlock again.

He was locking himself in. That didn't seem a prelude to flight.

Quiet an instant, as if he, too, listened, then the creak of floor boards, going past the door by which I crouched. Far past. The cot creaked.

A shoe slid to the floor.

He was getting back into bed.

He wasn't coming for Cottie. He wasn't coming for me. He wasn't flying. He was staying. Whatever had been done in the resort tonight, for whatever reason a woman had screamed, he was staying. The cot creaked lengthily as he lay down.

30

I tried, with an effect of pressing a lid down on a kettle that bubbled and boiled over, to suppress my expectant terror.

I whispered, "He doesn't intend to murder you. He can't. You're in his own house. He wants you for his son—to care for his son. You're as necessary to his son as shoes. He'll protect his son, and you'll come under the same protection, no matter what he is."

That was calming. I even tried to think up some innocent reason for his having been gone. But I couldn't do that. He hadn't taken the car. He couldn't have gone out on the lake in a swamped boat. He'd been gone for hours. He wouldn't have gone for exercise or pleasure over grounds that would soak him to the knees.

And someone had screamed.

I wrapped myself in all the courage I possessed and unhooked the door again. My feet were more quiet on the porch than his had been, but he heard me coming. His voice met me, a groaning whisper.

"I might have known you'd be a quick-ears." Disgust. Not a hint of wariness, of readiness to spring at me, of fear at having been caught.

"A woman screamed," I whispered, keeping the revolver pointed at where I thought he was. "Twice. Somewhere here. And you were gone."

"Listen." The word was barely audible. "If you find out in the morning that any crime has been committed you can talk then."

Even my emotion-clogged mind got that he didn't think there had been any crime, that the woman had cried out for other reasons.

Or else he thought the crime had been so skillfully hidden it wouldn't be discovered.

The impetus with which I'd come out pushed me on. "That woman may need help."

"She isn't still screaming for it, is she? Go to bed."

In that last was a warning. If I tried to leave the cabin he'd prevent me.

Again I stood at a complete pause. The man remained quiet on his cot. If I defied him, went out, went from cottage to cottage waking the sleepers at this hour of dark night, would I find nothing? Would I find myself the victim of hysterics, of a sound my own disturbed and apprehensive ears had manufactured?

He was so sure I wouldn't find a crime.

Slowly, still frustrated and uncertain, I went back to bed. There wasn't any lessening of my tension that night. I lay with the revolver under my pillow, stiffening to every vague night sound.

On the porch Steve Corbett, too, lay long awake; it wasn't until the light came up that his breathing changed to the rhythm of sleep.

Rationality came seeping in with daylight. I quit being a bubbling vat of alarm and surmise and began to think collectedly. I began to see a sequence again. The scream and Steve Corbett's night absence from the cabin—they might be two more links in the chain that had begun forming when he asked me to come here. He had asked me to come, given me the gun, maneuvered me into appearing as his wife, because he had some business in this resort of which he wanted to keep unsuspected.

My problem was what I should do in the morning. He couldn't keep me from leaving if I were determined.

But even now—did I want to go? As before, tendrils of fascinated interest played with what I knew, clung to it. If I pulled myself loose now I'd have to go around forever after with those tendrils of curiosity broken and unsatisfied.

And I still liked Cottie; the afternoons with him had been strangely contenting.

In the end I decided that when full morning came I would find out for certain whether a crime had been committed this night or not; I'd hunt up the proprietor, sound him out, if necessary go from house to house. I owed it to myself—owed it to Cottie—to find out if Steve Corbett was or wasn't a murderer. If there had been a crime I'd tell what I knew.

If there hadn't I'd stay and see what next happened in the chain.

I must have dozed with my decision made because I started awake to the weight of Cottie's elbows on my chest.

His voice demanded, "Mamma, I *need* oatmeal now."

All the urgencies of the night were on me, but they had to wait on Cottie. It wasn't until he was gulping oatmeal that I had time even to look at the world the morning presented.

On his cot Steve Corbett slept heavily, his back to the porch, his face thrust down into the blankets so that only the back of his neck and head showed. On the floor were his high boots, sodden.

Outside the porch coppery sunlight fell on wet-glistening grass, and through the trees the lake showed suddenly blue, with a brisk cool breeze slapping its surface into motion.

"Let's go by all 'at water!" Cottie drew in a breath of charmed surprise the first time he let up on the oatmeal.

I hadn't remembered, when I made my plan to scrutinize the resort and its inhabitants, that I'd have Cottie on my hands. If anything evil was to be discovered in the resort that morning it would be criminal to expose him to it. But I couldn't leave him in an unlocked cabin. After last night it didn't enter my mind that I might wake Steve Corbett and leave the boy with him. I had to decide between waiting and taking Cottie along; I decided on the latter. For our protection I tucked my handbag holding the

33

revolver tightly under my arm.

The horn-tagged key lay openly now on top of the khaki shirt on the chair nearest the cot; the man didn't stir when I took it.

I stood on the stone at the foot of the porch steps with Cottie's warm impatient hand in mine and looked out.

I was still jittery from the night I'd spent; I was ready to hear evil in a crackling branch, see it in a disordered cabin, find it suddenly facing me at any step I took. What I saw just made me feel a baffling contrast between what had happened last night and the way the place looked now. At the foot of the high-banked shore water glinted in sunshine, the bank was thick with birches, oaks and pines, lovely green lawns stretched from the row of cabins to the bank, and behind the cabins a hill of yellow stubble undulated upward in billows and was crowned with thick bushes at the top. Beyond our cottage was a sumac thicket, a high mesh fence, and beyond that the hill curving to jut out over the lake in a single craggy bluff.

The end cabin, and two uninhabited cabins between us and the other resorters. Why that? Only one possible answer. Steve Corbett didn't want to be observed.

Could it have been in one of the empty cabins that a woman had screamed? As we passed I paused at each one to see that it was locked, apparently undisturbed. The next cabin had a car parked beside it; the porch was empty but the curtains were unhooked, a sign the occupant had probably been up and around that morning. The next cabin was the same way.

At the fifth cabin we saw people: a boy of five and a girl of eight or nine playing at the doorstep. As we came along the girl hit the boy in the face with a sand shovel and he went down yelping; apparently life was normal there. We didn't see anyone else until we reached the last of the small cottages. At the table by the open screen sat the first woman I'd seen there, a dark behemoth of a woman. Had she been the one who screamed? If she had she was over it now; she was eating with the utmost calmness, her head turning to watch us pass.

The big log house was separated from the big woman by what, in a town, would have been a half block of lawn. The house was set in a hollow, with a barn of the same weathered logs in the trees behind it. Cottie ran away from me to cling like a limpet to the glass cases. I had to take time out from my purpose to tell him what the arrowheads, ax heads, beaded belts, baskets, jars and pipes inside it were. As I did so a small oldish man opened the porch door.

He began pleasantly, "You're admiring my relics——" Then, "It must be Mrs. Corbett and the boy. I didn't come down yesterday. Such a downpour. I'm not as young as I was. I'm John Loxton, the owner of the resort, you know."

He was the one to aid my search then. I started automatically to say I wasn't Mrs. Corbett, took in his respectability and swallowed the words. He was built like a slender boy, but he wore what my grandmother would have called best Sunday blacks. Little black eyes twinkled and snapped over a smiling mouth set in a trimmed gray spade of beard; he stood straight but leaning forward a little as if he were listening, waiting, an expectant, anxious host.

He didn't look as if he had been disturbed by screams in the night.

Cottie retreated to my pajama leg.

I thought I had better begin obliquely. "It's lovely here."

He asked briskly, "You'll be wanting milk? This way."

He pattered so rapidly away from me I had no time to get farther.

He led us through his house—it was old fashioned and scrubbed, with old walnut furniture on a board floor, bare except

35

for one round hooked rug under the dining table in the center—through the back door and down a plank walk to the barn. He chattered as he went, almost like Cottie. In the barn we entered a cement room almost as scrubbed as the house. A thin hungry-looking boy of perhaps eighteen with colorless stiff hair and a big nose was straining milk.

"This is Elmer." John Loxton's speech had something in common with a 1904 primer. "Elmer, this is Mrs. Corbett. The boy wants milk, eh, son? Give them some milk, Elmer."

"Yes'r." Elmer took a bottle from a table, opened the door of what looked like an oven full of bottles, slipped that one in and another out.

"'T's my ster'lizer." Elmer spoke so fast he had time for only half his syllables, and he worked like an express train. By the time the milk was in the bottle—a few seconds—I'd learned perforce about Elmer's making an old oven into a sterilizer and that he might get it patented. Cottie buzzed about like a fly, Elmer tipping him out of milk cans and water tubs at the psychological moment.

I was impatient to be back at my hunt. John Loxton followed me, beaming, from the barn, rubbing his hands. I asked without preamble:

"Who screamed last night? Was someone ill?"

The hands stopped in mid-rub, and the smiling eyes started.

"Someone ill? That would be a pity. I'm a little hard of hearing, but I'm sure I'd have heard anyone scream. Or if anyone had been ill I should know by now. You see, living as I do by the gate, no one drives in or out without my being aware. I'll show you."

He pattered to the front of his house and pointed out a rubber hose laid across the driveway. "It rings a bell in my room if anyone drives across. No one went in or out except Mr. Jordan, cottage three. He came last night about nine. I'm sure no one left."

I kept Cottie from picking up the hose.

"I'm still quite sure someone screamed," I insisted. "Twice. The first scream woke me. I was wide awake at the second. I don't see how I could be mistaken."

CHAPTER FOUR

ANXIETY LEFT John Loxton's face for crinkling laughter.

"Mrs. Corbett! Of course you don't know them as we do. Screaming. It's the loons. You heard the loons."

I'd heard of loons, heard they had a queer call. I asked more uncertainly, trying to tune that remembered cry to a bird's throat, "Do loons scream like a frightened woman in the middle of the night?"

He beamed at me. "They do, Mrs. Corbett. Exactly. Very strange sound. Fascinates everyone who comes here. You know the name of this lodge?"

His head tipped to the side like Cottie's in an ingratiating moment.

I said, "Yes, of course. The Crying Sisters."

He told me then the story that was to take its own place in the chain.

"That's a name that means something, Mrs. Corbett. There are really two lakes here. Swampy shallows between them. We're on Big Sister. The smaller lake to the south is Little Sister. Legend says twin Indian sisters once lived here with their tribe—daughters of a chief. One was to marry into her own tribe, but the chief wanted the other to marry into a neighboring tribe—some question of a treaty. Rather than be separated, the sisters jumped from a canoe into the middle of the lake. I've been told the lake is a hundred and twenty feet deep out there. Their bodies came ashore—that's another legend of the lake, that nothing ever sinks in it. Something about the springs and the waves. Sooner or later any loose object comes

38

ashore. But anyway, our sisters. As punishment for their willfulness and disobedience the Great Spirit separated their souls. One dwells at the foot of Big Sister, the other at the head of Little Sister. Only at night can they speak to each other, and then they cry across the lakes, a wait of lost and lonesome souls."

He ended on an incongruous note of beaming cheer, still rubbing his hands, with as much evident pride as if his legend were a personal possession. "Now of course, Mrs. Corbett, some people insist it is the loons that cry. You'll hear them. Undoubtedly you *have* heard them."

It was on the tip of my tongue to say that I had another reason for thinking that something had gone on last night, to tell of Steve Corbett's absence from the cabin. Perhaps I didn't say it because Cottie—Steve Corbett's son—was holding my hand.

John Loxton must have seen I wasn't convinced. He added anxiously, "You're maybe a little nervous in a strange place? I'll just show you all the people here. I'd be nervous now myself if I didn't check over my visitors. Screams in the night! Dear, dear! I can't have anything like that going on."

He trotted ahead; I followed with Cottie and the milk. At last he'd gotten the idea. This was what I wanted, a house-to-house canvass.

The dark woman in cottage one had our first call. I didn't expect much there; she'd looked too stolidly calm. As she stepped from her porch I wondered why fat women are called shapeless; this one had a variety of personal porches, front and rear, that certainly gave her shape. Her black hair hung in a Dutch bob; her youth must have coincided with Colleen Moore's reign. Eldreth has relic hairdresses like that from 1890 on. The only change she had made was to pin back the side hair with small barrettes of pink, blue and yellow celluloid flowers. Eyelids, puffed both above and below, tilted her hazel eyes, and her skin was a brownish yellow. I wondered if she drank.

Mrs. Rudeen said, "Nice day," shortly when introduced. But she wasn't disinterested; the slitted eyes watched me, watched Cottie. "Your kid?"

I glanced hastily at my situation and lied. "Yes."

"Cute."

Loxton laughed in apology for my shortness. "Mrs. Corbett was bothered last night. By the loons. She thought she heard a scream. You hear anything last night, Mrs. Rudeen?"

The woman considered, her eyes still on me. "Nobody in this place likely to be screamen. More'n likely those loons."

It was a clipped Texas drawl. As she talked on she made no mention of anyone else in her cottage; she seemed to be there alone. The car beside her cabin was that year's Packard, but she didn't look used to fine things.

I thought there might be things to find out about Mrs. Rudeen.

The second cottage had a '36 Ford beside it, but the porch was still empty.

Loxton paused. "Willards live here. They sleep late. I'm afraid they'll have to wait."

I marked the Willards to be checked on later.

At the third cabin a single male came out at our knock, smiling, he too apparently undisturbed by screams or anything else. He was one of those blond men who can spread glamour over themselves like a net, and he had the lazy eyes men have whose upper lids never rise very far and are decorated with heavy lashes. As soon as the eyes hit me I knew that if I stayed and wanted masculine company I could have it.

He turned out to be a bond salesman named Earl Jordan.

40

His own laughing words, in a tone that took the curse off the brag, were, "New York. I'm big-town stuff."

"Did you hear any screaming last night?" I asked at once.

He looked startled. "The lady hears things—oh, the loons. I guess you did hear something. Didn't Loxton tell you?"

That made three witnesses against my ears. Loxton was slightly deaf; Mrs. Rudeen wasn't a woman on whose testimony I'd put much faith, but now this man, too. My certainty was badly shaken.

Earl Jordan said we'd like the place; the bathing and fishing were good, and if we liked there was good gambling across Big Sister.

That was when I first heard about the Flaming Door. He walked me to the edge of the bank; I had to bend to see it through the trees—a red roof and the glint of glass.

"Only other habitation on the two lakes," Loxton explained proudly. "This is pretty wild country up here. Not even a road around Little Sister."

Cottie was squatting to look, too, immediately demanding, "Let's go see it now."

Earl Jordan laughed. "No place for you, kid. What's your name?"

"I'm Cottie."

He turned to me. "What's that short for?"

Starting, I wondered how I could explain that lack of knowledge. I said lamely, "That's just his baby talk."

"He reminds me of a kid I knew once, only his name was——" He halted abruptly, and I was glad enough to have the subject dropped.

Earl Jordan added himself to the group as we went on to the next cottage where the children played.

The girl called as we came near, "I'm Joanie, who're you?"

Both she and the boy, whose name turned out to be Bits, stared at Cottie as a woman came out of the cabin.

"We're around getting acquainted," John Loxton told her, introducing me.

Mrs. Clapshaw carried herself like a small dragoon and had a nose like a thin white claw. I thought she'd be the acid test.

"A scream?" she repeated rapidly, reaching upward with the nose. "Mrs. Corbett, I'm so glad you heard it. It's the Reds. I've told Mr. Loxton here. There are un-American activities going on at that Flaming Door. Nazis." She bit at her decisive words as they went past her teeth.

Earl Jordan grinned at me, and I felt completely silly. Mrs. Clapshaw had pushed my scream into melodrama.

When we left her John Loxton asked anxiously, "Now, you see, Mrs. Corbett? Except for the Willards—I'll see them as soon as they get up—you've seen most of the people here. The only others are Mr. Lewis and Mr. Sprung, and they were all right when they came for bait this morning." He made certainty doubly sure by counting on his fingers. "Cottage one, Mrs. Rudeen. Cottage two, the Willards. Mrs. Willard is a very sensible woman. I don't believe she would scream. She was once a nurse. Cottage three, Mr. Jordan. Cottage four, Mrs. Clapshaw. Cottages five and six, Mr. Sprung and Mr. Lewis. Cottages seven and eight, empty. Cottage nine, you, Mrs. Corbett. Any screaming must have come from somewhere else."

He even took his keys and opened the two empty cabins; they were as undisturbed as ours had been when we came yesterday. He was so pathetically worried and eager to have me believe the best of his resort that I had to say I'd been mistaken.

Well, sound carries far across water. Perhaps that scream had come from the Flaming Door. If the Willards and Al Sprung and Harry Lewis were also undisturbed it would look as if I'd had

42

my night fears for nothing, and perhaps Steve Corbett had just taken a walk.

Steve Corbett wasn't in the cabin when we got back. He'd made up his cot neatly and eaten, but left the dishes for me to wash. Later we found him down on the lake shore, in trunks and nothing else, bailing out a boat. I'd been right about his shoulders, they looked a foot through. To the waist he was a solid brown, but his legs were a contrasting white; he must have spent the summer shirtless. He turned his head as we came down the steps in the bank and for once spoke first.

"Find any casualties?" It was a taunt.

I said as easily as I could, "Not so far."

"Find bosom souls, I trust, in whom you can confide?"

"I didn't talk, if that's what you mean."

"Could that possibly be an instinct for self-preservation?"

"No," I told him coldly, "just wanting to know what I'm talking about before I talk."

He'd been shooting words at me. His whole face loosened and warmed as he turned to Cottie. "Hey, kid, I saw a frog under that boat."

"I need him," Cottie said, and started serious hunting.

I remembered something then. "What's Cottie short for?"

A beginning answer formed on his lips, but he cut it short to say instead, "It's just as well you don't know."

Yesterday's resentment flew up in my chest. "You can decide to treat me like a person or I leave. I don't like being pushed over or taunted or overruled or spoken to contemptuously. I can leave here today. It's my car."

"Sure. Why don't you?"

Why is it that being invited to make good on a threat makes

you want to change your mind? As usual when I'm pushed over the edge of anger, I couldn't find words, and stood sputtering.

What brought me around was a small, meek, placating "Don't be mad now, Mamma."

Cottie had stopped his frog hunt to stand picking at the rim of the boat his father was bailing, his blue eyes on me, stiff and frightened. I saw suddenly what I looked like to him: a new person, one he didn't know very well, and yet one on whom he had already fastened dependence in this wilderness of strange people, strange place, strange lake; his abrupt withdrawn father the only other person he had. And now both his people faced each other in anger, forgetting him.

I remembered what I'd read about parents fighting before a child.

I did the quickest job I've ever done of hauling myself up short, lifted the boy in my arms and carried him with all the blandishments I could muster on such short notice toward the bay to the north where I could see people lying on the sand.

At the beach I met Mrs. Willard and knew at once she hadn't screamed.

She came inshore from a swim, wiping water from a plump, lightly freckled face, pulling off a green rubber cap to shake loose red hair that stayed smooth even under that treatment. She had a nurse's manner, cool and efficient and prepared, even when stepping out of a lake.

When Mrs. Clapshaw introduced her she smiled briefly, said, "Hello. Oh, you're the one who heard the scream then, aren't you? Mr. Loxton was all perturbed, poor old soul. I assure you it wasn't at our cabin." Then she went on to a pile of bright towels and cushions flung on the sand halfway down the bay.

I had seen them all now, all the women in the resort. Mr.

44

Loxton had counted them and Mrs. Clapshaw confirmed the number. Mrs. Rudeen, Mrs. Willard, Mrs. Clapshaw, Joanie.

I decided I had heard a loon. I decided I'd stay and have fun with Cottie. I decided I'd quit looking for links in a chain.

I didn't hold to that very difficult last resolve any length of time.

By afternoon I had seen the three other people who lived at the resort and who were to be principal actors in its drama. Mr. Willard came in from swimming a few moments after his wife; a big young man who looked as if he had shrunk, with loose pale skin and light hair clipped to the scalp.

Mrs. Clapshaw whispered when he'd gone past without looking at us, "Very queer man, very queer. I wouldn't be surprised if he was a Red. Or a Fascist. Why does he wear that bathing suit?" She clipped off the last with an effect of triumphant logic.

The suit to which she referred was odd; it swathed Mr. Willard in 1910 black jersey from knee to neck. It even had sleeves.

Earl Jordan came to lie lazily in the sand. When Mrs. Clapshaw herded her charges home for lunch he told me amusedly, "Women whose faces stay on when they jump in lakes shouldn't be tied down with kids."

I looked out where Cottie was blissfully building a sand house. "I wouldn't be untied for anything." I felt that way after hours of sitting in the sun with my suspicions lulled.

"Ever have any time of your own?"

He was trying to flirt with me. I remembered that on Saturday I had wanted to be flirted with—that seemed a little alien now. But I also remembered I wanted to check on kidnappings.

I said, "Cottie takes interminable naps after lunch."

He was a bit surprised; his lazy long lashes lifted a little from

45

eyes that were very dark blue and quite wise enough to estimate just what effect they were having on me.

"Anything I can do about that interminable business?"

I phrased my answer carefully, "I haven't even a radio in my car."

He invited promptly, "You could do my radio a favor."

It didn't seem important if he got the wrong idea.

It was when I went to listen to his radio that I got what was, if not a new link in the chain, then a completing segment of one I already had.

I left when Cottie was settled for his nap, with the excuse that I was going for more milk. Steve Corbett, who had fished unsuccessfully all morning after bailing out the boat, was brooding again on his cot; he didn't comment.

As I left Elmer with the filled milk bottle in my hand I saw the two men I had yet to meet. They were talking to John Loxton on the north lawn of his house, near a colorful stretch of flower gardens. When Loxton called to me I picked a way across the still-wet lawn.

"These gentlemen are anxious to meet our new visitor." Loxton's black eyes twinkled above his gray beard, and his shoulders bent in their hostly stoop. "This is Mr. Lewis, Mrs. Corbett. And this is Mr. Sprung."

Mr. Lewis was big, with iron-gray hair and a fresh pink well-creamed face. He was built on the lines of any U. S. President about 1900, and many women would call him handsome. He'd been holding up a thick panting fish for the admiration of the other two men.

"You make me sorry I'm leaving today, Mrs. Corbett, but I'll be back. Does your husband loan you out for fishing trips?" His voice had a sonorous roll, and his compliments a professional ease.

"That's one nice thing about having a small boy," I said. "He makes such an efficient chaperon."

"I thought you was bringin' your own wife down here pretty soon," the man introduced as Mr. Sprung said.

If Mr. Sprung had lived in Eldreth he'd spend his time in the pool hall and sponge money from relatives. He was about forty and small, showing the unmistakable signs of malnutrition in childhood, but he was decorated with a Colman mustache, and his eyes were bold, traveling from my face on down.

Mr. Loxton was explaining. "Mr. Sprung is an old resident. In fact it was from Mr. Sprung that I bought this resort two years ago, after his mother's death."

"Yep, this is old home week for Al," Mr. Lewis contributed. He laughed largely. "I heard you laid awake hearing things last night, Mrs. Corbett. Sorry I didn't hear anything. Al here—the state Al goes to bed in he never hears anything."

I could believe that.

"Never was nothin' to do up here but sleep. C'mon, Harry, if we're gonna fish, le's fish." Mr. Sprung recognized no stops between words.

"You're taking me away from awfully nice company," Mr. Lewis said, and held the fish up for my admiration before he followed.

Mr. Loxton smiled at their backs. "Our resort seem more homelike to you now you know the folks, Mrs. Corbett?"

"Very much so." I didn't say I was reserving judgment on some of those people. The Al Sprung I had just met, Mrs. Rudeen. Mr. Lewis could be a confidence man. And the man in my own house . . .

Again John Loxton seemed to sense my reservations.

"Wouldn't you like to look at my flowers?"

It was the first time I'd paid any attention to that boundary of the resort. Against a shoulder-high wall were banks of cosmos and tall daisies and long beds of zinnias. John Loxton walked lovingly along the grassy edge of the gardens. A few leaves and petals lay tattered on ground that was still as wet as plaster, but before the storm the place must have been as neat as his house. Farther along the wall he had a bed of salvia, dripping its small crimson flowers like eardrops, and at the end what was evidently his special pride, a new variety of dahlia, faintly pink like roses, but with heads as big as chrysanthemums.

He twinkled as I praised, then returned with regret to what he'd kept me for.

"Odd fellow, Mr. Sprung. You mustn't let him annoy you. He does drink. But this being originally his home, I hate to ask him to leave. He doesn't usually stay long."

"That's all right," I assured him. "I'll keep out of his way."

I didn't know then how difficult it was going to be to keep out of Mr. Sprung's way, or for what a long section of the chain he was going to be responsible.

I got away from Mr. Loxton in time to get to Earl Jordan's cottage for the one forty-five newscast. Mr. Jordan didn't miss that I'd combed my hair and put on a clean shirt and slacks.

"Why don't we drive while we listen to this radio?" he asked at once. "Your husband wouldn't mind, would he?"

No, he wouldn't! But I excused myself. "I'm lazy from all the riding we did yesterday. Let's just stay here."

His car was a battered Buick roadster. We sat in it with the last of a music program on low. Earl Jordan said he was originally a Canadian but since then he'd been everywhere, he liked excitement.

I sent out at hazard, "Find anything exciting here?"

He laughed. "In this dump? I come here to rest up, same as I'd take a Turkish bath."

"Sh-sh-sh," I said, because the newscast was beginning. "Not having a paper makes me wonder if the rest of the world is hanging on."

The news was about China, Spain, Hitler, a murder trial in Pensacola and a dog lost down a crevasse in Montana. If Cottie had been kidnapped it wasn't known yet. The police bulletin came on, and then the announcer's mellifluous voice uttered words that had me rigid.

"Janet Ruell, who is believed to be traveling in the northern part of Minnesota, is asked to get in touch with George Train in Eldreth, Minnesota, immediately. Anyone else knowing the whereabouts of Miss Ruell is asked to inform her."

CHAPTER FIVE

MY EYES MUST have been popping.

Earl Jordan asked quickly, "What's the matter? You know anything about this girl? What's her name?"

"Janet Ruell. No—yes." I pushed words around with complete disregard for truth. "I work in a library, too—I mean I did before. I used to know a Janet Ruell. I wonder what's——"

"That's easy. You could call this man and find out. I'll drive you in to Maple Valley."

"No, wait." I had to think.

For what reason could George Train be calling me? My right hand twisted over my left, where George had tried to put, only last Friday night, his mother's unburied engagement ring. I had trouble even imagining that George Train still existed, that his pale eyes still peered through the wicket of Eldreth State Bank. Why in heaven's name should he radio for me? I'd told him definitely I'd make up my mind about marrying him only after this vacation.

Maple Valley—if I knew small towns I wouldn't be able to make a long-distance call without being listened in on by the operator. Earl Jordan would soon know from the operator, if he took me there, that I wasn't what I was pretending to be. And I didn't know yet whether I wanted him to know that fact or not.

I said, "After all, I haven't seen the girl for a long time." That was true enough, with the sort of mirror our cottage had. "I wouldn't be able to tell this man anything. And I must be getting back. My little boy will be waiting."

He demurred, but I got away quickly. I wanted to see if Steve Corbett knew anything about this.

When I told him he asked coolly without rising, "Who's George Train?"

"A man I know in Eldreth."

It didn't seem to mean anything to him. He said negligently, "I'll take you somewhere you can call as soon as the kid wakes."

He'd take me, in my car. Just an employee being allowed to meet a personal obligation. I began firing but stopped. What was the use? I knew where I'd come out.

The town he took me to was Duluth, forty-three miles. He wasn't having it known locally that I was Janet Ruell.

At the entrance to a department store he told me abruptly to look at my watch: it was three forty-seven. I was to be back out there in an hour. The car drove off, Cottie's head out the window, looking back.

I stood under the canopy of that store, a free agent. I had money in my bag; it would be very easy to get away now.

I went into the store, got a good supply of change and made for the nearest phone booth.

George's voice came thin and suspicious over the wire.

"Of course it's me," I said, trying to feel that at the other end of the wire was home and security. All I felt was impatience. "I heard your radio call. What do you want?"

"Some man named Corbett called up about you, Janet. Late Sunday afternoon. Called the operator here. You know, Bertha Lind. Asked her who you were. What you did. Bertha says he sounded a very rough man. Everyone in town is saying you've gone off with a man. Now Janet, if you've gotten yourself into any——"

I listened for six sputtering minutes, every one of which cost me money. Then I stopped it.

"George, you're being just silly. Didn't you ever hear of references? I was trying to get a job. As a companion. No, not to a man. To his wife. She's an invalid. I got it. I don't have anything to do with the man. If you want to reach me write to general delivery, Duluth. And quit worrying."

Having done all that tampering with fact, I hung up. The forty minutes I had left of my hour I spent buying wash suits for Cottie. At four forty-four I was under the awning, and at four forty-seven the car came.

Cottie climbed all over me. "Did you buy me somesing?"

He was becoming as skilled at reading me as his father. I presented the suits and an all-day sucker.

Over his blissful head I asked, "Why didn't you tell me you called Eldreth for references? Now they're saying I've gone off with a man."

He actually grinned at a cable car he swung out to miss.

"It's the truth, isn't it?"

"You could have been less suggestive."

He shrugged. "I couldn't trust my kid with a strange woman."

It rounded out that initial link of my hiring. I saw in his asking for references a man taking honest care of his son.

My distrust of him lessened. Perhaps I had misjudged him. I felt almost amiable toward him on that homeward drive.

Cottie dropped asleep at the table that evening. As soon as his head touched the table his father took something from his shirt pocket and threw it toward me.

"It might be a good idea for you to wear this," he said.

The box I pulled my knees hastily together to catch was blue velvet, and the ring inside was a chased circlet of yellow gold.

52

It struck me with a queer incoherent emotion. "Oh no, I can't wear it. It's——"

He said, "You can give it back when you're done with it."

His face was, if anything, rockier than ever. "Isn't it time you got the kid to bed?"

Putting Cottie to bed, realizing that now again night lay ahead, cleared me of emotion quickly. Tonight should clear up whether anything strange were going on here or not.

During the day I had listened, on and off, for bird cries. Chirps, twitterings, the buzz and fly of insects—there had been plenty of sounds, but nothing that resembled a cry.

Even as I was thinking that a cry came. It seemed to descend from Little Sister to the south, a high thin wail, lost and despairing. It was answered almost at once from some point high but nearer. Again and again the calls came, beginning faintly, rising to a crescendo of wild pleading, fading as if with lost hope, rising again.

When I got to the door I saw that Steve Corbett was listening, too. He had risen from his cot to go to the porch screen.

Of one thing I was certain. This wasn't the cry I had heard last night. I could easily imagine this call as coming from a bird; it was eerie, inhuman, its shrill despair not tuned to a human throat.

I said, "That cry I heard last night wasn't like this."

He said, "The less you talk about that cry last night the better off you'll be."

A slight beginning tautness moved up my back as he went back to his cot and lay down upon it. Would he go out again tonight? And if he did what would that mean? Would there be another scream?

I lay down on my bed without undressing, determined to see what happened. His breath became measured and even; he was asleep.

The night outside the cabin became quiet; the loon calls died away. Once someone walked along the hill in back of the house. Then there were only the silky insinuating whispers of leaves and water, the thin crackling of the cicadas.

Easy to hear when the rhythm of Steve Corbett's breathing changed and his feet slid to the floor. Easy to hear his step crossing the porch, the rasp of the key in the padlock, the whining swing of the screen, the padlock being fixed again on the outside.

He was gone again, leaving us locked in.

Tonight, whatever else I did, I wasn't going to become frightened. I stole on barely audible feet to the outside door. There was a little light; the sky overhead was seeded with stars hanging suspended in high air like glinting snowflakes. No moon, but the lake had a faint light instead—a pale, pearly nimbus.

I had been so quick that I saw a shadow disappearing behind the next cabin.

He must be going toward some one of those cabins that had stood so ordinary in daylight. Toward some one of those people I had checked over so carefully that day: Mr. Loxton, Elmer, Mrs. Rudeen, the Willards, Mr. Jordan, Mrs. Clapshaw, Mr. Sprung. Mr. Lewis had left as he said he was.

To which of those people was Steve Corbett stealing out? Why, if he wanted to see someone, didn't he see him or her by daylight? During the day he hadn't appeared to pay any attention to anyone. He had slept late, gone fishing alone, stayed brooding on the cot on the porch until we had gone to Duluth and after we came back.

Curiosity to know what he was up to pulled at me so strongly I almost decided to cut through the screening in the door and follow. If it hadn't been that that would have left Cottie unguarded I think I'd have gone. I wasn't afraid any more; the day had done away with that. I just had an awful, consuming desire to *know*.

Again I ran over the gamut of possibilities. Steve Corbett might have been here before, hidden something here, and gone out to find it. He might be spying on someone. Kidnapping was almost out. He might be planning something with some other resident. Whatever it was, was important enough so he'd spend a lot of time brooding about it. It must be secret, because he'd gone to all the trouble of providing me as camouflage. And it must have elements of danger or he wouldn't have given me the gun, which I suspected now was to protect Cottie.

I stood at that door until my legs were asleep to the knees, until my elbows cramped, and my mind just drifted.

No one screamed that night; I was sure of that.

It was after three when a shadow moved again at the back of the next cabin. I retreated to my bed, and a key clicked lightly against the padlock. In thirty seconds the man was on his cot.

I lay almost smothered under unanswered questions. I would have liked to shake the man into telling me what he was about.

But I knew I could just as well have shaken a stone wall.

Morning showed the resort wearing its normal daytime face again, and again I had to take it at its face value, but I stayed watchful. People slept late, went fishing, drove to Maple Valley for groceries. Elmer came around with lake ice for the boxes, and milk for those too lazy to carry their own. Between ten and twelve most of the inhabitants turned up at the bathing beach for swimming or sunning. The only people not following the routine were Elmer, Mrs. Rudeen and Mr. Loxton. The boy worked all day long, milking, mowing the lawns, cleaning the barn and the Loxton cabin. Mrs. Rudeen kept to herself. Mr. Loxton usually spent most of the time on his garden, Mrs. Clapshaw said. He was fussing that morning because the ground was still too wet for him to work there. Mrs. Clapshaw wasn't certain so tender a preoccupation with flowers was American—in a man.

Early that Wednesday morning Steve Corbett struck up an acquaintance with Earl Jordan and Al Sprung, and the three went fishing. I spent the time wondering if that meant Steve Corbett's business had something to do with those two men, and trying to clean the cottage, with Cottie's devastating help. I found he had no clean suits left. When I set about remedying that he spooned out my suds into an ancient coffeepot. His father came back just as a last spoonful spilled over to the floor.

"Too full," I told Cottie. "I'll empty out some." And did.

The boy threw himself on the floor kicking his heels. "No! I want it spills!"

"Here!" His father shoved his fishing tackle on top of the cupboard—all dangerous articles were up there by that time— and stood over the boy. "What you need is exercise. Let's us get out of here."

The two of them left, Cottie at once happy. Later, when I went out with my clothes, Cottie was swinging on a stuffed grain sack hanging from a tree behind the house. On the next tree hung a larger object made of two grain sacks. Steve Corbett stood with his hands in his pockets watching Cottie.

"You're going to be football stuff or my name is mud," he was saying. "Now watch this."

He took a running start and threw himself at the other stuffed object.

I didn't know then just how it fit in, but I'd learned one thing more about Steve Corbett. The hanging objects were rough tackling dummies, and the man went at his with a practiced ease which suggested that at some time he had played football, probably good football. He'd said he was a highway engineer; he'd learned a sailor's walk, and he'd played football. It was a lot, but somehow it wasn't incongruous. He was a man who would crowd his life with activity.

What I wanted to know was what activity he was up to here.

Cottie was so thrilled with Osco and Bosco, as he called the dummies, that he didn't even want to leave them for lunch. When I finally got him away I thought Osco and Bosco looked a bit unpleasant, suspended there side by side. Almost like hanging men.

That night came the first sign that I wasn't alone in wondering about Steve Corbett's night errands.

Earl Jordan and Al Sprung came to get him for a poker game after supper. When Cottie and I went up for the evening's milk we saw the three men on Sprung's porch, with a bottle on the table where they played.

Clouds had been gathering rapidly since dusk; the first drops of rain fell as I was putting Cottie to bed. The loons cried again. I was sleepy from my disturbed rest, but I was uneasy, too, because the porch screen was unlocked so Steve Corbett could get in. What would happen tonight? The smell of rain deepened, as wet and sweet as white clover. It rained hard through an evening when I half slept and half waited. I roused entirely at midnight when Steve Corbett came in; the rain had lightened then.

He stayed on his cot only a few minutes before he went again.

It hadn't done me any earthly good to watch the nights before; I decided to stay in bed. I wondered if I would get so used to his night prowls that I wouldn't even wake. I thought that his daytime consorting with Earl Jordan and Al Sprung was probably an offshoot of his night business, that the three men must be up to something together.

I think I'd have slept again if he hadn't come back so quickly. He seemed to fumble as he fastened the padlock on the inside; his breathing sounded labored as he slipped immediately to his cot.

At once I was alert, waiting, feeling that something more had to happen. Nothing showed at the room door but a faintly seen rectangle.

Then suddenly there was one brief beam of bright light. Not in at my door, but to the left of it. By the door to the porch.

Involuntarily my muscles lifted until I was sitting. Something would come of this night business now. I had in an instant a hundred blinding expectations—a shot through the door, harsh angry voices calling to open, Steve Corbett rushing to attack the source of the light, men tramping in to say he was caught. My internal arrangements drew out into a rope and then tied themselves into one tight knot as I sat there with all animation suspended.

But nothing happened. The light didn't come again; one faint, light footfall sounded on the grass outside and that was all.

Slowly my heart forced room enough for itself to thump. Five minutes, ten, fifteen. Waiting for the light to come again, and something else with it.

Steve Corbett must know what this meant; might know what was going to happen. When my legs would hold me I crept toward his cot.

A tight low whisper struck me. "Back to bed, you idiot. Someone's around with a flashlight."

His voice was such that I obeyed.

But not without learning something. Steve Corbett didn't want the person who had held that flashlight to know he had been out, to know that any unusual night activity went on at our cabin.

And the corollary to that was that someone in the resort suspected him of that activity—and objected to it.

His warning conveyed to me that the objection might be violent. Somewhere along the chain there would be conflict.

I determined on doing some talking when morning came.

I had a hard time doing it. After that uneasy night it was midmorning when I woke. For once Cottie must have slept late, too, and when he did wake he must have explored the bureau instead of waking me, because I opened my eyes on a startling object. Streaks of red crisscrossed his face from lip corner to ear, from eye to chin.

"Cottie! What——"

He said smugly, "I nice now."

It wasn't blood. Lipstick. The one cosmetic I use.

When I hauled him to the porch for a protested scrubbing Steve Corbett's cot was already empty; a knife and plate on the table suggested he'd eaten and left.

That was on Thursday. As on the other days, no sign of the night's activities showed. No one seemed to hold it against me that Steve Corbett went out at night. Yet I can see now that the links in the chain were forming with inexorable swiftness.

Steve Corbett had gone fishing with Al Sprung and Earl Jordan; the three men ran into a school of crappies and had a good catch. They returned in boisterous good spirits. They came running down to the beach where I was with Cottie. I sat on shore in a sort of throttled exasperation, watching them race and play and tumble in the water like schoolboys.

Al Sprung, to my surprise, could dive beautifully; when he headed for water even his chest seemed to straighten out. Earl Jordan was clumsier, as if he'd learned water habits late. Steve Corbett was careless but completely at home.

What annoyed me was why was he doing it? The moment he was alone with Cottie and me at lunch he relapsed into glumness.

I settled Cottie for his nap with dispatch and returned to the porch to do the talking I determined on last night.

"What did that flashlight business mean?"

He took on his manner of its not mattering what I believed. "Maybe someone thinks I leave here at night."

"Then someone would object?"

"Possibly."

I dared an outright question. "What are you trying to do—find something?"

"You might call it that."

"You stay right here in the resort."

"How pleasant, to have a little detective in one's home."

"I've got to know what's going on. I can't——"

"Life's interesting here, isn't it? Much more so than in Eldreth, Minnesota?"

I choked down what I might have said for another attempt to get what I wanted. "What could there be to find in this place? No one here has money. Just the most ordinary——"

"You might be surprised."

"You mean someone here—are you spying on someone?"

He said, "See here, I brought you along because I thought it was a good idea for the kid." He grinned. "And, Mamma, your niceness is almost blatant. Fine for me. But if you throw any monkey wrenches into my game you're going to be appalled at what the human mind—mine—can think up to do to you. I'm not asking much. Just keep your nose where it belongs. One peep to anyone here about my goings on and you'll never see the kid again. Like that?"

Things I could say nearly burst my throat.

But instead I found myself slamming the house door behind me. I sat on my bed watching Cottie sleep.

When Cottie woke I took him to the porch to wash and dress, and had that immediate awareness of something going on that comes from another person's tension.

Steve Corbett walked toward us smiling, took Cottie from my arms, and sat down to dress the boy himself.

"Hi, kid, have a nice rest? Look, how'd you like to row over to the little island? I stopped off there and it's a nice spot."

"I go in a boat, too, Daddy. Don't I go in a boat?" Cottie didn't miss opportunities even when barely awake.

"Sure," the man said. "You have to sit in the front seat. You'll have to wear shoes. Mamma, how's about shoes?"

No use asking what this loving-father business meant.When I came back with the shoes he was washing Cottie's face.

"What's the matter?" he asked in general. "Doesn't any-one around here have any ideas except me? Why don't we have a picnic? We could run in to Maple Valley, get wieners and buns——"

"Mellows!" yelled Cottie. "I need mellows!"

"Sh-sh-sh. All in good order. Marshmallows, too."

I began then to get not only what was going on, but also what had gone on in the lake that morning.

He was averting suspicion. He had a reason, too. Sitting on the edge of the bank directly before our cabin, with her back to us, was Mrs. Rudeen. Undoubtedly listening.

At last I could definitely tie down the activities in that resort to one other person beside Steve Corbett.

And for the first time, too, I thought, the activities of the night were beginning to break through into daylight. Had Mrs. Rudeen held that flashlight?

It wasn't to be the last time that day that I felt surveillance.

Steve Corbett turned off his camaraderie on the way to town and back, but as soon as he was in the resort he was once more the attentive husband and father. He helped me into the boat with a Clark Gable effect of awkward gallantry.

61

"You sit there in the end and hold Cottie." The tone was genial. "But God help you if you drop him."

Heaven knew I was careful; I held onto Cottie as if he were an eel in buttons.

There were two islands in the lakes: a large one almost overgrown with trees and bushes in Little Sister, and the small island in Big Sister. Like this:

It was to the little island, which was to be so important later, that Steve Corbett took us now. It was like a crown roast: trees around it, and in the center a level grassy plain. Children must have played there because Cottie at once lit on what had been a board hut.

"Did any kids live in it, you sink?"

"No, it's a playhouse," I told him.

"I need a playhouse."

"We should be able to do something about that," his father promised agreeably. He hunted along the shore for two smooth rocks.

"Mamma and Papa will now build their little boy a playhouse," he ordered.

That was what we did all that Thursday afternoon. By five Cottie sat in awe under what he considered his own roof.

"Come in," he invited. "Lets us eat now. Mellows."

I suggested a fire and the wieners first. Being host, he had to halt a howl in mid-arrival. His father set about the fire, and I wandered off for roasting sticks.

I was on tiptoe tugging at a stubborn branch when through a bush right ahead of me—a bush that was otherwise thickly green—I saw one black patch, and as I looked that black patch moved.

I dropped, the branch fortunately coming with me, hiding my face. Something, someone, was crouching behind that bush. I stood rigid while ice water replaced the blood in my arteries. Mrs. Rudeen had worn something brightly printed. This must be a man. Perhaps she was here, too. Perhaps I was surrounded. My head jerked so quickly I got one of those paralyzing pangs in back of my neck. I began backing, then realized that would look suspicious, and tried to walk normally back to what seemed now almost like safety—Steve Corbett.

When nothing stopped me I began running. He heard me, and his eyes were immediately quick.

"Mamma, never get excited," he said coldly.

"We've—got—company," I got out in jerks, and sat down because my bones were threatening to become ice water, too.

He asked quietly, "Mrs. Rudeen? Sprung?"

A patch of black.

"I didn't stop to look."

"You're getting sense. Just stay here. Everything's under control."

He went off to a piercing untuned whistle. Cottie came toward me, asking, "You hurt, Mamma?" He must have felt my apprehension, because he sat down on his ankles beside me, looking gravely off the way his father had gone.

I began telling myself I was a silly fool. Just because this spy was startling and unexpected I had let myself be frightened. Sense began coming back. Anyone who watched Steve Corbett might have a perfectly legitimate reason for doing so.

Just the same I was glad when he came back, behind enough foliage to be Macduff coming to Dunsinane, asking, "Anyone helping me trim these sticks?"

Cottie sprang up, his world at once right again. "I help."

I stood up, too. "Who was it?"

He looked surprised that I'd ask. "Oh, some man."

"Is he still here?"

"Went off in a boat."

"He was spying on us."

He asked carelessly, "What if he was?"

CHAPTER SIX

ALL AT ONCE I was angry. I had been startled, and he took it so lightly.

I accused, "You mean we were giving him a good show."

"Weren't we?"

"That flashlight. Mrs. Rudeen. Now this. It's all—part of a chain. Why're they doing it?"

He said definitely, "Mamma, you ask too many questions."

I stripped twigs from branches. Five minutes later I found I'd been holding my mouth so tightly clenched that my lips prickled.

Except that he seemed alert to sounds, Steve Corbett finished the picnic as if nothing had happened. Clouds began coming up as we were leaving; we were in for more rain. On the way back I spent my time wondering what this night would bring forth.

It began quickly.

Al Sprung was hovering at the top of our steps, and it seemed to me, in my upset state, that he was like a spider waiting for its prey. His prominent dark eyes swung from me to Steve Corbett.

"Me 'n' Jordan 'r' running over to the Flaming Door. Want to come along, Corbett?"

I wanted to shout, "No!"

But Steve Corbett was saying, "You took me for plenty last night. Oh, I guess I can stand it."

He said it lightly, but he tensed too. I knew it as soon as he laid the sleeping Cottie on the bed and turned to me. His eyes

65

were too bright. He was expectant, taut. His hand went into his breeches pocket and came out with the padlock.

He said tersely, "Keep your gun handy tonight. Lock yourself in. Don't go out or open the door to anyone except me."

It'll break now. That was what my mind said. All those links in the chain had just been something I saw. Now they were breaking into the open.

The man looked at me and read my emotion and smiled. "Don't you worry about me, Mamma. I can take care of myself."

"I'm not worrying about you. What about Cottie? You don't have to leave us here. We'll go, too. Anywhere——"

He took me by one shoulder, shook me by it. "Listen. If you go in for hysterics I'll slam you down. Nothing is going to happen to you. You're just nervous over those people watching. Sit down there and get a grip on yourself."

He pushed me to my bed: I sat there, watching him get ready to go with my apprehension not lessening but increasing. From his zipper shaving kit on the cupboard he took a wad of money. Then he came back into the room to bend over his Gladstone.

It was while he was doing that that I saw the flakes of white ash to the left of the dresser.

"Look."

He turned on his heel as he squatted, the easy, oiled motion with which he always turned. His eye caught my finger and its direction.

For once he was caught outside himself; his tone was quick, speculative. "They've been here all right. Cigarette ashes." Then he caught himself as he turned to me. "Anything missing?"

The scene began not to be real. My gun first. It was still in its place. Steve Corbett took it from me for a quick scrutiny.

"Nobody's touched that," he said, and gave it back.

I kept it in my hand while I went over the rest of my possessions. Because we'd gone to town first I'd had my handbag along; only my clothes had been left in the cabin. They were a little disarranged but all there. The same with Cottie's things. The man was checking his own.

"Nothing gone." He repeated my findings, it seemed to me, with hard cheerfulness. "Not a thief. Just someone wanting to find out if there was anything to find out." He was taking a canvas holster from the shirt fold of the Gladstone and a revolver from the bottom.

So he had a gun, too. He started strapping on the holster, and the same motion that had stirred when Cottie called me mamma, stirred again, to a different purpose.

I said unsteadily, "You'd think this was war."

"Maybe it is." He moved so quickly he'd soon be gone. He was pulling a tweed jacket over his heavy shoulders. It must have been tailored to conceal the gun, because no outline of it showed.

The apprehension in my throat thickened so I could hardly get words past it. What he was preparing for was violence. His face was tightening to an inner rigidity of preparedness.

I clung to one support. "You wouldn't leave Cottie here unless it was safe."

He was pulling a felt hat low over his eyes and starting for the door. "You'll be safe enough if you do as I said."

He didn't repeat his orders, but at the door he stopped short, came back. His eyes slid once over Cottie, then were on me, wooden. His right hand came toward me with my car keys in it.

I took them.

He said deliberately, "If I'm not back by morning keep the cabin locked until ten o'clock. Don't go out for any reason. At ten take Cottie, get in your car and beat it. Don't bother about getting any of this junk. Just grab the kid and get out of here without talking to anyone or stopping for anything. Get that? Take the kid to your home town and hold on to him until I turn up."

I said through the thickness, "Suppose you don't——"

His lips stretched sidewise. "You'd like that, wouldn't you? The kid would be yours. Okay, you've got the idea."

He was off then. I heard two cars leave.

Mrs. Clapshaw came by with Joanie while I was stiffly brushing up those telltale ashes, throwing them away.

"Is Cottie asleep? Why don't you carry him to our cottage? We could play cards."

"I'm worn out from a picnic," I told her.

Don't open the door to anyone. Could that include Mrs. Clapshaw?

"Granny says she'll make candy if you'll come," Joanie coaxed.

They stood outside my padlocked porch talking a while, obviously more and more surprised and displeased because I didn't ask them in, and went off at last patently hurt.

I knew I couldn't sleep, but I was just deciding to go to bed for what rest I could get from lying down when Mrs. Rudeen came.

I was at once on the defensive. She spoke casually. "Nice night for walken. Too bad you got that kid on your hands. Heard your old man went off with the boys. That right?"

"Yes, he went."

"Men, they're all alike," she said, and went on without asking to come in. For all her heavy body she was quite light on her feet; she moved with quick thrusts of her body. Her feet were small and stepped fast.

The rain had held off, but shortly after that it began pouring. I lay down, without undressing, on my bed, my right hand on the

68

revolver. The loons didn't cry that night; they never stayed out in rain. Was there any activity hidden under that sound of falling water? None that I could hear.

Slowly the illuminated hand on my watch dial circled the hours away. Ten o'clock, eleven, midnight. Two. Three. Did I think Steve Corbett would come back? What was going on now where he was? Was he at the Flaming Door, or somewhere else? *If I'm not there in the morning . . .* No, he had expected to return when he said that. His words and his manner, now that I thought them over in quiet, were those of a man preparing for an eventuality he doesn't really expect to happen—yet.

I wondered what I hoped. If Steve Corbett never came back, then Cottie might be mine. To keep.

I listened to the breath from the next bed; it seemed to me the soft warmth of the boy's body was something I could feel without touching. Never to say good-by to Cottie. I had a wave of emotion so intense it was painful.

No other emotion I'd ever had was as strong as this wanting to keep Cottie for my own. I knew I'd be willing to stand anything, do almost anything, just to live so that when I woke at night I'd always know he was somewhere near. Safe.

If Steve Corbett was caught at whatever secret action he was engaged in tonight . . .

I rose on my elbow to look at the sleeping child. The room was almost lightless. I could just see a dim bundle.

I even forgot to be afraid.

Steve Corbett came back just before five o'clock.

It was a terrific letdown. I knew he was coming when I heard a car's motor. I felt myself falling through spaces of disappointment, then I sat on the edge of my bed to whisper over Cottie.

69

"Not tonight."

I was waiting at the porch door when the wide figure came down the path; the gray dawn showed a dark unfeatured man I knew by size. Back of him rain mist.

He saw me through the screen, whispered, "Okay, it's me."

When I slipped the padlock from its staples he pushed the door open, came in and took the lock from my hands to replace it.

I asked, "Did it happen?"

All his tautness was gone. He chuckled. He'd been drinking; I could smell the faintly bitter whisky even from his coat.

"Al Sprung won eight thousand bucks. From a guy named Hoxie Mueller from Kansas City. That's all that happened." He walked past me, depositing the hat and his jacket on the icebox as he went. The holster with the gun still in it dropped on the table. He sat on the cot to unlace his boots.

I retreated to my inside room. He wasn't entirely drunk, but I suspected that if I'd stayed on the porch he'd have gone right on undressing.

Had nothing at all happened in his night business? This was the first night since our coming that he hadn't been out into the resort. I wondered if Al Sprung's winning all that money would have any significance in the chain.

By the next night I was to know about that.

In the morning I was dead for lack of sleep. I knew that when Cottie napped I was going to nap, too. Steve Corbett, for once having an alibi, slept all morning.

That was Friday, and as before, morning showed nothing to do but take up the routine. Cottie had another pile of clothes dirty. Not to bother Steve Corbett's sleep I took them to the lake for washing, together with Cottie, his spoons and two coffeepots—he'd foraged the extra pot from the Clapshaws.

Earl Jordan and Al Sprung came along the shore about ten.

Earl Jordan called, "Where's your husband?"

I put it briefly. "Sleeping."

"What's the matter? Can't he take it?"

"He can't keep up with bachelors."

Earl Jordan laughed, but Al Sprung didn't. His face had a dazed, half-hypnotized look.

"Jeez, I won eight thousand bucks off a guy. Cold cash. Tie that, will ya? I took it as easy as diving off that tower. Eight thousand bucks." He seemed incredulous of his own good fortune.

"Come on, guy. You need to work off some of that whisky you poured in last night," Jordan advised, and the two went on.

I was rinsing the last socks when the splash of oars sounded above the splash of water pouring from one coffeepot to the other in Cottie's busy hands. I straightened to see a boat moving in toward the dock; two men were rowing it with four inexpert oars. The blades slapped water instead of cutting in, and the timing was more that of a spider's walk than a well-rowed boat. I didn't want Cottie in the way of those oarsmen.

"Come on," I invited. "Let's go hang up the clothes now. Near Osco and Bosco."

"I help?"

"Of course you can help."

But then he saw the boat. "No! I need to stay here!"

He waded confidently out toward the approaching boat. I grabbed him by the back of the trunks just as the boat swerved toward him under what was probably a frantic effort on the oarsmen's part to swerve the other way.

Cottie squawked in mid-air. "No! 'Ey wouldn't bump me!"

"That's what you think! Stay on shore!"

"Gosh, lady, I never did get the hang of the way this thing steers."

I looked crossly over. The speaker was the popeyed, fat little man closest. He had pink hair, or else his scalp showed through. His face wore consternation, but as that faded a smile came on, a smile that looked like a permanent fixture.

The boat grated up over the pebbles of the shore, propelled by the second man, a thin man, very dark, who didn't even glance up.

I balanced the pan of clothes on one hip and got Cottie's hand.

"Wait a minute, lady." The fat one spoke again. "You know anybody in this resort name of Al Sprung?"

"I know who he is."

"You know where he's at now?"

I nodded with my head. "At the bathing beach."

"Thanks, lady, thanks!"

He clambered out of the boat on his hands and knees, but quickly. He was shaped like the roly-polies I played with as a child, narrow in the shoulders, heavily weighted at the bottom. He waddled up the beach toward where Jordan and Sprung were swimming in the blue sunlit water. The thin man stayed in the boat.

When I went into the cottage after hanging the clothes, leaving Cottie swinging on Osco, Steve Corbett was shaving, a job it took him ninety seconds, flat, to do.

He asked, "Who came in at the beach a few minutes ago?"

I described the boatmen.

He pulled his chin sidewise to get at the area to the right of his mouth, and out of that wry grin commented, "That'll be Hoxie Mueller. I thought he'd show up."

He hadn't a trace of his last night's tautness; instead he seemed to be enjoying something. I was too tired then to care much

72

about links or chains or anything else. As soon as we'd had lunch I put Cottie into one bed and myself into the other and slept.

When we woke it was after three. I saw from the porch that several people were on the beach. We got ready for the lake, too, and so walked unwittingly into drama.

Al Sprung was there. Even from the top of the stairs I could see he was quite drunk.

"——a thousand bucks in my chips," he was declaiming at a wide-eyed Mrs. Clapshaw. "Then that damn Corbett cleaned me down to my last fi' bucks. I said, don't say die. This guy from K. C. come along with a pal. I says, 'Come on in, guys.' My luck always did go better in a big game. I could tell he had the dough all right; I could tell by just looken at 'm. So he says, 'Cripes——'"

Cottie learned new words all too readily. "Come on, let's you learn to float," I coaxed, and ran with him into the water.

I noticed—even while trying to make Cottie lie down on water he wanted to sit on—that out beyond the arm of the bay was a boat with two men; Cottie's father for one, I saw by the size. I stayed out until Cottie began gasping, but even then Al Sprung was still spouting when I went back to shore.

"So when this Mueller comes over this A.M. I says to him, 'I'm no sucker. I won't play again till I get damn good and ready. I'm going to shoot some of that dough first; I'm going to have a damn good time first——'"

Beyond the two adults Bits and Joanie were wading in to shore, too. Cottie must have started toward them as I turned and bent to pick up his towel, bumping into Sprung as he flew. I was still bending when I heard the howl, and whirled to see Sprung kicking at the boy.

Cottie had tumbled face downward in the sand at the first kick. I saw the pointed shoe catch him a second time in the side.

I yelled, "Stop that!" Butting, I realized later, isn't done by ladies, but I wasn't thinking of being a lady. I remember that one moment I was kneeling on Al Sprung's chest, the next I was picking up Cottie.

It couldn't have taken long; Cottie was still face downward in the sand. When I lifted him wet sand was plastered over his cheeks, his nose, his eyelashes; his mouth was full of sand. After that first cry he hadn't uttered a sound; he was holding his breath. For a moment I thought he was dead. I held him up by his heels and slapped at his back as if he were a newborn baby. He caught his breath then and began howling and spitting sand.

I suppose that howl is among the more pleasant sounds I'll ever hear.

I sat down weakly with him on the sand. Someone put the towel in my hand; I began wiping sand from his face, his tongue. He turned in my lap until he lay face downward, rubbing his gritty forehead against my legs.

"He kicked me!" This was outrage. "He kicked me!"

Mrs. Willard had come to kneel beside me. She ordered curtly, "Here." Her fingers ran rapidly over his back, his sides, his abdomen. "I don't believe he's seriously hurt."

Cottie twisted when she touched his side.

"That hurts him," I said.

"There's a bruise coming down over his hipbone. I think that's where he was hit."

"I'll have to get him to a doctor." I stood up. "Someone get his father. I——"

Mr. Willard said, "He's coming in; I think he saw it."

I got a little of the scene then. Al Sprung was gone, running up the beach toward the stairs. I just glimpsed Mrs. Rudeen at the top of the bank looking down. Mrs. Clapshaw and the children stood by, aghast. The whole thing must have taken only a minute, but the boat was coming in, the oars striking up before they seemed to hit water.

Cottie yelled in my ear, "He kicked me!"

"I'll get Cottie in the car," I told Mrs. Willard. "Tell his father to hurry."

The car keys—I still had them. I thought of that as I stumbled up the stairs. They were still in my handbag.

I had them, had the car unlocked and the motor running when Steve Corbett jerked the right door open.

"I'll take him. You drive."

Cottie slid from my arms and I was at the wheel, the car going.

He asked tersely, "How bad?"

"He's all right, I think. Just shock. Sprung kicked him."

"He kicked me," Cottie howled. "Daddy, *he kicked me!*"

"*I saw him,*" his father said.

I'd heard that thin, high tone before. I'd heard it walking along a country road with telephone wires over my head and a wind in the wires. It was eerie in the wires. It was deadly in the man's voice.

The car whirled past Loxton's cottage. I glimpsed John Loxton running white faced from his house as if he knew—but how could he? No one would have had time to tell him unless Sprung—— But Sprung wouldn't have run to him.

Cottie's howls quieted to sobbing as we drove, with a loud, astounded catching of the breath between each sob. I spared one glance from the road for his father's face. It loomed dark and intent over the boy, vengeance if I ever saw it.

The Maple Valley doctor was in. Over the hardware store.

I learned about relief when he stood up from the office table on which Cottie lay and said, "I don't believe the boy is harmed. There's no expression of pain when I press here in the soft part of the side. One kick seems to have struck just above the knee here in back of the right leg, the second on the left hip."

Cottie had quit crying to be interested in the doctor, but his eyes were still astounded and wide.

"He kicked me," he explained.

The doctor turned to me. "You have witnesses? I'd see the sheriff. His name is Boxruud—lives right here in Maple Valley."

Steve Corbett said evenly, "The sheriff won't be necessary."

The doctor looked at him from the corners of his glasses as he helped me tug Cottie's wet bathing trunks back on. He smiled nicely.

"Be sure I don't have you brought in next. By your wife *or* the sheriff."

"I'm quite adapted to caring for myself."

He gave the doctor a bill that produced a whistle and, "I've taken out an appendix for less. Come again, any time."

The stairs going down seemed strange until I noticed I was stepping on their splintery boards with bare feet, and that above the feet I had on a damp suit.

I was almost lightheaded going back. Cottie went to sleep with his head against his father's shoulder.

Steve Corbett said, "I told you not to let the kid get hurt."

The car swerved; I had to bring my startled eyes away from his accusing face.

"It wasn't conceivably my fault. I was right there. Sprung was drunk and all blown up over having won that money. He——"

"He wouldn't have kicked the kid if I'd been there."

"In his state of mind it wouldn't have made any difference."

"It would afterward."

76

"I did what I could." I felt the top of my head.

"Don't worry, Sprung's got more coming," he said with finality, and shut up.

Cottie hadn't been kidnapped. I knew it for sure then. I never again went to listen to Earl Jordan's radio. Cottie's face in sleep was a little drawn; his eyebrows, faintly brown, were pulled down toward the nose exactly like the darker eyebrows of the darker face above him. With the blue eyes closed I saw that their sockets, too, were deep.

The boy was the man's son, and the man loved him almost with agony.

Yet last night he had walked out of the cottage into some circumstance he thought might be so dangerous he might never come back.

I wondered if he'd risk his possession of the boy he held with such fierce tenderness now for money. For personal vengeance. For . . .

What was his purpose in being at this resort?

I stumbled again against that question. The dark, secret face beside me kept the answer as carefully withheld as ever.

Steve Corbett flung off the moment he had carried Cottie into the house. I knew he would be hunting Sprung, and waited for the reverberations of the battle to come. I had been surprised, returning, to see that Sprung's car still stood beside his cabin; he hadn't run away.

John Loxton came in almost at once, in such perturbation and anxiety he could scarcely talk.

He kept asking, "You're certain the boy is all right? I wouldn't have had this happen for anything. It's terrible. I don't know what to do."

He seemed more upset than was necessary. Mrs. Clapshaw

followed on his heels, and Earl Jordan, for once respectful and subdued, after her. Even Mrs. Rudeen came, although I thought that was more out of curiosity than sympathy.

Mrs. Willard came last.

"I saw your husband; he says the boy's all right." Her voice had a husky, pleasant modulation. "I'm so glad."

"Cottie's still sleeping." I motioned for her to sit in the one rocker. "Had he—Mr. Corbett—found Mr. Sprung yet?"

She smiled at me. "I don't blame you for being nervous. But I don't think you have to worry. Mr. Sprung seems to have lit out."

"He's gone?" I didn't want Steve Corbett to beat him up too badly, but on the other hand I didn't want Sprung to escape punishment entirely, either.

She kept on smiling. "I'd never have thought you so blood-thirsty, Mrs. Corbett. You did a good job on Mr. Sprung yourself. It should be days before his digestive system works without protest."

"He might have killed Cottie."

She sobered. "He might have hurt him badly, at least. I should think Loxton would ask him to leave, if he hasn't gone himself."

"Funny he didn't take his car and go. He'd have had plenty of time while we were at the doctor's."

"He's probably too drunk to realize you'd take it seriously— just hiding until he thinks the thing has blown over."

"If he'd seen Cottie's father he wouldn't be that optimistic."

She said, "What an odd way to refer to your husband."

"What? Oh, I was thinking of him as Cottie's father then."

Steve Corbett didn't come back until after seven. The planes of his cheeks showed muscles bunched to hold his mouth in tight fury.

I told him, "Cottie was awake a while. I gave him some broth and tomato juice, and he went to sleep again."

"Let him sleep; best way to get over shock." He stood over the washdish in the sink, shaking his hands free of water, then flung himself into a chair by the table. "I don't want much."

"Did you find him?" I dared to ask as I put food before him.

"He's hiding out," shortly.

"Where could he be?"

"Not in the barn. I'm going to start on the bushes."

He went out again openly as soon as he'd eaten.

All through that evening I waited for the noise of fighting. I read, darned Cottie's socks. I found a larger pair with no heels and darned those, too. A small clear moon came out; it wouldn't rain that night.

Steve Corbett hadn't said anything about locks when he went; the house was open. At nine I fixed the padlock on the inside and went to bed, trusting myself to wake when he returned. Whatever was going to happen would happen whether I stayed awake waiting for it or not. On that thought I went to sleep, exhausted.

I woke with the impression that oars had splashed near by.

The sounds seemed to be drawing away, merging into the ceaseless silken susurration of the lake. The only other sounds to hear were Cottie's light breath, the light rustle of leaves. I stood up and ran my hand along the inside of the board until I had my gun.

The watch on my wrist said two thirty-three.

I bent over Cottie. There was so little light I couldn't see his face, but he seemed deep in sleep.

From the porch nothing was visible toward the bushes on the right or the lawn in front; nothing except the bulk of my car and the next cottage on the left.

Beyond the second cottage the resort lay hidden in the dark; quiet, its hidden activities, the desires of its inhabitants still unknown. Somewhere out there Steve Corbett was hunting Al Sprung.

If he hadn't found him before this.

This night at least I thought I knew his errand. Or was he back at his secret business? Was that more important to him even than revenge against Al Sprung?

There was one difference between tonight and the other nights I'd stood at that door. Tonight the padlock was on the inside.

If I wanted to go out I could, padlocking the door from the outside, taking the key with me. Cottie never woke at night. He'd be as secure, almost, as if I were here with him.

I felt temptation to go out pulling me with strings until my very skin felt pulled outward like pinches. I was sick of staying timorously in the cabin; I wanted action.

I had the gun. I should be able to take care of myself.

Without any more thought I slipped through the door, fastened the padlock on the outside. The horn handle wedged the key tightly into the breast pocket of my pajamas. I stood listening. Cottie, within, didn't stir.

The front trail seemed so open. I stole along the side of our cabin toward the rear. My eyes became a little adjusted to the darkness. There were clouds over the moon, no stars; just the dim opalescence radiating from the lake. I saw the shape of trees behind our cabin, and two dark shapes hanging.

The gun lifted itself in my right hand; my left was at my throat. Then I remembered. Osco and Bosco.

If I were going to be as easily panicked as this I wouldn't find out much, however well I prowled.

I slipped quietly behind the two empty cabins. The night was as innocent around me as a black taffeta dress. Past Harry Lewis's cabin. Still only the innocent night sounds.

The fourth cottage from ours was Al Sprung's. A small dark shape beside it showed the car still there. I ran lightly across the open space, still keeping to the rear.

Directly in back of Sprung's cabin something soft touched my foot.

CHAPTER SEVEN

I HAD BEEN uselessly startled by the tackling dummies; I told myself I wasn't going to be frightened by this. It was too dark there in the shadow of trees and the cabin to see anything. I pushed gently with my toe at the obstruction. There seemed to be a lot of it. I peered downward, could make out only a dark mass, bent.

My hand touched cloth. Rough tweed. A man's coat.

My hand flew frantically then; my left, because my right still held the revolver. Limp flesh under the coat, arms in the sleeve. A man lying huddled and still, face downward.

My hand found the left check. *No hollow there.*

I think I drew a sigh of relief.

But when my hand next ventured it knew what it would find. Yes. A mustache on the upper lip. I sank back on my heels. Only one man in the resort had a mustache—Al Sprung.

When I moved again it was to feel for the man's wrist. I found it, and my fingers closed around it. No pulse and the skin was cold.

I stood up, shaking my hand, shaking it as Steve Corbett had shaken his over the washbasin, trying to shake off the touch of death.

Any other movement seemed impossible. I tried to move one foot, away from Al Sprung, dead, away to do what must be done, to let people know.

One leaf crunched behind me.

I whirled, but a thick enveloping blackness was over my head before I could see or cry. I fought against it, dropping the gun so that both my hands could be free to tear at the black fabric that covered me and the iron muscles that opposed me. Something wound around me. My hand reached that once—it was smooth and bare and hard—an arm. It seemed slippery and cold and unbelievably long, a boa constrictor winding around me, twisting me lifeless in its inexorable winding.

Then a quick weight struck at my temple, once, dulling the world, twice, blotting it out.

There was wet grass under my cheek.

My ears woke. Someone was crying. Was it Cottie? My body was too heavy to wake, to see. Grass pushed up against my heavy head. The chain—the chain had come alive, flinging itself around me, binding me, weighing me down.

I moved my head forward; it seemed too far back. The wetness went with it, dripping down my cheeks.

Not Cottie crying. Me.

I opened my eyes at the black world. But it wasn't black now. Gray. I tried to lift my shoulders, but my back wouldn't follow. At the effort washes of dizziness swept up my throat.

When the earth settled a little I remembered. Al Sprung was dead.

I had found him and been struck down. Someone hadn't wanted me to find Al Sprung. Someone must still have been near by when I found the body; for all I knew might be near by now.

I opened my eyes again. My left eye was far enough out of the grass to see the shadows there were to see. A bush. Trees. Familiar. But no person.

Slowly I rolled my nose in the grass until my head rested on the other cheek. A cottage was right in front of me.

I thought it was Al Sprung's cottage.

Slowly I fumbled to my knees, sinking as the dizziness struck, rising again. I crawled along the grass. The first thing my hand struck was metal. The gun. Left beside me.

But no dead man was beside me now. The light was the first gray light of dawn. I could see the entire plot behind the cabin. No body anywhere. Quietly I worked toward the corner of the cabin, exploring the ground for any object; I felt only the cold crumpled grass. At the corner of the cabin a small breeze hit my face, reviving. I looked down and saw the car still there. And from the east stronger light coming.

I stood, clutching at the rough log ends of the house corner.

I must get back to our cabin to see that Cottie was all right. It must be almost four o'clock. I'd been gone an hour and a half. My hand went to my pocket; the hard outline of the key was still there.

I hoped that meant no one had broken in on Cottie. I took two shaky running steps, stopped to brace myself, went staggering and weaving back the way I had come.

I was thinking, I've got to get back before Steve Corbett comes. The best thing I can hope is that he isn't back yet.

I needn't have bothered to hope. At the corner of the last empty cabin something like a hard wind blew at me, hands had my wrists, shaking me.

"*You went out.*" Not a question. Acid. To bite and eat me.

"Al Sprung is dead," I said. My head wobbled back and forth from the shaking, but I got it said. "I found him. In the grass."

"You left the kid all alone." More acid sprayed. "I could kill you."

"I am almost killed. Someone hit me." We were talking in a jangling duet.

He was still too full of his own fury to hear me. "By God, I'll pay you for this——" His voice faded. "What did you say?"

At last I had a chance to be heard. "I found Al Sprung. Dead. Behind his cottage. I was going to run when someone hit me. Then when I woke up he was gone. Someone——"

"You've lost your mind."

"No. I went out to see where you were. I stumbled. Over a body. It was limp and getting cold. I thought it was you. But it had a mustache."

He jerked me forward, bending his head until his eyes stared at me not two inches away. There was light enough now for his face to be a gray mask.

"You've been crying."

"I woke up crying."

"You're inventing this to put me off the track. You were up with Jordan. I knew as soon as I found you were gone."

"I wasn't!" The dizziness washed up again. I clutched at his arm, but he took it from me. I slipped to his feet.

A flashlight played over my face, my hair.

"She was struck," he said impersonally. "There's a cut." The light snapped off; he stood over me like a pillar.

It was at that moment I asked myself the question that was to fill my days and nights.

Who?

It seemed in that first sick moment that there couldn't be any doubt. Without process of thought at all I knew Al Sprung had been murdered. I wouldn't have been struck down, the body wouldn't have been moved, unless someone had guilty knowledge of his death.

It was Steve Corbett, the man who stood over me now, who had wanted vengeance to visit Al Sprung.

It was the man who had told the doctor, "I won't need the sheriff." The man who had brooded over his son in the car, the man who had gone out hunting the man I found dead.

85

What would he do now? What was he thinking now? I stayed where I was, not daring to look upward to his face, to see his planning. Would I be next? But he had met me as if he hadn't known where I was. He had met me as if he didn't know what I was talking about. Would that be his game? Another set of pretenses?

Hands came down to pull me by my shoulders to my feet. "I'll go look at this place. Show me."

Pretense. Was it pretense? He had an arm along my back, almost carrying me. Behind Sprung's cabin his light played over the grass. Beaten-down grass. Tufts sprang into prominence, each blade distinct, faded again as the light moved on. A patch of wide-leaved plantain.

"Wait," I whispered. The light halted as I knelt to pick the leaf I had seen. "Look. A dark spot on this leaf. See? It smears. That's blood."

"There's a little blood on that cut in your temple."

"I was farther from the house. Sprung's body was here."

"He was probably drunk. Cut himself falling."

"He was getting cold."

"You can get plenty chilly lying outdoors at night."

I forced myself finally to meet his dark stare. "You," I told him openly. "You were looking for Al Sprung." I was in so much danger now this little more would make no difference.

He said quickly, "I never found him. Most of the night I was beating up the bushes on top of the hill. That was the only good hiding place I could see."

He'd never done any explaining before.

He turned from me abruptly to play the light in wider circles, against the cabin, into the trees. "Wait here. No. I'll get you home first."

He wasn't pretending any longer that he didn't know I was dizzy; he carried me back to the cabin.

86

I was too dazed to think well. I wondered vaguely if I should make an outcry, get away from him, but his voice arrested me, matter of fact and impersonal.

"I got in through a screen to see Cottie was all right. Where's the key?"

"Cottie—he is all right?"

"No thanks to you. Where's that key?"

My hand moved toward the pocket, but his hand was already there, over my breast. He set me on my feet while he unlocked the door, then carried me to his cot, left me, turned back.

"You'd better give me that gun."

I'd held it so long it seemed a part of my hand. "No. I——"

"If there's any monkey business going on we can't be found running an arsenal." He plucked the weapon from my hand and went inside. When he came out he was wearing his jacket. The pockets sagged.

He was gone, the padlock snapping after him.

A damp, small ball in my hand. The plantain leaf with Al Sprung's blood on it. I threw it on the floor.

Al Sprung was dead. That incredible fact was so big in my mind that my thoughts could scarcely move around it. Al Sprung was *dead!* Not badly beaten—that would have been credible. I had expected Cottie's father to beat him up. But kill him . . .

I tried to think of Cottie as the son of a man who could go out to murder a man in cold blood because that man, while drunk, had kicked his son. A man who could strike me down because I interfered with his crime, get rid of the body, and then play this game of pretense. Somehow it was unbearable.

It couldn't be true. *Someone else must have killed Al Sprung.* I wanted so hard to believe it that a flash of white light seemed to go through my head. There were other people here. Mrs.

Rudeen. I had marked her as strange. Or . . .

Again a blinding light.

Those two men who had come in the boat this morning from the Flaming Door. The one man, the smiling one, from whom Al Sprung had won eight thousand dollars.

I had such an upswing of relief I felt delirious; I'm not sure I didn't babble aloud. Hoxie Mueller. He had wanted Al Sprung to play again so he could win his money back. Sprung had refused. I remembered the words I had heard on the beach. Easy to think of Hoxie Mueller's bland persistent smile bending unperturbed to the work of death.

I felt I could almost force that to be the truth; will it to be the truth. I must have slipped into sleep or unconsciousness because the next thing I knew I was being shaken; Steve Corbett bent over me. I looked up at him with the emotions that were to rule my days: hope and fear. Hope that he wasn't a murderer. Fear that he was. Hope and fear, fear and hope.

All the planes and shadows of his face showed now. He was alert, defensive, the eyes not so much in retreat, the hollow almost flat. Stronger light was striking into the porch. At least an hour later than when he had left.

"What did you find?" Did I think that by asking I could get anything from that strong face?

"Nothing. I still think maybe he was drunk. He was drunk yesterday. He came out of it and knocked you down and beat it."

"He couldn't. He was dead. My mother died. I——"

I was arguing that Al Sprung was dead. With a man who either knew it better than I did or else was honest.

"Anyway, that's my story. Get it? You're going to be sick tomorrow. You don't say a word to anyone about Al Sprung. Get it?"

"I can't. He was dead. The police—the sheriff should

know. He was murdered. I can't let——"

"I'm not arguing. I'm taking you in——" He stooped over me but straightened again. "What time did you start on this trip?"

"About two-thirty."

"How far did you go?"

"Along the backs of the cottages as far as Sprung's."

"What woke you?"

"Oars."

"Going or coming?"

"Going. I think."

There was a silence, with the pin points of light watching me in the deep sockets.

"Why did you follow me out?"

No use not admitting it now. "I wanted to know what you do every night."

He drew in a long breath. "By God, I——"

From the corner of one eye I saw his hands move and tense, the fingers apart. I thought, "If he's the murderer I'll die now, and it's so easy."

I didn't seem to mind. It must have been the blow still holding me dazed; fear, even self-preservation weren't working; I knew their lack without regret.

But the hands relaxed as if forced by his will.

"I'll repeat that my business is my own affair and you'll keep out of it. I hired you to care for Cottie. Now you'll do as I say. Stay in bed and keep your mouth shut."

When he'd carried me in to my bed his fingers moved against my temple, exploring. I gathered myself to meet the pain but instead slipped into the warm comfortable dark of unconsciousness.

When I woke I couldn't remember where I was or why; I thought I was in my rose-and-brown chintz room in Eldreth until I saw the bare boards overhead. Slowly then, piece by piece, all the things that had happened since Cottie's frog jumped into my plate came back.

Sun lay on my bed. From the south rectangle of window. The sun was high then. It must be almost noon. From the porch came Cottie's light voice, punctuated—not often—by a deeper voice.

I put a hand to my temple; touching it was like a dentist's drill, and when I moved my head my stomach moved, too.

But I could think well enough to know that Steve Corbett was on the porch to guard me.

I didn't intend it but I moaned once. The screen door darkened, opened and closed.

"Want anything to eat?" The man stood at my bedside looking down; nothing now was apparent in his face except control.

I had to ask. "Have they found—him?"

"Everything's normal here this morning."

"Has Sprung——"

"Still hiding," he said significantly, and then, "You don't need a doctor. You were just knocked out. You'll be all right."

Cottie was climbing on my bed, to look at me with deep surprised blue eyes. He, too, had been injured yesterday, but he showed no signs of it now; the blue eyes were clear.

"Mamma, did you got sick?"

"Yes."

"Did you got kicked?"

"No."

"I did. 'At man kicked me and kicked me, but I didn't got sick." He shook his head at me comfortingly.

"You keep her company, kid." His father went back to the porch, and a kettle clinked.

He was getting lunch. Calmly cooking.

I thought over his every word after I told him. His reactions. His gestures. I couldn't tell. He might have been guilty and pretending. He might have been honestly surprised. I knew what people in the resort would think when the death was discovered. Everyone knew how he had been hunting Sprung.

Part of the chain. Before the chain had been something I had seen. Now it had weight. Pressing down, winding around me.

There was Hoxie Mueller . . .

Cottie's voice flowed. "Mamma, would you like to play we go on streetcars? Up the steps, little boy. 'At's right. Now give 'at man your penny. I sit by a window. Now I see a house. Now I see a train. You see 'at train, Mamma?"

Only Hoxie Mueller had a motive as strong as Steve Corbett's.

Cottie was silent, waiting for answer. When I opened my eyes he was bending above me, forlorn, tears beginning.

He offered, "Mamma, I'm your pal," hesitant, begging me to be near and approachable again, to like him.

How could his father be a murderer?

I closed an arm around him. "I see an airplane out the streetcar window, too. See? Right over there."

He sat up at once, beaming and reassured, with the tears still wet on his checks. "I see a tsurts, too. See 'at tsurts?"

"Church," I said.

A lake resort was a handy place for a murder. With deep water ready to hide the body.

Then a vague memory floated back—what was it John Loxton had said when he told me the legend? Anything cast into the lake came out.

"Are you hearing me, Mamma?"

"Yes, isn't this streetcar going fast!"

Perhaps Al Sprung wasn't in the lake. Perhaps he was on land. Hidden somewhere. But after a while people would wonder at his absence, if his car stayed here, his belongings stayed here.

Steve Corbett walked into the room with a bowl in one hand, a glass of milk in the other.

"Milk toast." He put the bowl and glass on the level edge of the bed. "Come on, kid, we eat now, too."

"I'm not hungry."

"Try it and see." He picked Cottie up and went out again.

The hot buttery milk smelled good. I took one tentative bite. The toast had been cut neatly into squares, buttered thickly before being dropped into the hot milk.

I ate it all.

Today a nurse. Last night . . .

Fear and hope. Hope and fear.

In revolt against the ceaseless turning of my mind I slept again. When I woke in midafternoon I was still rocky but better. Cottie was sitting tousle haired in his sleeper on the next bed, with eyes still sleepy from his own nap.

He asked dulcetly, "Did you waked up, too, Mamma?"

Mrs. Willard appeared in the doorway, Steve Corbett behind her.

"I didn't know you were ill until Earl Jordan told me this afternoon." Her husky voice was unreal, a part of a pleasant, ordinary world, far removed from the nightmare I looked at again as soon as my head started functioning.

"Sit by Cottie, Mrs. Willard," the man invited, and turned to me. Smiling. "Well, Mamma, how're you coming?"

I said briefly, "Better."

"Sick headaches are so apt to follow a shock," Mrs. Willard went on cheerfully. "Take some salts. Cottie looks chipper enough."

"I got a black," Cottie told her proudly, and pulled off his sleeper to show his bruises.

His father picked up a wash suit from the foot of the bed and sat down beside Mrs. Willard to insert the boy into it.

Informal. Ordinary.

I asked my question. "Has anyone seen Mr. Sprung today?"

"You people seem to have scared him off completely. Mr. Loxton's been looking for him, too. Say's he's going to ask him to leave. After all he can't have children get kicked in his resort. You never found him at all, did you, Mr. Corbett?"

Steve Corbett stood Cottie upright to button the back buttons.

"Nope. I've still got my beating spoiling for the guy."

His eyes over Cottie were on me. Warning.

"What about his car?" I asked.

"That's the odd thing," Marjorie Willard answered me. "The car's still there. He must be hiding near here—I can't imagine where."

Steve Corbett dropped in careless words. "Probably rowed across to the Flaming Door. He can stay over there drunk for months on what he's got. They've got bedrooms over the place."

"Oh, that's undoubtedly where he is then." Mrs. Willard smiled at him frankly. "I imagine what you have for him will keep." She stood up. "That reminds me I have a husband to keep. Sorry about that headache, Mrs. Corbett. Don't forget the salts."

She swished away; she was the only woman in the resort who put on lipstick in the afternoons and a gayly flowered dress-up dress.

When she was gone I asked, "What day is it?"

"Saturday—you haven't lost any days."

Cottie had climbed on the bed to sit on my knees. "Could we go get srogs now?" He was restless from being cooped up all day.

"No. Mamma's staying here." The order came deliberately. "Mamma's got a job on her hands. She's going through everything she owns so there won't be anything to suggest she isn't—Mamma."

"Oh," I said.

He did know—or think—that Al Sprung was dead. He expected trouble.

Trouble. I was in it now. The chain was around me. No use thinking I could leave now. If Al Sprung was found dead then anyone who had left hastily would be under heavy suspicion.

I said, "Yes."

"Okay. Cottie, how'd you like a trip to town?"

Even two-year-olds are witnesses.

"I suppose you're locking me in?" I asked through Cottie's vociferous approval. Not much use asking, but I asked.

"What do you think?" He started leading Cottie out. In the doorway he paused to ask, with his back to me, "I don't suppose you did anything with that knife—the big one on top of the cupboard?"

"Why, no. It was there when——"

"It isn't there now. You'd better do a good job, Mamma."

Our knife. Gone. I looked at the implications of that and didn't think I could get up at all.

The cracked and wavering mirror above the dresser showed eye shadows that spread halfway down my cheeks; one rope of hair hung loose down my back. I looked at the blue checked seersucker pajamas I still wore—the pajamas I had worn when setting out to spy on Steve Corbett. There was a grass stain up one leg. In a pocket mirror I looked more closely at my temple; the skin was faintly blue, but against the darker blue under my eyes it was scarcely noticeable, and the healing cut was hidden under my hair.

Nothing anyone would notice. I might be glad of that.

Water on my face felt cool and good; I held wet hands against the bruise until it, too, seemed to cool, combed my hair and changed into a wash-silk sports dress. Then I did as I'd been ordered; I went through my things and destroyed the name Janet Ruell wherever it appeared, feeling that I was cutting myself off even farther from my own identity. Traveler's checks, bankbook and driver's license were the only problems; I couldn't wear them; I thought I might be searched. As a last solution I knotted them loosely in a dirty cleaning rag and pushed them through a wide crack in the flooring. I could see the rag through the crack, lying on the bare earth amid the old tin cans, pans, poles and cartons that gather under lake cottages. All the cabins were open underneath, held up by slabs of cement at the four corners. When it was safe I could easily fish out my possessions with a pole.

Why did I follow Steve Corbett's orders? I don't yet know. It was as if I couldn't do anything else. Yet all the time I thought I should be seeing the police instead. I was just kidding myself I couldn't tell. I could call, scream, rattle at the padlocked screen—people would be at the door inside two minutes.

I could tell them—what?

You couldn't prove a murder without a body. I'd read that.

Still they could see Al Sprung was gone. They could search. Get the sheriff.

As I mulled it over the Willards crossed the lawn toward the nearest stairs, pausing to wave at me. I waved back.

I thought how silly it would look to them if they found out that the man they believed to be my husband had locked me in.

The first thing Steve Corbett did when he got back was to jerk out all the dresser drawers, checking on me. Then he went over his own things; I heard his Gladstone hit the floor. Later I had to reclose all the drawers; he always pushed them in more strongly with his right hand than his left, so that they were crooked.

Earl Jordan came by when we'd had supper.

"Hi, Mrs. Corbett, glad to see you're up!" He looked blondly scrubbed as usual even inside an unbuttoned shirt and dirty fishing slacks. "Did you know you did me out of a fishing partner today? Keeping your husband home to play nurse? You might make up by going along with me tomorrow yourself."

Steve Corbett said, "I'll go tomorrow. Mamma hates fishing. Don't you, Mamma?"

"I never have any luck. By the way, Corbett, did you ever get hold of Sprung? I haven't seen him all day."

I wanted to get out, to see if anything could be seen. It seemed to me there must be some trace somewhere of the ghastly thing I had run into last night.

"I'm going to be there when he gets hold of Mr. Sprung," I said.

Earl Jordan laughed. "You don't think Sprung could do anything to your husband, do you? He could knock Sprung's breath out in one knock and never show a scratch."

And never show a scratch. I hadn't thought of that. One glance at Steve Corbett's face showed it unmarked. It would be.

I stood up. "Why don't we all walk up to Mr. Sprung's cabin to see if he's back?"

"I'll referee if he is there," Jordan said.

The four of us walked along the track; Earl Jordan with me, Cottie with his father. Steve Corbett hadn't offered a word to hinder our going; he'd stood up as if with alacrity to go, too.

Eerie, to hear Earl Jordan knocking at Sprung's screen, when I was so sure the owner wasn't alive to answer. No answer; not even a clock ticked inside.

"Door's unlocked." Jordan pulled it open. "Want to go in?"

Into the house of the dead. I shook down a shudder and said lightly, "Housebreak? Certainly not. You don't think he could have fallen asleep in his car, do you?"

That might be one hiding place.

We all looked in the car. An untidy, unpolished sports roadster, the gray plush seat spotted, an empty whisky bottle on it.

"No neat housekeeper, your friend Sprung," Earl Jordan commented. "What's the use of looking for him? He's around somewhere, drunk. Look at that bottle. Maybe he went to the Flaming Door."

"That's what I think," Steve Corbett spoke. "As long as his car is here I know he'll be back; that's all I care about."

"No use looking," I agreed, but instead of returning along the front way I went toward the back.

There, behind the cabin, was the place. The grass was long, with strands of brown in it like graying hair. Most of it lay over from weight. There was the patch of plantain, too.

"You're still rocky, Mamma. Better get back." My guard, watching.

We went slowly along the rear of the cottages.

As we came toward ours Earl Jordan asked, "Good lord, what've you got hanging under those trees?"

Cottie cried, "'At's Daddy's Osco and all-my Bosco!" He flew at his small dummy and swung, dropping his head back to laugh.

"Tackling dummies! What do you know!" Earl Jordan ran, crouching, at the larger dummy, threw himself at it, but almost before his arms touched they dropped wide and he fell sprawling.

He lay where he had sprawled for a moment. Cottie laughed over at him, still swinging.

Earl Jordan picked himself up from the ground, brushing mechanically at the leaves and grass that stuck to his shirt, even after they were gone.

He moved oddly, getting up; he stood facing Osco, and his movements were jerky as if he were a large blond, jointed male doll. He turned toward us, his face for that instant almost blank.

"Corbett, I want to talk to you. Your wife and the kid better get away from here——" Not ending the sentence with a drop of his voice, just leaving it up.

In my ears Steve Corbett's voice snapped like crackling fire.

"Get the kid in the house."

CHAPTER EIGHT

AL SPRUNG was in the big tackling dummy.

I knew it as soon as I saw Earl Jordan's face. From then on what happened was automatic. Steve Corbett tearing Cottie from Bosco. Cottie yelling, "No! I need to swing!" Myself moving with him, still roaring, toward the porch of our cottage.

I knew, sitting there huddled, what Earl Jordan was saying.

Not in the lake. In the dummy. That was where *that* had been. All that day while I slept, right outside my window. So safe. Who would think of looking for him there? Steve Corbett hadn't used the dummy since the day he made it. The murderer must have intended to remove the body—tonight perhaps, when it was dark. Because in the end, of course, it couldn't be left there. The dummy was a quick temporary hiding place. Tonight the murderer could have put the body in the car, and all Al Sprung's belongings with him, and driven off, and everyone would have thought it was merely Al Sprung come out of hiding and driving away before Steve Corbett caught him.

That couldn't be done now. The killer's hand had been forced by the discovery of his hiding place.

One thing I saw as clearly as a noonday sun. *I couldn't tell now that I had stumbled over the body last night.* Not after keeping it quiet. I'd almost certainly be considered an accessory after the fact.

I had started out lying when I came to the Crying Sisters. I was going to have to tell big lies now.

Steve Corbett couldn't say that I had stumbled over that

body, either. He would have to protect me to protect himself.

The two men came rapidly onto the porch. Earl Jordan's face was the color of pale cream, his blue eyes sick. Steve Corbett only carried his neck a little stiffer, his head back.

"You can't stay here." He flung clipped words at me, and reached to take Cottie, who was still kicking and struggling on my lap to get back to Bosco. "We're going to Loxton's to phone."

"I got to swing on Bosco!" Cottie kept on.

"You can't," his father said. "Osco's hurt."

Cottie stopped with his mouth half open for the next yell. "Did he get kicked?"

"Yes, be good now." The two went off, Cottie pattering solicitude.

It wasn't until I stood up to follow that I found I was shaking, a shaking that didn't have anything to do with me. I felt quite calm inside as if I had a great deal of vacant space there; only the outer shell of my body shook. Earl Jordan came to help me.

At the second cabin he called to Steve Corbett as if he had difficulty getting breath. "Wait. Maybe one of us should—watch."

"Why should we? No one'll lay a finger on that."

We went the rest of the way in silence. John Loxton must have heard our feet on his porch because he opened his house door before we knocked.

"Why, it's the Corbetts and Mr. Jordan. Come——"

"Mamma, stay out here with the kid. Come along in, Jordan."

The three men disappeared inside, leaving the door open.

"Could we go look at all 'ose Indian sings?" Cottie had already forgotten Bosco.

"No. Sh-sh-sh."

"Could we go look at flowers?"

"No. I want to listen."

100

That appalled twitter was Mr. Loxton. Then Steve Corbett was at the phone. "Maple Valley—get me the sheriff, please. He's what? I don't care where he is, we have to reach him. There's been a crime. Comb the county until you find him. Call John Loxton at the Crying Sisters."

The three men returned together to the porch.

John Loxton was moaning, "This is terrible, terrible. My resort." He looked ten years older than when we came to the resort, his lower lip and jaw were relaxed. He mumbled as if he had difficulty forcing his lips to usual sounds. He held up his hands to look at them wonderingly; they were shaking as mine were.

Cottie said, "Mamma, you're wriggling."

He had become sober, beginning to feel the tension and shock.

His father smiled at him. "It's going to be a party. All the people are coming. You stay here with Mamma and Mr. Loxton, and Mr. Jordan and I will go invite 'em."

He added to Earl Jordan, "We can just as well break the news and round 'em up. They'll have to be here anyway."

Loxton sank trembling into a beach chair, his face as gray as his beard against the incongruous green and orange stripes.

"In my resort. Terrible." Over and over.

I sat there wondering what the attitude of the people in the resort was going to be. Someone there, the wielder of the flashlight, knew or suspected Steve Corbett's night errands. Mrs. Rudeen and someone else had spied on us. Everyone knew of Cottie's having been kicked. What the sheriff would think would depend a good deal on the picture they gave him.

Mrs. Rudeen was the first to come.

She began, "My God, what——"

I interrupted. "Cottie's here."

She turned her eyes from Loxton to me, rocking slightly on her heels. Her cheeks were bunched and hard, her eyes still and intent, the puffs around them bigger than ever.

She spoke inimically. "This is no place for a kid."

"Bits and Joanie will be here, too," I reminded her.

She sank into another of the beach chairs, her eyes licking from me to Loxton. "Who done it?"

I lifted Cottie to my lap to hide the ripple I couldn't keep my knees from making under my skirt, and kept my hands behind him. He was quite subdued now.

"I can't imagine," I said.

The puffs under her eyes rose until the irises were a mere line. "Funny, isn't it, this should happen right after Sprung kicked your kid?"

"That's ridiculous."

I was there as Cottie's mother, as Steve Corbett's wife. I was in the chain with them. Whatever my own fears might be I had to take the position of believing in Steve Corbett's innocence.

"The man that Al Sprung won money from was here looking for him yesterday. It would be interesting to find out who has that money."

The quiet that followed my statement must have lasted two minutes. John Loxton's head rolled slightly, trembling, as he looked from Mrs. Rudeen to me; Mrs. Rudeen stared at me unrelenting.

Mrs. Clapshaw came then with Bits and Joanie, all of them in a flurry of agitation.

"I'm leaving. I'm leaving at once." Mrs. Clapshaw, too, was trembling, seemingly with indignation. "I won't stay. I won't keep these innocent children in a place where—— Really, Mr. Loxton, I don't see how you could allow such a thing! Murder! You can't expect respectable people to stand for it!"

I wasn't in any state of mind to see humor. I told her, "I don't believe you can leave now. The sheriff will want to see you."

She turned on me. *"You* and your precious husband! Don't think I've forgotten what happened yesterday on the beach! And the way your husband was out hunting poor Mr. Sprung last night! Well! I guess nobody is going to suspect me!"

Nothing like a time such as this to wipe the veneer of surface friendliness and helpfulness from human relationships. Everyone for himself now, even if it meant batting other people on the head.

She flounced to a chair to sit with her claw nose lifted. Bits and Joanie, as soon as she sat down, howled. "I want to go home to my mamma! Grandma, if you don't let me go home I'll yell! I don't like a dead man! I'll yell, Grandma, I'll yell!"

Mrs. Clapshaw promised candy and ice-cream cones, but the children made good on the threat. One thing about it was that Cottie was completely entranced and sat mouse-quiet on my lap.

The Willards came. Mrs. Willard, walking into the hubbub as if she didn't hear it, hadn't been affected by the news; she'd stopped to put on fresh lipstick. Her eyes darted not to the people but to two chairs at the far end of the porch in shadow.

"Come on, Fred. We'll sit over here." She led her husband by the hand, like a child. He followed, stumbling, his shrunken face looking dazed.

"Dead," he said. "Dead. Man dead."

His wife said, "It didn't have anything to do with us, Fred," incisively, as if she were trying to etch that fact into his mind.

He relaxed into a vacant stare. Yesterday, when Cottie was kicked, he had seemed almost normal, jumping forward, telling me Cottie's father was coming in in the boat. Now his head turned gropingly from one face to another as if he hunted something. His wife moved so she could hold his hand.

Inside the house the phone rang. John Loxton seemed to shrink. "I can't," he said.

"I'll do it." Mrs. Rudeen lifted her bulk from her chair, and lumbered through the door. Over Bits and Joanie came only the intermittent twang of her Texas speech.

"The sheriff, he'll be right out," she announced, as if that pleased her, coming back.

"Oh my gosh, what'll this do to me?" Elmer was coming in just ahead of Steve Corbett and Earl Jordan. The boy's face was blue with fright. "Mixed up in a murder. I never figured to do that. It'll ruin all my ambitions 'n I'll never get to be anybody. I——"

He took in that no one was listening much, stood a moment with his mouth open, then slunk to lean against the screen close to the Willards. All the chairs were taken.

Cottie's father walked toward me. "Sheriff call?"

"I talked to 'm," Mrs. Rudeen told him. "He'll be here."

"Good."

Earl Jordan suggested nervously, "Maybe we should do something before the sheriff gets here. Take him out of that sack. God, suppose he's still alive."

Steve Corbett said, "You know damn well he isn't."

After him Cottie piped, "Damn well he isn't." He was nodding his head in corroboration, backing his father up. I wondered if he, too, felt the wall of suspicion rising.

I said, "Cottie, nice little boys don't say damn."

The presence of the children thwarted speech; the adults looked at each other, eyes careful, as if each pair peered from behind armor. Only Steve Corbett and Earl Jordan moved restlessly about the porch. Steve Corbett brushed Mrs. Rudeen's chair once.

She lifted evil eyes to say, "It ain't so hard to figure who did Al Sprung in."

The hollow drew out thin, the thick brows drew together. "If you mean me," he said to the group at large, "I'll go on record now. I didn't kill Al Sprung. I never saw him again after I saw him running up the beach when he'd kicked the kid."

He said it as if he were confident.

No one replied.

Over the cacophony of Bits and Joanie howling, we didn't hear the car until it was almost in at the gate; it slid to a quick stop before the house, and two men got out.

The one in front, advancing toward the porch with an elephantine step, had the authority. He was huge, a man with a large frame encased in layer after layer of flesh with a rumpled blue serge suit outside the final rolling layer. He pushed his hat back from his forehead as he came, showing a hairbrush of thick colorless hair over a shrewdly genial, purse-lipped face. He might have been a veterinarian or a hay-feed dealer.

Steve Corbett held the door open. "Sheriff?"

Both men came in; the second was as tall but only half the width, with long ropy bones and long ropy muscles.

"Yep," the first man answered. "I am the sheriff. I am Carl Boxruud." He spoke as if he were addressing children. "What's this about you got a man kilt?"

What I had expected came.

"Here's the guy that did it, Sheriff." Mrs. Rudeen stood up to point dramatically at Steve Corbett.

I said, "That's nonsense. Sprung had been gambling. He won a lot of money from a man named Hoxie Mueller at the Flaming Door. And he wouldn't play so the man could win it back."

The sheriff, the long man, everyone looked at me. Even Steve Corbett. I wasn't shaking any more.

"Well, now." The sheriff blinked from me to Mrs. Rudeen.

105

"Anyone here see this man get kilt?"

"I didn't have to see it," Mrs. Rudeen began. "Yesterday this——"

"So?" the sheriff asked mildly and unexcitedly. "Now I'll take charge here. All you folks stay right where you are."

Eldreth was full of people like him. I knew every accent of his speech, the speech of a man who had learned Norwegian before English: the double *o* where one *o* is right, the slight overstressing of consonants, the whistling *s*, the slight, slow swing to the speech tune. The faces of Mrs. Rudeen, Mrs. Clapshaw and Earl Jordan showed an immediate belief in the man's stupidity, but I wasn't fooled. I'm Norwegian myself. The sheriff was an intelligent man.

He turned to the man with him. This here is my deputy, this is Chet Leegard." Then he asked of us all, "This man who got kilt, where is he?"

"Behind my cabin, Sheriff," Steve Corbett answered swiftly. "There are children here. I'd suggest——"

Boxruud nodded. "You come. And you." He pointed a thick forefinger at Steve Corbett and Earl Jordan. As he turned to the door I caught the swing of a heavy gun against his hip under his coat.

Mrs. Rudeen said contemptuously when he was gone, "That dumb guy. He won't see anything you don't stick in his eye."

When she had stood up to accuse Cottie's father I had squeezed Cottie so hard he had said absently, "Ow," without taking his attention from the spectacle. Because I felt in some dim way that when she was accusing Steve Corbett she was trying to accuse Cottie and me, too. She meant it that way. She was inimical to all of us.

She settled back in her chair now to look with her slitted cats' eyes not at anyone else but at me, as if she had some personal, deep, and now triumphant reason for wanting to sweep me out of her path. Almost as if she had been afraid of me but wasn't any longer.

106

I'd seen that open rejoicing vindictiveness on the faces of people once before in my life. Why should she have had that emotion against me? Why had she spied on us?

Had she been connected in any way with Sprung? He was too old to be her son. Sister? Loxton hadn't said she, too, was a Sprung. Wife? They'd lived in two cottages. Or did her dislike hook up to Steve Corbett's private business—his night business here?

After all, why was she here, in this quiet, withdrawn resort? She was a woman you'd expect to care more for beer taverns.

It was soothing to relax my suspicions of Steve Corbett in order to suspect Mrs. Rudeen.

CHAPTER NINE

THE SHERIFF came back to the house once to make a phone call, walking through the assembly on the porch as if it wasn't there. On his way out he turned at the door for a brief order:

"Don't go off this porch until I give you leave."

His face had taken up slack in the time he was gone; the rolls of fat along his jaw looked harder, smoother. By moving in my chair I could see him walking quickly down the track, his heavy body bent forward as if he were butting into space.

Again there was the waiting. Cottie's neck went through its night-time drill, stiffening until he suddenly relaxed to sleep. I pulled him around to rest with his head on my shoulder.

John Loxton tendered, "Would you like to let the boy sleep on my bed? You'd be welcome."

Cottie was something to hold to. "Thanks, he isn't heavy."

Bits and Joanie, hoarsened into occasional lapses of quiet, finally lay on their stomachs sobbing into their arms. John Loxton went into the house for pillows for them, and they quieted to sleep that left the silence on the porch unbroken except for breath, the creak of chairs as someone moved, the ticking of a clock inside the house that grew louder and more metallic as time went on.

A car's motor became audible; that, too, increased in volume until the machine whirled by the porch without stopping.

There had just been time to glimpse the four men in the car. One was the Maple Valley doctor. Doubtless he was coroner as well as physician.

I tried to shut my mind to what was taking place behind our cabin. The tackling dummy on the ground now, its grain sacks ripped apart; Al Sprung on the ground again, staring his secret into the sky.

It would take strength to lift him down.

It had taken strength to lift him up. That was one quality the murderer had to have.

Steve Corbett wouldn't have had difficulty placing the body in that ironic hiding place, hanging it from the branch.

Who else? I looked around the porch. Nearest me was Mrs. Clapshaw. She had difficulty carrying water from the pump. Mr. Loxton. He, too, was too frail. Mrs. Rudeen—she was strong enough. Elmer I thought too slight; I'd seen his hands shake after lifting the heavy milk pails. The Willards—the two of them might manage. Earl Jordan—he wasn't as strong as Steve Corbett, but he was strong enough. Hoxie Mueller—I wasn't forgetting him. With his henchman he could have managed easily.

I asked, "Could anyone—someone from the outside—have come in here last night?"

Loxton answered dully, "The bell didn't ring. No cars crossed the hose. The gate was shut this morning, too. Just as I shut it."

Mrs. Rudeen pointed his answer. "No sir, it was someone right here did Al Sprung in. Not many people hereabouts."

"Someone could have got over the fence, or the wall."

"Who on the outside would know about that big dummy you put up?"

"Hoxie Mueller was here yesterday. He might easily have seen it."

"Yeh, there's him," she admitted contemptuously, as if I were trying to crawl out of something.

I persisted. "He came over in a boat during the day. He could have come again last night. I thought I heard a boat."

Elmer came in. "That Flaming Door's only got one boat. They don't use it much. They keep it locked up in a boathouse, and you got to ask the propri'tor for the key. He'll sure know if anybody come across."

"Aren't there any other boats on the lakes?"

"Nope. Except ours."

Already I could see the possible list of murderers, then. Hoxie Mueller—if he had taken out the boat. Anyone else who had used the Flaming Door boat that night. John Loxton, who seemed impossible because of physical frailty. Elmer, a poor suspect for the same reason. I had heard Sprung cursing at him for being late with the milk, but that was a weak motive. Mrs. Clapshaw, most unlikely of all. The Willards— a little strange, but they had seemed so indifferent to Sprung. Mrs. Rudeen. I would have been glad to guess she was the one. Earl Jordan,

The only motive I knew of against anyone there was the money.

Steve Corbett. He had another motive.

I shifted his son's head to my other shoulder.

The evening darkened, sunset showed red-orange streaks in the west with great gray feather plumes of cloud above; I forced myself to watch that beauty instead of thinking. But what I felt was the incongruity of the scene: that flaming pyrotechnic sunset, people sitting on the porch to all appearances like any friendly group spending a summer evening. And murder in the place.

The sheriff came at last with his deputy, pausing in the door to look us over speculatively.

"Kids asleep. That is good. Now I guess the best will be for me to ask you a few questions, one by one. In the house."

Steve Corbett and Earl Jordan came in behind him; he turned to address Cottie's father. "You first. Come along, Chet."

Steve Corbett's face as it went past me was completely quiet, the hollow not even pulled tight. He moved through the door with his arrogant, efficient, rolling walk as if he were stepping inside for fishing tackle or a magazine. He'd glanced once, nodding as if with satisfaction, at his sleeping son; me, he didn't seem to see.

The door closed behind the three men.

Mrs. Rudeen said, "The sheriff picked the right guy to ask."

I said, icing it, "Perhaps he feels Mr. Corbett is the most intelligent person to question."

Earl Jordan moved to stand behind my chair.

Elmer asked, "Gosh, Mr. Jordan, was he really dead? What killed him?"

"He was dead all right," the answer was grim but incomplete.

I repeated the last part of Elmer's question.

"Sorry, Mrs. Corbett, I was told not to talk."

Mrs. Rudeen's eyes burned more brightly, moving from me to Earl Jordan.

"I hope it won't be long." I tried to put all the casualness I could into my words. "Cottie should be getting to bed."

It was long. I looked at my watch: almost nine. The last sunset light was fading. Earl Jordan pulled on the light overhead.

All the faces sprang into prominence, shadowed below, high lighted above by the fall of yellow light. Mrs. Rudeen, in that uncompromising glare, was more nervous than I had thought; a thin shine of perspiration showed on her forehead and heavy nose. John Loxton had been reduced to pitiful despair.

He said again, "Terrible. Terrible." Then a new facet struck him. "Poor Sprung. To think it should happen in his boyhood home.

111

And I was going to ask him to leave." The black eyes went soberly from face to face as if asking backing for his sympathy.

That was the only expression of sorrow I heard then or later over the passing of Al Sprung.

It was nearly ten before Steve Corbett pushed the door open. He was serene; if he'd been in danger of being arrested for the murder it didn't show.

"You next, I guess," he told Jordan.

Jordan, still pale, went inside.

I asked, "Does the sheriff know how Sprung was killed?"

"Sure."

"Aren't you supposed to talk, either?"

"No."

"Does he have any idea who did it?"

"If he does he didn't transfer that idea to me." He went to rest against the ledge on my side of the porch, alone.

I noticed then how little grouping there was. Except for the Willards and the children, each person had drawn off by himself or herself in an aura of aloofness.

I have never heard people so quiet. Every ear might have been straining for the conversation inside, of which not the slightest murmur reached us. Quiet on the porch was so heavy it had weight; it pressed against me from the sides, from above, oppressive, wearying. For a moment the light and the faces had drifting streams of smoke between them and me; I remembered the blows on my temple last night; my illness that day.

Last night and today seemed a hundred years away.

Steve Corbett's voice came, steadying. "I'll take the kid."

The boy rolled without jarring from my arms to his. He turned toward the ledge again, but I stood up.

"You can't hold him there. He's heavy."

"Keep your chair."

"It feels good to stand."

Words fell into the quiet like slow balls of sleet falling singly through deep air. Cottie's father sat down. It did feel good to stand. I stretched my muscles and walked to look out over the lawn. The lawn was almost gray, but as I looked a cloud slid away from an eyebrow of light—the moon. The lawn whitened, trees sprang into darker shadow.

The door opened again and Earl Jordan came out. Behind him was the sheriff's large face.

"These kids, they should get to bed." He looked from Cottie in Steve Corbett's arms to Mrs. Clapshaw. "You I will see." He pointed at her.

"The name is Clapshaw. Mrs. Clapshaw." The speaker rose in gray-haired majesty; the door closed behind her.

"Guess I'll stick around and help Mrs. Clapshaw get those kids home." Earl Jordan had started to leave, but stopped. He came to lean against the ledge near me, looking almost cheerful.

"That sheriff isn't such a bad man," he told the company. "Seems to know what he's doing."

"He don't have no stone walls to look through," from Mrs. Rudeen.

"We may all get some surprises before this thing is through," Earl Jordan said directly to her. Mrs. Rudeen's thumb worked in and out of her handkerchief, and the rough Dutch bob moved so that she stared directly at him. Loxton moaned once.

Mrs. Clapshaw was inside only ten minutes. When she came out she was beaming and still vigorously talking.

"—it'll be as I say. I'm so glad you agree with me, Mr. Boxruud; it's nice to know there's a real American with sense running this horrible affair, at least!"

113

She turned to us, tossing her head, bent to shake Joanie.

"Wait." Earl Jordan moved forward. "I'll carry the girl. Elmer, would you want to take the boy? Too heavy for Mrs. Clapshaw. That all right, Sheriff?"

The sheriff's head, visible in outline beyond the screen, nodded. "You come right on back here," he told Elmer. "Don't hang around and don't do no talking. You, Mrs. Corbett, I will see next."

My turn.

I was walking steadily toward the door he opened for me; I thought, my hands are quiet now. But the palms are damp. Then I was through and standing in John Loxton's scrubbed living room. The sheriff shut the heavy log house door behind me.

Here, too, an unshaded bulb shed yellow light over the room, over the round oak dining table in the exact center of the round hooked rug, with reaches of unfinished board flooring to all sides. Light fell on a carved cabinet organ against one wall, its round top stool still serviceable, because Chet Leegard sat solemnly upon it as if he were posing for an 1890 photograph. The whole room had an 1890 look. When the sheriff set me down in a straight-back chair by the table what I had ahead of me was a framed motto in blue-and-red wools: God Bless Our Home.

This had been Al Sprung's home, his mother's home. I wondered if she had worked that motto and hung it there.

The sheriff settled himself into a chair with the motions if not the gusto of the dwarf, Happy, settling on his stool. An open notebook, the edges of its leaves frayed and gray with wear, lay before him. He picked up a two-inch stub of pencil and held it ready.

"Now, Mrs. Corbett, when did you decide to come to this place?"

That began the tangled web of lies I must weave. I moved forward so my hands would be hidden from him by the table edge.

114

Then I got the strategic position of Chet Leegard against the side wall; his gaze was seemingly vacant, but something told me he wasn't missing a motion. I forced my hands and knees to rigid quiet.

What had Steve Corbett told him? The sheriff's face was shrewd, but it was provincial; any explanation of my actual entry into the Corbett family and I could see him leaping to conclusions. From living in sin to murder is a slight step to the Eldreth mind.

I said, "My husband heard of this resort from a friend. Good fishing, you know. A quiet place for the boy, with lots of sunshine."

"Uh-huh." The sheriff seemed to make a mental comparison, the pencil stub held stiffly between his thumb and thick forefinger moved jerkily forward and back, and there appeared on the page I saw upside down the copperplate lines of a tiny, exquisite handwriting that might have been a woman's.

"You never have been to this place before?"

"No. This summer is the first time. We came last Monday."

"You make reservation ahead?"

"No. I—we stopped at some tourist cabins." I wondered frantically what I'd say if he asked what tourist cabins, and went on hastily, "That was a week ago today. You remember how hot it was. Sunday the boy and I stayed there while Mr. Corbett drove here to see if he could rent a cabin."

"Uh-huh!" It was agreement. "You know any of the people in this resort before you come here?"

"No."

He took me through my meeting with the resort people, my relations with them, what we had done every minute of our stay. When the dummies were made and what they were for and what people would have known about them. He didn't ask and I didn't proffer any information about Steve Corbett's night habits. The visit of Hoxie Mueller on Friday took some time.

"I have a man now asking this Hoxie Mueller will he please come to see me," he assured.

Over the incident of Al Sprung's kicking Cottie he went in plodding, minute detail. He commented, frowning at his notebook, "His mother, Mrs. Sprung, she was a nice woman. It was too bad the way this Al turned out."

He arrived then at yesterday evening.

"Now, Mrs. Corbett, it seems this Al Sprung died last night. Doctor Hansen, he says so."

I moistened dry lips and asked a perfectly idiotic question, I suppose with some idea of appearing innocent. "Did he—did he die naturally?"

An eye-widening surprise went momentarily over the sheriff's face. He chided me. "Could a man put himself into a sack and hang himself on a tree?"

"But someone might have found him and been—well, afraid or startled——"

He shook his head.

"But what did he die from?"

He shifted his head upward so that the light struck his face fully. I saw that the round blue eyes weren't mild or absent; they merely looked that way because of their paleness. They were instead quite intent and hard, with points of light in the pupils.

"You have not heard?"

"No."

He went for a moment into quiet, watching thought. Then he said as directly as if it were an accusation, "You are afraid this man Sprung died from a beating?"

"No. I——" There was something else I was afraid of, too.

"You think that would be—unlucky for your husband?"

"Oh no! My husband can't be——"

116

"Yes, it was lucky for your husband. Mr. Sprung has one blow on the head, yes, which perhaps makes him unconscious. But what he died from was a knife stuck in his back."

CHAPTER TEN

USELESS TRYING not to faint, but I fought against it, as if fainting were a danger.

Al Sprung had been killed by a knife in his back.

And our knife was missing.

I knew then what I had been trying so desperately not to think. Cottie's father couldn't, *couldn't* stick a knife in any man's back. Not even if that man were Al Sprung. I could imagine—yes, imagine and accept that he might have leaped at Al Sprung in hot anger, shaking him, drawing off to batter at his face with his big fists powered by the muscles of those bulging shoulders.

But a knife was a coward's weapon. To knock Al Sprung unconscious, and then when he was unconscious stick a knife in his back——

The next thing I knew I was lying across the dining table with the yellow light flaring in my eyes, a dark flapping object passing between me and the light, a glass at my mouth. I opened my lips and gulped once. Above the waving hat were the sheriff's matter-of-fact blue eyes and wide mouth.

He said, "Now she will be ookay."

I sat up on the table. He hadn't called in anyone else. With a deft and seemingly effortless motion he transferred me from the table to my chair, stayed bending over me. I looked up to meet his contemplative gaze.

"Mrs. Corbett, you have had a blow to the head."

I shut my eyes a moment to get back into that immense

118

pathless wildwood of lies I had to tell.

"I did that reaching for Cottie—the little boy—in the water. I slipped and bumped my head against the dock."

Again exploring fingers moved against the bruise, and I tensed myself for pain.

"You are lucky you did not drown then." He hinted, "If you were alone with the boy."

"I was alone. It did almost knock me silly."

He went back to write in his notebook for quite a long time. He wasn't as friendly as he had been.

"So now we will go over what happened last evening. What did you do, please?"

"My little boy was asleep. He suffered some shock from being kicked. Right after supper Mr. Corbett went out again——"

"Where?"

"Up the track past the cottages. He was looking for Sprung."

"You?"

"I was worn out; I went to bed almost at once."

"You did not see Al Sprung again before going to bed?"

"No."

"Go on please. When did your husband come in?"

I couldn't tell lies that Steve Corbett might contradict. "I don't know. I fell asleep almost at once."

"Go on please."

"That's all. I woke a couple of times, not feeling very well. This morning I had a bad headache. I was in bed until afternoon."

"Your husband, he was in the bed when you woke?"

"He sleeps on a cot on the porch. He was up and dressed when I woke this morning."

"You did not hear any sounds in the night?"

I thought hastily. "Once I woke I thought I heard oars splash."

"Going or coming?"

"Going, I thought."

"You did not notice what the time was?"

"Yes, I did. It was two thirty-three."

He pounced. "How do you know?"

I held out my wrist. "My watch. It's illuminated."

"Oh, so." He stared at me. "But you did not get up?"

I evaded. "It might have been someone night fishing."

He took me then through today's events. Our visit to Al Sprung's cottage. The discovery of what was in the dummy.

"Mrs. Corbett, this dummy hangs maybe twenty, thirty feet from your bedroom window. Your husband, he says this window is open. Yet you say you heard no sounds there."

I said lamely, "I sleep very soundly."

I had been lying unconscious behind Al Sprung's cabin while the murderer had carried or dragged Al Sprung's body to the dummy. The murderer had known he had nothing to fear from my ears while he pulled the dummy down, strewed the hay inside it over the hillside, and replaced the hay with that grisly enclosure.

But Steve Corbett——

Why hadn't he noticed that activity? He had said he was on top of the hill, in the bushes, hunting there for Al Sprung. Either the murderer had known he was there, or else the murderer had nothing to fear from Steve Corbett because he was Steve Corbett.

The inevitable questions, the hope and the fear, beating their drums again. I shut my eyes to the throbbing.

I said, anything to get away from my thoughts, "I should think he—it would have bled."

"There is blood on the sack. You would have seen if you had looked. But most of the blood is in the clothes."

Suppose Cottie had gone out to play . . . Against the horror of that thought I had to fight for rationality.

"The murderer, wouldn't he have blood on him?"

He shrugged. "Maybe a little. Water is easy to get at."

I was thinking desperately now. "And the money. He had eight thousand dollars. What about that?"

He said softly, "Oh yes. There was no money, either on the body or in the house. That does not make it so easy. Many people will do much for money. There is the money to trace. And then there is the knife."

The knife! How soon would he find ours was gone? What had Steve Corbett told him? I sat waiting for him to ask more about the knife, but he didn't; his questions petered out into a sort of anti-climax after the early tension, and he let me go.

When I stepped out to the porch Steve Corbett looked at me strong and hard over his son's head.

Elmer had come back; the Willards, Mrs. Rudeen and John Loxton still waited, too. As I went toward Steve Corbett, Elmer moved in response to the sheriff's beckoning forefinger.

I asked, "May we go now?"

"To your cottage, but not to leave the resort."

John Loxton made a deprecating sound of worry for himself and sympathy for us. "That cottage—I could let you have another."

"No," Cottie's father told him, rising. "I'll look out for us."

"Also I will have men here." The sheriff might have been giving threat or promise of safety, his voice didn't imply which.

Cottie's father held the door open for me; we walked out into the calm and peaceful, palely moonlit night.

Not talking.

Let go. For how long? In fifteen minutes, in thirty, would the sheriff come to our cabin . . .

When we were in front of Mrs. Clapshaw's cottage two head-lights switched on ahead; a motor started, and a car lurched past us.

A long black car. A hearse. It must have come while I was inside being questioned.

Suddenly I was shaking again, clutching Steve Corbett's arm. He wasn't shaking, but the muscles hardened as my fingers grasped; it was like touching a sleeve holding a warm marble arm. Had this been the arm I fought against last night?

I gasped, "I don't like hearses, I never did, they're an omen of what we've all got to come to sooner or later, and in this place it's sooner! I don't——"

He snapped, "Hold it! You can't throw fits now!"

But I couldn't stop. My teeth were chattering. "All the time— all the nights I've been here I've felt it coming. Ever since I heard that scream. Death riding in a wagon. That's one of us gone out of here!"

His hand slapped once, stinging, across my mouth.

Cold air crashed through my opened lips, crowding my lungs.

"Why you unspeakable——" I choked on it.

He grunted. "That's better. I can count on your shutting up when you're mad."

I got along after that; got back to seeing what went on around me. A light in Al Sprung's cabin. Lights flashing on the hill. The two cabins before ours were normally dark and empty.

When I was putting Cottie to bed I noticed that his pillow was on top of the blanket instead of underneath as I usually left it.

Steve Corbett had been right in hiding the guns. Someone had gone over our cabin. My first thought was for my hidden pos-sessions, but they were still there; I could see the rag through the floor boards, apparently undisturbed.

The knife.

I thought wildly that Steve Corbett must have been mistaken; the knife must still be here. I dragged a chair to the cupboard, to fumble around in the dust on the top, feeling it must have slipped down somewhere. But there wasn't any place it could have slipped.

"No use looking." Steve Corbett had come to watch me. "Get inside the house."

When I did so he backed me against the bureau. "There are men all around. Keep your voice down. What did you tell the sheriff?"

"I didn't."

"Okay." The eyes above me had the same blue-metal gleam as the revolver's mouth. "Stick to it. And if you ever feel like changing your mind, remember this. You can't leave now. The sheriff won't let you. Do I have to tell you what would happen all his life long to a boy whose father was in jail for murder?"

He didn't have to tell me. I could see it all, in one blinding succession of quick scenes.

He said, "Okay, you see it." He turned and went through the door, to pause just on the other side, smiling. "If that won't hold you think what happens to the wife of a man taken up for murder. Or even a woman just living with a man taken up for murder. Her picture in all the papers. Even the Eldreth papers."

He chuckled as he went toward his cot.

I lay down on my bed, but I didn't feel muddled or questioning then; my mind was hard and clear and cold.

If Steve Corbett was arrested for Al Sprung's murder I might have Cottie, but the two of us would be left to slink and hide around the world, our very names a falsehood. My job and my professional standing, such as it was, would be ripped from me; neither the Eldreth library nor any other library would hire a woman with this story in her life. No library would hire me under a false name, either, with no proof of experience, no references.

My life, Cottie's life, depended on keeping Steve Corbett free of the charge of murder.

I stepped from my bed and to the porch. The man lay on his back on the cot, his hands under his neck, elbows wide. He turned his face as I came near.

"It might look honest," I told him, "if you went at once to tell the sheriff our knife is missing. I gather you didn't tell him before."

"Someone went over this place."

"But we aren't supposed to know that."

One twist of his body put him on his feet. "I missed out on that one," he said softly. "Baby, the brain is working now."

He padlocked the door behind him when he went.

When he came back I asked, hoping, "Did the sheriff have it?"

He shook his head. "That was a good move of yours, Mamma. The sheriff's men reported no big knife in our cabin."

"Let me think." I sat down. "When did you notice it was gone?"

"This morning. It hasn't been here today."

"We didn't use it yesterday. The last time we used it was the day you caught the crappies."

He nodded. "Thursday. We left the cottage unlocked when we took Cottie to the doctor. Anyone could have taken it."

"Yes," I said. "Easily."

"You should sound more convinced," he said. "Why don't you get it off your chest?"

His face was quiet. I plunged. "It would have been easiest of all for you to take the knife."

"You want me to tell you I didn't kill Al Sprung, so that your conscience can be clear about concealing evidence."

"Yes."

"You couldn't work for me if I had killed him, I suppose?"

"No," I said. "Not even with what it would do to me. I don't like—murder."

"All right. I didn't kill him."

I said with despair, "You say that too easily."

"What do you want me to do—swear?"

"Yes."

"All right, I swear to God——"

"No. By Cottie."

He halted. A moment went by.

"No," he said then, "I'll stick to God. Look. I hated Al Sprung's insides. After what he did to the kid, I'd have been glad to kill him. With my hands. But I didn't stick a knife in his back. I never stuck a knife in any man's back, and I never will."

"That's what I can't believe." Hope trying to struggle free.

"Oh." He had finished his last statement strongly; this came more lamely. "That's—nice."

"Did you see Al Sprung at all last night?"

He repeated gravely after me, "I did not see Al Sprung at all last night. I did not see him from the time he ran up the beach after kicking Cottie until Sheriff Boxruud neatly unstuffed him from that dummy. Remarkably like a frog."

I shuddered, "Don't."

"Death isn't so much in the Andes."

"The Andes? What? Were you——"

He said quickly, warningly, "That slipped. Don't ever repeat it. Keep my biography quiet."

I warned, too. "Death is a lot here. You——"

He put on his old lightness. "But I'm not capable," he reminded me, "of sticking knives in backs. You said so yourself."

"You were out all that night. Like the other nights. What were you doing? If the sheriff finds out he'll want to know.

125

Suppose someone here—the person who came here with a flash-light that night—should tell. You'd have to explain."

He stood up, his face featureless in the gray moonlight. "Mrs. Corbett"—it came formally and dangerously—"you are getting your nose into my business again, and I do not like a nose in my business, however beautiful, intelligent and otherwise acceptable the nose may be. I think you had better——"

I stood up, too. "One more thing. You say you'd have gladly killed Al Sprung. Is there anyone else here you would like to kill?"

He answered as casually as if I'd asked him if there weren't any more books in my library he'd like to read.

"I know at least two I'd like to polish off."

CHAPTER ELEVEN

I WONDERED, lying awake on my hard flat bed that night, if I didn't owe it to the other people in the resort—no matter what it did to me—to tell the sheriff everything I knew about Steve Corbett.

But I couldn't bring that deliberate ruin on Cottie. I told myself that tonight at least everyone should be safe, with the sheriff's men patrolling. Steve Corbett wouldn't go out tonight.

Besides, he had said he didn't kill Al Sprung, said it at last with what sounded like sincerity. And I myself couldn't connect him with that knife in the back.

Weariness mingled with uncertainty; I slept. When I woke it was because Cottie was bouncing my bed. His father immediately appeared at the door, washed, shaved and dressed.

So he hadn't been arrested that night.

"Want me to take the kid?" The question was an order, an order to get on with life as if we had nothing to fear.

Murder hadn't entered Cottie's mind. Yet. At breakfast he asked, "Did Osco still got hurts?"

"I'm afraid we'll have to get along without Osco. The doctor took him away."

"Not Bosco. I got to swing on Bosco."

"I'm afraid not," his father told him. "Bosco went with Osco."

Cottie slammed his spoon down. "No! I *need* to swing on Bosco!" There was a breath-held pause, and then, "I got to had Bosco or I wull yell!"

One thing he'd gotten. The example of Bits and Joanie. I knew what to do about that.

"You just go ahead and yell," I told him. "You can be all by yourself in the other room all morning." I carried him screaming to the bedroom. "Be a big boy and yell loud."

He was obliging as I returned to the table. His father reached uncommenting for another slice of toast.

"You don't like that. But murder or no murder, Cottie isn't taking on Joanie Clapshaw's manners."

"I didn't say anything."

No. And I couldn't tell anything from his exasperating face. I couldn't see if he approved, objected, or would take it out of me later.

He said, "It's a beautiful Sunday morning, isn't it? You know, it wasn't until the middle of the night that I saw a possibility I'd overlooked. After all, you were around and about on the night of the unlamented Sprung's demise. You're a very competent young woman. Say Sprung met you on your errand, and proffered a few unwelcome invitations—you were pretty well bunged up."

Heat flashed over my face, my neck, down my chest. "I don't stick knives in people. Why would I have the knife along? I had the gun."

"I can see you faring forth, the gun in one hand, the knife in the other. In sleeping pajamas."

He was joking. I said, "The fun is all yours," but fear lifted a little and let more hope in. If he could have wondered if I killed Al Sprung, then he would be innocent himself.

I looked at his face again, confident, laughing, the eyes glinting in their depths of socket. Or was this just cleverness, to make himself look innocent?

128

He changed the subject. "We have silence within except for a faint knocking at the door."

When I opened the house door Cottie trotted out beaming, proclaiming, "I good now." He didn't hold the discipline against me. As soon as he'd finished his oatmeal he wanted to know, "We go lake?"

"We may be busy," I said. "The surest way of proving you didn't do anything is to find out who did."

His father took me up. "Meaning who?"

"Hoxie Mueller. He's the only one who seems to have a stronger motive than you have. I wonder if the sheriff found him."

"I'll go ask one of the men around."

"I might get more information."

He stopped halfway to the door. "You know about your face, don't you?"

"I'm under less suspicion than you are." I held my temper.

For once anger broke over his face; color as dark as red barn paint flooded under his skin. He said, "I'll be damned if I'll skulk behind——"

Then muscles sprang out like cords under his jaw. "No doubt you'll do better at worming out information than I would. Come on, kid, we'll go to the lake."

"In my clothes on?" Cottie asked, astounded.

"In I don't care what." His father stalked ahead over the grass to the bank's edge, his hands in the pockets of his khaki breeches, his back stiff, Cottie hop-skipping to keep up.

Involuntarily as I got ready to go I looked out the back window. Emptiness now where the dummies had hung. The grass beneath was trampled; otherwise there was no trace of the activities of last night or the more horrible activities of the night before.

The resort when I walked out into it was an incredible setting for murder. Clear baby-blue sky with drifts of outing-flannel clouds, a light breeze lifting the leaves to show their pale green undersides, sun enameling the grass and putting a shine on the lake.

But behind the cabin, halfway up the hill, was a man sitting with his knees hunched up before him, eating a banana.

I went up, stubble scrunching under my feet, grasshoppers skittering out like rays. "Hello," I began as soon as I was within hearing distance. "I'm Mrs. Corbett from the end cottage. Has the murderer been found yet? Has the sheriff——"

The banana eater began simultaneously, "I been here all night just watchen. Nothen happened and I don't know nothen."

He wore civilian clothes—an old gray suit and blue shirt. His hair was red and he had no visible eyebrows.

I sat down companionably. "This is the first time I've been near a murder. I suppose they're common to you."

The unbrowed eyes were still uneasy. "I help out the sheriff. First thing he needs a deputy, why he calls on me. But I don't know nothen. We had a bank robbery once."

He was a naïve youngster, torn between caution and the desire to please.

"I'm sure I read about your robbery," I said. "The sheriff said last night he'd sent someone out to get Hoxie Mueller. Was that you?"

"No'm. Now like in our robbery we——"

"You mean Hoxie Mueller hasn't been found yet?"

"No'm. I mean—I ain't supposed to talk—say, there comes the sheriff now!"

He took the remaining half banana in one gulp and threw the peeling, his eyes relieved.

The sheriff, with a second man behind him, was plodding up the hill from the direction of Loxton's cabin, the forward bend of his body increased by the climb.

130

"Hi, Sheriff," my intended victim hailed. "This is one of the ladies. I told her I didn't know nothen."

"Good morning, Sheriff," I said.

He drew up level with me. "Well, Mrs. Corbett. Jack, you go on home now, get some sleep, report back in eight hours. Maybe I'll want you some more, I don't know yet."

Jack left, running. I attacked the sheriff.

"I can't keep my curiosity down."

The round blue eyes didn't smile back at me. "The bump to your head, how is it this morning?"

"Oh, fine. I don't feel it at all. I——"

"Your knife—it has not suddenly been found?"

"Not in our house. Mr. Corbett told you about that, didn't he? We were out. Anyone could——"

"Every other cottage has its big knife. I have now gathered them all. Doctor Hansen says it was with such a knife as the cabins have that the killing was done. I sent all I have to the university to be examined——"

"Could one of them have been cleaned?"

He shook the heavy head with the black hat far back on the brush of wheaty hair. "Those scientific doctors at the university, they are very good. I use them before."

"Someone may have had an extra knife."

"I have thought that."

"And anyone here could have stolen ours."

"Mr. Corbett, too, said so. Now I will have to——"

"Wait. Mr. Sprung's eight thousand dollars. Have you——"

"They have not been found."

The guns. I couldn't ask him if he'd found those. I started to ask him if he'd searched all the cabins for the money, then thought that might not be politic.

He was going on. "Hiding places here are many. A hole in a tree, a hole in the ground, anywhere. I have my men look. Now——"

"Just one more question. Hoxie Mueller."

"The owner of the Flaming Door tells me Mr. Mueller left before suppertime of the Friday night Sprung was killed. This early morning I send out a radio call for Mr. Mueller."

That was the definite end to the time he'd give me. He beckoned Chet Leegard with a crook of the thick forefinger, and the two went on up the hill; I saw them near the top just below the bushes, pointing and waving their arms as if they were planning military maneuvers over the terrain.

At least he wasn't concentrating on Steve Corbett alone.

I told him so when I found him sitting on the edge of a boat, moodily watching Cottie spoon sand into his coffeepots— four coffeepots now.

"You didn't do so bad," was his comment.

"We should be working on Mueller."

"We might do a little a sleuthing. I'll ask the sheriff if it's okay. Allow me that much?"

He strode straight through the brush up the almost vertical bank and disappeared over the edge. He was back at the cottage before I had the sand out of Cottie's hair.

"Come on. You don't have to doll up."

That was evident as soon as we got to the Flaming Door. The tavern was a long gray stucco building on the general lines of a factory, but some upstairs windows showed curtains. A graveled driveway led to a front door painted a brilliant scarlet and studded with brass. Over the exterior wall above the door leaping flames appeared in blues, reds and yellows; obviously the intention had been to suggest the door of hell. The interior didn't live up to the entrance; it was in a drab state of Sunday-morning desertion. A

132

long hall, gloomily dark at the center, lit a little by high windows at the ends; what little sunlight entered lay coldly on the waxed floor and chair-piled tables.

"Dark," commented Cottie, reaching for my hand.

"Let this stay with you as an introduction to a house of sin," his father said, going purposefully toward the abandoned bar, to rap on its top.

Slithering feet sounded on the stairs, a door beside the bar flew open and a man flew out. He took in Cottie's father first, then Cottie and me, the last with obvious relief.

"Oh, gosh, I thought mebbe it was the sher'f again. You shoulda seen 'm clean out this place las' night. Sat'dy night, too. Enough to ruin bus'ness, that's what it is. Could I do anything for you folks?"

He was a stringy man with scanty gray hair brushed crosswise on his skull, Mona Lisa eyes and a jerky Adam's apple.

Steve Corbett leaned on the bar. "I was over here Thursday night. Remember me?"

"Thursd'y—oh, sure, sure. Yeh. You was in that game——" He swallowed hastily on the Adam's apple that seemed threatening to climb out of his throat.

"Yeh," Steve Corbett repeated. "That game. Fellow I was with took Hoxie Mueller for eight thousand bucks."

The man reached for a handkerchief in his pants pocket, but not finding any, substituted by wiping his grimy gray-striped shirt sleeve across his face.

"Mister, do I remember! I'll say. I talked myself hoarse all night tellen the sher'f about that game."

"What'd Hoxie say?"

Care and craft were in the Mona Lisa eyes. "Well, now, mister, Hoxie wasn't here last night. He left here Frid'y afternoon."

"That right? That let's him out of the killing then, doesn't it. You heard about the murder?"

"Mister, I sure did. But it wasn't Hoxie Mueller. Not his friend neither. They was both real nice guys. From Kansas City." He was a little overanxious. "It was just like I'm tellen you. Hoxie Mueller come to me about fi' o'clock on Frid'y——"

"You run a hotel here?"

"Well, sorta. We got some rooms upstairs we rent out, across the hall from us. My wife she—rents 'em."

I could imagine for what usual purpose.

"I hear you've got a boat here. The only one on the lakes except the lodge boats. Anyone use it Friday night?"

"No sirree, no sirree, mister. I got that boat under lock and key, see? Right here on my key ring." He fished a dangling tangle from a rear pocket, singled one out and pointed it at Steve Corbett's abdomen. "That there's the boathouse key right there. It ain't been used since Hoxie Mueller used it Frid'y afternoon."

Quickly, "He came over to the lodge Friday afternoon?"

"Well, yeah. He went once in the morning. I guess he wanted to work up another little game. But this Sprung says nix. So Hoxie goes over again in the P.M. for another try and he packs along a quart of scotch for a softener. You can't blame a guy for wanten to get his dough back. But this Sprung ain't around, he says. He was sorta mad when he come back and give me the key. He says the low life was hidin' out because he kicked a kid. Say, that ain't your kid that got kicked, is it?"

The mildly mournful eyes peered at Cottie.

So Hoxie Mueller had come to the lodge that Friday afternoon while we were in town with Cottie. He could have stolen the knife then, seen the dummies then, laid his plan to get his money back. It seemed to me the only thing lacking was proof that he had returned to the resort in the night.

Steve Corbett was asking to see the boathouse.

The proprietor's feet in bedroom slippers shuffled him rapidly toward the door. He blinked outdoors as if he were a ground animal unused to sunlight, and took us around to a small boathouse at the rear. The boathouse had one end on land and one in water; he unlocked a door in the landward end. Steps inside led down to a small dock where a white rowboat rode in black water. The oars were still in the locks, but a padlocked chain twisted between the boat's anchor and a post in the dock.

Steve Corbett went down the narrow steps to pull and tug at the chains, but he quickly gave up. "No one could use this boat without unlocking that padlock."

"That's right, mister, and I got the only key. Right here. It ain't been off this key ring since Frid'y afternoon. And looky here. This door at the end to let the boat out, it hooks on the inside." He unhooked the lakeward door, let it swing open, to an inswirling break of water. "You couldn't open that door from the lake even if you swum around the boathouse."

I went closer. "Could I look over the boat?" If I could find a plantain leaf, a spotted plantain leaf——

He held out a restraining arm. "You oughten to get your fingerprints on that boat, lady. The sher'f, he said I wasn't to let anybody touch it."

There was nothing else we could do; the three of us stood silent while the man relocked his boathouse. He stood by, jingling his keys and telling us what good business he had while we got into the car, and bade us good-by as if we were personal guests.

"What chance he's a liar?" I asked as soon as the car was going.

"Ninety-nine and forty-four one hundredths."

I pointed out that Hoxie Mueller could have stolen the knife.

"If Hoxie left that knife around, Boxruud will find it. I hope it has his prints on it."

Was there any chance it could? I said, "I hope the sheriff doesn't find those"—I spelled—"g-u-n-s."

Cottie asked, "Mamma, you talking about guns?"

His father told me, "You underestimate the Corbetts."

I wondered what the sheriff was thinking about the Corbetts.

CHAPTER TWELVE

RUSTIC REPOSE had fled from the Crying Sisters by the time we returned. A half-dozen youngish men in tweeds, their hats pushed to the backs of their heads, clustered around John Loxton's door; through the screen I glimpsed the lodge owner, harried, at bay, his little beard moving up and down in agitated speech.

Reporters.

Someone else had arrived, too. We'd no more than locked ourselves into our cabin—all the cabins in the row had presented an appearance of siege—than the sheriff knocked at our screen.

Behind him stood a man with all a politician's easy surfaces, complete with thin, curling brown hair, eyes that didn't quite meet mine, a syrupy damp small mouth, and jowls. His well-fed body followed Boxruud to our porch.

"Mr. and Mrs. Corbett, this is County Attorney Joe E. Vind, who will be in charge of this investigation." The sheriff kept a straight face saying it, but I suspected his emotions.

"Well, well, and a little boy, too, eh?" County Attorney Joe E. Vind spread on the geniality. "Now, I know a charming little family like this could have nothing to do with a murder. Sorry to trouble you, nothing we want less than to trouble you good city folks who come up here to relieve the cares of city life in our beautiful lake region. Just as a matter of formality however——"

"County Attorney Vind is hearing everybody's evidence over," the sheriff interpreted. "He would like to hear yours now. If we could go into the house, maybe, with you first, Mr. Corbett?"

Mr. Corbett agreeing with no grace, the men went inside and shut both doors. The questioning was shorter than the one the night before; inside thirty minutes Steve Corbett came out and I went in.

It was an informal room for any legal inquisition; Vind sat with crossed knees on the one rocker, the sheriff on my bed and I on Cottie's. Vind did the questioning, but he did it with the pages of the sheriff's copperplate script before him, adding nothing new.

"Just a formality," he assured me again when he finished. The small gray eyes still did not meet mine, but they dwelt on my figure, and the damp mouth became more syrupy. "I'll keep an eye out for you, Mrs. Corbett. If any reporters trouble you, just come to me."

The sheriff entered the questioning obliquely there.

"You are interested in Hoxie Mueller?"

I began, "I can't help seeing—— We don't want to come under suspicion ourselves. It seems so obvious that Mr. Mueller wanted his money back very badly."

The county attorney approved, but the sheriff took me through every word and action of the tavern keeper's that morning.

"I'm certain he could have been bought to—let's say improve on the earliness with which Hoxie Mueller left the Flaming Door on Friday," I ended.

No one took that up. I added, "Of course Mueller could have left the Flaming Door before supper, and still have killed Sprung. He could have come back late that night, perhaps taken the key when the tavern keeper wasn't watching. There were those oars I told you about, that I heard at two-thirty. He must have been coming here then; I must have been mistaken about thinking the boat was leaving. He would have plenty of time to kill Al Sprung"—and to knock me out, though I couldn't say that— "and get the body into the dummy, and still be back at the Flaming Door before daylight. He'd probably think he'd have a couple days' start before the body was found."

Vind began, "Good reasoning, Mrs. Corbett——"

But the sheriff's voice broke mildly through. "You believe that Sprung was put into the dummy *after* two-thirty, Mrs. Corbett, instead of before?"

Where does the sudden cold that hits you when you've made a bad error come from? One moment my hands had been warm, the next they were ice. I'd grown careless with self-confidence. I opened my mouth for self-defense. Then I thought wildly, no! I must think first! I looked from Vind's surprised deprecation to the sheriff's quietly watchful small popeyes, and forced one breath down through the ice block that had taken possession of my chest.

"We—my husband and I were talking about the possible time of the murder this morning. You know my husband was looking for Sprung that Friday evening. It was quite late when he came back and he hadn't seen Sprung anywhere—if Sprung was hiding he'd probably stay hidden a while longer, afraid my husband might come back—then, well, I did hear that boat after two."

It was halting and lame, and I didn't handle my voice well.

Vind tried. "That's reasonable, Sheriff."

The sheriff stood up, and I knew terror. What if I, *I*, should now be arrested for the murder! If he found out, forced me to admit I had seen Al Sprung's body after two-thirty; that that was how I knew he had been put into the dummy after that! Yet I had concealed this evidence. I thought with despair of the way I had let Cottie's father rule my actions, thought with despair of my own indecisions. How could I explain them?

But the sheriff was saying, "Maybe we will speak to Mrs. Corbett again. For now, thanks."

He lumbered toward the door. Vind followed him, spouting warm assurances of belief in my aloofness from crime; I was so numb from what had just happened I hardly heard him.

But I sprang to alertness again at the sheriff's voice outside. "Mr. Corbett, we're trying to decide when Sprung could of got kilt. What would you say?"

I stood behind Vind, helpless to give a worded warning. Steve Corbett sat at the porch table making Cottie a large cocked hat from newspaper; he raised his eyes to the sheriff, but not openly to me.

"That's an interesting point, Sheriff. We were talking about it this morning. The way I figure, it must have been after I quit looking for him and came home—I don't know when that was, but I guess it was midnight. Then my wife says she heard a boat about two-thirty. If the murderer was in that boat, then the killing probably was just before or after that, depending on if he was coming or going."

Talking around, not saying anything.

The sheriff turned on his heel and made for the door; Vind backed out after him. Outside the door they were greeted by the newsmen; a cluster formed around Vind like bees around a queen. Vind's drone came over the buzz; he might want to save me from reporters, but for himself he evidently didn't mind.

Folding up the brim of the newspaper hat, Steve Corbett asked, low and amused, "Did the clever Mrs. Corbett trip?"

"Yes. For just that reason."

"Good thing she has a husband to fall back on."

"It must have been obvious."

"The sheriff wasn't hoping that when he asked me."

Vind started up the track, most of the reporters following. Three turned toward us. I hastily hooked the screen.

"How do you do, lady, I'm from the Minneapolis *World*." The speaker was the fair-haired, innocently chubby youth in front. "How'd you like to make a little dough, say twenty bucks, for an

140

exclusive inside story of this murder? You wouldn't have to do any work, just talk."

"Sorry, she isn't interested," Steve Corbett said over my head. When I looked around Cottie wasn't on the porch; his father must have shunted him hastily inside.

The reporter wheedled, "Okay, but you're Corbett, aren't you? Is it true your kid is crippled for life by being kicked by this guy that got bumped?"

"The kid hasn't a scratch. The man was too drunk to touch him."

"That isn't what we heard. Now, Mr. Corbett, you're in a spot. We could work up a lot of sympathy for you. Picture of the kid, statement he's lamed—— Say, you got a good-lookin' wife, too. We could take shots of her holdin' the kid. Say, guy, I could do stuff for you so a jury would just say go in peace and God bless you."

"Sorry." The answer was hard. "I'm in no danger of having to curry favor with the public or a jury either."

One of the men raised a camera but lowered it. "Aw hell, I can't get a pic through that screen in this light."

The blond youth presented his cherubic back, but threw over his shoulder, "Okay, tough guy, take what you get. I can find others will play ball."

They hurried to catch up with the others ahead.

Cottie's father turned, shrugging, to let the boy out. "Now you can see what you've got coming. If."

Except for sporadic entreaties from other reporters we were left alone until after midday. Cottie was restless from inactivity and didn't want to nap; I finally got him to lie down by telling him Epaminondas. Just as Epaminondas was dragging the bread home by a string around its middle, I saw through the side window a man's head break through the bushes on the hilltop, then a second head. Slowly a file of men became visible. They walked crouched over after they were out of the bushes, about three feet apart; it wasn't hard to guess their purpose.

They were combing the hillside, inch by inch. Hunting the knife. Hunting the money. Any other clue.

For hours that slow methodical caterpillar advanced side-wise along the hill. Once I saw the sheriff move elephantine along the file, with figures bobbing up and down in his wake.

"They've haven't found what they're hunting," was Steve Corbett's comment. He had come in to watch, at my beckoning, but he soon lounged out to the porch again, to sit in his old attitude on the cot.

Toward three I told him, "We need milk. Eggs, too. I feel like getting out. It should be safe enough."

He lifted one corner of his mouth. "Don't take up with any strange men."

Except for the file of men moving steadily down the hillside the resort was very quiet. A gray head popped out Mrs. Clapshaw's house door as I went by, as promptly vanished. But at Earl Jordan's cottage his feet hit the porch floor from a hastily untilted chair.

"Mrs. Corbett! You out alone braving the tigers? Wait for me." He ran down his steps. "Lady, am I glad to see a human face. God didn't do much for that county attorney. Getting milk?"

"And what liberty there is."

"I've been wanting to tell you I'm sorry all the way to hell and gone for the spot you're in." He'd recovered some of his old insouciance. "I never thought your husband had anything to do with this mess. That Rudeen woman—she's just jealous. The sheriff won't pay any attention to her. Mueller—that's his guy."

The world seemed to swing a slight bit toward normal— toward hope at least. I told him about visiting the Flaming Door; he pooh-poohed the tavern keeper's evidence.

"For ten bucks he'd probably swear you didn't do a murder he'd seen you do with his own eyes."

Elmer was scrubbing the cement floor of the milk room, but his heart wasn't in it; the brush sloshed slowly around in the soapy pool.

"Sure you can get some milk and eggs." He stood up listlessly to get them, so slowed down he almost drawled. "Gosh, do you think they think I done it? I been thinkin'. I ain't got no alibi. I was right here that Friday night. Sleepen on my cot on the other side of the cows. There wouldn't of been a thing to keep me from stealen out in the dark night. Only I didn't. But I can't prove it. I said so, honest, to the sheriff. I'm an ambitious man, I says to him, why should I blight my c'reer by a foul deed such as this to start out? I got ambitions of owden this resort; would I——"

"Of course the sheriff doesn't think you did it." I did what I could to restore his morale. "We're under more suspicion than you are, because of Mr. Sprung's kicking Cottie, and the place he was found. You don't have to worry, Elmer."

His eyes were shocked. "Gosh, Mrs. Corbett, I know you or Mr. Corbett wouldn't of done it."

"Out of the mouths of babes," Earl Jordan said when we'd gone. "Don't you wish the sheriff had his faith? And talking about faith, I have faith in the mails. Let's see if there is any."

"It's Sunday."

"Someone may have gone to town."

Someone had. Three well-handled letters lay in the old cigar box nailed to Loxton's front porch.

"Mrs. Clapshaw one, the Willards two. None for us. Life."

I couldn't help seeing the legend in the upper left-hand corner of the top envelope, one addressed to the Willards. It read: Office of the County Attorney of Ramsey County, St. Paul, Minnesota.

Earl Jordan said, "That's interesting. The Willards, for some reason, are acquainted with county attorneys before. I keep thinking I've seen that Willard before. His picture, something."

I didn't have a chance to comment. Two men eased around the corner of Loxton's house, and I turned for hasty flight.

"Hey, guys, here's two of 'em loose!" The cherub was evidently a fair hunter. Three more reporters joined him.

"If it isn't Mr. and Mrs.—no, *not* Mr. Corbett. Lady, should you be out bringin' home the milk with a guy that isn't your husband at a time like this?" The cherub grinned amiably, hurrying to keep step with me, but I couldn't forget what a menace he was. "Let's have a sociable little talk, huh? This Sprung ever make any passes at you, Mrs. Corbett?"

"Don't let 'em bother you," Earl Jordan defended.

"You could be a great big help to your husband, Mrs. Corbett. *Cherchez la femme*—some femme, too, Mrs. Corbett. Say, why don't you and me have a date tonight? We could go to that tavern. I'll go along—hell, we'll all go. You don't have to walk so fast, do you?" Almost every phrase was in a different masculine voice.

I'd wanted adventure, I thought grimly. If any man smiles at you, smile back. . . .

One man ran ahead, walking backward in front of us, raising a small stereoscoped box to his eyes. I saw Eldreth seeing that picture, and squinted my eyes and pushed my lower jaw forward and slightly off center.

The camera lowered. "Aw, baby! Don't be that way!"

I walked the rest of the way with my face like that.

Steve Corbett stood at the screen to unhook it for me. "Thanks for playing guard." He grinned at Jordan. "Come in?"

"Sure!" The answer was in chorus.

"Sorry, I'll throw a party for you guys some other day."

144

A few of them stood around grumbling, then hurried after Earl Jordan. It wasn't until I was setting the bottles on the table that I saw I still had the Willard letter in my hand.

Later when the reporters had disappeared I ran with it to the Willard cabin.

Mrs. Willard came to the door. When I gave her the letter she said just one word.

"Thanks." She almost grabbed the letter out of my hand and turned her back on me.

Darkness halted the work of the searchers, daylight found them working again. Again we spent a guarded night. I heard the scrunch of feet on the hill, and slept between security and fear; security because we were guarded, fear that the guarders would find something and come to charge us with the murder.

As we ate breakfast on Monday the searchers were working along the lawns in front of the cabins, Cottie watching them fascinated.

" 'Ey lose somesing?" he asked, over and over.

At midmorning John Loxton pattered down the trail, a newspaper under his arm. He burst into agitated speech before he was up the steps.

"I knew this would be horrible. It is horrible. Look."

The paper he opened over the table was that morning's Minneapolis *World.* Nazi outrages held the page headline, but we were prominent enough.

Tackling Dummy Holds Body of Murdered Minneapolitan

Al Sprung, Vacationing at Crying Sisters Resort,
Is Victim of Knife Killing

145

Beside the headlines were pictures of two tackling dummies hanging from a tree behind a cottage, a black arrow pointing out the larger dummy with the legend: "Vacationist's exercise dummy in which the murdered man was found."

Evidently the reporters had been busy making dummies; I was certain the sheriff hadn't let them use the originals, and the cottage wasn't even ours.

John Loxton pointed a shaking finger at a picture of a man with a beard. "That's me. The resort is ruined. Mrs. Clapshaw wants her money back. And who else will come?"

Two other pictures were of Sprung's cottage and his car, and of County Attorney Joe E. Vind, in charge of the investigation.

My eyes leaped to the article, hoping I might find tangible facts. Behind me stood Steve Corbett, reading, too, and Cottie crowded to get between me and the table.

The events of Friday—the day preceding the murder—were given in detail, with emphasis on the eight thousand dollars and Hoxie Mueller's coming to get Sprung into another game. The kicking was told about, but no inferences were drawn, and the dummies were said to have hung behind "one of the cottages."

I thought then we were lucky. The melodrama of Hoxie Mueller overshadowed us.

"Descriptions of the Hoxie Mueller concerned today led authorities toward the belief that he may be Hoxie Moebbels, leader of the Kansas City Moebbels gang, who is known to have fled that city after the Kansas City First National Bank holdup.

"The Moebbels gang came under strong suspicion of the holdup, but the members so far located proved alibis, and none of the stolen money was found in their possession.

"As most of the loot—claimed to be about eighty thousand dollars—was in bills whose numbers are known, Kansas City police

146

have been waiting the first appearance of the money, but so far none of the known bills have appeared. Moebbels was never questioned in the robbery, the Kansas City police not being able to discover his whereabouts."

Hoxie Mueller a gangster—I could believe that easily.

A paragraph followed on the efforts being made to locate Mueller: the state police, the radio calls, the country-wide warnings.

I thought, as John Loxton left with his paper, probably to moan over it with the other inhabitants, that Hoxie Mueller had at least given us a breathing space. I thought, letting hope swing upward, that he, not Steve Corbett, must be the murderer. But as the day wore on to noon, I came to feel an expectancy almost like that I had felt on the night we came to the Crying Sisters, the night when the woman had screamed. Exactly one week ago today.

I wondered if anything would come out now about that screaming woman. If she would prove real at last. I hadn't even mentioned her to the sheriff; she had seemed too tenuous. I wondered if the sheriff's hunt would discover her, too, link her to her place in the chain, explain her mysterious presence.

Steve Corbett stayed almost without moving on his cot; I wondered if I caught some of the expectancy from him.

It broke just after noon.

There was a shout outside, from the men now working down the bank at a point north of us, between our cabin and Sprung's. Heads moved up and down in a knot of blue-shirted backs with here and there an odd strand, the jacketed back of a reporter.

Sheriff Boxruud emerged.

He walked steadily toward our cottage, holding something white before him on the palm of his left hand. There was an angry, almost threatening forward surge of the mob of men, but he turned to wave with his free right hand at the bank, obviously giving orders to go on. The men hesitated but broke and went back.

The sheriff turned again to come on, his deputy and the reporters at his heels.

CHAPTER THIRTEEN

THE SHERIFF CAME straight to our steps.

"Mr. Corbett!" It was an order. "I want to see you, please!" He turned to his deputy with a swift order, "Get Mr. Loxton here."

There was something about the sheriff's advance that had been like a marching army's; it had solidity and force, and he looked at us now as if he was penetrating enemy country—he was wary. He bellowed to the reporters to stay off the porch, and hooked the door so they had to.

I was glad Cottie was napping.

It was easy now to see what the sheriff held in his hand—a triangle of handkerchief over something long and flat. Steve Corbett's eyes were quick on that hidden object.

"Don't tell me you've found the knife—the right knife!"

"Guy, we'll tell you!" The reporters had moved to stand in front of the porch, looking avidly upward.

The sheriff ponderously moved to the table, laid the handkerchief upon it, and lifted the top fold.

"Do you recognize this?"

Our knife. The nick was there.

The fore part of the blade was shining and clean; gray dried earth clung to the metal in an irregular rim three quarters of the way up, and above that was a darker brownish stain.

One of the reporters whistled.

I think I stood perfectly still, but I felt myself rocking, forward and back, as if I stood in a swing. Only my feet were quiet.

It was my head that rocked.

"Yes," I said dully, "that's our knife."

"As far as I can see it's ours, all right," Steve Corbett repeated after me. He had come to stand close beside me.

"So," the sheriff said. "I do not think this knife was used alone for cleaning fish. I will send it where I sent the other knives and the grain sacks. I will soon know."

There was a large quiet on the porch; even the reporters had quieted. It was broken by Leegard, bringing in John Loxton.

The sheriff addressed the owner. "I asked you to come because I thought these people might deny it." He pointed to the knife. "Could that knife have come from any other cabin but this?"

Loxton blinked, looking down, his little beard thrust forward in surprise, his eyes horrified. He said mournfully, "I recognize it by the nick. No other knife here is nicked. They are all quite new knives."

The sheriff drew a deep breath. "I do not doubt this is the knife used for the murder. After the murder it was stuck there in the bank, under the bushes. Maybe the murderer thinks county sheriffs are lazy, they know nothing, they will not look."

His singsong was intensified, almost droning, as his emotion rose, and inside me the expectant fear rose with it. I felt rather than saw Chet Leegard's hand on his hip, and his eyes like a waiting grass snake's.

Beside me Steve Corbett waited, too. Quiet.

I asked, "Why wasn't it thrown in the lake?"

The sheriff seemed to recede an inch, not stepping back, but just his expanded flesh relaxing as if he had hoped for something but hadn't got it.

"You are a smart woman, Mrs. Corbett."

"Lady, you got something there," one reporter called, and another, "Yeh, and you better get something, too, baby."

150

"Hell, yes." Steve Corbett was fighting now, too. He stood as if he had only waited for me to strike back first, as belligerent and rocky as Gibraltar, his head and shoulders thrusting forward. "Do you think either of us would use our own knife on the guy, and then plant it right on the bank where it was a ninety-to-one shot it would be found? When there's a lake out there a hundred feet deep? Think again, Sheriff. If that knife was used for the murder it was stolen to throw suspicion on us. If it was stuck in the bank that means the murderer didn't want you to miss the trap."

He swung on Loxton so swiftly the man jumped, and the thin hands flew to a protective clasping at his breast.

"Anyone else in camp know about that nick?"

"I—I am not sure. It happened this summer when a previous occupant of this cottage used it on a wire clothesline——"

"There you are, Sheriff. Anyone in this camp might have known about that nick. Or Hoxie Mueller might have taken it just because we were the only ones gone that Friday afternoon."

"Good going, guy," came from outside.

The sheriff was a receiving set; he took it all in, but it wasn't making any appreciable impression. He came forward a step.

"Mrs. Corbett, where was this knife kept?"

I pointed to the top of the cupboard. "Up there."

"So. And where was it when you moved here?"

"There." I pointed out the cutlery drawer in the table. "We moved it so the boy wouldn't get it."

"Open the drawer to show me, please."

Wondering, I did. I showed where, as well as I remembered, the knife had lain amid the dime-store knives and forks and spoons.

"Thank you, that is all." As I closed the drawer the sheriff turned impassively to Steve Corbett. "Now you, please."

"That was right, where she showed you."

"You show me, please."

Cottie's father took the one stride necessary to bring him to the table. He jerked the drawer open.

"Right there!" he said sharply. "That suit you?"

"Thank you, yes."

"Of all the monkey business!" The drawer slammed in under impatient hands; it went in as drawers always went in under his hands, too far in at the right, sticking out at the left.

I had the same sensation I'd had yesterday morning when I let the sheriff know I knew Al Sprung had been put into the dummy after two-thirty. Not from anything I saw, but from something I felt in the sheriff.

"So," his voice was a needle point, inboring. "You. Not Mrs. Corbett. I see in the other room yesterday morning a drawer closed like that. I see it in no other cottage. Except one. *The cabin of Al Sprung.* After Al Sprung was dead, Mr. Corbett, you go there to look. You shut the drawers there as you shut this one. In a hurry. Perhaps that, too, is done by someone else to throw suspicion on you?"

Silence.

Then Steve Corbett was talking again. "Lots of people close drawers that way. What do you think? I'm the only one does? Al Sprung was a nervous guy, he probably slammed 'em in the same way."

The words were good, but the voice had the same hollowness I'd heard in my voice yesterday. Of course I knew. *That* was what Steve had done early that Saturday morning after I wavered home from finding Sprung's body. In addition to hiding the guns he had searched Sprung's cabin. For what? For money? Or for some other thing or clue, for the thing he had hunted every night of our stay?

The reporters were completely quiet; I think that if they

152

could they'd have ripped off their eyes and ears to throw them in on the porch.

The sheriff asked, "You were never in the cabin of Al Sprung?"

"I don't say that. I was there one night playing cards."

I wondered if the sheriff got as I did that he didn't say he hadn't searched Sprung's cabin.

Boxruud didn't comment on that. He said, "Your fingerprints on the table, yes. But our murderer is clever; he wipes his prints from the chest of drawers."

So they had our prints. They must have been taken from articles in the cabin.

And while I was thinking of fingerprints the sheriff's small round eyes were moving from Loxton to Steve Corbett to me, and what he said came on me without warning.

"If I am wrong I am sorry for the hardship I am causing, especially for the little boy. But I think it would be better, Mr. Corbett, if you should come with me to Maple Valley. Here there are too many reporters."

He stepped forward, and his hands slid over Steve Corbett's shoulders, his hips, his pockets.

It had come, the thing I feared. And all I felt was a sort of dull despair, as if the expectancy were worse than the certainty, as if I were done with waiting and the worst had happened.

The man under the sheriff's hands asked harshly, "Am I being arrested?"

The answer came after a hesitation. "No weapons. Let us say detained for questioning."

"I don't want to leave my kid here alone. Or my wife." He took the jolt without perceptible emotion; his first words were these practical considerations. "Look, Sheriff, be a sport. I didn't do this

153

murder. The knife is an obvious plant. That drawer stuff may sound good, but it's full of holes. How'd you like presenting evidence like that to a jury?"

"It isn't required I should give all my reasons. The wife and child"—the eyes went to me with lifting lids— "they will go, too. That will be best."

He folded the handkerchief over the knife again, and picked it up carefully. "Leegard, these people may go in their own car, but you will be along. I will be there soon. With Vind."

Even the reporters didn't seem important now.

I said, "I suppose we'll need some things. If we're going to stay overnight."

"Don't bother about me," Steve Corbett told me shortly.

He turned his back on Boxruud's and Loxton's departure, went to stand staring out at the reporters.

They called, "Hot stuff, fella. How's about playin' ball now? You're a Minneapolis guy, aren't you? Where you live? What you——"

Inside the cabin I was waking Cottie.

"Go someplace?" he echoed, instantly awake.

It was a hard job, but I managed. "We're going in to town, and we're going to stay in a cute little house with little rooms. Maybe you and I will both be in one room there, too. We'll play games and I'll tell you a new story."

Chet Leegard was kind enough; as soon as we got out on the steps the cameras started clicking, but he pushed our way through. Steve Corbett carried Cottie, holding the boy's face in toward his breast. His own hat was low over his eyes; he wasn't skulking, but all they got of him was an outthrust chin. I'd pulled my hat askew, too, and jerked my chin sidewise again; it was all part of a daze, something I felt I had to do to protect myself.

154

A settling frown creased a line over Cottie's pale little brows, once we were inside the car and moving. "Why you don't drive, Daddy? Why you sit in back?"

"I want to hold my big boy today," his father told him; it was the only thing he said on that journey.

Two women on the opposite sidewalk paused to stare as Chet Leegard herded us into the small gray concrete box that was Maple Valley's jail. The room we walked into was a bare office. Two small barred windows in opposite cement walls were inset a half foot; a scarred mission oak desk was flanked by a mission oak settee and three golden oak armchairs, a green steel filing cabinet. Opposite the door a small arched-over corridor led back past four cells, two on each side, their grilled doors standing open.

Cottie asked in wonder, "Is 'is a cow barn?"

"This is a man barn," was his father's brief comment.

Leegard waved a ropy arm. "Jest set down, folks."

The sheriff came quickly; he walked in looking merely businesslike, but Vind, behind him, looked shocked reproach, as if we had betrayed a trust. Reporters crowded after, but the sheriff shoved them back without words and slammed the door in their faces.

Shut up. In jail. At first it had almost seemed opera *bouffe*, a play jail, with the principals inside and a few gathering children as a chorus outside the door. But it was real now with the door shut, the sheriff grim, the county attorney perspiring, half apologetic, but ready to swing into a solid belief in our guilt any time it was safe.

"All a mistake, I'm sure," Vind offered uneasily again.

The sheriff pulled the limp black hat from his square hair, and flipped it to the top of the filing cabinet. The round tight eyes were on me.

"Chet," he said deliberately, "maybe Mrs. Corbett and the boy would like to take a walk."

155

He didn't want me to hear Steve Corbett's evidence.

There wasn't anything to do but go. I wonder if I'll ever take a walk under circumstances as queer. Cottie chattering in the middle, holding one hand to me, one to Chet Leegard, who had to slope sidewise to reach it. Behind us three reporters trailed, occasionally beseeching, while we went past fly-speckled store windows festooned with dusty twirls of once-bright crepe paper, bank, railroad station, creamery. Long streets of square-porched 1918 houses— hours of them. I barely noticed; I was too busy thinking.

Suppose this time Steve Corbett told how I had found Al Sprung's body. The sheriff would know I had lied. I tried to build a suit of armor for my own turn. This I must say. This I mustn't. I walked in a trance, sorting facts into two careful piles, one tellable, one not.

The sun was quite low when Chet Leegard suggested we go back.

"Carry me, Mamma. I tired."

I'd been expecting that.

Chet Leegard offered, "Here, kid, I'll lug you."

He did, too, with no lessening of his solemn taciturnity. At the jail door our reporters joined the others, disgruntled.

"To hell with this case," one grumbled as Leegard elbowed our way through. "These country guys never play ball."

In the jail office Steve Corbett sat in one of the golden oak armchairs, his khaki shirt unbuttoned halfway down his chest, his tie undone, his hair stranded as if he'd pushed impatient fingers through it again and again. The dark eyes burned at the bottoms of their brow-shaded sockets, and the hollow in his cheek was dark red in a plane as flat and rigid as steel plating.

He hadn't broken. He had a grin for his son riding in on Chet Leegard's shoulder.

156

"Hi, kid, got a new horse?"

The county attorney was more clammily uncertain than ever; the sheriff worn but still persisting. He stood up as we came in.

"My wife, she will have something fixed for you folks to eat."

Cottie's father stood up, too, offering gravely, "The county pays for this, I hope? We wouldn't put you to any expense."

Boxruud just slid a look at him.

Vind's nervous eyes were on me. "I hope you won't question Mrs. Corbett tonight, Sheriff. I'm afraid I won't be able to stay. I have—ah—a meeting of the Republican county leaders."

"You go ahead. I don't guess much will happen here."

He was to be wrong about that.

Vind backed out bowing; the opened door saw him lost in a surge of reporters. The sheriff shepherded us through the same obstructions.

"I ain't found out a thing yet, boys," he answered shooting questions. "When I get to know, you get to know."

"Any news of Mueller?" one called.

"No news."

We were driven two blocks to one of the square white 1918 houses, where a bustling woman with three chins under a pink face set us down to Swiss steak and mashed potatoes and carrots and jello. At the head of his table the sheriff talked about outrages against Jews in Germany, about taxes, about seizure of oil lands in Mexico, asking for opinions, as if he were trying to form an idea of Steve Corbett's character.

Cottie's father was noncommittal until the sheriff mentioned Mexico; he said he'd traveled there, and for the first time I heard him talking easily and well, like a competent executive, hard bitten but just, detailing problems he knew.

"Mexico's got too few people with governing brains; the

157

others are splendid as far as character goes—simple minded, friendly, cheerful people. Cute little beggars, too. But they have to be told when to get up and when to go to bed. Sanitation's terrible. An American would die in a week eating in the houses or even the Mex restaurants. The women carry one kid on their backs and another under their belts year in and year out, and baby coffins are sold in the market like radishes. You can't industrialize that country now . . ."

How well I was to remember that talk about Mexico later.

He creased lines in the tablecloth, showing sanitation systems that would be easy to install. But I didn't miss how wary he was being. He didn't pin himself to dates, didn't give any traceable facts about his past life. He was being completely anonymous.

When he stood up from the table he was vigorous and smiling, as if talking had revived him.

We were taken immediately back to the jail; the sheriff said he'd like to ask me a few questions that evening. But he never did. When we drove up before the jail door a state police car stood there, the heads of eight reporters in at its windows. Two uniformed men occupied the front seat, and in the rear were one uniformed man and two others. The two others were Hoxie Mueller and his dark companion.

CHAPTER FOURTEEN

"HI, SHERIFF!" One of the state patrolmen backed out of the car. "I got a couple of guys here I guess you want to see. I caught 'em trying to do a sneak into Canada."

The sheriff climbed out. "Come along, please, Mr. Corbett. You could recognize this Hoxie Mueller?"

"We had to bump 'em around a little—took a revolver off the dark guy—but I guess they can still be recognized," the trooper apologized.

"I know he's Mueller without coming along." Steve Corbett was out of the car, too, striding after the sheriff.

After that nothing was audible except reporters until the sheriff bellowed, "Quiet!"

He shoved reporters away to jerk the rear door open. The three men there stepped out, two of them handcuffed to the third.

"You don't want to see me, do you, Sheriff?" It came, oiled and ingratiating, from the blond young man with the narrow-topped, wide-bottomed body. His coat was ripped, his necktie had one end, and his face was swollen and cut. His follower was even more battered.

"I'm only riding around the country on my vacation, Sheriff." Hoxie Mueller rolled forward, crossing his short right arm to clasp the cuff on his left wrist. "I stayed near here a couple of days at the Flaming Door. If there's anything wrong about that Flaming Door—why, I don't know a thing about it, see? I only stayed there. What call you got to drag me in?"

The patrolman who'd done the talking gestured at him with his thumb. "His story is he don't know what happened, he don't know what he's wanted for. We haven't told him anything."

"Good." The sheriff turned to Steve Corbett. "I will first take care of these people. Come with me, please."

There wasn't much please about it. He herded us with dispatch toward the two back cells, pointing to the one on the right.

"Mrs. Corbett, you in here with the child. You, Mr. Corbett, across here, please."

Cottie had fallen asleep in the car. As I laid him on the cot his father stepped across the corridor without a word; the sheriff clanged the grilled door behind him and turned the key.

I stiffened defensively for the clanging of my own door.

But Boxruud was saying thoughtfully, "You, Mrs. Corbett, I will not lock in. You can close the door when you want." He left quickly.

I sat down on the foot of the cot, which with one sink, one toilet fixture, one shelf, comprised the furnishing of the tiny cell. Cottie was sleeping in a jail now, but it was sleep as sweet as any to him. Across the corridor his father's eyes were on him.

This was Steve Corbett's battle, Cottie's battle, my battle, which the sheriff would fight with Hoxie Mueller now. We didn't even have to enter.

Tramping feet announced the coming of Hoxie Mueller into the office. There were several voices; the troopers must have come in, too. The sheriff put in a call for Vind but didn't wait. "Here's the loot we got when we searched 'em." Objects clanked against wood.

"Good gun," came the sheriff's voice. "Which one had it?"

"The dark guy."

Paper crinkled. "This all the money? Only six hundred? I am hunting a sum of eight thousand dollars."

"That's all I got. Look 'em over yourself."

Grunts suggested the sheriff acted on that. Then he questioned Hoxie Mueller directly.

"So you're from Kansas City. You know this Moebbels gang that robbed a bank awhile back?"

"Not me, Sheriff, I'm a law-abiding man." I could imagine the soft words issuing from the ever-smiling pink face.

"Your name, it couldn't be Hoxie Moebbels?"

"Nope, Hoxie Mueller. Second-hand cars, that's my business."

"What's your name?" That must have gone to Mueller's companion. Only a splutter came in answer, then Mueller's soft voice again.

"His name's Dave Spendler, Sheriff. He can't talk. He's dumb. You know, like deaf and dumb. Only he hears all right."

"Leegard, you get that fingerprint stuff out."

Mueller objected, tried to kid him out of it; the sheriff plodded on, sending Leegard to mail the prints to the Minneapolis police. As soon as the door closed the questions began again.

They went on for hours. Mueller said he had never been in Minnesota until that summer, that he had come for vacation, hit by chance on the Flaming Door, liked the life there, stayed three days. The sheriff was particularly interested in Thursday's poker game.

"Where you got this eight thousand dollars you lose?"

"Like I say, I'm in the used-car business, Sheriff. A bunch of men come around, said they was goin' prospectin'—I don't know, that's what they told me. Said they was goin' to load up outfits and drive into Colorado or Montana or somewheres looking for gold. I sold 'em sixteen cars. Spot cash. That's when I thought I would take me a vacation."

It was decorative lying; the sheriff passed over it to take up Mueller's search for Sprung on Friday.

"Sure. I went over lookin' for Sprung in the A.M., but he was mad with a hang-over and won't play. So I goes again in the P.M.. But he ain't around. He's hidin' out because he kicked a kid."

Where had Al Sprung hidden that afternoon, while Hoxie Mueller hunted him, while Steve Corbett hunted him? That question hadn't yet been answered. And Steve Corbett would have been thorough. Had some other inhabitant hidden him? Mrs. Rudeen—suddenly I remembered that she had been at the top of the bank looking down when Cottie was kicked. Had she seen where he went? I was certain she hadn't told the sheriff so.

The voices down the corridor had faded before my thoughts. Now I heard them again as Leegard came back in, and the sheriff ordered him sharply to bring in the tavern keeper, Niddie.

Mueller didn't comment as the door closed again.

"Now this last time you rowed across the lake. Didn't you have a hard time getting back into that boathouse?"

Meaning in that; the sheriff was trying to trap Mueller into admitting he had made a third trip after dark. I saw, too, as time went by, why Steve Corbett had had his shirt unbuttoned when his questioning ended. The voices beat incessantly—the singing drone of the sheriff's Norwegian ancestors, broken to American words; a thin whine creeping into Mueller's tone, a whine he fought to keep down, succeeding, failing.

Across from me Steve Corbett's shadow dimmed and went out with darkness; for a long time the questioning went on in darkness, too, the sheriff hammering on one point: it was after midnight when Mueller took a third trip. Mrs. Corbett had heard his oars.

And Mueller couldn't betray he knew why he must deny a night trip. The whine broke into a scream.

"Why you want me to say I went over in the night? I never! That's all I got to say!"

"There is a reason." The sheriff was telling him at last. "That night Al Sprung was murdered."

"He—— Aw, Sheriff, you're kidding." The control of desperation.

A quick pounce, "Maybe you can't read newspapers?"

"I never got a paper today. Did I, Dave? Why would I buy a paper? I'm on my vacation, see?"

From this side, from that, the sheriff attacked.

"Your eight thousand dollars, it was not on Sprung."

"It wasn't on me, was it?"

"You have passed many hiding places."

"I never even seen that dough from the time Sprung scooped it off the table." It was insisted earnestly.

"I find the knife——"

"*Knife!* Jeez—you mean the guy was knifed?"

"The knife you steal from the end cottage in the absence of the people that afternoon."

"I don't know what you're talkin' about! I never stole no knife!" He was screaming again.

On and on. Baiting. Evasion. My watch showed twenty minutes of midnight when the outer door opened again and Chet Leegard entered.

"Gosh! Dark? What the——"

As the lights clicked on I came to a slow realization of myself. My legs and back were stiff from my strained, unsupported position on the cot. Where Steve Corbett's shadow had disappeared was now a dim half-moon—the distant light reflecting from the plane of bone over his temple, along his cheek, angling off his chin. His eyes, the rest of his face, were lost in the cavernous dark.

"Niddie's cleared out, Sheriff," Leegard was reporting. "His wife said he went to Minneapolis to get supplies."

The sheriff answered curtly, "Put out a call."

"That God damn fool!" That was Mueller raging, but forcing himself to quick quiet. "That ain't got anything to do with me, Sheriff. A man's got a right to buy groceries."

Advance, retreat, feint; the sheriff was a skilled, experienced valiant fighter. But he got nowhere. I grasped that at last; sometime during the night Hoxie Mueller might break, but I was too tired to listen longer. I pulled off my dress and lay down beside Cottie, pulling out the one thin blanket to cover us both. The beating voices finally were lost in sleep.

I woke cramped and cold. Morning light was quiet; there were no voices. Cottie's warm little body was close against my chest, his sweet hair under my chin. His breath was almost soundless, but from somewhere near came breaths that weren't.

Hoxie Mueller and Dave Spendler must be sleeping, too, released at last from questioning. How? Because they had broken, or because they had outlasted the sheriff? I slid to the floor and into my dress and shoes. The cell door barely creaked as I pushed it open. Across the corridor Cottie's father slept heavily, his head in his arm.

On tiptoe I went on; the two front cells had shutters drawn up over their grills; they were closed and locked. In the office at the front Chet Leegard slept in a complicated semicircle, his head on a coat in one chair, his body on a settee and his feet in another chair.

He grunted once, "Uh-ah," and sat up hastily as I came in.

"Did you break Mueller down?" Only one thought in my mind.

"We didn't get nowheres." There was disgust even in his yawn.

164

Where did that leave us? All through that impatient morning, while our breakfast came on trays, while I took Cottie out to walk and we were chased like pariahs from a small girl's sandbox, while his father just quietly waited, that question ate at me. Not until the sheriff turned up at ten did I have a faint lift of hope.

"Mueller is Moebbels, all right." Boxruud addressed Leegard buoyantly in the office. "I got a telegram about those fingerprints." His footsteps came down the corridor as far as the first cells.

"Good morning. Maybe you still aren't Hoxie Moebbels?"

The answer was as easy as if the speaker hadn't fought bitterly over that point. "Sure, I'm Moebbels. You can't blame a guy for tryin', can you? But I didn't have a thing to do with robbing that bank. You can't prove I did. And I didn't croak that Sprung. You just get hold of that Niddie and ask him. I ain't even askin' for a lawyer. I don't need none."

The sheriff took time out for thought. Then what he said came softly.

"Maybe you don't want your gang should know where you are?"

"This ain't in the big papers, is it?"

"In Minneapolis, the fact you are Moebbels is in the papers this morning."

A silence. "Say, you got any bigger jails around here?"

"We got a pretty big jail at St. Helens."

"How about moving me and Dave over?"

"I also had a phone call this morning; the Minneapolis police got Niddie. I will wait to see him first."

He went back to his office.

Cottie demanded a story; all through the rest of the morning in that place of expectation and fear I retold "Rumpelstiltskin" and "Rapunzel" and "The Little Tailor." I'd never noticed before, but I

165

thought then how full children's stories are of cruelty and injustice and vainglory and death.

Hope and fear. Fear and Hope. And the chain lying very heavy indeed.

It wasn't until Cottie was napping after lunch that a car door slammed outside and I heard the sheriff's satisfied comment.

"That'll be Niddie. Leegard, you go in and sit with Mueller. If he looks like he would want to say something, shut him up."

CHAPTER FIFTEEN

NIDDIE WAS NO MORE than in the door when the firing started.

"So! Niddie! First you lie to me, then you run away!"

I could guess from the splutter what was the activity of the Adam's apple.

"You know what happens when you hide evidence? That makes you accessory after the fact. Whatever the guilty one does, you also become guilty of. Here a man does a murder. You help him hide it. That makes you a murderer, too."

"Sheriff, I—I never—I don't——"

"That is the law." The sheriff appealed for support, evidently, to the Minneapolis policeman who had brought Niddie in. "Mr. Thoms, is that not right?"

"Yep," Mr. Thoms corroborated cheerfully. "That's the law."

"Taking money to hide evidence, that makes it worse."

"Ask any jury in the country," Thoms's good spirits weren't lessened.

"Now, Niddie, I know you lied. That Mrs. Corbett from the Crying Sisters Lodge saw Mueller over there after midnight that Friday." If tampering with truth was illegal, the sheriff was a bit unlawful himself.

"She couldn't see, it was black as pitch," Niddie denied weakly.

"So there was something to see!"

Niddie wasn't the stuff of Hoxie Moebbels; once the sheriff had an opening wedge he weakened rapidly.

I thought of Moebbels and Spendler, in their cells, hearing this. What must they be feeling? I walked to my door and saw hands gripping the grill of Spendler's cell; the fingers clutched so tightly they were as white as bone. They shook but the grill didn't rattle.

From behind that door came a harsh, discordant "G-g-g-g." Dave Spendler, standing there dumb while another man, perhaps, was getting ready to talk his life away. And Moebbels, throttled in his cell by Leegard.

If Cottie was to have a decent life Niddie must go back on his previous evidence.

He was saying now nervously, "Sher'f, supposin' I could of been mistaken about that boat? What could you do for me now?"

"Well, seeing if you was to turn state's evidence, that would let you off pretty light."

"Light? Gosh, Sher'f, you mean I—supposin', I mean——"

"Supposing you was to stick to lying, why, I'd say you'd get ten years in the pen, the way we could prove it by Mrs. Corbett. Wouldn't you say so, Thoms?"

"Ten—closer fifteen, I'd say."

"Gosh, Sher'f. Gosh, I—— That Mueller is a tough guy, Sher'f. I——"

"You don't have to worry about Mueller. The state troopers got him. He's in jail now. A good strong jail."

"He is? You sure about that, Sher'f? Gosh, I wouldn't want that Mueller to get at me. He scairt me almost to death, Sher'f." Terror, gasping and open, in the voice now.

"I'll take care of you, Niddie. See, I don't even ask you should say anything. You write it."

Paper slid, crackling slightly. There was further indecision, coaxing, weakening, but in the end pen traveled over paper, fumbling, pausing, scratching out, then moving frantically fast.

168

The jail was as quiet as if all the people in it were dead except that one, the writer.

The writing ended.

"Now, c'n I go?"

Paper folded. "You can go to the Flaming Door. Don't you go away from there, though."

A flying figure crossed my vision, as I stood at my door; Niddie fleeing like Ichabod Crane before the headless horseman. The door jerked open in his hand, but he met a wall as solid—the reporters. He struggled, kicking, in the many grasping hands.

"You want this guy, Sheriff?"

"Not now."

"Whoops! Then we do!" The group fell back, taking Niddie with it; the sheriff moved to shut the door.

"Now we will hear what Moebbels has to say." He came down the corridor with elephantine calm.

I stepped back as the key turned. "Bring him out here, Leegard." The clink of metal accompanied the steps that followed.

"Holy Joseph!" That was Thoms. "Boxruud, you know who you've got there? That's Hoxie Moebbels! You mean you've got him jugged in this cracker box? Why if his gang——"

"I got him well handcuffed." Curtly. "Leegard, take off that gag."

No more smiles now in a voice completely sullen. "Smart for a country guy, ain't you, Sheriff? No dame saw me that night."

"One heard you. And now Niddie tells the rest."

"Yeh? What did he say?"

"Not said. Written and signed and locked away. He says he keeps the boat keys hanging on a nail back of the bar. He says about midnight that Friday night he sees the keys are gone. You do not come back in the boat until three o'clock, nearly——"

Three o'clock, I thought. Oh no! Al Sprung was put into the dummy after two-thirty. Perhaps after two-forty. It had taken me a while to get to Sprung's cabin. How could Moebbels have put Sprung into the dummy after knocking me out, and been back across the lake, almost an hour's row even for a skilled oarsman, by three o'clock? It was impossible!

I heard with quickening fear, now, the sheriff's voice.

"You go running to your car. You throw to Niddie the keys and a fifty-dollar bill. You say, 'Niddie, keep your mouth shut; if anybody asks you, we never come back tonight. We left at six o'clock and never come back. If you talk we'll come back and tear your guts out inch by inch.'"

The terrible words rolled out loudly; I was hearing them as Moebbels would say them—tight, light, sinister.

But not at *three o'clock!*

"I want a lawyer."

"Maybe you would like I should just keep you in this jail which Thoms says is a cracker box?"

Feet shuffled. "You get me to a bigger jail."

"You talk, and I see about getting you to a stronger jail."

"You never pull no rough stuff, do you, Sheriff?"

"It is not necessary for a man with brains to use rough stuff. Talk."

"Okay, I'll talk."

A small, tense, listening silence. What was coming? Would he confess now, clearing us, leaving us free to go, leaving me free not to suspect Cottie's father again?

The voice began slowly. "So I did go over that night. So what? I didn't croak the guy. Somebody else did."

My heart slid down my spine in a shivering trail. He wasn't

going to confess. But he had been at the resort. He might have seen . . .

Fear again. Waiting for a new blow to strike.

"Dave and I rowed over, it was just on midnight. It was as black as hell. Nobody couldn't of seen us. We went in Sprung's cabin and looked around with a flash. He wasn't there and the dough wasn't there. After a while we heard little noises out back; we thought maybe it was him. We went out. I almost fall over something. It's that guy Sprung. He was croaked. *He was croaked before I saw him."*

That insistence he repeated, over and over.

And he repeated that he had been back at the Flaming Door by three o'clock. He and Dave hadn't wasted time after finding Sprung.

A voice near me whispered, "That lets us out."

I jumped, almost screaming at the shock. I had been so absorbed in the story I had forgotten Steve Corbett, forgotten he was equally absorbed with me. I turned now; the eyes in the deep sockets smiled.

"You'll be free, Mamma."

My body might have been cotton batting.

I whispered, "But he's telling the truth now. I'm afraid it's the truth. He couldn't have done all the things the murderer did, and been back at the Flaming Door by three."

"Say so, and where do you get? Where does Cottie get? How sure are you it was two-thirty when you went out? Suppose it was one-thirty, instead?" The whisper came back.

"Two-thirty. I'm almost sure. I thought the boat was leaving, then. And it must have been. Moebbels didn't put Sprung in the dummy."

"You're almost sure. You better wait. Think it over."

"If Moebbels goes to trial I'll have to tell the truth."

171

He didn't answer for a while, but in the end he said, "That will be your privilege."

Moebbels was locked into his cell, Thoms left, the reporters were allowed to surge in. From behind my closed door, now, I heard the sheriff give a meticulous account of what he'd learned.

He finished. "Now, the guy who is giving this is Joe E. Vind, county attorney of Poleckema County. If he don't get the credit, I don't get elected sheriff again."

Some reporter produced a raspberry, but it was drowned.

"Thanks, Sheriff! Any time you want a break from us! This is swell!"

Someone asked, "This let those Corbetts out?"

My breath caught on that one.

The answer came equably. "I will now release Mr. Corbett from being held for questioning."

He made good on it as soon as the reporters were gone, cautioning us only not to leave the county.

"Don't worry," Steve Corbett told him, coming to take his son. "We won't leave the Crying Sisters."

"No!" I cried in protest.

I didn't want to go back to that cottage, alone at the end, three cabins away from the spot where I had found Al Sprung, with the trees still standing from which Al Sprung had hung, and the loons crying at night.

"Come on, Mamma. Haul your nerves together." The words were jocular but the look accompanying them wasn't.

The last thing I heard in that jail was Moebbels calling, "Don't forget, Sheriff, you're moving me and Dave to a bigtime jail."

I felt as if we had been away from the Crying Sisters for

months. As if when we came back time must have aged the inhabitants, sagged the cabins, worn at the very shore line.

As it was, nothing was changed except that the reporters were gone. We'd been gone twenty-four hours. When our car passed over the signal hose John Loxton's head popped up on his porch; he came running out beaming, rubbing his hands, and Cottie's father stopped.

"Mr. Corbett! Does this mean—but I'm sure it does!"

Steve Corbett told him the progress of the sheriff's work.

"I haven't heard such good news since this awful thing happened. I was sure it couldn't be any of my people."

Other heads peered at our passing, too. Away from the Crying Sisters I had felt I couldn't face it again, but I found I could even look at the trees behind our cabin. Imagination is so much harder to face than reality.

"John Loxton tells me you're out of it." Earl Jordan was the next to welcome us back. "That's great. Golly, that sheriff turned out to be quite a guy."

"We're not out of the woods yet," Steve Corbett answered, and I thought he was thinking of what my testimony would do. "This thing isn't ended yet."

It was far from ended. I was to find that out.

The two men went fishing, Steve Corbett saying he had to get some wild air in his chest.

The moment they were gone I was looking through the floor crack; the cleaning rag was still below, seemingly undisturbed. And the sheriff hadn't said anything about finding any guns.

Cottie and I climbed to the top of the hill and then ran down as fast as we could go, the hay stubble crackling and complaining, the grasshoppers flying out like spray. Cottie ran exulting in freedom, his head back, arms and legs flying; he fell and rolled, got up

173

and ran on until he fell again; the moment he was at the bottom he started up. I was exhausted before he was; I sat at the bottom to watch him come down like a five-winged kite. The hay stubble was aging; in the depressions it was almost lavender, but in the sun it was the color and lightness of Cottie's hair. The earth and the sunbleached grass were so clean I wanted to rub my face in them.

Cottie threw himself, hot and gasping, into my lap.

"I runned, I runned, I runned," he yelled triumphantly.

I didn't hear Mrs. Rudeen come; the first I knew she was drawling her slow words over my head.

"You sure did. I never saw a kid run so fast."

When I looked up, startled, I saw she was making an effort to be pleasant.

"We're rejoicing in release," I told her stiffly. "Were you ever detained for questioning in a jail?"

For just a second light so hot it might have been a neon bulb turned on behind her slitted eyes. The upper lids blinked and the light went out.

"What do you mean? I don't get into things like that."

"I'm not trying to be insulting; we've just been in a jail and we're innocent enough," I reminded her.

"Oh." A pause. "Yeh. You folks sure got yourselves into a mess of trouble." She moved until she was farther up the hill, and sat down. She was wearing a Mexican crash dirndl as if she were trying to be young and gay and casual.

"I s'pose we won't be seein' you much longer. I'd sure beat it out of here the minute I could if I was in your shoes."

"But we can't leave yet," I reminded her. "The sheriff isn't sure Hoxie Moebbels is the killer. And he'll want us for witnesses."

"Oh," she said lamely. "Well, that's too bad."

174

I hardly heard her. The corner of my eye had caught the stubby white patent-leather sandals on her feet.

Caught between the heel and the instep of one sandal was a dry scrap of plantain leaf.

CHAPTER SIXTEEN

I TOLD MYSELF that leaf couldn't mean anything.

Al Sprung had been killed Friday night. Today was Tuesday. Only four days later. It seemed so much longer than that.

While I told Mrs. Rudeen about what had happened in jail—to her avid prompting—I tried to look her sandals over without staring at them directly.

The sandals were that summer's fad, a mess of crossed strips with a hole at the toe from which a stocking tip was supposed to protrude beguilingly. These examples of the fashion might have been width B at the outset, but they were width D now; the patent leather showed gray cracks where it had spread. There was no fresh cleaner over the cracks. If they hadn't been cleaned since Friday . . .

No one knew as well as I that perhaps Hoxie Moebbels hadn't been the one to put Al Sprung into the dummy.

How much might that plantain leaf mean? Plantain is a common enough weed. It might be all over the lawns. And even if she'd picked it up from that patch behind Al Sprung's cabin, how could I tell when? Only those few hours Friday night were important.

I got rid of her by telling her it was suppertime. As soon as Cottie had had the toast, poached egg and apple sauce of freedom I started out looking for plantain.

It was a job. Cottie got tired and wanted to be carried, but I covered the ground. I couldn't imagine Mrs. Rudeen walking far up the hill; I started halfway up. Fortunately plantain is a very dark green; I could see all the dark green patches in that light stubble from far off. I found only wild ground cherries and dark patches of red-and-white clover.

The lawn was harder. I settled Cottie with Bits and Joanie, temporarily, and wandered back and forth alone, trying to look casual.

There was that one big patch behind Al Sprung's cabin. That was the only place plantain grew on the lawns. The bank and the shore below produced plantain profusely. But Mrs. Rudeen used the stairs when she went down the banks. Almost everyone did. And she'd scarcely walk along the beach in those high-heeled sandals.

No. The chances were she'd picked up that leaf from the patch where I had picked a leaf showing a telltale drop of blood.

One question it seemed likely I couldn't answer. When?

Steve Corbett didn't come back from fishing until after eight; he had two small bass and a towering appetite. I fed him the fried fish and my story of Mrs. Rudeen. He merely nodded as I finished, pushing his chair back to sit tilted against the screen ledge as I washed the dishes.

"If you're going to testify at the trial that you know Al Sprung was stuffed into that dummy after two-thirty, it'll be a good idea to have an alternate murderer to bring up," he said. "I've been wanting to have a look at Mrs. Rudeen's cabin. But she sticks too close. How about you keeping her busy while I search?"

I asked, "To see if she has Al Sprung's money?"

"That or any other thing that might be—interesting."

I paused. Lately we had seemed to be in this affair together. But I couldn't forget that he still had had secret business here.

"You're sure your reason for wanting to search her cabin has something to do with Al Sprung's death?"

"Yes, Mamma," he said evenly. "I really think it would."

I finally let him go to tell Mrs. Rudeen I was lonesome and would like to play cards.

"You were so kind to come to see me this afternoon." I didn't know I had that much falseness in me, but when I wanted it, there it was. "My nerves are upset. And my husband said he was going out."

I scarcely faltered over that *husband* any more.

"I was glad to come down," she told me largely. "Nothin' to do toni—— I mean, nothin' to do around here anyways."

We played Russian bank. I learned that Mrs. Rudeen cheated without thought whenever she had the chance of getting away with it and sometimes when she couldn't have believed she could get away with it. Also she missed plays under her nose.

After one game we played rummy. Two hours went by before Steve Corbett came back; two hours in which she became almost friendly. She had, she said, a husband who "traveled in business."

"I get mine. And I salt it down, too. Not but I believe in getting the best there is, either. You seen my Packard? Swellest car on the market. It's different from—I mean—it's different than I started out. I believe in getting ahead."

"Didn't you discard two cards stuck together that time?"

"What do you know? Yeh, you ought to see my bracelets."

I had a wild idea. "You don't keep them out here, do you?"

"Don't you worry, I've got 'em where they're safe."

It must be for clues that Cottie's father was looking. I laid down three kings and tried probing. "I should think you'd find it quiet here. It's not very lively."

She grew a trifle less expansive on that. "Oh, I sort of got used to the joint."

Thirty minutes of Mrs. Rudeen made me want to scream.

178

She returned to her hint of the afternoon, that she should think nice people like us would want to leave after all we'd been through, and she pounded on it. It was with a good deal of relief that I saw Steve Corbett returning.

He said, "I couldn't find Earl; went up and talked to Elmer for a while. What's going on here, rummy?"

"Mrs. Rudeen's beating."

"I'm lucky at cards," she laughed, attempting archness, the tilted eyes rising at the corners as the under puffs lifted. "I ain't saying about love."

If ever there was an evil-eyed harridan, I thought, she was it. I wondered what had built the immense familiarity with the worst impulses of men, that lay in her eyes, the thickness of her slow, significant voice, the turn of her hands, the slide of her thick hips.

Steve Corbett joined the game, but he yawned so steadily she took the hint and left.

"Did you find anything?" I asked before she'd reached the next cabin. I'd helped; I should be able to ask.

He hadn't risen when Mrs. Rudeen left; he slung the cards across the table in a long unfurling fan.

"I didn't find a damn thing." His brows came down, his features seemed to thin and sharpen as he thrust his face forward. "Shut up. I want to think."

He paced the porch like a prowling leopard while I went inside and hooked the door. If he didn't want to talk it was no use urging.

I wondered what Sheriff Boxruud was thinking now and if he had taken Hoxie Moebbels to a stronger jail, and if there was new evidence either against Moebbels or—anyone else. I tried to examine my conscience. Was I so certain my watch had said two-thirty that Friday night when I woke? The trouble was

179

that two-thirty fit in with Niddie's new evidence, too. If that had been Moebbels leaving when I heard the oars at two-thirty, then he might have reached the Flaming Door shortly after three, as Niddie said he did. But if he had come then, if he had found and killed Sprung immediately, and knocked me out, and then put Sprung into the dummy, it should have been four when he got back.

· No. If the accusation against Hoxie Moebbels stuck and he went to trial, gangster or no gangster, I would have to testify in his behalf.

I avoided looking at Cottie.

Out the window was a moon perceptibly wider than the last moon I remembered; the Japanese-print shapes of trees were etched against the pale night sky. Were any of the sheriff's men still around? Nothing moved within sight.

But something was moving within hearing; feet pounding.

Outside our door Mrs. Rudeen bellowed "You low-down loafer! You think you're going to get away with this? I'll have the law on you! You think I'm not smart, huh! Why, you———"

What came next I shoved aside among the words I don't remember, grateful that Cottie was asleep.

When I got to the porch Mrs. Rudeen stood shaking our screen door, her face burgundy, and her eyes almost shut with rage. One of the celluloid barrettes had slipped, and her hair whipped backward and forward as she shook.

At the sink Steve Corbett was calmly brushing his teeth. He took the brush from his mouth to ask, "Anything the matter?"

"You! You went through my house, that's what! Come up there asking all mealymouth won't I play cards with your wife. Oh, I know what———"

She stopped right there as if she'd been slapped, but for an instant longer she stayed staring in at us. The puffs seemed to be stretching apart, both above and below her eyes; the eyes came out greenish and almost round. She backed down the steps with her breath coming in heavy gasps and stumbled away, going backward for three or four steps and making odd, inarticulate motions with her hands as if she were warding something off. Then she turned and ran up the path.

Steve Corbett was reaching his toothbrush to the cupboard top.

"You must have left marks."

His shoulders moved. "I had to cut a slit in a window screen. And take it out. The bitch padlocked her door when she left."

"If she goes to the sheriff———"

"She won't." He turned that aside as if there wasn't a chance.

"You took a screen out. If anyone wanted to get in here———"

"You've got the—— No, you don't have the gun, do you? Well, if anyone starts coming in, yell. I'll be here tonight."

He began unbuttoning his shirt.

At first I thought there was an earthquake, the bed shook so, and the boom was still in my ears. I woke, standing by Cottie's bed with my hands hunting him. The second boom couldn't have been one minute after the first; the floor under me shook again and the bed shivered as if it were alive and afraid. But when my hands found Cottie he was sleeping and safe. I ran with him toward the door; a dark figure clouded the other side.

"It's across the lake. At the Flaming Door, I think." Steve Corbett spoke as if he were deciding for himself rather than reassuring me, but he was quick to see I had his son. "No use waking the kid. There's nothing going on near here. Put him back."

There were no more shocks. I put Cottie back in bed and went to the porch. Somewhere in the resort were excited calls and feet running.

"You stay here," Cottie's father ordered. "I'll see if I can find out what's happened." He ran in the direction of the middle stairs in the bank. As I watched I saw first one figure, then another, poise briefly at the top of those stairs before running down.

"No one knows what it is," he reported, coming back in a few moments. He hadn't dressed at all; he stood in the pale light in rumpled pajamas and with rumpled hair. "But it sounded to me like something being blown up."

"Could the sheriff possibly be——"

"No use guessing."

A figure came up the bank again, and turned toward our cabin; it was Earl Jordan. He'd dressed sketchily. "I'm driving over to the Flaming Door to see what's going on over there. You want to come along, Corbett?"

"Sure I——" He hesitated. "No, I guess I better stay with the kid—and my wife. She's nervous."

"Okay, I'll take Elmer. Be back with the news." Jordan left.

After he'd gone there seemed a difference in the air; a difference growing steadily stronger until I knew what it was. Smoke. Through the trees a yellow light appeared and spread.

"Fire," Steve Corbett seconded me slowly.

As we watched the light grew until it arched over the tree-tops like a wide spade-shaped flame above a gigantic lamp wick. It kept that height one moment, then receded.

"It must be only the boathouse. If the tavern were burning it would be a bigger fire."

"If you think you ought to go——" I didn't want him to, but I had to offer.

He didn't answer, but stood watching the glow with his face intent. The fire died quickly; I went back to bed at last, leaving him still watching.

At dawn Earl Jordan and Elmer came back, smoke grimed, their hands and trouser knees black.

"Screwiest thing I ever saw." Earl Jordan was excited, almost elated. "We heard a car driving away, fast, just before we got there. Niddie and his wife were tied up in chairs in the taproom. The boathouse was blown to bits and the bits were on fire, those that would burn. The boat went, too. We let Niddie loose and hunted——"

"Call the sheriff?"

"Yes'r!" Elmer contributed; his face, too, was alert with adventure. "That was the first thing I done when we got Niddie untied. Only I couldn't get 'm. He was out somewheres. His wife said he got a call over to St. Helens jail. She didn't know what for."

"St. Helens," I repeated. "That's where Hoxie Moebbels was taken. Do you think he's escaped? Maybe he came back to get even with Niddie. But I should think he'd have done more. Niddie was the——"

"Wait a minute," Jordan broke in on me. "Niddie swears Moebbels wasn't in the gang that came. He said he saw 'em all. He said they drove up in one big car—six men. They pounded on his door. When he went down and opened up one of 'em hit him on the head with the butt end of a revolver, and the next thing he knew he was tied up in a chair, his wife the same way across the room, screaming bloody murder. The noise of the boathouse blowing up must have brought him around, because he heard the second charge go off."

Cottie's father asked thoughtfully, "Anything done inside the tavern?"

"One of the bedrooms upstairs was about ripped open. Niddie's wife said the men did that before going out to the boathouse."

"Room Moebbels had when he was there?"

"That's the one."

"Did you try the county attorney?"

"Vind was out, too." Elmer seemed to have done all the telephoning. "Wife says he got a call to St. Helens jail, too. Gosh, I never see this much happen around here. I sure am glad nobody can think I was in on this. I wasn't *there!*"

The two left, still excited, to tell their news to anyone else who might be waiting and awake to hear it.

The facts of what had actually happened that night came seeping in through the early morning, I suppose by mailman and telephone. John Loxton came down to say he'd heard a rumor Hoxie Moebbels and Dave Spendler had escaped the St. Helens jail.

Mrs. Clapshaw, an hour later, came running to say she'd heard that the bodies of Hoxie Moebbels and Dave Spendler had been found by Sheriff Boxruud and his men, up a lake road not far from the St. Helens jail. Both men had been riddled by machine-gun bullets.

Wednesday evening's papers gave the continuity. Most of it they'd gotten from one Hank Benjamin, car thief, who had occupied the cell next to Moebbels in the St. Helens jail.

In the middle of the night, Benjamin said, he heard something in the front of the jail that sounded like a crash, only it wasn't very loud. A short time after that a light flashed in his face from the corridor and a voice whispered, "He ain't the one."

Right afterward the same voice whispered, "Here he is, boys."

After that, according to Benjamin, several things went on at once. There were slight buzzing, singing sounds, a faint pink light in the corridor, and three voices.

One voice was the whisperer's, a thin, intent whisper that carried like a spoon rasping across tin. It said, "Why, hello, Hoxie, you didn't expect to see us, did you, Hoxie? Ain't it nice to think we've come to get you out of jail? You ought to thank us for that, Hoxie. Aren't we the smart guys? We started to get you the minute we read about that Hoxie Mueller. It sure sounded like you. You wouldn't do anything like you done if you could do it over, would you, pal? You wouldn't run off with the take all to yourself again, would you, Hoxie? Now we're getting you out of jail you'll be glad to tell us where the dough is and divvy up, won't you, boss? We know you lost eight thousand bucks of that dough in a poker game, but you got it back for us, didn't you, boss? Just sit quiet and we'll have you right out."

Or something like that, Hank Benjamin said. He remembered all those things, but there was more of it.

The second voice had almost the same thin whine as the whisper, but it was intensified to a scream.

"Listen, gang, that dough was hot, see? The cops had the numbers. If we divided up, where'd we be? We'd all be fryin', see? You know the way the boys are, the minute they get their hands on dough they got to start shoving it around. I was just holding on to it until it got safe, see? Gosh, boys, you got to remember we bumped a guy on that job. I'm the boss, ain't I? I was comin' back. I figured I'd get the dough to a fence, see? Change off what I had for dough that wasn't hot, maybe send it down to South America—listen, boys, listen, pals——"

The third voice was the strangest of all. It said, "G-g-g-g."

The reporters had a field day.

They dovetailed the story as neatly as any superplot in a magazine. Hoxie Moebbels, gangster, had run off with the eighty thousand dollars take in the Kansas City First National Bank robbery, taking with him only Dave Spendler, mute gunman for the mob. In a north woods hide-out he lost eight thousand dollars in a poker game, had to dig into the eighty thousand dollars to pay his losses.

He knew the serial numbers of the bills were listed; knew that if Al Sprung spent any of that money he was not only going to have FBI men hot on his trail, but his former helpmates also. He made vain efforts to get Sprung into another game, thinking he could win his money back. That failing, he rowed over the lake at midnight, found Sprung, knifed him or had Dave Spendler do it, took his money and fled.

The blowing up of the Flaming Door boathouse, the newspapers said, indicated that Moebbels must have hidden the eighty thousand dollars there, afraid of having the money found on him and thinking he could come back later to find it. He had then fled toward Canada only to be caught by the state police. With his name in headlines he knew his ex-gang would be after him; he got Boxruud to move him to the St. Helens jail. But St. Helens, with its two guards, was no hindrance to the gang; they entered it at three in the morning as simply as if it were a bank they were rifling, clubbed down the two night guards and cut Moebbels and Spendler out of their cells with acetylene torches.

By the time county and state police were told of the jail break the trail was cold. The gang must have gone directly to the Flaming Door after finding out from Moebbels where the money was hidden.

The rest, the newspapers indicated, was up to FBI men.

So that was the jigsaw puzzle into which Al Sprung's murder fitted. It seemed to go in so very neatly.

Or did it?

CHAPTER SEVENTEEN

I WOULD NEVER have to testify now that I thought I had heard that boat leave shore before Al Sprung's body was stuffed into the dummy.

A wave of terrible heat swept over me. Was it my fault Hoxie Moebbels and Dave Spendler had died? If I had told the sheriff all my story yesterday . . .

No. The sheriff couldn't have released the two men, even then. Couldn't have let them free to fly their pursuing vengeance.

Behind me Earl Jordan commented, "People, am I glad I didn't get to the Flaming Door before those gangsters left!"

It was he who had brought the papers over. I stood up to ease the cricks in my back, and he and Steve Corbett, who were bending over me to read the sheets spread on our porch table, perforce had to straighten, too. Cottie was trying to worm his way past my knees to get his nose over the table edge.

I said, "It doesn't explain why Al Sprung was—why they made the disposal they did of the body." This at least I could talk about. "It doesn't explain why they took our knife. The Flaming Door must have had knives. Why go to all that trouble to throw suspicion on us?"

"They'd be sure to plan some way of getting out from under," Earl Jordan suggested. "That Moebbels was a smart guy. He probably thought it all up after he heard Sprung had kicked your kid. He probably thought the suspicion against you would be so heavy he'd be all in the clear and free to get away."

"But how could he hope so? In the circumstances he'd know some suspicion would fall on him—the way he'd been over here twice that day, hounding Sprung. He might know the sheriff would want to question him. And just being held for questioning would be fatal to him. He must have known it."

"You should worry," Steve Corbett put in warningly. "You'll never have to bring your doubts into any court now."

We soon found out we had one more questioning to go through. Chet Leegard came that evening to order us to attend an inquest into the death of Al Sprung at nine the next morning at the Maple Valley schoolhouse.

We went, leaving Cottie with the sheriff's wife after the sheriff told us that the inquest would probably last all day.

I shan't give all that testimony; there was too much of it, and I learned so little that was new. I learned that John Loxton gave his occupation as retired antique dealer, formerly of Chicago. That fit him; I could just imagine him proffering a Chippendale chair. Al Sprung was proved to be a professional gambler. Earl Jordan's home address was a New York hotel.

In the opinion of the experts, our knife was undoubtedly the one with which the killing had been done. Its handle had been washed, there were no fingerprints.

Mrs. Rudeen, in a pink georgette dress that fluttered the Maple Valley housewives, said she hadn't noticed where Al Sprung had run when he came up the bank after kicking Cottie. She thought he had gone to his cottage. The memory of Steve Corbett's searching her cottage still seemed to rankle; she gave most of her testimony with her eyes fixed vindictively on me. But she didn't tell about it.

Not one person admitted having an inkling where Al Sprung could have hidden between the time he kicked Cottie and the time he appeared in the dummy.

Only when Mrs. Willard testified was there any real surprise. She sat in the armchair beside the desk at which Dr. Hansen sat as coroner very calmly; even her smooth red hair looked cool over her white dress.

"Your occupation, Mrs. Willard?"

"Housewife."

"Your husband's occupation?"

She looked at her husband, who hadn't testified yet, smiling steadily. Then she said proudly, "My husband is a pilot. He flies passenger planes for Trans-Continent Airlines."

All the heads turned in Fred Willard's direction; his pale thin face was steeled to meet something.

Marjorie Willard went serenely on. "My husband was the pilot of the plane which crashed this spring just outside the St. Paul airport as it was coming in from Chicago. You will remember that a wing cracked. It was due to his skill that the plane was landed without killing any of the passengers, although several people were seriously injured, including himself. We came to the Crying Sisters to be away from people. But my husband is quite recovered now."

She still smiled at him with the utmost confidence; I saw color creep under the skin of his face. He turned, after a moment, to meet without flinching the eyes staring at him.

So that was Willard's secret. That was why they stayed aloof, why Fred Willard had been dazed by death, why they got letters from the county attorney of Ramsey County.

I felt an impelling rush of desire to have Steve Corbett's secret turn out to be as innocent. But I didn't really hope.

When my turn to be questioned came I told the story I had told before. I couldn't help Hoxie Moebbels now. Steve Corbett followed me giving away nothing, and after him Niddie and Hank Benjamin.

The jury brought in the verdict just before five o'clock. Al Sprung had met his death by violence at the hands of Hoxie Moebbels or David Spendler, now both deceased.

People crowded up to shake hands as if we'd had a personal success. Steve Corbett said, "Duck," as a flashlight went off, and I noticed then that there were only a few men who looked like reporters in the country crowd. The newspapers had been so sure of their verdict they'd sent only scouts.

"Nice work, Mamma," I was told on the way to pick up Cottie. "You should be damn grateful to that whispering guy who bumped Moebbels off. Now you can go back to Eldreth unsinged when your vacation is over. There won't be any trial, you won't get any publicity, you'll have the bridge wide open back to your job."

My job. My old life. I said, "My conscience hurts about Moebbels."

"Aw, be your age. Moebbels was a murderer already, wasn't he? Didn't you hear they'd killed a man in that robbery?" His conscience evidently didn't hurt.

The sheriff's wife handed Cottie over smiling; someone must have phoned her because she was congratulatory, too.

I asked Cottie in the car, "Did you have a nice time at the lady's house?"

"She gave me candy."

"Wasn't that nice? What did you do?"

"I talked."

His father cut in ahead of me, "What did you talk about?"

The boy nodded a solemn, remembering head. "I talked about Mamma and about Daddy and about Dooby and my srog went in Mamma's plate."

I groaned, "That was smart, wasn't it? Parking him there?"

His father chuckled. "Safe for the kid."

"How about us? If the sheriff puts two and two together——"

"Why should he worry his head? He's got a verdict now."

"If it's as settled as that, then we can leave the Crying Sisters. We could go to some other lake. People are expecting us to leave. If we stay on it will look as if we have a *reason*."

"We do have a reason," he said pleasantly, and I knew both that we weren't leaving the Crying Sisters yet, and that its chain hadn't been finished.

He left the cabin again that night.

I stood at the porch door—how many nights I stood at that door—seeing the narrow moon come up, seeing small clouds pass, seeing the dark meander of the cinder track, the car, the next cabin, the trees. Hearing the lake, the leaves, the cicadas, nothing else.

When he came back soon, within an hour, I stayed. I said:

"So it isn't ended."

"What do you mean? I just went out to get your chaperon back."

He took my gun from his breeches pocket, and held it toward me.

The sheriff had found the knife but not the guns. I asked as I reached for my revolver, "Where were they hidden?"

He was smiling. "In old Loxton's flower gardens. I figured the sheriff might pass over worked earth there; I raked over a nice big piece. Nice of Loxton to leave his tools against the barn."

I couldn't help what I next said. "If you had killed Sprung, there wouldn't have been a sign to show, would there?"

He still smiled. "You flatter me. Go on back to bed."

He left at once again and didn't come back until after three.

No more than before was there any sign of his work in the morning. I took Cottie to the beach; the sun was warm and the water blue. The Willards lay in the sand.

Mr. Willard called to me, "Nice to get out here again, isn't it?"

He was alert and cheerful; I could imagine he'd expanded under the concealing bathing suit, which I now guessed covered scars.

"Isn't it nice to have that horrible affair ended?" Marjorie Willard turned over to say cozily. She didn't mean the murder alone.

I asked if they were planning to leave; they said no.

"I've bearded this bunch now." Fred Willard grinned. "I'm making sure of myself before I tackle another." His wife had shaken him into facing reality, but there was a little waver over his face as he met my eyes.

I said warmly, "You're nice people," meaning it, feeling a rush of confidence in them because I knew that at least they, now, hid no secret and awful activity.

The waver went away. "Thanks," Fred Willard said quietly, and I went on with Cottie. That was the thing to do, leave them alone.

As soon as Cottie napped that afternoon I snaked an old bamboo pole out from under the cabin, and went around to the north side of the cottage where I thought I could fish out my possessions undisturbed. No one was around when I went out, but I'd no more than angled the cloth within reaching distance than Mrs. Rudeen's feet became visible under the house.

After what had happened I was startled that she'd ever turn up near me again, but instead of explaining her presence she asked curiously, "You lose something under there?"

She had me in the ridiculous position of having to think up an excuse for fishing out a dirty old cleaning rag. "I didn't remember to take any cleaning cloths along. I had to take a towel. And then Cottie pushed it through a crack." I reflected that I now lied quite glibly and with almost no effort.

She eyed the cloth suspiciously. "Uh."

I had to carry the thing, which was twice as filthy as when I pushed it through the floor; had to carry it as if it were a cloth with nothing in it. On the porch I put it under the sink and washed my hands thoroughly. Mrs. Rudeen followed me, still eyeing the rag as if she'd like to investigate but didn't quite dare.

She was trying to act as if Steve Corbett had never searched her cabin. She said bluntly, "Well, I thought I'd better come down before you wasn't here any more. You'll be leaving tomorrow, I expect."

I asked pointedly, "Are you leaving, Mrs. Rudeen?"

"It's different with me, not having any kid, and anyway, I wasn't in the murder. But I was saying to Loxton, 'Those Corbetts, they'll be leaving. *Nice* people like them, you can't expect nice people to stay after what they've been through,' I said to Mr. Loxton."

Why was she so anxious to have us leave? "Mr. Corbett likes it here," I said. "And it's so good for Cottie."

"Oh, sure," she said vaguely. Then, "How your friends take it, you being suspected this way?"

How did my friends take it? My friends didn't know I was suspected. Steve Corbett's friends . . .

No friend of Steve Corbett had come forward, either. It was as if he, too, traveled under a false identity.

She was going on, sitting bolt upright in a chair by the table, her slitted eyes as watchful as a cat's at a mousehole. "I should think they'd anyway write. I stopped by the mailbox to see if I could bring your mail down and there wasn't any. Then I thought you must've told 'em to hold your mail in town. The least friends can do I always say is stick when you got trouble."

I stammered, "After all, our friends have hardly had time yet; I haven't expected——"

She pounced. "They know you're up here, don't they? So they wouldn't miss it was you in this trouble?"

I suddenly wanted it very clear that friends of ours knew where we were. "Of course my people know we're here. I called my sister long-distance from Duluth——"

I added lie after lie. The tilted eyes stayed on me steadily, the thick hands twisted a timothy stem.

She went back to her earlier theme. "Well, you'll be seein' your friends soon now when you leave, anyhow."

If I hadn't been so exasperated I'd have laughed. Did she think I was being taken in?

"Why, Mrs. Rudeen," I said. "I might almost think you had some *reason* for wanting us to leave!"

Under that simple deduction she grew sullen and left, swallowing almost open anger.

I told Steve Corbett about it when he came back from fishing with Earl Jordan. He listened with a thoughtful, lowered head.

"I don't like it," I ended. "It's practically as if she was warning us to get out."

"That's fine," he said. "One of the best pieces of news I've had yet." And actually he seemed to feel that way about it; he stood at the screen smiling to himself and whistling.

When I had rescued my possessions from the rag I went in to put them in my handbag. Three new ten-dollar bills I hadn't had before were in the coin purse. I took them out, puzzled, not able to imagine how they came there. Thirty dollars . . .

Cottie's father was paying me thirty dollars a week. For lying awake nights and being taken to jail, for discovering murder and being hit on the head, for lying to the sheriff.

He glanced at me brusquely when I held the money out to him, saying I'd rather not take it.

194

"Maybe you'd rather I sent it to Mr. Train in Eldreth to credit it to your account?"

And he laughed out loud when I hastily shut the bag on the bills.

That mention of George Train came up in my mind when we drove to Duluth that afternoon as a treat for Cottie. At the post office I was handed a letter from George, written on Tuesday, the day we had been let out of jail.

"Dear Janet, I think you should come home immediately. The Minneapolis papers are full of a horrible murder that's taken place up there. Janet, as I remember it, the name of the man who called up about you was *Corbett,* and the papers this morning carried pictures of a Mr. and Mrs. Corbett and their child being taken off to jail. Janet, I hope you're not working for those people. The woman, especially, looks quite abnormal. Now, Janet, you know a banker's wife has to be very careful . . ."

It would do George good to know that abnormal woman was me.

I'd expected the Clapshaws to leave that Friday, but they didn't. Mrs. Clapshaw took the trouble to explain when I took Cottie up for milk that evening; she came down from her porch to walk to the barn with us, her sharp nose leading the way.

"I expect I could leave now, but as I was saying to Mr. Loxton, I could see how it wasn't his fault really, Mr. Sprung's getting murdered here. It could just as well have been at the Flaming Door. And after all at sixty-five dollars for the season. I could hardly get back more than fifteen dollars on my rent, and where could we go on that? Besides, I really feel for poor Mr. Loxton; he'll never get any more people out here this summer now."

She wasn't quite right about that last. When Cottie and I left her we went down to the beach to see the last long sunrays

195

make the lake mysterious and shadowy, and when we came back a car was moving down the cinder path at the slow jounce accustomed drivers used on that path.

The man who stuck his hand out the window to wave was Harry Lewis, the portly man who had been at the resort the day we came. Beside him I glimpsed a head with a kerchief around it, and wavy tendrils of extremely golden hair.

I remembered that morning less than two weeks ago when Mr. Sprung had asked Lewis if he wasn't bringing his own wife out. Evidently he'd done so now.

He brought her to our porch to introduce her, later that same evening.

"Here's my wife Carol." He had the jovial, condescending, fatuous look men of his type get when they're talking about what they call a "little woman."

Carol didn't seem to mind; as she clung to his arm her smile was quite self-satisfied. She was the sort of blonde I'm not; the blowing curls were too metallic for reality and her make-up was extremely pink. She was a big woman in her late thirties, highly polished and plumped out until her flesh looked firm and hard.

"I finally got her out here," Harry Lewis went on. "She's an awful hard girl to make change her mind."

Carol gurgled, "Ooh, you silly, you know I love to come on your silly fishing trips. You just never asked me before." And she pouted at Steve Corbett. "You men never want a woman along when you're all busy on men stuff."

Steve Corbett was rising from his cot with what looked like interest.

I worked in an inane "It'll be nice to have another woman here; we're so few," in spite of the fact that I thought Carol wouldn't be much interested in women as long as there were any men.

196

Then Cottie's father said, "I can't imagine not wanting *you* along," and I felt my eyes stretching as he came forward with all the airs of a gracious host to offer the Lewises chairs, pulling one close to himself for Carol to sit in, smiling and talking and casting blandishments at her.

It was the first time I'd seen him show personal interest in a woman.

So that was the sort of woman he liked!

I can't remember that it even crossed my mind that I should join the group and be polite; I turned mechanically to my unwiped dishes in the sink. Later I found I'd been wiping the same plate for ten minutes.

"You should have been here last week," Steve Corbett was saying. "We had a murder. More excitement than a fire. Didn't you read about it? Papers were full of it. We had reporters on six sides."

"I've been wanting to hear about that," Lewis cut in. A slight frown had come above the large, dark, slightly pompous eyes at Steve Corbett's open interest in his wife. "Poor old Sprung. I used to fish with him. He was a fool for gambling, that boy was."

"I said to Harry," Carol cooed, "he ought to be glad he was in the city with me instead of up here. Wouldn't it have been awful?" She shivered, smiling. "He might have been put in jail. You were, weren't you, Mr. Corbett? How perfectly terrible!"

Her worries might be over Harry, but her tone indicated she'd be willing to accept admiration from Steve Corbett, too. She asked avid questions about the murder, seemingly curious as to each detail.

"We're keeping these people from their sleep." It was Harry Lewis who rose to go.

Carol rose at once with little screams of dismay. "You just

mustn't let me bother! But we'll see you again, won't we? I think we should see just lots of each other!"

She scattered smiles so impartially that some even fell on me.

Going up the path she walked trippingly as if she felt Steve Corbett would be watching, and he was. He didn't turn from the door until they were past the next cottage. I was right behind him at the sink; he turned and took my elbow in a grip so hard it hurt.

"Why didn't you tell me that woman had come?" His eyes shone.

"Why should I? I didn't know you'd be interested."

"Interested? Lord, I've got to know everything that goes on here."

"It wouldn't surprise me if they weren't married." I don't know why that catty comment came out—at least I didn't know then. Now I have an idea.

The withdrawn eyes grew harder, brighter. "Trust a woman," he said, and walked away. He prowled the porch with a quick step, but he paused sometimes in mid-stride as if he were thinking so hard it halted even the reflexes of walking.

I knew that in some way the coming of Carol Lewis, too, was a part of the chain.

Once during the evening I heard a car leave; I found out the next day that Earl Jordan had gone to spend the week end in town. As soon as it was dark Steve Corbett left the house as quietly as an excursioning cat, and didn't come back until dawn. When I got up I went to look at his sleeping face. Was it Carol's coming he had been waiting? Had anything happened that night?

The thick brows were pinched together in a frown as he slept, but I couldn't tell anything from that.

I knew later that something significant had happened that night; something that was to alter entirely the rest of the chain.

198

Then I saw only the resort as before, unrippled. The night had been cool, one of those mid-August nights foretelling autumn, but the midday was almost hot. At eleven when I took Cottie to the beach the Clapshaws and the Willards were already there; Fred Willard played with the children like a well man. To my surprise Mrs. Rudeen came to the beach, too, all dressed up in the pink georgette dress she had worn to the inquest; she stalked past the group of us without speaking and went to sit on a rock by herself. The rest of us wore sunglasses; she stared bare eyed at the lake, her face stony.

A little later Carol and Harry Lewis struggled down the stairs; he was carrying a lunch basket, the oars, a rod, a bamboo pole and a tackle box. She carried only a white handbag.

"You're such a silly," she was saying. "Why can't I be a big girl and help carry?"

"You be a big girl and I'll catch you a big fish," he promised. He looked self-satisfied and pleased with life. He called, "Good morning, everybody, grand morning, grand."

We called hello in return, Carol prinking and smiling.

Mrs. Rudeen had turned her face in their direction; Harry Lewis, seeing her, seemed to jump.

"Good morning, Mrs. Rudeen," he said quite formally.

"Oh, someone else I don't know!" Carol waited, expectant, smiling now at Mrs. Rudeen.

"Hold on a minute till I get this stuff in the boat, will you?"

He passed close to me to dump the gear in his boat; the pleased self-satisfaction wiped off his face. He took Carol to Mrs. Rudeen, then. Mrs. Rudeen didn't rise, but the tilted eyes looked very closely at Carol.

I know now how much drama was hidden behind that meeting. Then I saw only that inexplicably Mrs. Rudeen seemed to look at Carol with the same hate she had held for me.

199

"Carol, I want you to know Mrs. Rudeen." It was nervous.

Even Carol couldn't misread that face. She tried hard but her greeting was flat. "It's so grand here, I don't know why I didn't come before."

Mrs. Rudeen said, "Uh," as if it choked her to say that much.

The Lewises came hastily away, Carol's eyes directed toward the beach clogs in which she was picking her way among the pebbles. A backless red-and-white print halter and spotless white slacks made no secret of her figure. A handkerchief, matching the halter, tied down the flying curls, but at this moment her face didn't match the gaiety of her clothes.

When they were thirty feet out her voice rippled back— water carries sound in a way that people unused to it don't realize.

"Harry, who was that *awful* woman?"

Harry's reply was low enough not to carry.

Mrs. Rudeen's face didn't change its granite stillness, but her head turned as if her eyes were magnetized by the boat.

Mrs. Clapshaw nudged me to whisper, "You know I think something must have been going *on* between Mr. Lewis and Mrs. Rudeen. Look at her! She's all upset because he brought his wife out! Well! Murder is one thing, but I never thought anything like this was going on at this resort or I'd certainly have something to say to Loxton!"

CHAPTER EIGHTEEN

IT SOON BECAME evident that Mrs. Rudeen was establishing an incessant watch on the Lewises.

She stayed on her rock until the Lewises came back from fishing, and threw them two triumphant words.

"No fish!"

When they went up the steps she went, too. The Lewises probably napped after dinner—at any rate their shades were drawn—and all that time Mrs. Rudeen sat in a beach chair she had lugged to the lawn before their cabin.

"Scandal," I told Steve Corbett. "Mrs. Clapshaw thinks Mrs. Rudeen must have been making passes at Mr. Lewis when he was up here before, and now she's green eyed." The habit I'd formed of telling him things while we were suspected of Al Sprung's murder still held; I didn't seem able to stop it.

"That's fine," he said. He was more alert and cheerful than he had been since we came to the resort. When Cottie woke he took us to the island for another picnic; to my surprise when we got there he produced my gun.

"It might be a good idea for you to practice with this thing; never know when it might come in handy."

My eyes flew to his face, but he looked careless and urbane. Just the same, I felt a quickening, too. Did he think it more necessary than before for me to know how?

My first shots were very wide; painstakingly he showed me how to aim and how to allow for the kick. And how to reload.

We spent all afternoon at it, Cottie yelling with delight every time I shot, so fascinated he didn't even look at his playhouse. His father stood well behind me with a firm grip on him, not taking any chances of his running forward.

"Not too bad," he said at last. "Your eye is all right. All you need is practice." I'd just come within two inches of what I aimed at, and I thought that rather grudging.

When we got back to the resort the Lewises were just coming off their porch; they waved and said they were going up the hill to watch the sunset. Surely that was a guiltless diversion, but I saw Mrs. Rudeen leave her chair—she was in the pink georgette dress still—to stand among the trees at the foot of the hill, again watching.

Steve Corbett left as soon as it was dark; I was so used to it by that time I slept anyway.

We hadn't had much of Carol's company on Saturday; she'd been too exclusively with her husband. But beginning with that Sunday we saw a good deal of her.

She called to Steve Corbett from the nearest steps on Sunday morning. "Why don't you come fishing with us?"

Harry Lewis, a few steps before her with all the fishing gear again, turned hastily. "He wouldn't be interested in the sort of fishing we're going to do. Just sunfish, Corbett."

"Two's company, three's a crowd." Steve Corbett, who was eating breakfast, waved them on. His face in bright sunlight was darker, harder, thinner; that was the only evidence of lost sleep.

I said, "I don't think Mr. Lewis likes attention paid his wife."

"He'll get it just the same," was the truculent answer.

Mrs. Rudeen came along the edge of the bank while we still watched, stepping quickly, her face turned to the lake. She had on the gay Mexican crash dirndl, and a blue print handkerchief was over the black Dutch bob.

"It must be funny," I said. "Mrs. Rudeen, making a brave womanly effort to keep another woman's man."

"She's going down to the boats," Cottie's father commented softly. "Three is going to be a crowd, whatever Harry Lewis wants."

When I took Cottie down for his eleven o'clock playtime in the water I could just see the two boats, up at the marshy entrance to Little Sister, looking not more than fifty yards apart. It must have been amusing for Harry and Carol Lewis to fish with those malevolent slitted eyes fixed on every fling of their poles. Particularly, I thought later, it should have been amusing for Harry Lewis.

Mrs. Clapshaw told me John Loxton had sprained his ankle, and I remembered I hadn't seen him around. Cottie and I went to pay a sympathy call before lunch; he was very grateful and let Cottie play his organ.

"Mrs. Lewis' coming—do you think that might possibly be a sign people might not be as frightened off as I think?" he asked hopefully. He sat in a rocker with the sprained foot propped on another chair.

I didn't say that I'd gathered from Steve Corbett's manner that there was some special reason for Carol's coming. Instead I said I hoped so, and asked who cooked his meals. He said he could get around with a cane, and that Elmer helped. On the way back I saw that Earl Jordan was back; at least his car was, I didn't see him.

While I was at my usual afternoon chores of settling Cottie for his nap Carol Lewis appeared at our door.

She called, "Hello there, sleepyhead," gaily to Cottie's father. I heard his feet hit the floor and carry him quickly to the door.

"Mrs. Lewis! Don't tell me you're coming to see me!"

"Harry's asleep." She came in, waving negligently to me.

Cottie instantly sat up. "I can't rest now, Mamma."

"Oh yes, you can." I shut the log-house door firmly and told him "Little Black Sambo" until he fell asleep from sheer boredom.

When I joined the group on the porch the two were so absorbed they didn't even look up; Carol just flashed an absent smile.

"Your husband's been telling me some more about your perfectly fascinating murder." She had on a new plum halter and a fresh pair of the white slacks; she held her hands so that the maroon fingernails were poised against her thick white shoulders.

The recital went on. "When we were sure what was in the dummy we went up to Loxton's——"

"Who's Loxtons?"

"The man who owns the resort. In the main house at the entrance."

"Oh yes. Go on!"

Steve Corbett went on until Harry Lewis came hurrying up the track. He called, "Carol! There you are!" as if he were relieved and almost surprised.

"Mr. Corbett's been telling me some more about the murder. While you slept, you lazy thing, you."

"I thought you were going to stay right there. I wish you wouldn't go out like that." He stood looking down at the top of her very golden head, not seeming to notice that Cottie's father held a chair for him. "After all, this is pretty wild country up here. And they did have—ah—they did have an unfortunate occurrence."

What was the matter with him? Did he really think Mrs. Rudeen was a danger—that she might attack his wife?

She laughed at him. "Aren't men wonderful? So protective. Isn't it silly? As if I couldn't take care of myself! I'm a great big girl now, Harry. You just sit down and listen. Mr. Corbett is at the place where he got put in jail."

Harry Lewis sat down. He didn't seem quite as imposingly large and firm as when I had first seen him; his flesh fitted more loosely. How much was Mrs. Rudeen on his mind? Or was it Steve Corbett he worried about? His eyes were intent on the two.

Once he turned to me. "You and I ought to get together, Mrs. Corbett. The way our partners hit it off." But there was no heart in it.

I said maliciously, "That's a lovely idea. My little boy was promised a boat ride when he woke. Would you want to go?"

Carol clapped hands. "Oh, I want to go on a boat ride, too. I haven't been to the island yet. Can't we wake your little boy?"

He didn't have to be waked; he was standing in the doorway, flushed and sleepy eyed, his hair on end. He came along in his white sleeper, the back unbuttoned, to rub his head against my hands. And again I felt the incongruity of his sweetness in the midst of all the intrigue I sensed in what went on around us.

"Go boat ride now?"

"You bet you are, ducky," Carol told him. "Harry, isn't he a lamb?"

Harry didn't answer; his head was turned toward the screen. Mrs. Rudeen sat there on the bank, her back to us, as she had sat once before.

When we left we ignored her as if by common consent; the two men going ahead carrying oars, Carol between them. Both men had their heads bent to her, ostentatiously bantering.

At the shore Carol pouted, "Why can't I be two girls and go in two boats?" But she stepped into cabin six boat, and the Corbetts went *en famille*.

"This is the cutest little trip I ever went on," I said mildly.

"What's the matter?" Cottie's father asked. "Don't you like it? I am having more fun." He pulled so savagely at the oars they bent.

"You'll have more fun if the oars break."

"I like to break things."

205

I rested my chin on Cottie's nice-smelling hair and ignored him. Forty feet to the right of us the Lewis boat slithered on the water, rising and falling with the waves.

Carol called, "Yoo hoo, we're beating," and on that small hint succeeded in working up a race. Both men began rowing like mad, calling taunts to each other. Steve Corbett shipped so much water Cottie clung to me squealing.

"I getting wet, Mamma! I got wet on my suit!" As if he expected me to scold his father for it.

Steve Corbett won, but we hit the little island with such force I was knocked off the seat; I fell forward still holding Cottie, trying to keep him from hitting the seat in front of us.

"Look out for the kid!" Steve Corbett was reaching to grab the boy from my arms.

"I not hurt," Cottie assured him.

"I am!" I said in anger. I'd landed on my knees, and they hurt.

"I'm sorry," Steve Corbett said, and for the first time in our acquaintance he looked as if he realized he'd been brutally careless of me. "Could I get—could I help you out of the boat?"

"No, thanks." I got out of the boat by myself. Walking was an agony; my knees were scraped and bleeding, and under the short front-buttoning play skirt I wore over my shorts they looked awful, too.

The Lewises were beaching more slowly. As soon as they were in Carol rushed over to exude sympathy.

"But you mustn't blame your husband; he's so strong he just doesn't know his own strength, do you, Mr. Corbett?"

"I find out about it once in a while." He stalked ahead, to settle me with Cottie by the playhouse; I was in no shape to enjoy exploring.

Carol, as soon as we halted, slipped a huge blue-enameled compact from her handbag to repair what damage the row had done to her complexion. I was to remember that little scene later.

Then it was just something I barely noted. "Explore for hours if you want to," I said. "Cottie and I will be fine here."

Carol maneuvered herself between the two men, linking an arm with each. I thought that was the way she liked life—to have men, big good-looking men, walking one on each side of her.

As they left Cottie came out of his house to invite me in.

"Thank you, but we'll play I'm sitting on your porch. I like it out here. My, you have a lovely lawn, Mr. Corbett."

"I mower it," he said at once, delighted. "I mower it with a lawn mower like Elmer has. Do you have a mower at your house, Mamma?"

"I have one old one for mornings and one new one for afternoons."

"Would you like I s'ould make some lemonade maybe?"

"I would love lemonade."

He disappeared into the playhouse. I sat thinking about Carol Lewis and Mrs. Rudeen and Steve Corbett, wondering what the next scene in that odd drama would bring forth, what the next link in the chain would be.

Cottie came out holding something in his hands.

He said confidentially and happily, "Look, money. Look, Mamma, I got money in my house."

His hands were full of it, like leaves. Unfolded paper money.

My first wild thought was that his father must have lost his money there, but I knew immediately that wasn't possible; he would not have had that much money.

I gasped, "Cottie, where did you get that?"

"In my house. Mamma, can I get a cone now?"

He opened his hands so that the bills fluttered to my lap in a shower. As they touched me my flesh seemed to shrink away from them.

This must be Al Sprung's money. The eight thousand dollars.

I sat blinking at it stupidly. Al Sprung's money. How had it come here?

Slowly I stood up. "Show me where the money stays."

It was still play to Cottie. "In my house. Come in, Mamma."

I stooped to the windowless interior; enough light came in through cracks for the space inside to be no darker than dusk. In the left front corner of the hut a sod lay overturned, and in the place where it had been lay a dirt-soiled canvas bag with its mouth open.

Cottie hunched toward the bag frog-fashion, and thrust his hand inside to bring out more bills.

"Don't touch it!" I jerked him away from it. Would this money have fingerprints? Would it show that Hoxie Moebbels had had it last, or that someone else had had it last?

"All my money," Cottie protested.

"How did you find it?"

"I make lemonade."

"Oh." My mind made the imaginative jump required. He had been pulling up grass to make play lemonade, that being all there was in the hut. And when he pulled the sod must have come up.

What should I do now? I didn't trust Harry Lewis, and what I knew of Carol wouldn't recommend her as a trustee for that money, either.

Cottie's father—the best I could say of him was that I didn't know.

If I could put it back, swear Cottie to secrecy, get to the sheriff somehow . . .

I looked down at the bright uplifted face. "Let's put all this money back. Then we'll drive to town and tell Sheriff Boxruud about it. You remember, the big man?"

The small face clouded. "Can tell Daddy."

"It'll be a secret. We'll surprise Daddy."

That was a mistake. He ran from the door yelling, "Daddy! S'prise!"

The answering call came almost at once. It would, with Steve Corbett's ears always pricked for that voice.

I had to add my own call for appearance's sake. "Come here! Come back!"

"What's the matter?" Underbrush crackled as Steve Corbett appeared from the left. Cottie flew toward him. "You all right, kid?" He scooped him up.

"Money in my house!" Cottie bounced in his arms. "Now can I had a cone?"

"*What* in your house?" His father asked, and turned to me.

I pointed to the money Cottie had showered over me, which was still on the ground. "A whole bag of it in the hut," I said tersely. "It must be Al Sprung's."

That expression on his face—was it stupefaction? Or anger at the money having been found? He would know about the hut as a hiding place. He had built it.

Behind him Harry and Carol Lewis came panting into the clearing.

"What's up? Did anything scare——*Gosh!*" Carol came within seeing distance. "Look at the dough! All over the ground!"

Harry Lewis bent popeyed to pick up one bill. "My God, Corbett, that's a C note. What's it all about?"

Cottie's father took charge. "It must be the money Al Sprung had on him. The murderer must have hidden it here. Unless——"

Quickly he was gathering up the money from the ground, taking the one bill from Harry Lewis' unresisting fingers. Then he was asking, "Where's the rest of it?" and crowding his big body into the hut, the Lewises after him.

I said loudly enough for them to hear inside, "We should leave it here. Just as it is. Then get the sheriff."

Steve Corbett came out pulling the drawstrings at the bag's mouth.

Behind him Harry Lewis said, "That's the best idea, Corbett." A fascinated glaze seemed to have come over his eyes, but behind that curtain I thought his mind was working rapidly.

"Gosh," Carol breathed reverently, "I never thought I'd live to see that much dough piled around like rubbish."

Steve Corbett wasn't answering them or me; as I stood facing him his eyes were over my head. I turned.

Mrs. Rudeen was not six feet behind me in the center of the glade.

"I was out fishen and I sure thought I heard some yellen," she said, as if it were a prepared piece. Then she added, "What you got in that bag?" In words as quick as her eyes.

"Money," Harry Lewis said queerly. "They found a whole bagful of dough in there. It ain't eight thousand. It must be fifty, sixty thousand. They're taking it to the sheriff——"

He stopped abruptly.

All movement, even all thought seemed to be arrested. I stood as if I were marble, powerless to do anything but watch Mrs. Rudeen's eyes go from one to the other of us, with one brief, scrutinizing, estimating jerk for each face. She started with Steve Corbett, went from him to me, and then to Cottie holding my hand. Carol Lewis next. Harry Lewis.

With her eyes fixed on Harry Lewis she took one slow,

even step forward.

I hadn't really felt fear when I found Al Sprung's body. Not fear for myself. But I felt fear now. Terror. I felt terror pouring in on me like the water in the storm the day we came to the Crying Sisters.

Without thinking, I grabbed for something and ran for the boats. I knew inside two steps that what I had grabbed was Cottie; he was there, protesting in my arms. I thought he should be heavy, but I couldn't feel his weight; I ran fleetly and without effort, not even remembering my bruised knees, as if some reservoir of strength had flowed into my nerves and muscles.

Trees, the stalks of tall weeds tore past, and then I was in the boat. I must have thrown Cottie to the thwart because he was there and I was standing in the middle of the boat with an oar in my hand, shoving off, when Steve Corbett lunged through the trees behind me and ran down the shore.

"What's the idea? I'm going in that boat, too."

Mrs. Rudeen was right behind him; the Lewises in back of her.

I kept on shoving. The boat stuck because it had been shoved so far onto the beach; then it came free, water widened between me and the shore just as Steve Corbett reached it. He threw the bag over my head into the boat and splashed through three feet of water to swing himself over the bow.

What he said was, "Good girl." He slid forward to take the oars from me.

I backed to sit beside Cottie, hugging him. I felt a tremendous surge of relief, as if whatever I had run from was gone.

Cottie turned his head against my chest and said in wonder, "Mamma, you bump."

The oars dipped smoothly in his father's hands.

From a shore now fifteen feet behind us Harry Lewis called, "If you beat it with that dough we'll get the sheriff on your tail."

Mrs. Rudeen didn't call anything, but she was standing so close to water it must have wet her feet. On Carol's face, as she came up from behind to clutch her husband's arm, was such a look of shock that I wondered if she, too, had felt the terror.

I know now how right I was in feeling that unreasoning fear.

CHAPTER NINETEEN

AT THE RESORT Steve Corbett got us and the money into the car with all possible speed. As we went down the cinder track the Lewises were just coming up the stairs from the shore. To my surprise he stopped the car, and invited them to come along. Only Mrs. Rudeen was left behind. As the car started again she came running up the stairs, her face contorted with anger.

Harry Lewis spoke only once on the way to Maple Valley.

"If this dough doesn't belong to anybody we're in on it, too."

"Don't worry. It belongs, all right."

There could be no doubt of that after the sheriff stood up from the living-room table where he had hastily pushed vases and magazines aside to make place for the bag.

"This is seventy-three thousand and five hundred dollars." The round blue eyes traveled over the five of us awaiting his verdict. "There is no doubt this is the greater part of the Kansas City First National Bank robbery. I was given the list of the numbers."

Steve Corbett was thoughtful, looking down at the bills piled by the sheriff into neat stacks as he counted.

"Moebbels. He must have hidden it in the playhouse instead of in the boathouse as he told his gang. A double-cross to the end. He must have hidden it there on his way back to the Flaming Door that night Sprung was killed. He didn't dare let it be found on him."

The round blue eyes were intent on him. "Yes," the sheriff agreed softly. "But is it not interesting that there is only seventy-three thousand, five hundred here? The loot in the bank robbery was over eighty thousand. The eight thousand dollars which Sprung had is still missing!"

The eight thousand was missing. And it was still missing after Boxruud had literally torn the hut apart, and almost literally torn the island apart. For two days we had boatloads of reporters and searchers going back and forth between the shore and the island. It wasn't until Tuesday night that the sheriff gave up his search, and quiet descended on the Crying Sisters again.

"I did not find one thing more, except I find somebody has been shooting a gun over there, a revolver." He waited, after saying that, as if he hoped I was going to volunteer something.

"That's an odd place to be shooting," I said.

"It does not seem anything was hit except trees," he added, and not getting any response on that, either, left.

Steve Corbett went out every night as before; I wondered how he avoided the sheriff's men, if there were any about.

On Wednesday morning only the resorters were in residence. Cottie was taken to town on a grocery-buying trip; I grabbed the chance to clean the cabin and wash clothes. There had been another thirty dollars in my handbag on Tuesday.

When I went down to the dock with my load of soiled clothes the Lewises were on the beach. Carol lifted a head that glinted like brass filings to wave at me. Later she came to sit swinging her legs idly from the dock as I washed and rinsed.

"This is the first time I ever saw you without that kid."

"He went with his father to Maple Valley."

In a white rayon bathing suit her figure was as plushily luscious as an overstuffed pink satin davenport. I hadn't seen much of her since the discovery of the money; the resorters had stayed quiet while the reporters were around.

She fidgeted with casual subjects—the weather, fishing,

Cottie—but I thought she was working toward something, and it came out at last. She leaned forward to pitch her voice in a confidential undertone that wouldn't carry to Harry Lewis, still basking in the sun at the beach.

"Say, over on that island Sunday when we found that dough—you know. The way you ran; was there any reason?"

I straightened from the soapy circle I was making with one of Cottie's suits to see what she meant. She'd dropped coquetry; that was something she used only on men. The usually rolling hazel eyes were quite direct.

I said, "I don't know. I just had a feeling I should get away from there. And get Cottie away." I didn't see where honesty would hurt me. "I guess I was afraid."

"That's funny. Because I had a funny feeling right then, too. Scared. Scared all the way down to my lights. I was so scared I couldn't move. Then when you grabbed the kid and beat it—it was like it broke. The next thing I knew I was running after Harry myself." She was puzzled, open; I thought if she wasn't being honest, then I didn't know genuine emotion when I saw it.

"It was odd and not very pleasant," I agreed. "Have you thought——"

"It was that Rudeen woman," she said instantly. "She gives me the willies. I don't suppose you've noticed, but it seems to me I can't move unless she's right there watching. Even these last days when we had all the men around she's been camping right in front of our house. You don't think she could have been in with that gang—you know?"

Of all the suspicions I'd had against Mrs. Rudeen, the idea that she had been a member of the Moebbels gang had not entered my head.

"That seems unlikely," I thought as I talked. "This is her second summer here. Her husband is a traveling salesman."

215

Carol snorted. "What's a traveling salesman? Anything. She can't fool me. That woman is bad. I don't want anything to do with her and that's flat!"

"I've often thought she was spying on us, too. Maybe she's just snoopy, the way some small-town women get. I know——" What had I been about to say? I couldn't tell of my Eldreth background! I tacked hastily. "Have you seen her this morning?"

She pointed past the southern tip of the small island. "That's her out there in that boat."

A single figure sat in the boat, but the distance had been too great for me to see who it was.

"She came down the steps carrying her fishing stuff as soon as Harry and I walked down to lie on the beach. She fished offshore a while, then she rowed over there."

"Maybe she's trying to bolster up her story about that being a favorite fishing spot of hers—that's what she told the sheriff when he asked her how she came to be watching when the money was found."

Carol shrugged thick creamy shoulders. "I wouldn't put anything past her."

Her feet lagged in their swing, and when she spoke next it was in the tone of a woman who feels the urge to become entirely intimate and confiding.

She said, "You know, I've had a funny life. I was married once." She looked toward Harry Lewis. "I mean, I was married before Harry."

She was married *once*. Was that a slip, confirming my idea that she wasn't married to Harry Lewis? She was too much absorbed in herself to be noticing me.

"Funny, I wasn't thinking much any more about that time I was married, but lately—I came up here and that guy had been

216

murdered and all, it sort of brought it back. Did you ever think—did you ever think how many people get murdered and it never gets found out?"

That was startling enough to drag my thoughts from wondering if she was Harry Lewis' wife. "Oh, that doesn't really happen often, does it? It must usually be found out sooner or later."

She shook a slow head. "You'd be surprised. I was in a murder once that didn't get out."

I stood up again to stare at her, electrified.

She'd been in a murder that didn't get out. Suppose she wasn't exaggerating. Could that have anything to do with her being in this resort where Steve Corbett prowled at night, spying or waiting? Could it have anything to do with his excitement at her coming? Did it have any place in the chain?

She must have caught the expression on my face, because she jerked back to briskness, although she still spoke low.

"Don't get excited; it's as dead as doornails. Golly, was I excited when it was going on, though!"

"When was it?"

"Long enough ago to be dead for good. Only this Sprung business brought it back. Funny. The whole thing turned out lucky for me, too, and I got married on account of it."

Again she must have seen bewilderment on my face; she laughed.

"Sounds screwy, doesn't it? 1926. I don't forget that year. I was nursing an old guy that was all ready to pop off—he was over eighty. That's what I was once—a nurse."

I said, "Mrs. Willard was once a nurse, too." Casting about wildly for any link.

"The redhead? I never knew her. Well, this old guy I was nursing had two kids—two sons. They weren't young any more.

The old man's name was Martin Maartens." She repeated the last name, spelling it. "Imagine that, will you. I got to know it well enough, and I always had to spell it. This old Martin Maartens lived in one of those big old brownstones in St. Paul on lower Summit Avenue. The older son's name was James Maartens. He was forty-some years old then."

"James Maartens," I repeated. The name stirred some vague chords of memory; something to do with money—I couldn't recall what.

"There was plenty written about it in the papers. Anyhow, the younger son's name was Adam—he was thirty-seven then, and had a daughter Alice, ten. There isn't anything I don't remember about them when I start thinking. I was around in that house for months. The old guy was always right on the edge of dying, but he never did. Living right there in the house I found out a lot of things. The older son, that's James, was no good. He was the sort of man that just had to have money, not to hold on to, just to let it run through his hands, fast. I heard the old guy tell him he lost more money gambling every year than the President of the United States' salary was. Women. I guess he had a lot of 'em. Parties that got whispered about."

She paused as if to search back in some recess of memory. "The funny thing was he didn't look it. He looked like a preacher or something even after he'd put away two quarts of scotch; I saw him do it. The old guy used to get propped in bed and call James in and almost spit at him. He said James had been forging checks on him and stealing from him, and if he did it again he'd cut him out of his will."

I'd kept on trying to remember where I'd heard the name James Maartens, and finally I got something. "Wait. I read about a James Maartens in a Sunday newspaper. He disappeared the day after his father's death and never returned to claim an inheritance of a quarter of a million dollars."

"That's the one," she nodded. "They've been printing those pieces off and on for twelve years. I guess it gives the reporters the willies, to think of all that dough in the bank and no taker, and they don't know why."

"Do you?"

"Sure. That's what I'm telling you. The son old Martin Maartens liked was Adam. Adam was straitlaced enough for anybody. He lived in the same house, but he and James never said a word to each other, even all those nights they stood on opposite sides of the bed, expecting the old man to die.

"I don't know what James got into. First a woman came to the house asking for James and calling up, and then a man began calling up. I heard James stalling 'em off. He'd say—" her tone became mincing —"'You will simply have to wait. The present state of affairs cannot continue much longer.'

"I knew what he meant all right, the snake. He meant the old man wouldn't last much longer. Adam heard him, too; I saw Adam listening once, and maybe you think you've seen a tight mouth. It was that way quite a while, with the doctor saying old Mr. Maartens might die tonight and he might last six months, with those people calling James up and James cursing and Adam watching.

"Then one night I came in from my evening walk and James and Adam were having a fight right beside the old man's bed. Adam had it all over James on muscle. When I got there he was holding James' hands out in front of him, and James' hands was full of dough, a lot of it.

"'Father, wake up,' Adam was calling, and the old man did and there was a fuss. I guess the old man had been sleeping and James had sneaked in and got some money out of a safe. Adam was watching and saw him do it and caught him with his hands full. The old man said this was the last time and told Adam to get his lawyer in the morning, because he was cutting James out of his will."

She stopped there to go into a brooding that reminded me of Steve Corbett. I found myself standing stiff kneed in the water with a forgotten shirt in my hands.

"That was *asking* for murder!"

Carol jerked back. "He got it," she said grimly. "I still don't know how James got in that night. I was right in the next room—I had a cot because the old man didn't need close watching. I didn't hear a thing. In the morning the old man was dead. I called Adam and he called James and the doctor. The doctor said this was to be expected and signed the death certificate.

"It was when I was cleaning up the medicine table by the bed and was going to rinse out the drinking glass the old man used that I noticed the inside of the glass had little gray circles where the water had dried.

"Golly, Mrs. Corbett, talk about knees shake! I went to Adam. He didn't say anything, just took the glass. But that night he called me into the dining room. They were all there: Adam and James and Alice and the housekeeper, Lulie Webster. Adam had the glass in front of him and a revolver and a sheet of paper and a pen. He made us sit as if it was a dinner, himself at the head and me at the foot and James all alone on his right, and Lulie Webster and his little daughter on his left. James was sweating, but looking—you know—I dare you.

"So then Adam started talking. He said, 'James, you murdered our father. Miss Ridley'—that was me—'Miss Ridley saw the traces of dried poison in the glass.'

"James laughed and said, 'Prove it.'

"'I will,' Adam said. 'I will order a post mortem. With your reputation and the scene Miss Ridley witnessed here last night there won't be much doubt of the outcome.'

"James said, 'Why, Adam, you wouldn't disgrace the old family, and yourself, and your own little daughter, Alice, would you? Her uncle a murderer. My, my.'

" 'I don't think that will be necessary,' Adam said, 'because, my dear brother, you are going to write a free and full confession and leave that confession with me. After that it will be best for you to go to South America, I think. I'll give you five thousand dollars to leave with. Everything will be perfectly all right, James. Except that if you ever return to this country or try in any way to claim the money you inherit from our father, then I will turn this confession and the testimony of these witnesses over to the police. You shall not profit by this murder.'

"James swore; Lord how he swore! He came flat out and said he had murdered the old man because he wasn't going to see Adam get everything. I could see then how he hated Adam; gosh, how he hated him. He stormed and shrieked and yelled, with Adam getting quieter but not giving up any, and the little girl scared and Lulie Webster and I just holding on. James grabbed for the gun once, but Adam just moved it out of his way.

"We stayed there almost all night. James went once and ran through the house; we heard his feet in all the rooms, as if he could get away running. We just sat and waited until it got light for morning. James came back and screamed some more. I never saw a man that close to driving himself crazy. It was terrible. He did act sort of crazy in the end. He sat down and wrote on the paper; I remember how his hand jerked.

"Adam picked up the paper when he was done. 'This will do very well,' he said, and took a wad of money out of his pocket. James just grabbed it and ran out of the house; he didn't stop to get anything, not even his hat. When the door slammed Adam turned and said the first words he'd said to us.

"'James living without money will be more adequately punished than James hung,' and I could see how the way James hated him was nothing to the way he hated James. Then he said, 'You may wash this glass now, Miss Ridley, but first you will all sign this confession as witnesses, please. And you will all please remember my brother's oral confession. I will arrange with our lawyer that if James tries to claim his inheritance the claim shall be given wide publicity over the entire country for two months before the money is paid. Even if I am dead you are to come forward to press the murder charge; I will leave the confession to one of you in my will.'"

Carol stopped her story, shivering.

I asked, "You signed?" Carol had a feeling for drama; I'd been hypnotized.

She nodded soberly. "We all signed. Even the little girl. And promised, too. Adam didn't seem to worry much about Alice or Lulie Webster, but I guess he worried about me. I always did think that was why he married me."

I gasped, "He married you? Adam Maartens?"

"He sure did; that's how I got what I've got. We even lived together a couple of years, but it didn't work so good. I could of stood it, but I guess I just wasn't in his class." She said that with the calm clarity of a woman who can face reality when she wants to. "So we split up."

"Oh."

"I made up for lost time since then," she assured me, bridling and drawing on her coquetry again. "Mrs. Maartens. But it brought me in a nice check every month. Even after he lost most of his dough in the crash it was a pretty good check. Then when he died he left me a trust fund. He died six years ago. He was just the kind to be funny that way—you know, his wife even if I wasn't living with him."

"The confession—who got that?"

Her legs had begun swinging again; they stopped. The hazel eyes grew more secret, but she answered carelessly enough. "I dunno. Maybe Adam left that with the lawyer."

"Hasn't James Maartens ever tried to get his money?"

"Not yet."

"Did you ever hear where he went?"

She shrugged. "Adam heard once he was in Mexico. That's a long time ago now."

Mexico.

As if it were a picture being superimposed on the scenes I had just been seeing, I saw Steve Corbett sitting at the sheriff's dinner table, and heard him talking of Mexico with the firsthand knowledge that only a sojourn there could give.

But he couldn't be James Maartens. He was too young.

Mrs. Rudeen—Mrs. Rudeen wore a Mexican crash dirndl. She'd said she'd traveled a lot. But she was a woman.

I floundered, hunting, trying to see any connection.

"The girl—Alice—what about her?"

"Haven't seen her for years, either. I heard she got married—married a guy named Kernan. I think her father left me more dough than he did her. I'm going to look her up sometime. She was a cute kid."

"And the other—Lulie Webster?"

"She stayed on keeping house for Adam. I think Adam left her a chunk, too." She straightened, yawning. "Gosh, I've been spilling my whole life story. Keep it dark, will you? I wouldn't of opened my mouth this far if Adam was still alive, believe me! It feels sort of good though, talking. Gosh, the way it used to ride me!"

She talked inconsequentially for a few moments, and then went back to where Harry Lewis lay.

I went back to my washing, but my movements were automatic.

Steve Corbett—Mrs. Rudeen—could there be any connection? Al Sprung. Could Al Sprung in any possible way—he had been a gambler, too? I wondered wildly if he could have been James Maartens. But Carol had said James Maartens was in his forties in 1926—surely Al Sprung couldn't have been in his fifties.

That confession—could it possibly be that confession Steve Corbett was hunting? Did that explain his interest in Carol Lewis? Did she have it?

Of one thing I was almost certain—that this story had its place in the chain somewhere.

I know now how right I was in that. But how wrong I was in almost all the inferences I drew.

CHAPTER TWENTY

I SHOOK MYSELF out of my romancing to finish the washing. When I was done I went to lie with Carol and Harry Lewis in the sand, willing to rest.

We were still lying there talking casually when Mrs. Rudeen's boat scraped bottom near by. She stalked past us carrying a three-pound bass toward the cleaning table which was between our cabin and the dock.

Harry Lewis called, "Swell fish you got there, Mrs. Rudeen." She didn't answer or turn her head.

Soon afterward we went down the shore, too, Harry Lewis gallantly offering to carry up my wet clothes. Mrs. Rudeen was still cleaning her fish when we passed her, standing behind the long waist-high table, spattering scales to right and left with a knife that looked to me like a duplicate of the one with which the murder had been done. I thought that Boxruud must have given the other knives back, but not ours, of course. That, somewhere, was probably Exhibit A.

Just as we were opposite, Mrs. Rudeen lifted her head and smiled full at Harry Lewis. It was a smile that was intended, obviously, to be significant, though of what I couldn't tell. Then she turned her eyes on Carol and me, resting her knife as she did so on the fish, just in back of the neck.

The knife must have been sharpened to an incredible edge, even if she had previously cracked the backbone, which she must have done. Because the severed fish head rolled free without any apparent pressure of Mrs. Rudeen's hand on the knife at all. As if the fish were butter. As if she had just rested the knife on the fish and the knife had slashed through of its own weight.

Carol gasped, and as soon as we'd made the top of the stairs asked nervously, "Gosh! Did you see that woman handle that knife?"

There had been a sort of pleasure in Mrs. Rudeen's severing of the fish head that wasn't pleasant to look at. It was almost as if she were saying, *"Look, I could do this to you, too."*

"I'm beginning to wonder if she's unbalanced," I said. It was the only explanation that seemed to cover the facts.

Carol had been at the top of the bank for several moments, but she was still breathing hard. "It isn't safe to have that sort of woman around. She ought to bc shut up."

Harry Lewis had been easing the pan of clothes from his bay window to the ground. When he stood up he was trying to look unconcerned, but this time I had no doubt but that he had paled.

He said, "You don't want to pay any attention to Mrs. Rudeen. What if she is a little touched in the head? I'm here. I can take care of you."

Carol said, "Well, she's getting in my hair. I'm for getting away from this resort."

Her husband began, "I can't——" but changed it. "Oh, let it ride. I'll talk to Loxton about her, see what he thinks. Where do you want these clothes, Mrs. Corbett?"

It seemed a shame to shunt the whole matter on to Mr. Loxton, but as proprietor the business was more his than mine. Harry Lewis carried my clothes to the lines and went off with Carol; I thought Carol was a little sullen because he hadn't at once agreed to her suggestion about leaving.

When my clothes were hung and I walked toward our cabin

door I saw Mrs. Rudeen again. This time she was standing directly in front of the Lewis cottage with the fish dangling from her left hand by its tail. With her right hand she was making gestures, pointing first at the Lewis cottage, then up the track toward her own— and the gestures flashed. The knife was still in her hand. Her face was working, too; contorting into mouthy grimaces. When I started wandering toward her she saw me, whirled and sped up the track so fast the full skirt of her dirndl kicked up in back.

Harry Lewis stood alone on his porch, watching her retreating back. He had been dressing, buttoning a shirt—its skirts hung down over his trousers. But he had forgotten that; his hands hung at his sides.

"Did you see that?" I asked.

"I d-don't know what she meant by it," he said. His face was blank, the lower edges of his cheeks almost flabby.

"That woman's getting dangerous; I'll see Loxton about her if you don't." This was nothing to let slide by.

"I guess that wouldn't hurt," he said after a pause. He returned to some vivacity and began buttoning his shirt again. "Don't say anything to Carol about this; she gets nervous."

I could imagine Carol nervous; she'd be a tornado.

"All right, I'll see Mr. Loxton."

John Loxton, still kept in the house by his sprained ankle, welcomed me as a visitor warmly.

"It's lonesome, and I keep thinking of my neglected flowers," he mourned. "I hope you've come to stay a while."

The eagerness went out of his eyes as I told my story. "Oh dear, I do seem to be having so much trouble this summer. I have never noticed that Mrs. Rudeen had been making—ah—making advances to Mr. Lewis. Still if she acts as you say——"

"She may be mentally unbalanced." I proffered my own

conclusion. "You know, there's still a possibility Hoxie Moebbels didn't murder Al Sprung. That eight thousand is still missing. And she handles that knife as if she enjoyed it. I don't like it."

He was completely stricken at having the wound of the murder reopened; his hands and beard shook. "Oh, Mrs. Corbett! Why did that terrible crime have to happen here? What should I do? Should I ask Mrs. Rudeen to leave?"

"It's up to you. I'm not afraid of her—at least not most of the time. I—oh, I don't know what I think." Now that he put it up to me, it did seem presumptuous of me to force him to kick out one of his customers.

I said so and went home, giving Mrs. Rudeen's cabin a wide berth. Cottie and his father were back when I got there and Earl Jordan was with them, the two men lying on their backs in the beach chairs laughing at some joke, Cottie running from one to the other with a butterfly he'd caught, holding it by the tips of its helpless blue wings. They looked too peaceful after the unnerving morning I'd had.

"This place is getting screwier and screwier." I put some of my disgruntled crossness into words. "I'm all for leaving." I told the latest Rudeen incidents.

"Mrs. Rudeen?" Earl Jordan sat up, interested. "She never struck me as a Sunday-school teacher, but I thought she was harmless."

Steve Corbett lounged unstirring in his chair even when Cottie held the butterfly's grasping feet against the bare skin of his forearm, and advanced the insect by jumps down to the wrist and back again.

Steve Corbett appeared to be watching the butterfly's progress, not me, but he said, "That's like a woman, wanting to see how much trouble she can stir up."

I said hotly, "Anyone who goes around brandishing a

knife with a sort of ghoulish glee merits some attention. We had a murder here."

"Particularly it merits attention from people who know a lot of fancy words and like to use 'em," he said.

That was so rankly unjust I went into the bedroom slamming the door behind me. Once inside I knew that was exactly what he wanted—to shut me up.

As soon as Earl Jordan left he followed me, leaving Cottie crooning to his butterfly on the porch.

He said, "I take it you spent the morning with the Lewises."

I laid aside the magazine I'd picked up. He stood wide legged in front of my chair with his hands in his breeches pockets, and his head dropped forward to scrutinize me.

"Yes." I didn't feel communicative.

"Do any talking with Carol?"

"Yes."

"I don't suppose she could possibly have become confiding? Have let loose any hints about herself?"

It was uncanny. As if he could have guessed that Carol had something to tell and had told me. I looked upward, but the dark face was hard, the controlled muscles quiet.

When I didn't answer he asked again, "What did she talk about?"

"About finding the money on the island. Being afraid of Mrs. Rudeen."

"Anything else?"

At the distance of Maple Valley, how could he have known? I was being ridiculous. He was just guessing.

"Keep this dark." Carol Lewis had ended her story with that admonition. I could see why she wouldn't want that story repeated too widely. It must be illegal to conceal a murder.

Now Steve Corbett was trying to get her story out of me.

The hands came out of the pockets to reach for my shoulders; he lifted until I stood upright with my face only a foot below his, then he began smiling.

"Mamma," he said, cajoling. "You know I can read you like a book. Carol told you something and you're bursting with it. Spill it."

I still didn't answer.

He sobered. "Look. I know there's something about Carol Lewis I've got to know. I can't get it out of her; all the damn fool does with me is flirt. And I don't even know what I'm after. If she didn't tell you this morning, then I'm going to ask you to find out for me. Make a friend of her. Cultivate her confidence. There's something in her life somewhere—she's got something—or there was a crime——"

His jumble of suppositions was so like those in which I had floundered.

I asked, "Why do you want to know?"

"I can't tell you that. It might be dangerous. For you. Believe that, you're better off not knowing. Now what about Carol?"

"So you can hurt her?"

"I honestly believe it will be better for Carol Lewis, too, if I know."

How could I tell what I should do? He was Cottie's father. Mrs. Rudeen I now thought a more likely criminal than he. He was hard and secret and he lived withdrawn and brooding, but he loved his son and I had not actually seen him commit a crime.

I was very close to him. In spite of the rigid quiet of his face an emotion swept from him to me; if it had come from anyone else I would have said it was appeal.

In some dark interior part of my mind a voice said, horrified and helpless, "I like him."

He must have seen, after that, that I was suffering some

230

sort of shock, but he misread it. The hands gripped my shoulders harder and the eyes deepened.

"She did tell you something."

"Yes," I said unsteadily. "She knows about a murder. Not Al Sprung's. Another murder. A long time ago."

My voice, mechanical, began Carol's story and carried it through to the end. And while I talked Steve Corbett shook me, a shaking that was imparted either because of a quivering in his hands, or because he unconsciously tried in that way to shake the words out of me, make me reveal more, talk faster. The shaking seemed entirely dissociated from the activity going on behind his eyes. His lips, too, carried an abrupt, broken accompaniment.

"So that's it. So that's it. Oh, the damn little fool. A better guy. A better guy. The poor little fool. And Carol Lewis. She's a fool, too. Doesn't she know she's an idiot? Oh God, so that's it. So that's it!" Over and over, the same words repeated, almost meaningless to my ears, but backed by an emotion so intense it seemed agony and the words either cursing or a prayer.

I hardly heard. I was still, in the retreat of my own mind, trying to recover from the idea that whether I wanted it to be that way or not, whether I trusted him or not, I liked Steve Corbett.

I told Carol's story, I am sure, three or four times over before he let me stop. His grip on my shoulders was so tight my arm muscles felt squeezed into the bones, and I said so. He came to himself at that; slowly his face and eyes became controlled again.

"Look, Janet." It was the first time he'd used my name. "You mustn't tell this to anyone else."

I promised. I was glad enough to.

He left me to sit on his cot with eyes that remained dark and unseeing even when Cottie spoke to him, even when he ate lunch.

I spent the afternoon on the beach with the Clapshaws and

the Willards; the afternoon was outwardly serene. At about eight in the evening the Lewises both came over; Steve Corbett immediately roused himself. As far as I could see he treated Carol exactly as he had before; kidding her, flattering her, settling himself for the admiring, attentive joking she loved. Harry Lewis, somewhat abstracted, joined in at intervals; I was completely out of it.

What I was trying to do was work myself into a new state of mind. I decided I should shut curiosity out of my mind and not let it in again. What if Carol did know about an old murder? What if Steve Corbett was excited about it? I felt, I knew, that we were moving toward something. Something was going to happen; we were approaching some climax now. It would come in spite of any hindering I could do; I couldn't stop it.

The four of us sat on the porch while the loons' ululating calls came and went, sadly despairing. As I might have guessed, Carol didn't like the loons. A little later on I thought I heard a boat go out. Steve Corbett's eyebrows lifted, almost imperceptibly, but I thought it a mark that he had heard, too. The Lewises left about half-past nine.

"Go to bed," Steve Corbett ordered, as soon as they were off the porch.

Their footsteps had hardly died away before he was gone with the padlock fixed behind him; I stayed listening a while but the familiar night sounds came and nothing else. I who had fled in such instinctive terror from the island felt no instinctive terror then. I went to bed; what I lay thinking about had very little to do with Carol Lewis or Mrs. Rudeen either, and after a while I slept.

I woke with Cottie's head in my neck; he must have wakened early and crept into my bed for his last nap. When he roused he was in a rarely affectionate mood; he rolled against my shoulder, warm and small, murmuring in content. He trusted me, loved me.

These Corbett men. It wasn't enough that I should have to like one of them.

The morning outside was radiant. Steve Corbett was still sleeping. When Cottie had had his breakfast I took him down to the beach. The morning breeze was still brisk and chill with the crispness of cold water from the lake depths. We ran southward down the beach with our faces to the wind and brought up glowing and warm only when the cattails blocked us down at the southern end of the lake. Then we tramped back.

Cottie told me that we would both ride on his train when he got one.

At Loxton's we detoured to get the morning's milk on the way; on the side lawn we saw Mr. Loxton out hobbling about, trying to rake his garden over in spite of his difficulty in walking.

"Shouldn't you keep off that foot?" I asked. "It'll heal faster."

"It makes me feel bad to see my flowers go untended. And Elmer really doesn't have time."

He shook his head sadly over the neglected stretches of his garden, then remembered something more pleasant, and turned to me brightly.

"I believe I have good news for you this morning, Mrs. Corbett. You remember what you spoke to me about yesterday? That little difficulty has solved itself. Of course I did speak to her, but I did it in only the most friendly way. I didn't ask her to leave, at all. She went entirely of her own accord."

"You mean," I asked incredulously, "that Mrs. Rudeen has gone?"

He nodded, his cheeks as freshly pink as one of his dahlias over his good news.

"That's exactly it, Mrs. Corbett, exactly. She left last night."

CHAPTER TWENTY-ONE

OF ALL THE ENDINGS I could have imagined to Mrs. Rudeen's openly displayed enmity toward us and the Lewises, this was the least expected. That she should calmly and of her own accord pack up and leave. It just didn't fit.

I tried to make it fit. Tried, with one of those effects you get when you turn the bottom of a kaleidoscope, to fit all the pieces of what had happened into a new pattern that could include Mrs. Rudeen's departure.

I tried to see Mrs. Rudeen as an ordinary left-alone wife, a woman with few pleasures, spending her summers at the resort, becoming attracted to Harry Lewis, believing she was making an effect, growing insanely jealous when she saw his wife and his open devotion to her, throwing up her game and leaving in dis-appointed vanity and expectation when she finally saw it was no use. He might have told her it was no use. Yesterday, after that knife-brandishing scene.

Her watching me—well, Eldreth women with nothing on which to fasten their minds spent their lives spying on their neigh-bors, too. No one should know that better than I.

That plantain leaf on her shoe might have been coinci-dence. Her appearance on the island caused by jealousy over Carol.

Mr. Loxton was still waiting to hear me express my relief.

"She must have decided very suddenly," I said. "Did she say why she left?"

"Not to me; she didn't say good-by to me at all. I woke up when a car went over the hose. That was just after five, so she left early. When I went down I found her key and a note under my door. I've got that note somewhere here."

He fished around in his pockets, standing awkwardly on his one good foot, until he found the note in a back pocket.

The note I took was very brief and written in pencil, with heavily slanted tall letters that angled crosswise on the page.

Okay, I'll leave your lousy joint.
EDNA RUDEEN

I didn't know her writing, but there was no reason to doubt the authenticity of the note; the words were as characteristic as the Dutch bob.

Mrs. Rudeen, in a fury at being repulsed and reproved, had left.

John Loxton sighed. "I'm afraid she will never come back. She left the gate open behind her. She isn't the type of visitor I like most, but she was very prompt with her money. I wonder if I should advertise. Do you think that would help?"

I'm afraid I discussed advertising absently; I was in a hurry to get to Steve Corbett, and find out if this news meant anything to him. It was strange to pass Mrs. Rudeen's cabin and think of her as gone, but the Packard was gone, the windows closed, the oars stacked neatly against the house wall instead of lying carelessly in front of the porch.

The Clapshaw, Jordan and Willard cottages were still quiet, but Harry Lewis stood washing at his sink in crumpled pajamas, blinking at the sun.

"Hello there, early birds!" he called.

This would be interesting to watch, too. "We're one resorter less this morning, I've just heard," I told him. "Mrs. Rudeen has gone."

He asked, "What's that? Mrs. Rudeen's gone?"

As far as I could see he looked surprised but no more than that; he picked up a towel and came to the screen rubbing water from his face and neck and hands.

"I heard it from Mr. Loxton when I got the milk. She left early this morning."

"Well, I don't see the resort will be any worse off," he philosophized, and his voice dropped to confidence. "You know, I think that woman really did have a couple of funny ideas in her head. I put a flea in Loxton's ear yesterday afternoon. Maybe that had something to do with it. Carol won't be sorry. You folks fishing today?"

That seemed to be the end of his interest in Mrs. Rudeen. I wondered if Steve Corbett would be as indifferent. He was still asleep when we reached the porch, but he sat up electrically when I shook him.

"Mrs. Rudeen's gone. She left last night. Or early this morning, rather."

He was still half asleep; I'd caught him without armor. An emotion as openly shown as Cottie's came into his eyes, his mouth, the very dropping lines of his checks. He was flabbergasted.

He got out gutturally, "Say that again."

"Mrs. Rudeen left early this morning, taking all her stuff. She just left her key and a note under Loxton's door. I guess he talked to her yesterday about her unpleasant manners."

"Her unpleasant manners," he repeated, as if he still couldn't comprehend. He shook himself like a shaggy Saint Bernard, and rubbed his head against his hunched knees. "She's gone. Mrs. Rudeen. How could I guess that? God! I was watching Carol." The voice came smothered by blankets.

236

He asked listlessly after that if I wouldn't get out so he could dress.

If I'd wanted a reaction I'd had one. The only trouble was that I didn't know much more than I had before.

Except for Steve Corbett the whole resort seemed to brighten at Mrs. Rudeen's going. While I was washing dishes the Lewises waved to me from a boat headed north toward Little Sister; he was rowing, she trolling offshore with little screams and jerks as her bait caught on underwater weeds. They looked gay and carefree. The Clapshaws came along to our door with their shovels and buckets to ask if we weren't coming early to the beach on this lovely morning.

"Did you hear that Mrs. Rudeen went?" Mrs. Clapshaw asked. "You know, I sometimes wonder if that woman isn't a foreigner of some sort. Definitely she isn't an American type. Joanie! Don't poke holes in that screen! Children are so energetic, aren't they?"

We left hastily before Joanie's energy ruined the door. Earl Jordan met us at the head of the center stairs, in his fishing slacks and turtle-neck jersey, to stroll down with us.

"Mrs. Corbett," he started cajoling, "you never give me any breaks. Here I am, a lone, forlorn bachelor. Mrs. Clapshaw, you see how I pine, night after night, don't you? I must have fallen arches or B.O. Couldn't you go fishing with me today, Mrs. Corbett?"

"I'll watch Cottie." Mr. Jordan was a pet of Mrs. Clapshaw's; he ran errands for her, and sometimes took Bits and Joanie rowing so she could have an hour's rest. "Why don't you run along?"

"It takes endurance to watch Cottie."

Steve Corbett, who had disappeared down the track after gulping a hasty breakfast, came slowly down the stairs to stand looking at the lake.

"Your wife's a stubborn piece, Corbett," Jordan called to him,

237

smiling. "She won't go fishing with me. How do you handle her? You must have made headway with her once."

Cottie's father turned with his easy, liquid movement. "I'll take her fishing myself. Just the thing I had in mind. Come along, Mamma. Get the kid."

"What do you mean, stealing my stuff?" Jordan objected. "You never took her fishing before."

"Thanks for the idea. I was wondering what to do today. Hey, kid, want to catch some fish?"

"Tsiss!" Cottie agreed gleefully, scampering up from his sand house.

"Fish," I corrected as the three of us went up the beach. As soon as we were out of earshot I asked, "Did you find out anything about Mrs. Rudeen?"

He asked coolly, "What is there to find out?"

True enough. Against the finality of Mrs. Rudeen's packing up and leaving, questions were fairly useless.

"The sheriff might want to know. He questioned her quite closely about why she was watching the island when we found the money."

"I called the sheriff from Loxton's. He said the case was closed. He didn't have anything to hold her on."

So that was what he had gone to do.

We went fishing like any pleasant family. I sat on the back seat with Cottie, holding one arm around the boy and trolling with the other, a viciously hooked bassarino on the end of the line. We went north as the Lewises had, but Steve Corbett's object wasn't to catch them; instead of going through into Little Sister, he swung the boat as we neared the cattails and wild rice that filled the shallows between the two lakes. Slowly he rowed back and forth along the north end of Big Sister.

If silence is what fishing takes we had it; only Cottie piped up now and then. He lay crosswise on my lap, fascinated by the life visible beneath the thin sheet of water: the swaying, ferny water weeds, the darting bugs and sunfish, the rocks and snails and gasping clams. Halfway past the little island the rod jerked in my hands and Steve Corbett, reaching to take Cottie from my lap, said I had a fish.

I waited to be told what to do next. Eldreth has small lakes near by; I'd caught sunfish with poles, but rods with reels on them were outside my experience.

"What do I do?"

"Bring him in! Jerk! Start reeling!"

I jerked and started reeling; the fish jumped in the direction of my line, an arched silver back that looked gigantic. I tried reeling faster, but the pull became so heavy I could barely move it; not just the fish pulling, the mechanism didn't work.

Steve Corbett said in disgust, "You'll lose him now."

I dropped the rod to pull the line in hand over hand. A long time. Then the fish flew out of water again, near the boat this time. I jerked while he was in the air, and he swung over the boatside to leap flapping on the tin bottom.

Cottie was screaming, bounding in his father's arms to keep away from the fish.

"Tsiss! Jumps! Look, Mamma! Jumps!"

Mamma looked. Mamma was in the bottom of the boat herself, panting.

I slid hastily back to the seat. "I got him," I said.

Steve Corbett was roaring with laughter. "Where's your rod?"

I'd forgotten the rod; I looked for it now. The line leading from the bassarino hooked to the fish disappeared over the side of the boat. I grabbed at it and pulled in all the line I'd pulled in before

239

and a lot more, while Cottie's father put his face down into his son's hair and kept on laughing.

I hadn't lost the rod; it came up at last, heavily stuck with slimy weeds.

"I didn't lose your rod, either. Even the reel's on it. It'll be as good as new, won't it?"

He lifted his head, gasping. "I paid seventeen bucks for that rod and reel. It would have been worth it. God, you were grim. Oh lord, I'm beginning to think maybe women are human. Did you know you slung that rod over the side of the boat?"

Looking down at that protesting fish I saw how funny I must have been, and laughed, too.

That was the incident that started the amity with which we did the three days' fishing ahead of us, the fishing that was to end when that revealing bundle rose on the end of Steve Corbett's line.

I didn't know that on that first day. Then I noted only that Steve Corbett took on a different manner. He grew quiet again, but it wasn't the distant quiet it had been. He made casual remarks about the resort people, the trees on the island; he talked to Cottie about the lives of fish. He asked if my hands were cut by the line, and tore his handkerchief in two to tie them up.

In the afternoon we went fishing again, stopping only to drop off at the island for another hour of target practice.

At night he went out again. The next day we resumed the fishing, Cottie and I going along in the morning, Steve Corbett going alone in the afternoon. Always he kept along the same line—the northern end of Big Sister. He caught six bass that second day; we passed them around the resort. The night was like all other nights.

On Saturday for the third morning we went fishing again. He'd moved his ground a little; he kept the boat going back and forth just behind the little island. Cottie was tired of underwater life by now; he wanted to go shooting on the island, but his father refused firmly.

"If you don't want to fish we'll leave you with Mrs. Clapshaw."

Cottie hastily worked up a new interest in marine matters.

That was the morning Steve Corbett asked me why I'd never married, and I found myself telling him about Eldreth. About the days when I thought my life would always be wonderful. I had the most dates of any girl in high school, and I became engaged to Ted Williams, the only boy in the class going on to college. I didn't mind waiting while he went to college—why should I? I went to library school for one year myself. And then I got a job in the home-town library, where my mother was on hand to spoil me, and I had two letters a week from Ted, and his visits almost every week end. Three years of that. Ted Williams even came to spend the week end before his graduation with me. And then the day after he graduated I got a short note saying he was sorry, but he was married.

My listener didn't offer consolation. He said, "What of it? I'll bet he turned out to be a pill," and went on to talk about his own life.

He'd been so quiet about his background before that I could hardly believe my ears. He said his father had been a mining engineer and that he'd spent his childhood in the Andes tended by Indians; his mother had died when he was small.

"Death isn't so much in the Andes." He'd said that once and called it back as a slip.

He'd been sent up North to a private boys' school, and then to a technical college. He'd played football at both places. It was at the prep school that he'd gotten the scar in his cheek—a cleated heel caught him on the cheekbone, and the doctor had to dig for bone splinters.

An injury caused by football—was that the origin of the

hollow that had helped to make him seem so mysterious to me? A bullet, too, might have caused such an injury.

After college he'd had two years on a tramp steamer. That was where he'd learned the rolling sailor's walk. It was, he said, a steamer making South American ports, Rio and Barranquilla and Puerto Cabello. He told about those ports until I could smell the very rotting bananas on their wharves and the coffee in their warehouses and the acrid cheap alcohol of their drinking dens. Even Cottie sat up to listen, fascinated and round eyed.

"I quit the steamer when my dad died," he ended. "I came up here and got a job."

He stopped there. He didn't tell of meeting Cottie's mother, of how he had married her, lost her.

That story Carol had told and that had so excited him—I tried to see where it could fit into his life, and failed. That is, if the story he told today was true. I tried to think this might be camouflage to cover up his real life, but he had told it with that reminiscent fondness that goes with your real past and not with a lie. He had sat with his rod seemingly forgotten in his hands, his eyes as well as his voice holding that affection for things past.

And he added evidence of truth.

"You can hold your tongue when you want to, Janet. Don't let my past leak out; it might not be so good for the kid."

He hadn't said any more about having been in Mexico.

I thought how easy it would be to like him unreservedly if this were what he really was.

And then the rod bent for a second time that morning—he'd caught one fish before we started talking. This was no fish; the line stayed fast.

"You're just snagged," I told him, maneuvering the boat. I was having a turn at the slow rowing.

242

"That's about it." He was turning the reel with effort; there was no pulling as a fish pulled, but the line was coming in.

"You must have a log," I went on. Remarks as simple as that were permissible in the new atmosphere.

It wasn't a log. When what he'd caught came sucking to the surface it was a muddy mass as big as a water pail. Cottie twisted to watch, exclaiming. His father wound his legs around him to hold him more securely, but his eyes, too, were on the muddy mass.

"I can see your bait; it's caught in the top."

He didn't reach for the bait; he let the mass lie on water level, and with his left hand swished it slowly back and forth in the water. Mud floated away.

What I saw made me start forward, dropping the oars.

Inside the mud was a bundle of cloth. A bundle of cloth, and the outside cloth was a blue, green and orange print.

There wasn't a single possibility of mistaking what that print was. It was Mrs. Rudeen's Mexican crash dirndl.

I had just one instant in which to see it; in the next instant Steve Corbett's hands jerked the leader in two. The bundle plopped toward bottom taking his bait with it.

"Wait," I said. I felt as if weight pressed downward on my head. "Mrs. Rudeen. That——"

He hissed at me, "The kid's in the boat."

The whole world rocked with the boat as I stared at him.

He was back at being what he had been before these last three days. The eyes had receded into distant flints, the hollow was shallow and red in a muscle that seemed to rise and bunch under it, the head and shoulders hunched forward as if he were ready to spring at me.

My mind must have been working somewhere because it was sending out words.

"I can't keep quiet. Something's wrong. Why would she throw her clothes away?"

Not my mind but something in his fierce face told me one circumstance under which Mrs. Rudeen's clothes might have been thrown into the lake.

CHAPTER TWENTY-TWO

I FOUND OUT then how I had allowed myself, during those three days of amity, to let my suspicions of Steve Corbett be stilled.

The shock hit full. Somehow the oars came in my hands again and I sat clutching them as if they were a support. I felt the contact of my mouth rubbing across my knuckles, but I couldn't see anything; my head was too crowded by that welling wave of shock.

A loud voice said over my head, "Here. Get back. I'll row."

As he pushed me toward the back seat I felt around blindly for Cottie; when I didn't find him I came to enough to see that he was now sitting on the floor of the boat between his father's legs, with the oar handles moving rhythmically over his head.

"Pull yourself together," the voice ordered. "Take that line— hold the rod and pretend you're trolling as soon as we get around the island."

Mrs. Rudeen. Dead. Murdered.

When it was Mrs. Rudeen I had thought was the danger. When it was Mrs. Rudeen I had thought was the stalker, not the stalked. The spying. The plantain leaf on her shoe. The gestures with the knife. Her visits to me, her wanting us to leave.

I had interpreted all those as indicating that Mrs. Rudeen was involved in something, that she might be guilty of Al Sprung's death. And now, her clothes came up out of the lake into which they had been thrown, as an indication that she would never need clothes any more.

MABEL SEELEY

I said aloud, "I can't understand it. She—I thought if any-one she——"

"Cut it."

"Hoxie Moebbels didn't do this. He's dead now."

"Be quiet." The words came from between lips as flat and straight as sled runners. "If we've got to talk we'll do it alone."

We rowed all the way back to shore in the heavy ensuing silence; I crouched in the bow trailing that baitless line. He took me directly from the shore to our cottage, a hand under my elbow; I felt that if I tried to get away he'd have prevented me forcibly. It didn't escape me that he kept between me and the door while lunch was being made and eaten, and Cottie hurried off to his nap.

I said directly when I came back to the porch, "That bundle was big enough to hold seven or eight dresses. There couldn't have been any reason for putting all those clothes in the lake—except one."

He said, "I haven't thought of more than one."

"She's dead. Murdered. And this time there isn't a trace."

That was what had struck at my mind like a whiplash raising a weal, as soon as I guessed that Mrs. Rudeen was dead.

That was what I had thought after Al Sprung was murdered, that if Steve Corbett had done it there wouldn't have been a sign.

I said, "You can't hide murder. The sheriff will have to know. I'm leaving now to tell him."

He stood with his back to the screen door; I walked steadily forward to push past him. But he advanced to meet me, taking my arms in hands like steel clamps, pushing me backward until I sat upon his cot.

"Listen." Red had drained out of his face, leaving it an even brown except for the hollow, which stood out completely white. "You aren't going to tell anybody right now about what you saw me

246

fish out of that lake. I've got a reason for what I'm doing. I've spent an entire year getting to where I am right now. You're not going to spoil my game. Get that?"

"You can't possibly keep me from talking."

"I can try," he said. "Look at this." The paper he dropped to my lap came from his shirt pocket; a note folded twice.

I opened it, curious to see what he thought could hold me. The words in the note were handwritten, in ink.

"In case of death or any other misadventure which will make it impossible for me to continue the guardianship of my son, known to her as Cottie Corbett, the said son is to pass to the guardianship of Janet Ruell of Eldreth, Minnesota, to be her ward exclusively."

"STEPHEN CORBETT"

He said as I was reading, "That's just to show you how much trust I put in you."

Cottie. Mine in case—but he couldn't possibly hope to bribe me. I said so.

His answer was impatient. "It's not a bribe. What's more, I don't expect to get myself killed or jailed. Certainly I don't expect to go to jail for murdering Mrs. Rudeen. *I didn't murder her.*"

That was what he had said about Al Sprung.

I said reasonably, "If you didn't, then why do you want it hidden?"

"Look," he said. "All I'm asking is delay. After I've got what I want I don't care what comes out."

"When will that be?"

"Not long now. A few days. It can't hold out much longer." He was pleading, but pleading with all his secrets held, refusing to let what was hidden come to light.

247

My mind said that holding back information for a few days wasn't as bad as keeping it hidden forever. And then it asked why I always seemed to fall in with his wishes. I got no answer from myself on that.

"Not long," he went on pleading. "I'll let you know when you can talk."

I said slowly. "You say you didn't kill Mrs. Rudeen. Do you know who did?"

"Yes, I know who did."

I cried, "But it's all so useless! If you know someone else murdered Mrs. Rudeen, then why shouldn't I tell?"

He warned my rising voice. "Be quiet. Someone might be listening. I want something else to happen first. You can't worry about Mrs. Rudeen; she had murder coming. Sometime you'll know how well she had murder coming. The minute I have what I want, then the whole thing can blow."

He talked a long time, threatening very little, cajoling a great deal, never openly referring to the note. But always the note was right there in my lap. It, too, was a link. A link joining us. He was giving me Cottie in case anything happened to him.

I didn't doubt that if nothing did happen to him, then he would blithely take Cottie when his vacation was up, and I'd never see him again. But I pushed that doubt out of my mind.

The face I looked at was insistent and unyielding. In the end I promised not to tell about the clothes for a few days.

He went out then, leaving the door open as if once I had promised I couldn't possibly break my word. I went to put the note in the safest place I had—my handbag; that done I returned to the porch to think. I had promised not to tell about the clothes—for a few days. But I hadn't promised not to look into things myself.

I told Steve Corbett so when he came back.

"I don't suppose you could tell me who murdered Mrs. Rudeen—you say you know."

He came forward, pushing tobacco into his pipe. "I wouldn't think of it."

"And *why* was she killed? Do you know that, too?"

He sat down in one of the beach chairs, his face immediately gloomy.

"No. That's one of the things I've got to find out. I don't know where she comes in——" He stopped abruptly, as if he'd said too much.

"Mrs. Rudeen seemed to hate Carol Lewis. And me, for that matter. But who hated her?"

He wasn't being light now. "Have you thought of Lewis? She seemed to be making a dead set on him."

"That's so inadequate. He could just tell her to stop bothering him."

"Unless she had something on him. There's that possibility."

"What?"

"That's to be discovered."

"The murder must have been done the afternoon or evening before she disappeared. I saw her for the last time about noon. She was standing in front of the Lewis cabin making gestures at Harry Lewis with that knife."

"I doubt if she was killed in broad daylight."

"I'm trying to remember that day. I was on the beach most of the afternoon with the Clapshaws and the Willards. You were fishing. In the evening the Lewises came over."

He went on from there. "About eight o'clock. I've gone over this, too. They stayed until after we heard that boat. I suppose you remember hearing oars splash while we sat here with the Lewises that night?"

249

I hadn't, but I did then. I saw the connection.

"If that was someone throwing Mrs. Rudeen's things away— it couldn't have been Carol or Harry Lewis. They were right here."

"Exactly. It annoys me, too." He said that without apparent reason that I could see.

"You left as soon as the Lewises left," I accused directly. "You stayed out all that night. If you didn't kill Mrs. Rudeen, why didn't you see or hear what was going on? There must have been some activity. The car, the body."

He said with a groan, "I was watching the Lewis cabin. Carol, that's who I was concentrating on. I didn't pay any attention to anything else, didn't go anywhere else."

Was that the explanation of his night absences—was he out in the resort waiting for something to happen? Could he actually have been watching Carol's cabin so closely that he missed seeing or hearing the disposal of Mrs. Rudeen's body?

I shivered. "I wonder if she'll be found. Al Sprung was. Or if she's in the lake. There aren't any more dummies hanging. Cottie won't be going in the lake anymore."

"No," he said. "I think——"

But he didn't tell me what he thought. He went into one of his absences, roused himself out of it finally to be brisker, more sardonic.

"Would it help you in your researches if I try to reconstruct the crime? That's good detective practice, isn't it? Let's see. Mrs. Rudeen is in her cabin, let's say. Or in someone else's cabin. Or else it's dark. The spot must be either secluded or dark. Someone approaches, or else someone is already there. It is someone Mrs. Rudeen expects or trusts, because she makes no outcry."

No cry. No, that night there had been no cry. I had an eerie wonder if Mrs. Rudeen's cry could have gone back two weeks in

250

time; if it had been her premonitory cry that I had heard the first night of my stay in that resort. If it had been not from Mrs. Rudeen, but *for* Mrs. Rudeen that I had felt that instinctive fear on the island when we found the money.

Nerves. I'd have to keep myself away from thoughts like these.

Steve Corbett was going on. "So then our murderer gets in his blow. It may be a knife again. Or poison. Or strangling. Something nicely quiet as well as efficient, because again no noisy shots or other disturbances mar the serenity of this lovely spot."

My hands squeezed together in my lap. Death, which must come to all people, had come to Mrs. Rudeen in those trappings of sudden shock and horror from which people have prayed to be saved since the first dim human intelligence conceived the idea of a protective being.

I said, "I thought Mrs. Rudeen was stalking Carol Lewis. And instead someone was stalking her."

He looked at me, and his eyes became very bright and intent. "Me, you suspect."

I went stubbornly on. "I can't think of a single incident in the time we've been here that could be interpreted as anyone stalking Mrs. Rudeen. Unless that's what you've done at night. I can't get away from it."

"Why try too hard?"

"Because you're Cottie's father." I said that steadily, too.

"Even at the age of plus two my son protects me. My latter years should be spent in cotton wool."

Somehow or other he had worked me into my old position of being baited; he was smiling now, but the eyes were as steady as pistol bores in merciless hands.

"You say you didn't kill Mrs. Rudeen. But you're a skillful liar. I heard you at the inquest."

"You didn't do so badly yourself."

"I was forced into a position where I had to lie."

"How do you know I wasn't? Don't you want me to finish my reconstruction? There my murderer is, with Mrs. Rudeen neatly laid out at his feet, quiet forever. I can't leave him like that."

"What's more, you aren't disturbed enough by death. It's in every word you're saying."

Incredible that this should be going on; that I could be openly telling a man how deeply he was to be suspected of murder, and that he should be turning my words aside lightly and almost gaily.

"Hush. I'm talking. My murderer plans to get rid of the body and all the personal effects and make it appear that Mrs. Rudeen is leaving of her own accord. The lake is handy——"

My mind jumped to something. "That may be a clue. If he put the body in the lake, then it's someone who doesn't know the legend about the lake returning everything thrown into it. Mrs. Rudeen should come ashore."

"Today is Saturday. Mrs. Rudeen disappeared sometime between Wednesday noon and Thursday morning. If she's on land she should have turned up before this. Al Sprung did. He turned up inside twenty-four hours. Remember, this is warm weather."

I shuddered, sickening, but he went unfeelingly on.

"What hiding places are there for a thoroughly dead corpse?"

"The woods outside."

"Mrs. Rudeen must have weighed two hundred pounds. It would take a strong man to shunt Mrs. Rudeen around. I, Steve Corbett, admit the possession of the most muscles here. That's the way you figure, isn't it?"

"Whichever way I look, you're there."

"'Well, let's say the disposal of Mrs. Rudeen is a point yet to be solved. The murderer does throw her clothes in the lake—we know that. He probably also threw in such other possessions as he didn't want. Except for an accident"—he paused and repeated—"except for an accident we would never have seen Mrs. Rudeen's clothes rise from the mud of the lake bottom."

Accident? Was it? Few things happen by accident. My heart leaped to a throb of hope.

"You fished across that same line for three days. Why?"

I knew before I asked that somehow he had known those clothes—or something else—would be there. I remembered the morning after Mrs. Rudeen's disappearance. Cottie and I had run southward along the lake shore with the wind in our faces. The waves in the lake that night would have carried anything they caught northward until it was caught by the sucking mud of the shallows at the mouth of Little Sister.

"It would fit," I said aloud. "If you just suspected Mrs. Rudeen had been killed, and wanted proof."

He laughed at me. "Mamma, you're weakening. That's not up to your usual suspicious nature. Let's let this case against me appear in all its blackness. The murderer throws the clothes into the lake. Next morning he notices the waves. So then, being a smart guy, he goes out and pre-empts the fishing ground where anything float-able would have floated to. The Lewises rowed north that morning, too, didn't they? He might not want the Lewises to fish up that bundle—or something worse."

I tried to think what the inside of his mind must be like, and failed. Tried to see reason in his talking as he did, and failed in that, too.

I said instead, "Mrs. Rudeen's car is gone, too."

"Oh yes, the car. Now what could our murderer do with that? One, drive it into the lake——"

"No rain since Wednesday. The tire marks would show."

"Bright, aren't you? Two, drive it off into the woods somewhere near by. Three—well, Duluth with its secondhand car markets is only forty-three miles away."

"How would he get back?"

"Another point to solve."

"There's her cabin. It might have clues. That's why the sheriff should be told immediately."

"With our efficient murderer? I doubt those clues."

"I could ask Mr. Loxton to let me see that cabin."

"Don't let me stand in your way. Only don't do it in such a way as to arouse suspicion. And in case you're starting out as a knight-errant to clear the name of your beloved's parent—and incidentally your own peace of mind—isn't there one clue you've overlooked?"

What he had taken me through was such a welter I felt I could have missed anything.

"What?"

"That boat we heard Wednesday evening. Not only Carol and Harry Lewis, but also *I* was with you on this porch at that time. I couldn't have been out there casting Mrs. Rudeen's possessions into the deep."

Again a little hope lifted, but a precarious one.

"Someone might have been night fishing then."

"Interesting to know if anyone admits it."

"I can ask. But the Flaming Door might have a new boat, too."

"We'll row over and find out. Anything to let your mind rest."

I didn't know if he was taunting me into making inquiries or trying to taunt me into a silence even more complete than the one I had promised. As I walked up toward Loxton's I walked wrapped in a sensation of unreality as if I walked in a dream. Could this be I, Janet Ruell, whose life had once been desperate only because it was humdrum and restricted? Could this be I—had I changed so much in two weeks that now I could see a proof of murder rise from the lake, and then agree to conceal my knowledge? Could this be I, going almost calmly about the business of finding out for myself what I could about that murder?

Because I knew very clearly what things I intended doing. I was going to see Mrs. Rudeen's cabin. I was going to find out who had been night fishing Wednesday—if anyone had. Check for a possible boat from the Flaming Door. And look for tire tracks or the drag of any heavy body toward the lake, the woods, or any other hiding I could think of.

I admitted, walking along that meandering hot cinder track, that what I wanted was proof that Steve Corbett wasn't the killer.

I tackled John Loxton on his porch first, putting all the casualness I could muster into my tone as I talked flowers and weather.

Then as the conversation lagged I asked, "Heard anything from Mrs. Rudeen since she left?"

He moved his ankle to an easier position on the stool before his beach chair, and his mouth made the round, surprised opening men's mouths make in the middle of beards. He shook his head.

"So few visitors write. And Mrs. Rudeen—the way she left, angry, I'd hardly expect to hear."

"I suppose the sheriff must know her town residence; in case anything new came up about Al Sprung's murder, I mean."

As usual he was so appalled by the idea of having that trouble revived that he could scarcely be dragged from the subject.

"I wonder if Mrs. Rudeen took any fish in with her when she left." I angled him away from Al Sprung at last. "I heard someone out on the lake the evening before she left."

"Night fishing should be excellent now. About Mrs. Rudeen I don't know. The boats are so far away. And my hearing——"

"It is quieter down here than up where we are," I went on. "Is the cottage Mrs. Rudeen had just like ours?"

He picked that up with alacrity. "Cottage one has an extra room. Would you like to see it? It's five dollars a week more, of course. But if you'd care to move, it's a lovely cabin." He produced three loose keys from his pocket, and held one toward me. "If you'd go alone—I usually accompany people who are looking at my cabins, but you'll have to excuse me this time."

As I went toward cottage one I blessed the sprained ankle that made it possible for me to see that cabin alone. The key and the padlock were just like ours. I stood very quickly on the porch where I had so often seen Mrs. Rudeen.

Whoever had cleared out the place had done a convincing job; it was cleared but not cleaned, exactly as Mrs. Rudeen would have left it. Sink empty, but covered by a thin film of grease and badly stained. Water pail half full, rusting. Basin with a half-moon of dried soap.

The cabin was longer than ours; two rooms instead of one led from the porch. I'd never thought myself slow moving, but I developed a swiftness that surprised me; I knew I couldn't stay long. The bed in the bedroom was unmade and sheetless, with pillows and blankets thrown carelessly around. I dropped to my knees to look for blood stains under the mattress. None. Upper side the same way. I quickly unfolded and scrutinized the blankets. Same result. One rag rug covered the painted-gray board floor beside the bed; the rug was unmarked, as was the floor under it. Except for the bed the

256

room held only one wooden chair and an ancient gray-painted chest of drawers; perspiration started on my neck as I labored to slide those stubborn drawers silently out and in. They were empty of everything except stray hairpins, dust rolls and a tack.

The living room next. A chintz-covered wicker settee in violent purples and cerise, a matching chair. A magazine-stacked table. I ignored the rest of the room for the magazines. It was so easy to slip something into a magazine, so easy for a searcher to neglect them later. Rapidly I thumbed them through.

Stuck in the back advertising and story-continuation section of a confession magazine was a scrap of paper.

Footsteps sounded on the porch outside; I had just time to crumple the paper in my hand before Mrs. Clapshaw stood in the door.

"Oh! It's you in here!" The eyes over the claw were bright with curiosity. "What're you doing?"

"I thought we might like a larger place." I told my story. "But I don't know now—I don't think I could get along with that settee."

"It is loud, isn't it? But look there. A new mattress on the bed. Much newer than ours. I wonder if Loxton would exchange."

I saw she'd stay until I left; she was soon looking into the icebox, cupboard and chest of drawers. Curiosity—or did she have a reason, too? It seemed ridiculous to suspect Mrs. Clapshaw, but by this time I suspected anyone.

I got in my questions. She knew nothing of Mrs. Rudeen's background, but was willing to gossip endlessly about the possibility of her having had an affair with Mr. Lewis. She hadn't been night fishing, ever.

As well as I could under her sharp eyes I examined the tan grass rug of the living room, the unpainted flooring of the porch. No sign of blood, of any scrubbed spots. Grease marks on the porch floor proved it hadn't been washed lately.

In the end I decided that the murderer hadn't left a mark.

I left Mrs. Clapshaw walking to Loxton's with the key and a pile of the magazines which she wanted to read. I went toward the barn to find Elmer. The milk room was empty; in the small barn room beyond I heard the steady swish of milk hitting a pail bottom.

It seemed safe. I drew away from the door to smooth out the paper scrap I'd found, a scrap torn from a cheap sheet of ruled tablet paper. The writing on it was in pencil; a column addition of figures at the top.

$$\begin{array}{r} \$\ 652.25 \\ 3500.00 \\ 126.36 \\ \underline{417.82} \\ \$4,696.43 \end{array}$$

Under that was a sum in subtraction.

$$\begin{array}{r} 8,000.00 \\ \underline{4,696.43} \\ \$3,303.57 \end{array}$$

Over and over on the sheet, sometimes straight, sometimes crosswise, another figure had been scribbled: "50,000, 50,000, 50,000."

And two words appeared in the same way: "Good business."

CHAPTER TWENTY-THREE

TWO THINGS about that scrap of paper I couldn't miss. One figure was eight thousand dollars. Al Sprung had had eight thousand dollars.

And the two words were not in the handwriting which had been on the note thrust under Mr Loxton's door.

Mrs. Rudeen had had—or had depended on having—Al Sprung's eight thousand dollars. And if this note was in her handwriting, then she hadn't written the note which was thrust under Loxton's door.

She had surely been concerned in some way in Al Sprung's death. She expected to profit by it to the extent of getting his money. That plantain leaf on her shoe had been a pointer in the right direction.

But now she herself was gone! I turned and twisted that fact, trying to fit it in with what I read from that scrap of paper. Had she murdered Sprung solely for his money? Then had someone coolly taken up murder where she left off—murdered her, in turn for the same money? It didn't seem hard to imagine Mrs. Rudeen murdering for money; that concept of her had been behind my instinctive terror on the island. But who was left here now to be that coldly acquisitive?

Steve Corbett—no. I couldn't think that he would kill for money. John Loxton? I couldn't imagine his neat precision breaking into violence; I had never seen any violence in him. Elmer? An innocent country boy. The Willards? They had turned out to be people with a perfectly good reason for being what they were. Mrs. Clapshaw? She had always seemed conventionally respectable to me. Earl Jordan? It was hard to think of his laughing good nature as having such a cruelly sordid side.

That left the Lewises. I didn't think Carol would murder for money. But what about Harry? There had been a hungry gleam in his eyes as he looked at the money found on the island. He had wanted to be "in on it" if anyone was.

Still he'd made no effort to take it. Harry's mettle seemed a little weak, to me. My judgment of Harry was that he might want to do desperate things to get what he wanted, but that when it came to actual dangerous action he'd falter.

And Harry Lewis was with us on the porch when we heard the boat.

I put the scrap of paper into my shirt pocket and went on into the milking room to insert my questions in Elmer's ears.

Elmer knew nothing of Mrs. Rudeen that I didn't already know. And he didn't remember hearing that anyone had gone fishing last Wednesday evening.

"I alw'ys did sleep hard, M's. Corb't," he apologized. "N'now, ever since that Sprung got murdered—well, the min'te it gets dark I shut m'self up in this barn 'n' I stay here. I wouldn't go out of here for nothin'. Sometimes I hear mighty funny noises, too, but you couldn't get me out of here, no sirree!"

I tried to make him describe the noises.

"Sometimes 't seems to me I hear people walkin' around here almost all night. Once somebody leaned somethin' up against the barn. And them loons, they sure make funny noises."

That leaning something up against the barn was probably the night Steve Corbett hid the guns.

The Willards tried to be helpful, but didn't have much to

offer. They hadn't really known Mrs. Rudeen. They hadn't done much fishing, and none at night. Marjorie Willard's eyes watched me sharply as I went doggedly on with my questions, but she couldn't distinguish the night of Mrs. Rudeen's departure from any other night.

Earl Jordan guessed another purpose in my visit, jumping to open his door.

"I can't come in; Cottie'll be waking," I excused myself.

"Then I'll come to you." He did, squatting on his doorstep and patting the stone beside him in invitation.

I hesitated, but sat down, too. He promptly took my hand.

"It's a nice hand, but that ring spoils it." He turned the wedding ring. "You know, Mrs. Corbett—What's your first name?"

"Mamma," I said. "I've forgotten I ever had any other."

"That the way it is? All right. Only—well, I wish I'd seen you first. If you ever——"

There wasn't any doubt about what he meant.

And I didn't feel anything but indifference. What was the matter with me? He was blond and scrubbed and handsome. Practically any woman would find his eyes exciting. His manners indicated that he was the nice young man Steve Corbett wasn't.

And yet perversely I had liked Steve Corbett in spite of all he was, in spite of all I knew against him—and if he were cleared of this new suspicion I felt I might like him again. Had he hypnotized me? What? I couldn't explain his influence over me. I just knew he had it.

It was difficult to work Mrs. Rudeen's departure and night fishing into Earl's conversation, but I got them in. The results were as negative as before.

No use asking the Lewises. They hadn't been out in that boat. But as I passed before their porch Carol saw me and called me to come in. Both of them had been drinking highballs, and both greeted me with such enthusiasm I guessed they were covering something.

"This is the first time you've been on our porch," Carol chided. "That's just terrible. Harry, mix her a drink. You'd think we weren't fit to associate with, or something!"

Harry Lewis, hurrying to mix the drink, had the relieved alacrity of a man being saved from a scene.

He said jocosely, "You aren't wanting to go back to town all the time, are you, Mrs. Corbett? You stay here and set Carol a good example."

So that was it.

Carol's mouth resumed a sullen droop as she sat back in her beach chair. "There's something about this joint. It gives me the willies. Those loons. I don't know; I just feel it. I wish the rest of that money would turn up. I keep thinking everybody has it. Oh, not you, Mrs. Corbett. Or your husband. He's a grand guy if I ever saw one."

I asked quickly, "Who do you feel jumpy about?"

"That Rudeen woman was a pain. What if she comes back?"

I couldn't tell her how unlikely that was.

I sat sipping my drink, listening to Carol grouse; she didn't pin her uneasiness to any other resident. What I was thinking was that unless the Flaming Door had a boat again, some one of the people I had just seen had lied about not being out in a boat Wednesday evening.

The porch floor was deep in litter when I got back; Cottie had spent the afternoon cutting badly mutilated people out of magazine ads. His father came to unhook the door for me.

"If it's tellable, spill it."

"No one here admits going out in a boat that evening."

He motioned me inside, away from Cottie.

"Get inside Mrs. Rudeen's cabin?"

"Yes. There isn't a sign of any unusual activity. And by the way, we're going to have to tell Loxton we don't want to move."

"You're not downcast enough. What did you get?"

I hesitated, but after all I had no reason for not showing him the scrap of paper. I brought it out. "This."

What happened to his face when he took it was exactly as if the inside of his head had caught fire.

He said, "God!" with a sort of awful delight.

Then he caught me by the elbows and kissed me squarely on the mouth. I didn't get any wrong ideas; it was the sort of kiss French generals give with a Croix de guerre. "I've got something now. So that's where she came in. I could have guessed. Good girl, Mamma!"

I pulled away. "That eight thousand—I figured it must be Al Sprung's eight thousand. Do you think she killed him? She subtracted a sum of money from eight thousand, maybe something she was going to spend, because what she subtracted was the total from that list of added figures. But that other figure—look at that. '50,000.' Somewhere she had or expected to have fifty thousand dollars or fifty thousand somethings. Doesn't it look that way to you? Those words would indicate that. 'Good business.'"

"Don't talk so much. I'm thinking."

"And where's that eight thousand now, if she had it?"

"That'll turn up. Don't worry."

"Someone else must have it now. Even if she did kill Al Sprung."

"How do you know she did?"

"She had that plantain leaf on her shoe. And the money."

"Maybe that eight thousand was a payment. On something else." He took my arm. "Look, Mamma, don't let it be known around how much you know."

"Can't we go to the sheriff with what we have now?"

"No. But I don't think it will be so long, now." He went with long steps to open the door for a clamoring Cottie, his eyes commanding me to be quiet. The paper scrap he laid tenderly between bills in his wallet; I felt in him the excitement I had sometimes sensed in him before when he thought things were going his way.

"I'll take my family rowing around the edge of the lake now," he ordered. He picked Cottie up and threw him to the ceiling with wild exuberance.

"Look out!" I shouted over Cottie's gleeful shrieks. "You'll drop him!"

"Fat chance!"

"I suppose it would be useless for me to add that the writing on that scrap is quite different than on the note Mr. Loxton got?"

"Quite useless." He went, still with the same abandoned cheerfulness, to gather up the oars and stride across the lawn, Cottie riding one shoulder, the oars the other.

I, who had found the thing that made him triumphant, just tagged after.

We worked around Big Sister first. Except at the bathing beach it was possible to keep quite close to the shore; most of the shore line was mud, with weeds growing close to the water's edge. The bathing beach was the hardest to examine for marks, especially since several days had passed. Impossible to tell if Mrs. Rudeen had been dragged across it to a boat. But at least the car hadn't been driven off there; the slope was so gradual that water would have stalled the engine long before it covered the top.

The car could have been sunk only where the drop was

sudden right at the shore; not until we reached the southern-most point of Big Sister was the drop that deep. I watched for traces of a body being carried or dragged through weeds; I watched, with a crawly shiver along my body, for the sodden roll that would be the lake returning what wasn't its own. Yard after slow yard went by. Mostly the shores were too thickly wooded for a car or anything else to have broken through, after we got out of the vicinity of the lodge. We made the same slow passage up the eastern shore of Big Sister, the boat rolling alongshore in deep water. When we reached the Flaming Door we hadn't seen a sign.

"One thing about Niddie." Steve Corbett looked over the ruined dock. "He lets things be. He doesn't clean up evidence."

Chunks of cement and splintered hunks of wood were strewn high on the shore; jagged outlines of cement blocks showed under water.

Cottie asked, "Did somesing broke?"

His father was delicately maneuvering the boat among snags to the beach. "It broke with a great big noise. I don't see any boat around, do you? We better have supper here; it's getting on."

Niddie himself served us. "No sir, Mr. Corbett, I never bought no other boat. No sir, I guess I'll just get along without boats." He rubbed his thin palms. I caught Cottie lifting his face from his glass of pop—unprecedented revelry, but the most innocuous drink the Flaming Door afforded—to stare at the progress of the Adam's apple with his mouth opening for comment.

"Could I have the rest of your pop if you don't want it?" I asked hastily.

After that he tried to swallow all the pop at one gulp; I had to pound his back to bring his breath in. Through that commotion Niddie spoke calmly on.

"It's been awful good for business though, Mr. Corbett. I

265

hope those gang guys don't come back, but they were as good as an advertisement to me."

When we left Steve Corbett was whistling. I didn't get the idea until I noticed the tune was "Little White Lies."

"Not so white," I said, as we got into our boat. I knew for sure now that someone I had seen that afternoon had lied to me about being in that boat we'd heard. Mr. Loxton. Elmer. Mrs. Clapshaw. The Willards. Earl Jordan.

The Lewises were out. I watched the shore line after that with feverish intensity, but Steve Corbett shook his head at me.

"No roads around Little Sister. Not one chance in a hundred that the car will have gone off anywhere around here. Or that you'll see anything else. She isn't in the lake."

I didn't like those last words. "How do you know?"

He said quickly and curtly, "Reasoning."

We made the entire round of the lakes. It took hours. Past the little island, through the eastern passage into Little Sister, up along the big island and around the north end of Little Sister which I hadn't seen before, back along the western shore and the western passage. Cottie tired of the hard-board seat; he sat on my lap, lay on my lap, and helped his father row. My eyes stayed on the shore line. But there was nothing.

It was dark when we got back.

"Still a chance the car may be hidden in the woods beside the road somewhere," Steve Corbett said cheerfully, his tone suggesting I wouldn't find it. He had stayed in exasperatingly good spirits. Sometimes I thought his eyes, too, had been watching the shore; sometimes I thought he was putting on an act. It was impossible to tell if he was for or against me. And he had been so sure Mrs. Rudeen wasn't in the lake.

He said we'd drive along all the roads near by in the

266

morning, and we did. He got up at nine, after a night spent out as usual. The morning was gray and drizzly, the first rainy day we had had since just before Al Sprung's death. I thought of that as we started out on our searching.

The car crawled the mile and a half between the lodge and the main highway; trees and bushes crowded each other so thickly on each side of the narrow sandy track that they looked ready to crowd out the narrow hard-held path. Nowhere was there a sign of a break, of a car having crashed through. At the highway Steve Corbett turned the car left instead of right. We explored little farm roads leading to all sides for miles; we doubled back and explored the road leading to the Flaming Door. I saw Niddie's startled face appear at the door as we circled the tavern and went on without stopping.

Again I went over, in my mind, the morning after Mrs. Rudeen's disappearance. I had talked to Mr. Loxton very early; he was the one who told me she was gone. I'd gotten milk from Elmer, and stopped to tell Mr. Lewis the news. Mrs. Clapshaw had come for us quite early, and Mr. Jordan had met us at the top of the stairs, wanting me to fish with him. As I left to go fishing with Cottie's father, instead, the Willards had just been coming down the stairs.

How could any of those people have taken the Packard very far, and yet have been back so soon? But something had to have happened to it.

I said so.

Steve Corbett said, "It's just as well you don't know, perhaps. The less you know the better."

Something about the way he said it made me feel he knew where the car was. I accused him of it.

He said, "The trouble with you is you don't know what to look for."

That was all my hunt for clues brought me. The scrap of paper, the knowledge that one of the resort residents had lied to me about being out in a boat, the feeling that Steve Corbett not only knew where Mrs. Rudeen was and who had killed her, but even where her car was hidden.

We drove nearly to Duluth before I gave up. We had dinner at a roadside inn, and when we came back I got out at Loxton's to tell him we'd decided against moving, while Cottie's father took the boy home for his nap.

"You'd have liked the bigger place," John Loxton told me, but he didn't press it.

Near the center stairs I met Earl Jordan and Harry Lewis, laden with oars and tackle. The day had cleared of rain, but the sun still hid behind clouds.

"Want to go along?" Earl Jordan invited. "Gray day like this is the best for fishing."

"Not best for me," I denied.

"Stop and see Carol," Harry Lewis suggested. "She's been driving me jumpy."

I did stop for a moment, to be met by a grumbling Carol.

"I've put my foot down flat. No more fishing. Get out in the middle, and if it started raining, would they come back? Not much. I was out this morning. Came back like a sponge left overnight in ice water. What's your husband going to do this afternoon?"

"He said something about napping with Cottie."

"My gosh, the way men sleep around here!" I didn't say there was a reason Steve Corbett slept by day. "Well," she added disconsolately, "I suppose I could just as soon take a nap myself. I didn't sleep so well last night. Those loons! The place sort of gets you—it kind of closes in. Harry can have this place if he wants it. I'm going back to town."

Later in the afternoon she appeared at the door, dressed and combed and made up, looking a great deal more cheerful.

"I made my mind up. I'm just about all packed and ready to go." It seemed to be this that had cheered her. "Harry can come along or not just as he wants. One more night in this dump is all I can stand. Of course I'll be sorry not to see you folks any more, but you know how it is. When you gotta go, you gotta go."

Just before she left something else crossed her mind.

"Say, you know that Rudeen woman? What was her first name?"

I recalled the note to Loxton. "Edna, I think."

Steve Corbett had wakened to be his usual attentive self in Carol's presence; I thought he became more alert at this.

Carol laughed. "That's what I thought. I had an idea I spoiled a pass she was making at Harry, coming out here the way I did. I guess that was why she took such a hate to me. Look at that."

She opened her handbag to take out a picture post card; the side she held upward showed the Maple Valley schoolhouse where the inquest had been, violently colored. Then she turned it.

"Look at that," she repeated archly.

The post card was directed to Mr Harry Lewis at a Minneapolis address; the message at the side was short.

Make it this week end. EDNA

"Look at the date." Carol was enjoying the joke. "AUGUST 10. That was the Wednesday before he brought *me* out. Was she surprised!"

I was thinking that there was no moral indignation in Carol—if she was Mrs. Lewis. And then I was thinking that Wednesday, August 10, was the day after we got out of jail, the day after the boathouse blew up, the day it became apparent that Hoxie Moebbels would be charged with the murder of Al Sprung, even if he was dead.

Tenseness was growing in Steve Corbett; it had been ever since she said she was leaving. I knew him well enough now to know it even if he didn't show it.

He said, "That's a swell joke on Harry. Where did you find it?"

"In an inside coat pocket of his, when I was packing. He must have forgot it, I guess. Men! Honestly, Mrs. Corbett, aren't they the limit, though?"

I agreed that they were.

"Just you wait until I see Harry, will I light into him!" That was her last promise to us, after her good-bys were said.

That, I know now, was the beginning of the end. As soon as she was out the door Steve Corbett let it drop, and came striding back across the porch, rolling his shirt sleeves down, buttoning the cuffs at the wrists.

He said, "I'll be going in to Minneapolis tonight. I'll take the six-thirty bus from Maple Valley. You can drive me that far."

CHAPTER TWENTY-FOUR

I REPEATED STUPIDLY, "You're going in to Minneapolis—leaving me here? What about Cottie?"

"I'm leaving him, too."

What I was faced with hit me. I felt as if I were being abandoned to tigers, and I wouldn't stand for it.

"I just won't stay here."

"I'll be back."

"I absolutely refuse." This wasn't a question I had any doubts about. "Cottie and I will go somewhere else the minute you're gone. I won't stay here alone after what's been going on."

"You've got to stay here." There was complete finality in a voice like rock. He came toward me, took my wrists. "Listen. Today my vacation is up. This is the night I'm naturally supposed to go back to town. I'll go up the line telling everyone so long. You'll drive me in to the bus after supper. Then you'll come back. Act as if nothing was different. But lock your door. Stay inside the cabin no matter what happens. Don't go out of here before eight o'clock in the morning. Get that?"

"I don't, and I won't stay!" I was frightened enough already, without the portentousness of his looks and manner. Something was going to happen that night; I knew it and was pushed into a desire for escape that was so strong I wanted to grab Cottie and fly as I had from the island. "You can't force me to stay. As soon as you're gone I'll take Cottie and drive away. You can't force me to come back here."

He groaned. "We can't all leave on short notice. Not tonight. Don't you see that would arouse suspicion? Look. If there was real danger for Cottie, do you think I'd leave him in it? You've got the gun, you know how to use it, too, now."

A little of my fright fell away. I didn't think he would actually put Cottie in danger.

Or would he? His face now was harder than I had ever seen it; the whole face might have been not carved but roughly chipped from brown stone. The rim of the hollow stood out in a ridge. There was some desperation in him. He still had my wrists; he dropped one and began stroking the other as if he wanted to hypnotize me, mesmerize me into doing what he wanted. The eyes weren't distant now; they reached for me, striking into me like spearheads.

He was saying, "You'll be perfectly safe, and so will Cottie, if you do as I tell you."

"But how long will you be gone?"

He hesitated. "My story will be that I won't be back until next week end. But it may not be that long."

"Why?"

"I have to get something done—something has to be done."

"Something to do with this resort? What?"

He dropped my wrists. His voice came freely and easily.

"Hello, kid. You have a good rest?"

Cottie was pushing open the bedroom door. His father went toward him.

"Let's you and I take a walk and see all the people. Daddy's going in to town tonight."

Cottie's answer was as immediate as mine. "Me, too."

"You're staying here with Mamma."

"No!"

"Mamma'll give you a cone as soon as I'm gone on the bus."

His eyes were on me. "You will, won't you, Mamma? How's about helping me pack, too?"

Wasn't it too bad I couldn't be placated by an ice-cream cone, I thought grimly, as I went to obey orders. Almost every distrust that could be held against a man I had held, at one time or another, against Steve Corbett. Yet now I objected instinctively and desperately to his going. Not because he was going—I told myself that over and over. But because I didn't want to be left alone in that resort with Cottie.

I climbed on my bed to make sure my revolver was as it should be. It was. But even then . . .

I had until Steve Corbett got on the bus to decide whether I would come back to the Crying Sisters or not.

While he was saying good-by Harry and Carol Lewis came to our cabin on the same errand.

"Steve just stopped in to say he was leaving tonight," Harry Lewis told me. "So we said good-by to him then. I hate to think it, but Carol here says we're pulling out in the morning, too."

"You bet we are." Carol seconded that heartily. "I think we'll go up toward Lake Louise, Banff, that way. I've never been, and Harry says he hasn't either. I don't know why he was so stuck on this old dump, anyhow. I hope I see you again, sometime."

They went off in the cloudy afternoon. In spite of the invitation I thought I'd never see them again. Neither one had said anything about the post card, and Harry hadn't proffered any reason for insisting on staying at the Crying Sisters for so long. Like Steve Corbett. He never gave any reasons, either.

Supper was eaten in an atmosphere of tenseness unequaled even by the time we waited to be arrested for the murder of Al Sprung.

Steve Corbett nodded a curt "You drive," when we went out

to the car, and I wheeled slowly by the cottages. The Willards and John Loxton waved from their porches.

The road outside the gate was firm and wet from the morning's dampness; the smell of the trees and all the other green-and-brown wood growths swept in through the car windows, sharp and refreshed. The woods, the scent, the car—all these were real, throwing into contrast the spring-tight tension of the man who sat beside me holding Cottie in his lap, and all the things that tension implied.

He talked to Cottie all the way in, not able to keep the tightness from creeping into his voice.

It made even Cottie wondering and uneasy. He asked, "You come back soon, Daddy?"

"Yes, I'll be back soon."

"I'll be a good boy." There was a heart-rending promise in it; the promise of a small boy offering everything he has learned an adult wants of him.

I saw the face, and the arms closing, and looked away.

That was the anomaly. That Steve Corbett could be all the things he was.

He didn't speak to me until we got to Maple Valley. The bus stood ready before the drugstore where it made its start, but it was empty. Even the driver was inside the store.

"Draw up in front of the bus," my orders came. "All right, kid!"

As I angled the car in to the curb, careful but quiet hands moved the boy to sit beside me. He reached for his bag as I turned off the ignition, lifted it over the back of the seat and stepped quickly out backward. He stood at the curb then, looking not at Cottie but at me.

"You have your instructions. Follow them. Go directly to

the cottage. Lock yourself in. Don't let anyone else in. Don't go out until eight tomorrow. Is that clear?"

He might have asked, "Is that clear, men?" That was the way he spoke. Like an army captain commanding a company action. Impersonal and flinty and expecting unquestioning obedience.

I said, "I hope it doesn't rain again or the highways will be slippery."

He repeated, "Is that clear?"

I nodded.

"All right," he said, and slammed the car door.

He hadn't asked me to promise to do what he ordered. He took it for granted that if I understood, then I must also obey.

Cottie was on his knees at the window waving. "Good-by, Daddy, come again soon."

The door of the drugstore closed behind the wide back that hadn't turned since it left the curb.

"Cone now," Cottie reminded.

I wasn't going to follow that back into the drugstore to get the cone there; I drove slowly down the main street looking for another ice-cream sign until I saw one over a café. I remember that the proprietor had freckled hairy hands, but I don't remember leaving the car or walking back to it. I remember driving around the town, around and around, trying to make up my mind what to do. Past the sheriff's house, past the jail, past the schoolhouse. Wanting desperately to go anywhere but to the Crying Sisters.

I was alone with Cottie. Or I would be as soon as the bus left. I could go to the sheriff then, tell him about the mud-soaked bundle. Tell him I was certain something was going to happen, tell him I could feel it. Tell him all about the chain, about the frog jumping in my plate, and Steve Corbett's hiring me as a nursemaid, and giving me the gun, and teaching Cottie to call me mamma. Tell him of that first night I had spent at the Crying Sisters, of the scream I had heard, and Steve Corbett's absence from the cabin. An absence he had kept up almost every night since. Tell him of the story Carol Lewis had told me, of the plantain leaf on Mrs. Rudeen's shoe, of the scrap of paper.

I went over them all, during that bemused driving. All the loose links of the chain. Links that he wouldn't know about; he knew only about the links in Al Sprung's section of the chain. Al Sprung's section was all linked together, or at least most of it was. The trouble with the other links was that I couldn't link them together; I didn't know where they fit. Still I felt they were leading somewhere, and that end was swiftly approaching now.

If I told everything to the sheriff reprisal would hit me. But not right away. And if Steve Corbett was proved an unfit guardian for Cottie—driving with one hand I fumbled in my bag until I felt the reassuring crisp edges of a note. I still had that transfer of guardianship.

I reached the stop sign for the main street again, went into low.

Down the street in the gray late afternoon two head lamps blazed on.

I asked Cottie, "Shall we wait here to see the bus go by?" I wanted to see Steve Corbett gone before I went to the sheriff.

"See Daddy?"

"If you look hard."

The lights began drawing closer, swimming slowly up at us like two round golden fish swimming up out of deep water. The bus was still in second gear when it passed, thundering and lurching. Cottie stood on the seat, leaning forward to plaster his nose against the windshield.

When the bus was gone I, too, was trying to stand, the

wheel pressing into my abdomen, my face almost to the windshield.

The inside lights of the bus had been on as it passed. Each person in it was distinctly visible. The driver, stoop-shouldered over his wheel. Two busty, important women, one in a front seat right behind the driver, the other back toward the middle.

That was all. No Steve Corbett.

Unless he was lying across the seat or on the floor—a position I couldn't imagine him taking—Steve Corbett was not on that bus.

I sank back to the seat, trying to see the meaning of that.

Unless he had caught a ride with someone—which I thought too unlikely to be considered—Steve Corbett hadn't left Maple Valley.

Then suddenly that particular link slipped into place. He never had intended to leave. If he had he'd have said so long ago.

He had announced his departure only after Carol Lewis had come to tell us she was leaving. That was what had started him off. The whole thing had been abrupt, decided then. But he had actually never intended to leave. All he wanted was to have me and the rest of the resorters think he was leaving.

For a moment I wondered crazily what would happen if I drove back to the drugstore to ask where he had gone. In this small town I should easily be able to find him.

But my imagination presented so vividly a picture of Steve Corbett being presented with a balked plan that I knew very quickly I wouldn't do that.

Again I thought of the sheriff. I would have one more thing to tell him now.

But Steve Corbett wasn't gone. He was here.

I had long ago quit trying to imagine what the purpose of his secret activity was. I tried now to imagine why he had planned this apparent departure.

The answer grew in my mind without any steps of reasoning behind it at all.

Something was going to happen at the resort that night. It was for that reason Steve Corbett wanted the resort people to think him gone. His plan was matured now. He was ready to act. And Carol's leaving was what had brought his plans to a head.

I didn't know I had made a decision, but the car was moving back toward the Crying Sisters. As if I couldn't help myself.

Odd to drive through the resort, knowing now that it was the setting for a coming drama whose character I didn't know, but whose outlines I filled in with horror. Al Sprung and Mrs. Rudeen had already been murdered; that seemed only a prelude now to what was coming.

Thin wisps of fog had formed; they floated between my car and the cabins as I passed down the row, as if Nature, as on the day of our coming, was acting to keep the activities of the resort hidden and secret. Porches and windows showed yellow oblongs of light; people had become dark shapes moving in the radiance.

I said to Cottie as the car stopped, "Run for the house; see how fast you can run," and he scooted, laughing.

I followed, laughing, too, but feeling I ran through danger even in those few feet. I'd driven the car close against the side wall of the cabin for what comfort the thought of its closeness would give me. We'd left the outer door padlocked, so there was a moment of waiting while I unlocked it; then we scurried through so I could hurriedly fix the padlock on the inside. When I'd done it I stood hanging to that lock with a ridiculous sense of security that I knew was false, remembering the flimsy screens and walls that were the only barrier between us and anyone who wanted entrance.

For once I allowed myself the trick of looking under beds, even the porch cot, but the cabin was innocently empty. It was while I was making that tour of inspection that I happened to glance at the cupboard top, and saw up there the edge of Steve Corbett's brown leather shaving kit.

He'd forgotten his shaving kit, and he'd be furious—that was my first thought.

The second was that it didn't matter. He didn't intend to be gone long. Only until his "game" came off. And I felt that would be tonight.

Cottie wanted a story; I hooked us into the inside room and told him one, trying to force myself to a sane calmness. I would take care of us both. I had the gun.

As soon as the boy was asleep I prepared for the night's vigil I intended to keep. I took the gun from my handbag, where it had been during the trip to town, and looked it over carefully again. It was loaded and ready. I was grateful, at that moment, for those afternoons of target practice on the island; I felt quite confident of my ability to use it.

I propped two pillows against the head of my bed, intending to sit there all night. In the dark, so that I could see anything that approached as quickly as it could see me. In the dark, so that my hearing would be more acute.

Just before I pulled the light cord I remembered the shaving kit on top of the cupboard. It was from that shaving kit that Steve Corbett had taken an auxiliary supply of money when he went to play poker at the Flaming Door. I wondered if he still had money there now.

As long as I was guarding Cottie I could just as well guard that, too. I unhooked the door long enough to get it down. Inside, I laid it on the bureau top. Curiosity is an ignoble impulse, but it drew my hand toward the zipper around that case irresistibly. I was to be well punished for what I did.

The shaving kit opened, and the envelope in the lid. Inside was not money, but something else.

That something else was one of the celluloid flower barrettes which had held back the sides of Mrs. Rudeen's square black bob.

I stood before the dresser, holding to it, staring at the thing that lay on the écru cotton cover.

One of Mrs. Rudeen's barrettes. Cheap celluloid flowers, pink and blue and yellow, strung along a celluloid clasp. It had been stepped on. Or else it had been crushed—in some other way. It had been on the ground, in earth. Bits of black earth were ground among the flowers.

I raised my eyes to a face in the mirror that I didn't recognize as mine at all.

Only one person would have hidden that incriminating object in that place.

In that moment I gave up hope that Steve Corbett was innocent of murder.

CHAPTER TWENTY-FIVE

I DON'T KNOW how long I stood there. I came to with an electric shock at a sound outside, an unmistakable near whisper against the deep, incessant far whisper of the lake, a sound I had heard many times in that resort—the slide of quiet feet over grass.

The room passed into quick darkness as I reached my hand to the light cord overhead and jerked; at least then I didn't stand silhouetted in light, a target for anyone who wanted to peer in.

The sound outside ceased.

I hadn't loosed the revolver in my hand. My heart had started thudding, when, I didn't know. Minutes went by, but I heard no other sound.

Perhaps I had been mistaken. Slowly I eased backward until I sat on the bed. The springs creaked when they took my weight; I hoped that anyone listening would think I had gone to bed.

But I hadn't been mistaken. After five minutes, ten, the whisper came again, came closer this time without pausing. It seemed to approach from the rear of the cabin, and to pass along the side wall just on the other side of Cottie's bed. In the dark the gun in my hand followed its course until it reached the porch door. It paused there. I had just the fraction of an instant in which to wonder dizzily what the prowler would do, to see a slit in the screen and a hand reaching through with a duplicate key to unlock the padlock; surely no one could hope to wrench the sturdy staples from the doorcasing.

Then I heard the unmistakable *click* of a padlock being pushed home.

I didn't have to look in order to know what had been done. Someone had padlocked the door on the outside, so I couldn't get out. Someone was taking no chances on my leaving the cabin that night.

I had little doubt who it was. It was Steve Corbett who padlocked that door on the outside, habitually. He was the one who had told me to go to the cabin and stay there.

I thought—he's here already. He's going to begin now.

And then I knew, sitting there on the edge of my bed in that doubly locked cabin, that I had been forced farther than I would go. I would not sit quietly by while a third murder was done.

My knees and my whole body had been shaking in a sort of spasm. But as soon as I made up my mind the shaking stopped. The indecisions I had had, the weak obedience into which I had fallen under Steve Corbett's influence—all these fell away. I saw clearly what I must do and how I must do it.

I must go immediately to Sheriff Boxruud to tell him that Mrs. Rudeen had been murdered and that some danger threatened tonight. I could remove one of the window screens to reach the car— once I had the car going I should be fairly safe.

The problem was Cottie—should I take or leave him? In an agony of indecision I hung over his bed. Taking him might expose him to terrible danger. If Loxton had the gate closed there'd be moments when I'd have to be out of the car struggling with that. Leaving him seemed impossible, too. One small child, alone in the cabin in the midst of that unknown and hidden activity.

In the end I decided to leave him. He never woke at night, so he shouldn't be afraid. And he was the one person I was certain Steve Corbett would not harm. As soon as I had reached the sheriff I would speed back here to get him.

The next thing was to get the screen of the back window off.

Pushing against the frame from the inside had no effect. Two things I could do—cut out the screening with scissors or pry the frame out. I'd try the latter first. Still in darkness I tiptoed to the porch for the ice pick, coming back to slip its point between the window casing and the frame of the screen. The frame gave a little then; the nails holding it were mere shingle nails, and when I increased the leverage the frame moved out easily. I didn't dare let it drop with a noise; it had to be lowered slowly and silently to the ground below.

If Steve Corbett was trusting to his outer padlock he should be too busy elsewhere by now to be watching me, but I didn't take the chances of being noisy. Still tiptoeing I found my coat and slipped it on, found my handbag and the gun. The handbag I stuffed into a pocket so I could hold my car keys in my left hand, the gun in my right.

"God help me," I whispered, bending over Cottie. "If I'm not doing the right thing, leaving you here, I'll never forgive myself." He stirred a little in his sleep, rolling to lie flat on his back; I felt his breath on my cheek in the dark.

Suppose I were making a mistake? Suppose the thing to do was to stay in the cabin as I had been told? But Steve Corbett had Mrs. Rudeen's barrette. Crushed and stepped on . . .

Without allowing myself more time for thought I slipped to the window, got my legs over the sill and dropped.

The night outside was still cloudy and lightless, so completely dark I couldn't see even the shapes of the trees. I stood a while listening, but if anyone was around, he made no movement then. Swiftly I passed along the rear of the cabin, keeping the hand with the car keys against its wall, holding the hand with the gun before me. I found the corner and turned, and when I thought I was halfway down the cabin side felt outward for the car. I'd driven it so close it was right there; my hand touched a fender.

The darkness around me was still completely quiet. I turned in a complete circle, trying to see any shape, any movement, around me. With the keys still in my left hand I fumbled for the lock in the car door, but I got nowhere; I realized I'd have to transfer the gun to my left hand a moment. I did it, trying to be quick, feeling unprotected. Again I felt along the slippery fog-wet side of the car for the door handle, this time with my right hand.

The sound was very small, but I whirled, dropping the keys to the ground in my haste to get the gun back in my right hand. Even that wasn't fast enough. Something quick and hard struck me down from the darkness right at my side.

My head seemed to be hanging, and the world rocked from side to side as if it were a great rocking chair. But that was no comfortable lap on which I lay. It was hard, and my head ached with a dull insistent agony, and was wet. When I opened my eyes the blackness that met them was so complete I thought I must be blind.

I drew one hand up before my face to flex the fingers; still I saw nothing. But my hand had splashed upward through water, and water dripped from my face; my head and my hands had been in water, cold, rocking water. Something held me up under the stomach, something hard and flat; I slid backward until I was on my knees and my hands could reach and finger that support. It was wooden and flat. I felt along its end. Tin.

Not hard to know where I was. I was in a boat. A rocking boat. Boats rocked only when they were on water. And this boat was not only on water, but it also had water in its bottom.

I came a little out of the thick daze that held me, raising my face to look overhead. Still nothing but blackness—no. I could just make out a faint gray drift.

At least I wasn't blind. There was enough hope in that to

make me feel around the boat, trying to discover more of my situation. Water in the boat came well up over my wrist when I plunged my finger tips straight downward. A hand over the side told me the boat was riding much too low. No doubt about what that meant. The boat was leaking.

Slowly I twisted myself upward until I sat on the seat that had supported me when I became conscious. Bit by bit the events that had preceded my unconsciousness came back. This was the night Steve Corbett had picked to do what he had come to the Crying Sisters to do. I had tried to reach the sheriff, leaving Cottie.

Cottie! In a panting spasm of fear I fumbled from end to end of the boat, hunting him. He wasn't there. If he had been put in the boat with me and fallen overboard . . .

For a long time I knelt in the watery bottom, in such a craze of anguish I felt scorched. If that had happened to Cottie I was perfectly willing to crouch there, my head resting on my arms on the seat, until the boat went down.

Slowly a flowing ointment of hope welled up. It must be Steve Corbett who had put me here. And he wouldn't send his own son out to drown. If Steve Corbett was the murderer, his son was safe. I was the one he had to get rid of.

I could see, now that it had come, how it was inevitable that in the end he would have to get rid of me. I had known too much. He must have been near by while I was getting ready to leave, threatening to destroy his plans. And so he had simply acted to get me out of the way beforehand instead of afterward, when he would have had to get rid of me anyway.

I knelt there with the first burn of grief over Cottie dying away, but leaving a soreness in my chest that made every ingoing and outgoing breath a pain. For three weeks I had lived in Steve Corbett's house and cared for his son. I had lied for him, obeyed him—and I had liked him. Over that ridiculous weakness of having liked a man who in return could calmly send me out to die I felt a sort of wild shame.

I don't know how long I stayed there, numbly waiting for death. But death was so slow in coming. He must have expected me to stay unconscious a long time. From somewhere outside myself a slow anger began boring into my waiting numbness. That I should be sent out to die like this was cruel and brutal.

Suddenly the uprush of anger was swift. I wouldn't submit.

I suppose it was my instinct for self-preservation asserting itself even through shame; I suppose it called on anger to loose all the reserve strength my adrenal glands could furnish. Then I didn't bother wondering why; I only knew that returning strength flushed along my muscles as my anger flowed.

Water was deepening in the boat; I had been aware of that. A few minutes more and the boat would swamp and go down. If there had been heavy waves it would have done so before this; I owed the fact that I was still alive to the fact that the breeze had been light and the waves small. Acting still not on thought but on instinct, I moved to the back of the boat and began feeling along its bottom. I must hurry but I must be thorough. My hands slid from side to side of the heavy tin sheeting; they passed over dents and bumps and rust spots, over loose objects I didn't stop to identify, over seat bolts and the curved wooden framework of the boat. It seemed eternity before I found what I hunted—a bubble of water under my palm.

It was almost directly under where I had knelt for so long.

My dress was stubborn with wetness, but I got it over my head. The rip in the boat bottom was too narrow for me to force the fabric through with my fingers, but I folded the stuff to an edge and finally forced it into the tear far enough so that I no longer could feel water coming through. Any touch would dislodge the dress; I must watch for that.

If there were more rips they were too small to feel; I decided finally there was but the one. I sat back on my heels when I had gone over the entire boat, too stiff to rise, my chest still too sore to allow me much breath.

Water—a lot of it—sloshed back and forth in the boat bottom.

I thought that nevertheless I was temporarily safe. Unless a wind came up I could just stay there until morning, and in the morning I would be rescued.

But by morning Steve Corbett would have finished his work. He'd have succeeded. Succeeded in something he had tried to kill me to accomplish.

My anger said he wasn't going to succeed if I could help it. Even now, if I could, I would get back to shore to give the alarm. He wouldn't be watching for me to return now.

It scarcely paid to feel for the oarlocks; I knew the oars would be gone, and they were. The boat would be too heavy to row, anyway, half filled as it was with water. If I was to get anywhere I would have to get that water out. Those vague objects I had passed over as I hunted the leak—what were they? I hunted again. The first thing I found was a fishing rod.

I came closer to hysterics as I took that rod in my hands than I care to think about. I saw a scene as clearly as if it were on a movie screen—the boat out on that water on a sunny day, Steve Corbett laughing, Cottie dancing between his father's knees, and myself pulling the fish in hand over hand.

And just as clearly I saw in what manner I was supposed to have died. I was supposed to be a foolish dead young woman who, the moment her husband's back was turned, had locked the sleeping child into the cottage and gone off on a night-fishing trip on which, poor unfortunate young woman, she lost the oars in the lake and drifted until her boat snagged or swamped, and so she was drowned. I, like the twin Indian sisters of the legend, was to drift ashore dead, pulled by the waves. And everyone would say it was a natural death. There wasn't to be a hint of murder.

New spurts of anger spurred me on. I thought of calling out, but if I did, then Steve Corbett would know I was alive—he might get there first. I was sure of what else I would find in the boat, and it was all there. The stringer. The tackle box.

The last thing I found was the flashlight. The batteries were wet, of course; it was useless. I knelt there pushing the knob of that useless flashlight back and forth.

Poor unfortunate young woman nothing! I was getting back to shore if it was the last thing I ever did. And quickly. In time, if possible, to ruin Steve Corbett's games forever.

I didn't have much to go on, but I had something. I emptied the contents of the tackle box into the lake and began bailing. Bailing is supposed to be back-breaking work, but I didn't feel it. Only the soreness spread, until my throat, too, felt raw. Bend, dip, throw, with nothing around me but deep night and the lake, the lake taking what I gave it with a splashing protest. When the water in the bottom was down to an inch or so I quit. It didn't seem to take long. I wasn't tired; I'd been lifted out of tiredness. I got up to the middle seat and with the flashlight in my hand tried to paddle a little in the direction the boat drifted.

After all, there was land all around this spring-fed lake; I'd have to get to land sometime. I tried to remember where the wind was from; it seemed to me it was quickening; the push against my drenched body was colder and stronger. I looked where I thought the horizon must be, for lights, but if there were any they were hidden by the thick night.

I didn't know where I was going, but I was getting there; the water lapped and whispered that assurance against the boat.

The boat grated over pebbles at last.

I must be careful not to meet Steve Corbett now. Cautiously I put one foot over the boatside, felt firm sand underneath, not mud. I might be anywhere along the Crying Sisters beach. I pulled the boat up quietly; I'd want that boat for evidence. With the flashlight for a weapon I reconnoitered. There were still no visible lights, but it was late; I didn't know how late. Walking inshore I came to weeds before I thought I should, and then my reaching hand found a tree. The shore rose only slightly as I walked through more trees; I came into a grassy space and knew then where I was. The little island.

Washes of discouragement streamed over me. From the little island it was so far to any shore. And if the wind had taken me here then it would be dead against me going back—and I had no oars.

I was safe here. If I stayed here until morning someone would come fishing on the lake; I'd be rescued with nothing worse, probably, than a bad cold.

But by morning what Steve Corbett was doing would be done.

My mind wasn't working in its usual ways; I just seemed to act, moving in a sort of daze, propelled by a will from outside. I ran stumbling over the grass, hunting for the hut, falling, losing the flashlight, finding it again, running too far and bumping into trees. When I did find the hut I fell into it. The sheriff had torn most of it down. Only one corner was left nailed together; the other boards were strewn around the ground. It was the boards I wanted. I went quickly over them, accepting and discarding, until I had four that I thought might serve as oars. Nails tore my hands and arms, but I didn't stop to notice. I knew I couldn't fit the boards into the oar-locks and so could use only one at a time, but I wanted plenty in case of loss. When I had four I went with them in my arms to find the boat, bringing up short as the ends caught in trees, stumbling for a long time back and forth along the shore until the boat bumped me. With a splinter from one board I stuffed my dress more firmly into the tear, and then with all my boards inside shoved off.

The only way I could possibly keep direction was to point the boat's nose into the waves and not let it waver; the wind must have blown almost due eastward to carry me to the island. I dug my board into the water and then held it at the end of the stroke as a canoe is paddled. The water fought to push the boat into the trough of its waves; I fought back to prevent it. I became exhausted and went on paddling anyway; if I let up in my constant dig and hold the boat immediately swerved.

I lost that board, my hands too numb from grasping it to obey when I tried to grab for it. I shook my hands to get blood back in the fingers, knowing vaguely that they ached and burned; as soon as they moved again I reached for another board. That board broke almost at once. The boat lay awash now; I didn't know how much distance I'd lost, how far I'd drifted back toward the island. I dug into the water with the third board; the boat swung only slowly to repeated strokes. I felt that I worked without advancing, that I strained and pulled, wet now from the skin out, without getting anywhere, that the boat would rock eternally on waves that washed eternally to meet it. I felt that the lake moved but the boat did not; the boat stayed forever in one spot. I think I gave up any other eventuality.

Then sand grated under the keel. I hit with enough force to knock me to my knees. Weakness wanted me to stay there, but I couldn't; I rolled out of the boat into shallow water. The boat could wash where it would; I didn't stop this time to pull it in. I was late. I must hurry.

This time the shore was the right shore; the bank rose steeply before me. I started climbing on hands and knees until I remembered there were stairs, and moved along until I found some and went up, not knowing which stairs they were, the ones below our cottage, or below Mrs. Clapshaw's or below Loxton's. At the top I walked straight ahead, knowing I would reach some cottage; I came quickly up against a wall and felt along it to the side where there were steps and a door.

I thought again of calling, but again I didn't dare. Steve Corbett might be anywhere near. At the top of the steps I pushed gently at the door; it opened inward without hindrance. What cabin could this be, unlocked at night? Ours had been padlocked on two sides. The first thing my hands touched was a sink.

The sink was where our sink stood. It was my own cabin I had found. I ran, but even at the bedroom door I was sure of Cottie's light breath; he was there in his bed, safe, as I had left him. I had thought it would be that way, but even then I dropped at his bedside in sudden weakness and relief. Whatever his father was, Cottie was there, unharmed.

When I had strength to do it I found the back window. The screen had been replaced. I saw then what had been done. Steve Corbett had taken the outside padlock off. And then entered through the rear window, to remove the padlock from the inside, and replace the screen. Only why hadn't he padlocked the cabin from the outside again, when he left? That was unlike him. He must have been in a hurry.

I must hurry, too. I must get something around me; I was wet and in rags. I grabbed for the blanket on my bed and found my coat there, laid neatly at the foot. The handbag was still in one pocket.

And in the other pocket was the gun.

I knew how false any dependence on that gun was, now. It had been right in my hand both times I had been struck down.

This time if I met the death that stalked the resort of the Crying Sisters my death would be certain—unless I shot first. The killer wouldn't fumble again. And this time I didn't dare take time out to drive for the sheriff. I must get at once to the Lewises, to Mrs. Clapshaw and the Willards and Earl Jordan and John Loxton. Warn them.

My car was still beside the cottage; I followed along its side to the rear of the cabin, and from there to the rear of the next cottage, and the next.

The Lewis cottage was next. All I had to do now was make this one more cottage; from there Harry Lewis could carry my warning, get the people together where they would be safe. Unless Steve Corbett had already visited the Lewis cabin . . .

I thought at first the cabin was dark, but as I started across the open space I saw a thin pencil line of light along a window sill; there was a light on, with the shades drawn. I walked as quietly as a caterpillar and almost as slowly, weaving my head from side to side in search of danger on all sides of me, the gun straight before my chest and my finger tightly on the trigger. I was almost to the Lewis cabin when a voice drifted over me from beside a tree.

"Who is there?"

Only one thing kept me from firing. The whisper didn't come in Steve Corbett's voice. It came in the voice of Sheriff Boxruud.

CHAPTER TWENTY-SIX

MY FINGERS relaxed on the gun as the surprise went home.

I whispered, "The sheriff. What're you——" And then in the weakness of relief, of having won to safety and what I had set out to do, my knees gave way and I was falling in a coil at his feet.

He bent to me. "A woman. Mrs. Corbett," he whispered to himself. He was trying to pull me to my feet; I came up leaning to him for support, felt myself shaking against his body. I suppose I hadn't stopped that trembling since I was in the boat.

"You've got to hurry," I whispered urgently. "Steve Corbett. He's here. Something is going to happen tonight. Mrs. Rudeen must be dead. We found her clothes in the lake. Steve Corbett pretended to take the bus. But he didn't. I saw the bus and he wasn't on it. I tried to get to you to warn you and he tried to murder me. He put me on the lake in a boat."

I poured it out, a jumble of broken, incoherent whispers, my tongue tripping over itself in my haste to warn him, to get the things said that I had to say. I don't think now that he listened; he probably thought I was just half wild from worry.

He whispered, "Mrs. Corbett, be quiet. I know everything; I was warned. I must watch now and be quiet!"

One thing I got. He said that he knew everything.

Again relief swept me like faintness; I caught at the rough log ends of the house corner to hold myself up.

"Find him," I whispered. "Find him. Hurry."

He whispered again, "Quiet!" with a fierceness that might

293

have been Steve Corbett's. I reached for him with my right hand, the hand that still held the gun. He must have felt the weapon because he brushed it away from himself with his own right hand, and as he did so I felt the push of metal. He was holding a gun, too. As I calmed enough to sense anything I sensed first the listening tenseness around him. He was waiting for something, gun in hand.

I had found him, told him. Relieved of my duty, I found myself caught into his waiting, found myself listening, too.

For what? This was the sheriff to whom I held with the emotion portrayed by the girl in the old oleograph of the storm-swept cross. Sometime, somehow, Steve Corbett must have slipped. Somehow the sheriff must have guessed that something was to happen tonight. Or could he have been warned? Someone in the resort knew of Steve Corbett's night activities.

This was the Lewis cabin beside which we waited.

Whatever was to happen must have something to do with the Lewises. With Harry Lewis or Carol Lewis. Listening, I could hear faint sounds of voices inside, but not what was said. The voices seemed a little strained; they rose and fell. Once Carol laughed stridently.

Then all at once the cabin door flung open and I heard Harry Lewis calling, "C'mon, hurry up, we've got to get back 'n' get some sleep."

Carol came out, too. "Aw, what I wan' to say g'by to Lox'on for?" she asked. "I ain't even seen the guy all the time I been here. What I wan' to say g'by to him for?"

They'd both been drinking; that was what caused the loudness in their voices.

"I got to pay'm the rest of my rent. Come on along," Harry Lewis repeated.

"Aw right, he just can't get along without his girl, can he?" Carol asked coquettishly.

Their door slammed, and the voices receded down the cinder path.

The sheriff's hand came down on my arm. "You go home now."

"I can't. Don't you know? Something's going to happen." I was like a phonograph with one record; my necessity for saying those words had been so strong and accomplished with such hardship that I had to go on saying them over and over.

"I am taking care of everything. Go back to your cabin."

"I can't. I have to know what it is." Yes, that was the real reason I had to go on. The end was coming now, the end scene to which all the links of the chain led, the end scene that would fit all those links together in their proper places in the chain. Since that first time when I had seen Steve Corbett and Cottie together, a man alone with a little boy at Mrs. Golloy's table, my curiosity had been rising, until now my need to know the answer was as strong as starving hunger.

"I can't stay here longer talking." The sheriff broke impatiently away from me, to disappear in the way the Lewises had gone. I followed after by myself. Ahead of me the footsteps and confused voices of the Lewises still sounded with no attempt at concealment. I tried to count the cottages I passed. Sprung's, Mrs. Clapshaw's, Earl Jordan's, the Willards', Mrs. Rudeen's—the Lewises went past all those, walking on toward Loxton's. A light showed briefly on Loxton's porch and then was extinguished as the Lewises went inside.

I bumped into the sheriff again. He was crouched near the porch of Mrs. Rudeen's cottage.

"Hurry," I whispered to him. "You must hurry." It seemed to

me I had been hurrying a lifetime; the need for hurry was so great I couldn't stop it.

"No," the sheriff answered, low. "Wait."

His left hand closed again on my arm. No light came from Loxton's cottage; no sounds came, either. Overhead, clouds parted and a stray wisp of moonlight came briefly through before the clouds closed again. Hidden. Hidden in darkness. That was the way with this whole affair. I couldn't see . . .

The wind was chilling; I grew aware that I shivered in the wet rags under my coat. I knew that I was cold, but all I could feel was the expectancy, the heavy expectancy of knowing that something was coming and having to wait. Somewhere now in the black stretches of night around me Steve Corbett must be waiting to move, and right beside me was the sheriff waiting to intercept him.

The seconds fell, heavy, moist, dark, whispering only of trees and the lake.

At last a momentary flash of light, a much weaker beam this time, showed John Loxton's door opening again, and a big man coming out. A big man coming out of Loxton's house, into which Harry and Carol Lewis had gone. Could that be Steve Corbett now? He paused at the door as if he were locking it, then I heard his footsteps crossing the porch stealthily, with the sound of a big man trying to be quiet. He opened and closed the screen door; he must be coming outside. After that he made no more sounds.

No more sounds. As if he, too, waited. Again the seconds fell. Minutes going.

Then one indistinguishable sound that wasn't lake or trees. Quick and dull.

Immediately the sheriff was running forward, leaving me to stay or follow as I would. He went so fast I lost him, but I felt the currents of moving bodies around me, and reached outward until I touched a back. I think it was the sheriff's back again; at any rate I heard his soundless whisper.

"You got him good, Chet? We got to get that key off him."

Something thrashed on the ground. A panting, whispered answer came from Leegard, "I got him good. Here's some keys."

Some of the moving bodies went swiftly away.

I stayed. "Have you got Steve Corbett?" I whispered. "Is he safe now?"

Chet Leegard was breathing heavily at the level of my waist. He panted, "Mrs. Corbett, you go away from here. It ain't safe. Go away from here." Something moved again at his feet and he bent even lower.

I insisted, "Have you got Steve Corbett?"

"He's gone in the house," came his labored answer.

I didn't stay. I found John Loxton's porch door and opened it. Against the house door were men's backs and at the keyhole a tiny concentrated beam of light from a midget flashlight; a hand came into the light with a key, another hand took it, and a voice said, "Try this one." Still the sheriff's voice. The second hand turned the key in the lock, and I knew at once that the door was giving.

"We better take our shoes off," ordered the sheriff in the same soundless voice. The light was extinguished as they bent. They were very quiet about taking off their shoes, and I thought very slow. Finally the door opening under a noiseless hand.

Two backs—there were only two backs that I saw slip through that barely opened door. One I knew was the sheriff. The other—I began to be bemused, to wonder if the structure I had built was toppling. From inside the cabin, from beyond the two backs, came the sound of something falling, crashing.

Without knowing how I moved or how I got there I found myself inside the living room of John Loxton's cabin. The room I stood in had a soft light, coming not from above but below; between it and me were the two backs. They walked around something on the floor to stand with the sides of their faces toward me, looking down into the well of light.

I could see now without question who the other man beside the sheriff was.

It was Steve Corbett. And the sheriff was making no move to take him. The two men stood at the brink of an opening in the floor, looking downward, both faces so intent that they neither saw nor heard me. Not only light but noise was coming from the well below.

Irresistibly I was drawn forward to look, too. The light well was in the middle of the floor. Between it and me were the dining table and the crumpled rug; those were the objects the two men had circled.

I went the other way, to stand opposite the two men, I, too, looking down.

What I saw was an ordinary gray cement cellar, with a trap door on the side opposite the dining table. Immediately below me were three people. Harry Lewis, bound and gagged, struggling on a pile of sacks. Carol, gagged, too, and bound to an overturned chair from which she was struggling desperately to escape, her whole body convulsed and straining.

Standing over her, trying to get the chair upright but not to let her free, was John Loxton.

She jerked the chair, trying to catch his feet and overturn him; he jumped nimbly aside—on two feet. He had no sprained ankle now. With a deft strength I'd never suspected of him he stamped down, cruelly hard, on her wrist, and then at almost the same moment pulled the chair upward so that it was again upon its feet, Carol coming with it like a chairbound doll.

John Loxton's breath came in labored gasps, but even then he scarcely looked disturbed; his eyes were bright, fiercely bright, and the mouth above the little beard smiled. He swooped up a candle in a brass holder from the floor, to hold it over Carol so the hot wax dripped down on her bare shoulder from which the dress had been torn away.

I opened my mouth to scream, to scream that he must stop, but his first words halted the sound in my throat.

"My dear Miss Ridley," was what he said, in a voice that purred. "You won't try that again, will you, my dear? You'll be glad to tell me now where that confession is that I so mistakenly wrote, won't you, Miss Ridley? You're sorry now that you wouldn't tell Harry Lewis where that confession is, aren't you? He tried so hard to get you to tell, and you were so obstinate. He grew so fond of you, too. So fond he fought and fought to keep this from happening. But, after all, I couldn't give up now, Miss Ridley. I had to kill my own niece, Alice Maartens, that I hadn't seen since she was a little girl of ten. I had to kill Lulie Webster, too—you remember the housekeeper, my dear? Dear, dear, she was such a fool and caused me so much trouble by screaming. And all the time it was you, Miss Ridley—or should I say Mrs. Maartens—who had my confession. Lulie Webster told me at the last. Adam left it to you. My dear brother Adam. You'll be very glad to give me that confession now, won't You, Miss Ridley? Because such very, very unpleasant things are going to happen to you if you don't."

What kept me from screaming was the terrific shock of seeing at once two things so stunning that they swept aside, the immediate need for helping Carol.

The first was that John Loxton was James Maartens, the man of Carol's story. I no longer wondered who had killed Al Sprung or Mrs. Rudeen, or why a woman had screamed.

The second was that Steve Corbett was *all right*.

He didn't have anything to do with the crimes. He must be here—for some reason yet untold—to hunt James Maartens out. He hadn't been the one who sent me out in the boat to die. That must have been James Maartens, too.

I didn't even look up at him. I couldn't. I just stood swaying while something cool and sweet and healing flowed down over the inside of my chest that had been raw and sore. I took a breath, and air swept into my lungs easily and unhurting.

CHAPTER TWENTY-SEVEN

AS SOON AS I had breath in my lungs I made an uncontrollable sound, and John Loxton—the man I had known as John Loxton—looked up, showing me James Maartens' face.

Carol, in the chair, had her back to me; she was facing the sheriff and Steve Corbett. James Maartens faced me.

He seemed stunned, staring at me. He must have been very sure of not being interrupted. His face for a long time showed nothing but incredulity, and I remembered that he thought me dead. The mouth above the little beard stayed in a stiff circle; the eyes, as I looked down, seemed circular, too. His face was a triangle with three circles in it. I saw Carol's head sink forward on her breast; she must have become aware then that the two men were there, that help had come. Harry Lewis ceased struggling on his sacks. My eyes went back to James Maartens and became riveted there. Slowly through his incredulity realization was breaking, the realization that he was failing. As I watched the uplifted triangle of face it seemed to me I could see the very flesh decay, see it shrink and disappear, until the bony outline of a death's head showed—a death's head with a beard.

Behind him Steve Corbett spoke quietly. "That's right. It's all over, James Maartens."

Slowly James Maartens turned, until he looked upward at the two men.

"You," he said. The words whistled a little. "You. Why did you have to come here, interfering?"

"I'm Scott Kernan," Steve Corbett said. "I'm Alice Maartens' husband."

Alice Maartens' husband. The little girl who had been ten years old. I remembered Carol saying, "I heard she married a guy named Kernan."

So that was the answer for Steve Corbett, that was why he was here hunting down James Maartens, that was why he prowled the place at night.

"Alice's husband," James Maartens said thinly, the strange whistling note in his voice growing more pronounced. "Alice's husband. Of all the things I thought of, I never thought of that. He was away in Mexico. It's a whole year now since I killed Alice. Why should he come hunting me down now? And I could have killed him so easily. The boy then was her boy. I could have killed him so easily, too. I even knew there was a child. But this child had a mother. That was what threw me off. I knew Alice's child had no mother. Why do things have to be so confusing?"

As if he were complaining.

He was still looking upward at Steve Corbett, and suddenly he screamed shrilly, a high bleat.

"I had to! Don't you see I had to? They stole my money! My money I murdered my father for! They kept it away from me! What right did they have to keep it away from me? I couldn't stand it. I've got to have that money, you hear? You can't keep it away from me! That confession and those three women—that's all that's between me and my money—they're murdering me, why shouldn't I murder them? My money! My money!"

It rang out, echoing from that little enclosed space below. He raised the candle to shake it over his head. I remembered in Carol's story how the man James Maartens had run through the rooms of the old house in St. Paul, trying to run away from the inexorable

302

brother who was forcing him to write a confession of his murder. She said he seemed insane at the end. He seemed insane now, standing below us with the candle in his hand, arguing his mad defense of murder.

The sheriff must have thought so, too. His command came almost soothingly.

"You'd better come up here, Maartens."

The mouth opened as if to scream again, but instead said, "No."

I lifted my own eyes now to see that both Steve Corbett and the sheriff stood opposite me with revolvers leveled.

Steve Corbett said, "You can't get out of it now, Maartens. You can just as well come up here."

With rodent swiftness the man below darted backward until he was behind Carol's chair, crouching almost at my feet. I saw his hand snaking toward his pocket and realized that he, too, had a gun.

Carol was between him and the two men. He could shoot around her, but the two men couldn't hit him without endangering her; it was that risk staying their hands now. At one side of them was the trap door, at the other side the dining table; they wouldn't be able to shoot until they got around to where I was. They began moving but they wouldn't get away fast enough.

I knew that at the same instant I knew that I still held my own gun in my hand. I was at the end with James Maartens directly below me; Carol wasn't in my way. I saw a gun rising in James Maartens' hand; it was leveling not on the sheriff but on Steve Corbett.

James Maartens would be very glad to have Steve Corbett dead.

I pointed my gun and pulled the trigger. It did the rest.

Exactly as Steve Corbett, when he gave that gun to me, had said it would.

So much happened that night, and so fast.

I remember Steve Corbett hanging over Cottie's bed, saying, "He *is* all right," and again, "He's all *right!*" He rested his head for a moment against the small shoulder. "God, Janet, couldn't you have done what I said? He wouldn't have touched you if you'd just stayed quiet in the cabin."

He had begun running from James Maartens' house as soon as Maartens dropped, as soon as he had released his eyes from the murderer below and realized I wasn't with his son. The only thing he'd stopped for was to pull on his shoes.

I had run after, panting, calling that Cottie was all right, I'd seen him. What he called back as he ran isn't printable.

He relaxed a little when he stood up; I think he looked at me then for the first time. "My Lord, what happened to you?"

I looked at myself for the first time then, too. More particularly I looked at my hands. They were so torn and so crusted with mud and blood it was hard to see they were hands.

"Lord," he said, "I don't see how you pulled a trigger with hands like that. But thanks for saving my life. What happened?"

"I found the barrette in your shaving kit. I was sure you'd killed Mrs. Rudeen. I started to get the sheriff——"

"That barrette was my first evidence that Mrs. Rudeen was dead. I found it the morning after she was killed. Near the edge of the flower garden. How did you get those hands?"

I told him.

He groaned. "Maartens. He must have been afraid we were playing a trick. He knew I was around nights, but he didn't know what for. He was the one who came around here with that flashlight.

Tonight he must have watched the cabin a while to make sure you didn't come out. He had to be unwatched tonight. Look, I'll wash your hands. Then we'll go back."

"What's Cottie's name now?" I asked, as he washed my hands.

"Adam Scott Kernan. I began calling him Scott after . . . His mother called him Adam, after her father."

I wanted to ask about Cottie's mother, but he didn't offer it, and I didn't dare. I thought I'd soon find out now.

"I suppose you've got to come along," he said as soon as I'd put on the dry clothes he ordered. "I'll take Cottie as far as the Willards." He rolled the boy to his shoulder and stood a moment looking down.

He said, "I've done the best I could about your mother, kid," as if this whole avenging was something he had owed the boy.

When we walked back into the main room of the house I had known as Loxton's, Dr. Hansen was just straightening from bending over the day bed along the north wall.

"He'll do," he said curtly. "He can talk now."

The handcuffed and bandaged man on the day bed was James Maartens.

Dr. Hansen talked impersonally on. "Nice clean shot, who-ever did it. Through the right shoulder—just missed the top of the lung. He'll live to spend a good many years in prison."

The sheriff said, "Sometimes I think it is too bad we do not have electric chairs in Minnesota." He stood by the table, near the end of the open cellarway.

Near him sat Carol Lewis, her head forward on her arms, resting on the table. Almost touching her was a heap of objects— handbags, keys and jewelry and bills, a bankbook, and a little to the side a larger pile of bills.

The sheriff turned as we came in, pointing to that pile of bills. "There is the eight thousand we did not find before," he said sadly. "We find it in the cellar. And these things, too. I am afraid some of this belonged to your wife, Mr. Corbett."

Steve Corbett's hand picked out a brooch in petit point and gold filigree, and set it gently aside.

"I gave her this," he said.

"My men are digging in the garden as you said." The sheriff went gravely on. "They have already found Mrs. Rudeen. I have no doubt the others . . ."

Steve Corbett—I couldn't think of him by any other name—nodded, his face inexpressibly tired. "Under the flowers . . . I thought that must be the place after I'd gone there myself to hide the guns. It was a perfect place. No one would suspect freshly dug earth in the gardens."

He slumped slowly to a chair near Carol.

His wife. Cottie's mother. The mother who had gone away. She was buried under John Loxton's flowers.

Then I almost forgot her. When Steve Corbett sat down I saw what he had obscured. Against the far wall behind him sat two handcuffed men guarded by Chet Leegard. They were Harry Lewis and Earl Jordan.

Earl Jordan! Had he been in this, too? I heard my breath whistling in as Cottie's did when a wind hit him, and bewilderment wrapped me so heavily that the room blurred. "I got him good." It must have been Earl Jordan that Chet Leegard and Steve Corbett had struck down at the door of Maartens' porch; he must have been the lookout. But I thought he couldn't possibly have known what was going on.

And then I saw he had.

His face and Harry Lewis'—the two bore identical expressions of sullen defeat.

306

The sheriff was pointing at them now. "These two will not talk. But this one will." He walked over to pull James Maartens to a sitting position.

The man blinked once at each person in the room, and then began smiling. It was horrible, knowing what he was, to see that bland coaxing smile, as if he thought he were being clever and attractive.

"It will be such a pleasure to talk, Mr. Kernan, alias Steve Corbett. It will be such a pleasure to talk to you and the so charming young woman who is certainly not your wife—and to you, too, gentlemen." He looked upward at the sheriff and Dr. Hansen, standing at the head of the day bed.

"I am a wronged man, gentlemen, and—shall I say ladies? I am the victim of my brother's hate. It was my brother Adam who committed these murders, gentlemen and ladies, not me. Adam was a good man; Adam sat in the seat of the scornful. I am a delicate man. My life must be fine. My father did not appreciate me. My father and Adam—they stood between me and a fine life. And then there was another thing about my father. He wouldn't die. And when I helped him to die—I admit it freely, gentlemen—wasn't that a kindness? He was so old. And I couldn't let him live—he would have given all my money to Adam. My money, you hear?"

On the last words the voice left its pleasant honeyed monotone to shriek, "My money! Why couldn't you let me get my own money?" In spite of the bandaged shoulder he twisted the handcuffs in his lap with a sort of frenzy; I thought the steel might snap, and Sheriff Boxruud stepped quickly closer.

But James Maartens could still exercise control; after a moment he looked at us again with the smile, the eyes rolling a little, the pointed beard outthrust.

"It was my money, you know. A quarter of a million dollars.

In cash. It said so in my father's will. I defy you to say it isn't so. Even the newspapers admit I have that money coming. But Adam made me sign a confession I'd killed my father. He said he'd use it if I ever tried to get the money. He had three witnesses, his little daughter Alice, and his housekeeper, Lulie Webster, and Carol Ridley there, my father's nurse."

Carol had lifted her head from her arms to stare fascinated as the rest of us did.

"I went to Mexico. Did you ever live in Mexico, gentlemen and ladies, without money? What's five thousand dollars? I, living in a stinking hole with Mexicans. I, eating their filthy food. I, crowded in with brats that died like flies. I, without even decent American clothes to my back, forced to cadge drinks from tourists, getting what little money I got from cheating Mexicans in their gambling houses—I, James Maartens, hear that? I don't have to live like this! I've got a quarter of a million dollars in a bank! I'll prove it—laugh—I'll prove it!"

His whole face had become defiant, twisted; in his mind he must have been back in Mexico, living the dingy life he had lived there, with the sore of his murderous hatred festering.

He switched abruptly back to his murmurous purr. "Mrs. Rudeen came to Mexico City. Ah, Mrs. Rudeen. Mrs. Rudeen who had murdered her husband for his insurance and eloped with her lover, Harry Lewis. That was Harry's fine business, ladies and gentlemen, eloping with women who had money. Of course Harry didn't really want Mrs. Rudeen to murder her husband—it was all quite a surprise to you, Harry, wasn't it?"

Carol Maartens—I suppose she was still Mrs. Maartens— shifted until she could stare across the table at the sullen face of the man with whom she'd lived. Her face showed numb acceptance rather than anger.

Harry Lewis said nothing.

The purr went on. "It happened Mrs. Rudeen had read about my unclaimed money in the papers; she believed me. Of course I said it was only a confession of theft that stood between me and the money. I knew my brother had died. Really it was Mrs. Rudeen who proposed our—shall we call it an expedition—to recover my confession and so bring me into my inheritance at last. I was certain my brother would leave that confession to Alice, his daughter. Alice would be grown now. So Mrs. Rudeen and I looked around and we saw Mr. Jordan. Mr. Jordan was in Mexico because of a little difficulty with his Canadian bank. Mr. Jordan was glad—for twenty thousand dollars—to entice little Alice into telling him where the confession was. Weren't you, Jordan?"

Desperation and despair on the blond face that didn't look up.

On and on words poured while I listened in mesmerized horror. Because James Maartens was enjoying what he told. He told how the three—he and Jordan and Mrs. Rudeen—had come to Chicago and seen the Crying Sisters resort advertised for sale and bought it, because it was just the place they needed. How Jordan had found Alice Maartens in Minneapolis, a girl of twenty, with a small child and a husband who was away working in Mexico. She had told him willingly enough the story of her uncle, but said she didn't know where the confession was. He couldn't be too insistent. And so, after a summer of attentions, he agreed to bring her to the Crying Sisters for a week end. That was a year ago.

"Of course I told Jordan that once I had the confession I would let the girl go—but I couldn't do that, could I? After all, she was a witness. Dear, dear, Mr. Jordan was so distressed when he found out what had happened. But of course he could do nothing then; Mr. Jordan had to keep very quiet. And he couldn't go away;

he had no money. It was quite amusing. And I was quite distressed, too, because it turned out Alice didn't have the confession, and I'm sure at the end she told the truth."

Steve Corbett made an indescribable sound.

I couldn't bear it; I walked to the porch to cool my face, to crush down the welling sickness in my throat.

When I went back James Maartens was telling how he had enticed the housekeeper, Lulie Webster, to the resort. He had written her, extolling the delights of the place as a vacation spot, quoting very low prices. Finally she had written to reserve a cottage. She had come on the late bus Saturday night—the Saturday before we came to the Crying Sisters. Mrs. Rudeen had gone to meet her in the Packard. She never got out of Maartens' house; only he and Mrs. Rudeen knew the woman had ever been there.

It was Lulie Webster that I had heard screaming that first night I spent in the resort.

James Maartens apologized for that scream. "I killed her immediately—the gag slipped. It was she who told me Carol had the confession."

They had been working on Carol Maartens all the time they were working on Lulie Webster. Harry Lewis had been written to, asked to work his way into the graces of this well-to-do widow; he had agreed with alacrity.

"Poor Harry," James Maartens said. "He didn't know how serious his activity would prove to be, either. Mr. Lewis was very successful with Carol. He even got her to admit once when she had been drinking a bit, that she had the confession. But she wouldn't tell him where she had it."

He was smiling mockingly again at Harry Lewis; he quit that to sigh.

"And then we had a little trouble here—poor Mr. Sprung.

You see, when Mr. Sprung kicked the little boy and ran to hide, he was very drunk. And somehow what he ran to was his mother's cellar—this cellar right here. You all remember that this was the house his mother lived in up to her death. That was so bad for me. Because Lulie Webster was still in the cellar. I couldn't bury her because it rained every night. I couldn't put her in the lake, either, and have her coming ashore. So I had waited."

Through my horror I could see the links I had held, falling one by one into place. It was in the cellar of this house that Al Sprung had hidden between the time he ran up the beach and the time I found him dead behind his house.

James Maartens was nodding around brightly. "You do see I had to kill Al Sprung? He jerked the trap door open before I could stop him, and started down. He saw Lulie Webster on the floor below. He screamed and started back. Of course I couldn't let him go, then. I had to hit him on the head very quickly. Fortunately for me he fell down the ladder unconscious. I ran out."

I could remember John Loxton's face as I had seen it when we sped past taking Cottie to the doctor. I had thought he looked anxious over us. And instead he was distraught over having Al Sprung lying unconscious in his cellar beside the dead body of Lulie Webster.

He went on. "I told Mrs. Rudeen, and went to borrow the Corbetts' knife. Mr. Corbett had been such a nuisance to me, prowling about at night. I saw the dummies behind the house. Mrs. Rudeen helped me that night."

He hadn't been too frail. And Mrs. Rudeen had come rightly by that plantain leaf in her heel, and the eight thousand dollars.

"We heard Mr. Corbett up in the bushes at the top of the hill. We thought we were quite safe. But unluckily Hoxie Mueller was in the cabin. We had to drop poor Al and retire until the gangsters left.

Then Mrs. Corbett—I don't know your real name, my dear—blundered by. Mrs. Rudeen had to take stern measures."

So it was Mrs. Rudeen who had thrown something over my head and struck me down, that night.

"It was so sad, the way it turned out. Hoxie Mueller got all the blame, and the Corbetts stayed. Just when Mrs. Rudeen had written Harry Lewis to bring out his catch. Poor woman, she tried so hard to talk the Corbetts into leaving, but I'm afraid she wasn't very subtle, and of course I couldn't appear myself."

No, he had taken good care to keep his activity hidden.

Hidden. He was the source of all the evil this resort had hidden. All the evil he now unfolded so . . . happily.

"The first night the Lewises were here we held a conclave. It was decided we must postpone our little interview with Carol until the Corbetts left. Mr. Lewis was to keep Carol here, satisfied. And then a new difficulty arose. Mr. Lewis began to be quite fond of Carol."

Carol still stared steadily and unseeingly across the table; she might have stared at both men, her gaze was so wide.

"Dear me, it made Mrs. Rudeen very jealous. Poor woman, I felt for her. But one night she came to tell me she was going then to kill Carol and Harry Lewis both. I couldn't have that. Carol was still being stubborn about the confession. I had sent Jordan to search her apartment the first week end she was here."

I remembered how disinterested I had been in that trip.

"And he couldn't find it. But just the same, I had all three witnesses in my hands now. I had taken care of Alice and Lulie Webster. Carol was right in my grasp; since the others didn't have the confession, she must have it. I saw that Mrs. Rudeen had served her purpose. And so I soothed her, and the next afternoon invited her to have a cup of tea with me. She never recovered. It was inevitable anyway, you see that, don't you? She was so exorbitant in what she wanted—she wanted fifty thousand dollars as her share. Just for financing the expedition. It was, as I said, inevitable. And Mr. Jordan helped me clean up."

No, Earl Jordan hadn't been night fishing that night. But he had been out in a boat.

Steve Corbett said wearily, "By the way, Sheriff, I'll show you where Mrs. Rudeen's car is. In the bushes along the resort road. They'd transplanted bushes to hide the break. I knew what to look for when I thought of a gardener."

"Clever of you, Mr. Kernan, but clever of me, too, don't you think?" Again the head unbelievably tilted for approval.

"And now we came to this sad affair tonight, gentlemen and ladies." He smiled again. "Believe me, the night was not of my choosing. It was forced upon me. If it hadn't been for that, I still think I might have succeeded. But Carol insisted on leaving. Then when I heard Mr. Corbett was leaving I knew I must seize the opportunity. Mr. Lewis agreed to bring Carol to the house at night for a little questioning. I had to tell him he could take Carol afterward to some quiet cabin in Canada until I had my money. I saw Mr. Corbett leave, but I was a little suspicious of a trick. I padlocked Mrs. Corbett into her cabin but she tried to escape, so I knew I had been right. Dear, dear." The small black eyes now rested only on me. "How did you get here, Mrs. Corbett? Young women are so resourceful nowadays. I thought I had you so nicely taken care of."

He shook his head regretfully and went on without a break. "Mr. Lewis brought Carol here after all the cottagers were certain to be deeply asleep, as agreed. Mr. Lewis got quite upset after he got here—Mr. Jordan had to help me tie him up. And then Mr. Jordan went out to guard. I'm afraid he wasn't a very good one."

On that he stopped, sighing, smiling, looking around as if now he had done his part.

The sheriff said to Carol, "Is it true you have such a confession, Mrs. Maartens?"

She shifted her gaze from Harry Lewis to him. "Oh, sure," she said flatly. "I've got it." Her right hand fumbled dazedly under her left arm. "My handbag," she asked. "Where is it?"

James Maartens spat at her. "It isn't there. I looked. I tore it in pieces. Look for yourself on the cellar floor."

The sheriff gestured with his head at Steve Corbett, and Cottie's father went down the ladder to come back with filled hands. Torn letters, strips of lining, keys, the leather bag itself twisted and shapeless, the enameled compact broken at the hinges into two parts. He laid the fragments before Carol.

"I'd have burned and rotted before I told him," she said in the same flat voice. Her hands took up the half of the compact that had held the rouge and powder. The loose-powder compartment was empty, its lid swinging; the puff was gone from the rouge tray.

She pushed down on the ejector that expelled the little square plate of rouge to make place for a refill.

Underneath was a folded bit of paper.

I moved closer.

The handwriting of the note slanted—unmistakably it was the handwriting of the note signed Edna Rudeen.

This note said:

I poisoned my father. And you, dear brother, will never get my money now. JAMES MAARTENS.

A choked cry sounded. I turned to see that the sheriff and

Dr. Hansen and Steve Corbett were all bending over the note. And directly behind Carol stood James Maartens, vainly trying to push his hands forward to that note. There was froth on his beard.

I walked beside Steve Corbett as he carried Cottie back to our cabin.

He said just one thing on the way. "We'll leave in the morning."

So this was the end of the chain.

He had no further use for me now. His plans were done. He'd found out what had happened to his wife while he was away in Mexico, and caught her murderer. He could take Cottie back to Doobie, and even Cottie wouldn't need me any more.

I walked beside the lakes of the Crying Sisters with a man and a child, through a resort that had brought terror and death to one man and three women, who had cried or not cried, as they could.

I thought that I as well as they had a reason to cry out. And couldn't.

Inside the bedroom Steve Corbett laid Cottie on his bed as I pulled the light cord overhead. He turned toward me slowly; there was almost a looseness in the muscles of his face, as if the sustaining energy that had driven him for a year were drained out.

He said, "It's been sort of tough on you, Janet, but God, it's been tough." He dropped on the edge of my bed to sit looking down at his hands.

"I got back from Mexico last fall—I'd been down there six months working on the Pan-American highway. My wife didn't write much—she was angry because I took a job so far away. When I got back nobody was in my apartment. Not my wife. Not Cottie. I found a note. It said: *'Sorry, Kernan, your wife's found a better guy.'* I went through that building like a crazy man. I found the

315

kid downstairs, with a Mrs. Deubener. She said Alice had gone away for a week end two weeks ago and never come back. She was frightened, but didn't know what to do because she knew Alice went with a man. Alice. She was sweet and just a kid. I——"

It seemed impossible for me to absorb any more emotion, I'd taken so much. But I could feel sorry for Cottie's mother.

"At first I thought she'd just run off. Then I thought I'd try to find where she'd gone. I traced her as far as the Crying Sisters, don't ask me how. It took a whole year. My first visit here was the day you took care of Cottie in that tourist camp. I talked to Loxton on his porch. And I got a feeling—the same feeling I've had on the job when a rattlesnake is getting too close. So instead of asking questions I rented a cabin, thinking I could look around and see if anything strange were going on. I thought perhaps it was just a gang of men robbing women—Alice took quite a lot of money with her."

He was silent a moment again. "When I got back to the tourist camp you were there. I needed you to fill out the picture—make me unsuspected. I gave you the gun, but I didn't know how dangerous it would be. I'm sorry."

"That's all right," I said miserably. "I didn't help any."

He lifted his eyes, reaching forward to take my wrists, to pull me to the bed beside him. Then his head went down into the hands Dr. Hansen had bandaged before we came home. As Cottie had done he moved his face against my hands, back and forth, for comfort.

He said, "I'll be a tough guy for a husband, Janet, but you'll never run away. You'll never run away from Cottie."

Who knows about power and glory? Who knows the way the world can burst and open up an unguessed splendor? I could see all my life the way it would be. It would take a while, but I could make it. Eldreth, where was Eldreth? Gone? George Train? Gone?

Never to say good-by to Cottie, never to say good-by . . .

In the end it was I who made the gesture that was the completing link of the chain. The first link of a new chain.

As well as I could I curved my bandaged hands upward around his face.